"An ambitious novel . . . that shuns the formulaic pit-falls and conventionality of other bestselling paranormal fantasy sagas. This is Stacia Kane at the top of her game—it is a writer evolved, a storyteller matured, an imagination fully unleashed upon the world. . . . Dark, stylish, and wildly original."

—B&N Explorations blog

UNHOLY MAGIC

"This follow-up to *Unholy Ghosts* is full of supernatural suspense told in a fast-paced story. With a gutsy heroine, creepy paranormal elements and some page-turning action, it's a satisfying addition to the flooded urban fantasy genre. It all adds up to a very entertaining read."

—4 Stars, *RT Book Reviews*

"Like any drug, the first taste gets your attention but it's the second taste that gets you hooked. I thought the first Downside Ghosts book, *Unholy Ghosts*, was an impressive debut, but *Unholy Magic* is even better. I am well and truly addicted to this dark, seductive urban fantasy series."

—All Things Urban Fantasy

"In trying to come up with an adjective to describe the overall tone and feel of this story, I came up short. Gritty seems weak in reference to this book and just does not cover it. . . . Stacia Kane has written an amazing, spine-tingling novel in *Unholy Magic*, taking me by surprise by surpassing even the brilliance of its predecessor, *Unholy Ghosts*."

—5 out of 5, *The Fiction Vixen*

"The bottom line is this—never before in paranormal fantasy have I read a series that features the combination of grand scale world building, labyrinthine storyline, superb character development, and social relevance. Stacia Kane's Downside saga is taking paranormal fantasy to another level right before our eyes . . . I challenge anyone who has never read a paranormal fantasy before to read this series—I'll guarantee you that you never look at paranormal fantasy the same way again."

—B&N Explorations blog

CITY OF GHOSTS

"Book Three in the Downside Ghosts series lives up to expectations. Kane's dark and dangerous world is a unique setting for her anti-heroes. The heroine's realistic flaws make her more interesting and set her apart from others in the genre. Fans of urban fantasy will love the tight plot, swift pace and twists and turns."

—4½ Stars, *RT Book Reviews*

"*Unholy Ghosts* and *Unholy Magic* stayed with me long after I read them and it was no different with *City of Ghosts*. . . . It's full of witchy magic, action and romance. I literally couldn't put this book down until I had read the very last word."

—10/10 review, Book Chick City

"There are two words that describe this book perfectly: 'Nonstop action!' Other suitable options include: 'super book!', 'whoa Nelly!' or 'holy cow this book is going to be the death of me because I can't go to sleep yet because I haven't finished it and I must, must, MUST know what is going to happen next because holy cow this book is one hell of a ride!!!' Yes, I am aware that that is a few more than a couple of words, but they really do describe how I was feeling while I was reading. Stacia Kane hardly gives you a minute to catch your breath before the next wave of jaw-dropping action or gut-wrenching suspense or heartbreaking confrontation hits! Simply put, this book is fantastic from beginning to end."

—5 Stars, Yummy Men and Kick-Ass Chicks

BY STACIA KANE

Unholy Ghosts
Unholy Magic
City of Ghosts
Sacrificial Magic
Chasing Magic

CHASING MAGIC

STACIA KANE

BALLANTINE BOOKS • NEW YORK

A Del Rey Mass Market Original

Copyright © 2012 by Stacey Fackler

Published in the United States by Del Rey, an imprint of The Random House Publishing Group, a division of Random House, Inc., New York.

DEL REY is a registered trademark and the Del Rey colophon is a trademark of Random House, Inc.

ISBN: 978-0-345-52752-3
eBook ISBN: 978-0-345-52753-0

Printed in the United States of America

www.delreybooks.com

Cover design: Derek Walls
Cover image: © Ipatov/Shutterstock (woman); © Andrew C Mace/Getty (landscape)

9 8 7 6 5 4 3 2 1

Del Rey mass market edition: June 2012

To the doctors, nurses, and surgical staff
at Lister Hospital Stevenage, without whom
I would literally no longer be alive

Chapter One

All of the documents were in place: the Affidavit of Spectral Fraud, the Statement of Truth, two Orders of Imprisonment and two Orders of Relinquishment, and, of course, the list of Church-approved attorneys. The Darnells would want that—well, they'd need it, because they were about to be arrested for faking a haunting.

At least, they would be when the Black Squad got there to back Chess up. She didn't always want the Squad to come along; police presence tipped people off, made things more difficult, and most people came pretty quietly once they realized they were busted, anyway. The Darnells didn't seem like the come-quietly type, though. Something told Chess they weren't going to take this well.

But she'd told them she'd be there at six, and it was five past already and their curtains kept twitching. They knew she was there.

Right. She'd taken a couple of Cepts before leaving her apartment in Downside, so they were starting to hit—smooth, thick narcotic warmth spreading from her stomach out through the rest of her body, a pleasant softness settling over her mind.

That was the best thing about the drugs, really; she could still think, still be coherent, still use her brain. She just didn't have to if she didn't want to, and it was so much easier to keep that brain from wandering into all those places she didn't want it to go.

And she had so fucking many of those places.

She grabbed the Darnell file from her bag, locked her car, and started walking along the cobblestoned path to the front door, weaving around the flowers and plants scattered like islands across the impossibly green sea of grass. Bees made their way from bloom to bloom, doing whatever the hell it was bees did. Sure, she knew it was something to do with pollen or whatever. She just didn't give a shit.

By the time she reached the porch sweat beaded along her forehead and her body felt damp. Summer sucked. Only the middle of June and already it was scorching.

Brandon Darnell opened the door before she'd finished raising her hand to knock. "Miss Putnam. You're late."

Asshole. She faked a smile. "Sorry. Traffic."

At least they had air-conditioning.

The entire Darnell family sat in the pretentious high-ceilinged living room, slouching on the ridiculously overpriced suede couch and chairs that were partly responsible for the enormous debt they were in. Debt they'd planned to clear by faking a haunting and getting a nice fat settlement from the Church of the Real Truth.

Too bad for them, the Church wasn't stupid—being in charge of everyone and everything on earth for twenty-four years proved that—and had contingency plans for such things. Chess was one of them.

Brandon Darnell indicated an empty chair along the back wall. "Have a seat."

Alarms started ringing in Chess's head. He seemed a little too calm, a little too . . . cheerful.

But all the other chairs were full, so she sat, shooting a glance out the window to see if the Squad had arrived yet. Nope. Damn it!

The Darnells sat there, unmoving. Watching her. Because that wasn't creepy at all.

Mrs. Darnell—frowsy, bad perm, blue eye shadow up to her brows—showed her perfect white teeth in what could pass for a smile. "Do you have any news for us? When will you Banish the ghost?"

Chess's phone beeped—a text. A text from the Black Squad, thank fuck, they were almost there. Good. She didn't have to sit around wasting time with these people.

"I do have news." She pulled the forms from the file. "This is my Statement of Truth, copies of which I've already filed with the Church. This one is for you to sign. It's the Affidavit of Spectral Fraud, which is basically your confession, and this one—"

"What the hell are you talking about? We haven't committed any fraud, there's no—"

"Mr. Darnell." Normally she'd stand up for this part, but what the hell. The chair was pretty comfortable. "I found, and photographed, the projectors set up in the attic. I won't bother to point out to you where the holes in the ceiling are, since you already know. The 'ectoplasm' on your walls has been analyzed—twice for confirmation—as a mixture of cornstarch, gelatin, iridescent paint, and water."

She waited for a response and didn't get one. Good. "I also have pictures of the portable air conditioner you set up beneath the house—that's another crime, by the way, putting anything underground, but I imagine you know that—to fake sudden changes in temperature. One of my hidden cameras caught you breaking the mirrors, and another one very clearly shows you and Mrs. Darnell discussing your crimes."

Mr. and Mrs. Darnell looked guilty. Their children—

Cassie and Curtis, how cute—looked confused. Chess directed her next comments to them.

"I have two Orders of Relinquishment here. You two are going to be taken to the Church with your parents, but when they go to prison you'll be moving in with another family member or, failing that, a home will be found for you. You'll be safe there."

She could only hope that last line was true. It hadn't been for her. None of those "homes" she'd been sent to had been safe, or at least not more than a couple of them.

But that was a long time ago. That was before the Church was really settled. That was a mistake; she was an anomaly, or something, and it mattered only in her memories.

Because the Church had saved her. They'd taken her out of that life and given her a new one. The Church had found her and made her into something real.

The two children looked at each other, looked at Chess, looked at their parents. What was the expression on their faces? Shock, curiosity? Chess couldn't quite read it.

She squeezed her eyes shut, opened them again. Shit, she didn't usually have problems like this from her pills. And no way had she gotten a bad batch; Lex had given her those, and Lex might be in charge of the Downside gang in direct opposition to the one Chess's . . . Chess's *everything* worked for, but Lex wouldn't try to do her any harm. She knew that. Lex was her friend.

So what the fuck?

Her eyes itched, too; she raised her hand to rub at them. Struggled to raise it. In fact, she'd been sitting still for a few minutes, hadn't she? Without moving.

The room started to rock around her, as if she and the Darnells sat on the deck of a ship in stormy waters. Nausea slithered through her stomach, up her throat.

Her skin tingled. Not her skin, actually. Her tattoos—runes and sigils inscribed into her skin with magic-imbued ink by the Church—tingled. The way they always did in the presence of ghosts—or in the presence of magic.

It took forever to turn her head to the left, on a neck that felt like it was being squeezed by strong, hard hands she couldn't see. Who was . . . Fuck, someone was casting some kind of spell on her. Who was it, what was it?

She couldn't tell, couldn't see well enough to tell. Just a shape, a spot of darker shadow in the long hallway. But whatever it was—it felt like a man, she had enough presence of mind to know that—it was powerful, it was strong, and it was about to beat her.

Something inside her struggled. The noise of the Darnells' shouting faded, as if a stiff wind had come up and was blowing them all away. The adult Darnells yelling, cackling; the young Darnells panicked and confused.

And over it all words of power seeping into her consciousness, spoken in a deep smooth voice like smoked glass. Smoked glass with jagged edges; she would cut herself on them, they'd slice into her skin and her blood would spill out onto the floor, staining the carpet the Darnells couldn't pay for. Staining everything except her soul: That was filthy enough already, covered with grime and pain that would never go away, no matter how many pills she took or lines she snorted. She deserved to be punished for that. Deserved to die for it.

But she didn't want to. Not just because she was afraid of the City of Eternity, either. As her breath came shorter and shallower, as the black edge around her vision thickened until she could see only tiny spots of the room, all she could think about was Terrible. The only man in the world who made her feel . . . like she was okay, like she could be happy. The only one who understood her. The only one who loved her.

The only one, period.

She would not leave him. She refused to leave him.

His face grew in her mind: black hair pomaded into a rockabilly DA, thick heavy muttonchops, the face she'd once thought was ugly and now couldn't understand why or how she'd ever thought that. Because every scar showed how strong he was, those hard dark eyes thawed just for her, the heavy brow smoothed when he looked at her and it all added up to Terrible, and she was not going to let some shithead scam artists and their rent-a-witch steal her from him. He'd expect her to fight. He'd expect her to win, too.

Moving her lips hurt. She forced herself to do it anyway. "*Arkrandia arkrandia, bellarum bellarum, dishager dishager, arkrandia arkrandia, bellarum bellarum . . .*"

The Banishing words started to come faster, stronger. Not much, and her vision still hadn't cleared, but she could feel it. Something was building inside her—power was building inside her—and it was chasing away the choking fog of the dark spell.

She kept chanting, her voice creaky and rough, scraping against her throat, while she made her stiff fingers move. She needed to get into her bag; she had goat's blood in there, cobwebs and chunks of snake. If she could find a piece of iron to grab, it would help.

The witch loomed over her, his large body giving off the faint smell of sweat and cheap aftershave.

Were her feet on the floor? She thought they were, was pretty sure they were, and she guessed it didn't matter if they weren't, because she had to try anyway. She started to stand, her legs shaking and hurting beneath her.

The witch hit her, knocked her back. Fucker. That wasn't even a good punch; it was a wimpy little bitch slap. Now she was getting pissed. Who the hell did he think he was, this soft bag of shit in a shiny-cheap black tent and a pair of dorky-looking loafers? He thought he could come in to one of her cases, attack her?

Bullshit he could.

More anger, to make her even stronger. She was finding it now, that pit of rage deep inside her, the hatred for everyone, for everything they'd done to her. The hatred for herself that never seemed to end, would never end, would never lessen. It was there, and she needed it, and she took it and used it to clench her right hand into a fist, a good strong one. She'd never been too bad at fighting—not with her upbringing—but Terrible had shown her some new stuff, taught her how to do it, where to hit.

So she wasn't worried at all when she pushed herself up and punched him with all her might. And she had something nobody else had—or at least nobody who wasn't a trained witch who'd put some real thought into physical self-defense, which her opponent obviously hadn't.

She pushed her power into that fist, all of her energy, the anger and pain and everything else, and felt it reverberate when it hit him. Good. That gave her more strength, more will to fight.

Unfortunately, seeing her bounce back seemed to give the Darnells the will to fight, too. As she drew her fist to have another go, her energy returning in a rush as the spell was interrupted, an arm wrapped itself around her neck, yanked her against a well-padded chest.

Where the fuck was the fucking Squad? Yes, the whole thing had probably taken much less time than it felt like it had, but they should be there—

The witch dropped his shoulder, ready to hit her again. To hit her properly this time, while Mr. Darnell held her defenseless. Nice.

And, nope, she wasn't going to let them do that.

The witch checked his swing when she leaned forward

as much as she could, trying to bend over completely so Mr. Darnell would rise from the floor. He pulled back harder, his arm tightening around her throat. She kept leaning. Lights started sparking behind her eyes, red and green fireworks of imminent death bright against the figure of the witch, the tackily tasteful living room.

Just when she thought she couldn't bear it one more second, she stood up straight. Fast. So fast Mr. Darnell didn't have time to react; he kept pulling her, and they both tumbled to the floor, the witch's fist barely missing her.

With Mr. Darnell beneath her and the witch leaning over, she kicked out with her right leg, managed to catch the witch in his rather ample stomach, and sent him stumbling a few steps away. Her elbow dug into the soft space below Mr. Darnell's rib cage. His arm around her loosened—not a lot, but enough for her to sit up and start to roll off him.

Roll right into the barrel of the gun.

"Stand up." Mrs. Darnell's voice didn't shake. Her eyes didn't leave Chess's face. "Come on, get up."

Great. This was just great. How many people had she busted in her four-year career? Almost exactly four years, in fact. Dozens. Dozens of people. None of them had ever tried this shit with her.

That could have been because if she had any suspicions they might, she asked the Squad for backup, of course. Where the hell were they?

Her legs still felt weird from the spell. That energy hadn't faded completely. She risked a glance at the witch, saw him standing with his fists clenched, whispering something. Another spell. Wonderful.

"Mrs. Darnell, I don't think you want to do this."

"I think you're wrong." Mrs. Darnell's narrowed eyes shot beams of cold hatred at Chess. "I think you're really, really wrong."

"Killing a Church employee is automatic grounds for execution. Not to mention we get a special dispensation so we can haunt you until that execution happens. I really—"

"You idiot. How the hell did you manage to catch us, being that stupid? I don't want to kill you, no. But I will, unless you sign those forms and give us our money."

"They won't—"

"Shut up."

Chess shut up. What was she going to do, argue with the woman holding a gun to her face? Besides, she wanted to think.

Mrs. Darnell had obviously held a gun before, used one before. Both of her hands wrapped tight around the gun's butt, and her arms bent slightly to absorb its kick. Her entire stance indicated complete confidence. The safety was off. "Now. Get the forms or whatever you need. Slowly."

"You won't be able—"

"Oh, but we will. We're all ready to go. You didn't think we'd stick around here, did you?"

Mr. Darnell stood up. "I'll take the gun, Lois."

"No. If I take my eyes off her, she'll move."

No, she wouldn't. The witch's spell grew stronger again, and this time she knew if she tried to say the Banishing words she'd be shot. This was ridiculous. She did not spend her whole life fighting to end up shot in some over-mortgaged suburban ranch house.

Might as well take a chance. She dropped to the floor, pushing herself forward so she hit Mrs. Darnell's legs. The gun went off as Mrs. Darnell staggered back.

Chess hadn't been hit. Excellent. She was deaf but she hadn't been shot.

She raised her fist—like lifting a ten-pound weight through a tub of dense foam—and punched Mrs. Darnell in the knee as hard as she could.

Another explosion from the gun. Mrs. Darnell fell on top of her. Chess tried to roll over and push her off; the woman was surprisingly heavy, but she slipped a little. Enough for Chess to shift herself to the left, enough to find Mrs. Darnell's right hand still clutching the gun.

The witch's voice grew louder, the energy in the air darker and thicker. If Chess didn't get that gun away immediately, she was going to die, no question about it.

She kicked back with her right leg, catching Mrs. Darnell somewhere, she didn't know where for sure. Mr. Darnell had joined in the struggle, trying to pull his wife away and help her up, but Mrs. Darnell was apparently having too much fun trying to bite Chess and punching her in the legs and side. Chess kicked again, and again, her leg screaming from the effort—it was so heavy, so fucking heavy—until she somehow managed to hit Mrs. Darnell in the face.

The woman's grip on the gun loosened. Only for a second, but it was enough. Chess snatched it away, raised it above her head, and pulled the trigger.

The picture window at the front of the room exploded; shards of glass filled the air, a deadly tidal wave of sharp edges and splinters that could slice veins, dust that could choke.

For a second everything stopped. Everything except Chess; she'd been waiting for that pause, hoping for it, and she used it—it and the power rushing back to her, since the witch had stopped speaking—to push Mrs. Darnell away once and for all, to stand up and hold the gun on the two of them still on the floor.

The front door flew open—the Black Squad, their own guns drawn, their all-black uniforms and helmets like moving ink spots against the pale walls.

Chess lowered the gun, looked over at them. "You're late."

One of the Squad members glanced around the room, then back at Chess. "Any problems?"

She grinned. Now that she had the gun, now that the Squad had arrived, relief and adrenaline buzzed through her body, and she felt cheerier than she had since . . . well, since that morning, anyway. "No. Not really."

Chapter Two

The best kinds of surprises are intangible! The warmth of a sudden visit from a friend far outweighs material goods.
—*Mrs. Increase's Advice for Ladies*, by Mrs. Increase

Her body still ached three hours later, when she trudged up the stairs of her apartment building—a former Catholic church, renovated after Haunted Week proved all religions false—to the hall.

Hers was the only apartment on that side of the L-shaped building, and the stained-glass window that made up the entire front wall of her living room was only one of the reasons she loved it. The privacy, the space—it was hers, something that was only hers, for all that it was just rented.

Nobody came in without permission. Not anymore, not ever again.

That didn't stop people from visiting, though, at least it didn't these days. Proof of that stood right outside her front door, slumped against the wall in that elegant lean he did so well. "Hey there, Tulip. Starting to wonder iffen you come home at all on the anymores, aye?"

"Hey, Lex." As always, a confusing mix of emotions tumbled through her head, through her chest. Happiness to see her friend, the desire for him to leave before Terrible got there, annoyance at the way he always just showed up and assumed he'd be welcome—what if Terrible had been with her? Just because he didn't forbid Chess from seeing Lex didn't mean he approved or liked the fact that she did.

She didn't approve of or like it, either. Nor did she approve of or like the small, insistent tingle of arousal low in her belly, but she couldn't change it. For almost three months, seeing Lex waiting for her had signaled more drugs and at least a couple of orgasms. It took time to undo that sort of conditioning, no matter how completely in love she was with someone else and no matter how much Lex knew it.

He bent to give her a kiss on the cheek—that familiar Lex smell washing over her—and smiled. "Figured I'd give you the hellos, me, see iffen you needed all anything."

"I can always use more." A minute or so to unlock the three bolts on her door and release the magical wards she'd set up, and she led him into her kitchen.

"Figured on that." He reached into the front pocket of his battered jeans and tugged out a wrinkled plastic sandwich bag half full of her little white best friends.

She took it. Her pillbox was only about a third empty, she'd just refilled— Wait a minute.

She gave him a sharp look. "Why are you really here?"

"Ain't I can come on a visit? Thinking you ain't give Blue the what's-up she brings sheself here, so why I getting it?"

She washed four Cepts down with water. "Because Blue doesn't only show up when she wants something from me. And because I know you."

"Know you, too. Like how mean you is." He walked the few more steps into her living room, plunked himself down on her new couch. Well, maybe not exactly new—she'd had it for about two months—but it still seemed new.

Without asking she grabbed a beer from the fridge and handed it to him.

He nodded his thanks. "Coursen . . . now you mentioning it, could be maybe I got a favor you could do me."

Uh-huh. She let the totally-not-fooled expression sit on her face another few seconds. "Really. Like what?"

"Thinking maybe you ain't mind working me up a chatter with Terrible."

If she'd had any liquid in her mouth she would have sprayed it everywhere in shock. Luckily she didn't, but she sort of sputtered anyway. "What—but—why? Why would you want to talk to him?"

"Got my reasonings, I do."

Right. Like trying to kill him, presumably, since Lex wanted nothing more than to take over all the areas of Downside currently run by Terrible's boss—her regular dealer—Bump. Without Terrible, Bump would be a lot easier to defeat, and everyone knew it.

She eyed him with extra suspicion. "Why, Lex?"

"Gots some stuff to chatter on with him." He leaned forward, meeting her gaze. "Know what thought you got, I do, but ain't that way. Just wanna sit us down, is all, nothing on the extra."

Terrible would never go for it. Never. The only time he'd even acknowledged Lex's existence as anything but an asshole he'd enjoy killing was the night three months or so ago when she'd almost died, and the two men had driven around Triumph City to find her. And that had required her to almost *die*. Nothing short of that would make him agree to speak to Lex again.

"I don't think—"

He sighed. A heavy, put-upon sigh, the kind at which he excelled. "Shit. Gotta give you the swears? I swear on it, Tulip. Ain't gonna do shit to him, I ain't."

It wasn't that she didn't believe him. Well, it was, a little, but mostly it was just . . . shit.

"Notice you ain't got so much worryin on me, you ain't. Gotta give you the thanks for that one." His tone was dry, barely on the right side of sarcastic, but it pinched her all the same. Yeah, that was kind of shitty of her, wasn't it? Especially since anyone who would bet on Lex in a fight between him and Terrible—shit, anyone who'd bet against Terrible in any fight—might as well throw their money into the bay.

She hesitated, and he took his shot. The one shot guaranteed to work on her, and she knew he knew it. "Ain't never given you the asks on the befores, aye, and seems I recall doing you favors plenty."

"Fine." It went against everything she wanted, but he had her there. He'd done her a lot of favors, done a lot for her. The least she could do was ask Terrible to talk to him.

It might mean spending a night alone—Terrible didn't enjoy being reminded that she was friends with Lex, that for a while she'd been *naked* friends with Lex—but she didn't have much choice. Hell, she had a full pillbox and a nice-sized backup now, for free, and that was another favor.

He grinned. "Aye, that's real good, real good. Knew you gimme the stand-up. Counted on you, I did."

Yeah. She was certain of that.

She was also certain that Terrible would arrive at any minute and that, whatever she'd agreed to, he wouldn't be thrilled to find Lex there. She was also blessedly aware that her pills were starting to hit, her muscles relaxing, peaceful cheer seeping into her head and making her feel light. Making the situation seem not so bad.

Good thing, too, because the sound of the Chevelle's engine drifted through the window. One thing about stained glass: It was beautiful, and it made the room look like the inside of a jewel box when the sun hit it, but it wasn't particularly well insulated.

Lex heard it, too. "Hey, lucky chances. Sounding like he got heself here on the right now, aye? Just have myself the wait, catch him he gets inside."

"Yeah, lucky chances." Fuck. Double fuck. For one mad second she thought of kicking him out, pushing him out the door and slamming it behind him. But what difference would it make? Terrible would run into him in the hall or as they both crossed the lobby that had once been the nave.

Oh well. Worrying about it wasn't going to make it any better, and there was no way it could be good.

Terrible's key turned in the lock; her nerves gave a fluttering twist in her chest as he stepped inside.

His smile dropped like a guillotine blade when he looked past her and saw Lex leaning back on her couch, with his arm along the back and one foot propped on her battered coffee table. "The fuck you doin here?"

Lex opened his mouth, but Chess was faster. "Hey. Um, Lex just got here, he wanted—actually, he wants to talk to you, it's why he came. I didn't know he was coming, he just showed up."

Wow. That didn't sound guilty at all. She met his dark eyes, hoping he could see the truth behind hers. Trusting that he would, or at least trying to trust, because he needed her to trust and she wanted to.

"Wanna have me a chatter," Lex said.

Terrible glanced up. "No."

"Aw, c'mon now, only the speech, dig, not—"

Terrible shook his head. His left hand rose to grip the back of Chess's neck, a possessive gesture she wasn't sure he realized he was making. "Ain't saying no to chatter. Sayin no to whatany it is you want."

"Aye?" Lex lit a cigarette, leaned forward to pick up Chess's cheap plastic ashtray, and set it beside him on the couch. "Thinking you wanna make Tulip here happy, you listen up."

Terrible looked at her, *What the fuck?* written all over his face. Too bad she didn't know, either.

"Coursen, maybe you ain't wanting her happy? You just gimme the tell, then, I see what I can—"

Terrible lunged. Chess moved a second before, knowing it was coming. She leapt in front of him and wrapped her arms around his neck, ignoring the weird yelp that came out of her mouth in her amazement that she'd managed to catch him at all. "Don't, just . . . just don't, okay? Please?"

It didn't make much difference, really; he could have kept going without even noticing the extra weight of her body. But something—maybe her presence, maybe her words, maybe the fact that it was her house—stopped him.

"Talk." His anger vibrated against her skin even as she stepped away from him. This was so not the way she'd wanted the evening to go.

Lex smiled. He hadn't moved once. "Only a tease there, aye? Ain't meaning harm by it."

Damn him, that whole fucking thing had been a ploy, a game to see what it would take to make Terrible mad. Information Lex could use, a weakness he could exploit—as if he needed another one of those.

She hadn't figured out a way to neutralize the sigil carved into Terrible's chest, and she couldn't risk just slicing the skin off even if she could stomach the idea. For all she knew, that sigil, the one whose very presence was testimony to her crimes—killing a psychopomp hawk coming to claim his soul, and using her knife to make the sigil itself—was all that actually kept him alive.

She didn't regret it. Never could regret it; if she hadn't done it he'd be dead. But she did wish to hell it hadn't made him so vulnerable. Passing out in the presence of

dark magic was not a good thing, especially not when
Lex knew about it.

Lex indicated one of her lumpy chairs, waving his
hand as if he were lord of the manor or something.
"Ain't you wanting to have you a sit-down?"

"Talk."

"Aw, c'mon now, Terrible, ain't needing to get all
fratchy, aye? Let's us have a real chatter, friendly-like.
True thing."

Terrible didn't move. This was not going to go well;
Chess knew that, of course, but that stupid hope would
never go away, even though she knew how useless it
was.

Lex paused for a second, then shrugged. "Guessing I
ain't gotta give you the knowledge who's in charge my
side now, aye?"

When Terrible didn't reply, he continued. "I gots me-
self some plans, I do. Changes coming, if you dig me."

Great. Why didn't he just threaten Terrible outright?
Despite what some people thought—despite what he
himself thought—Terrible wasn't stupid. Especially not
about shit like this.

She glanced over at him, watching him pull a cigarette
from the pocket of his bowling shirt and light it with his
black steel lighter. The six-inch flame cast a faint glow
that told her maybe turning on some lights would be
a good idea. The sun wouldn't set for another hour or
two, no, but . . . it felt dark in there. Dark like Terrible's
anger, dark like the world. Dark like the emptiness inside her.

"Big changes. Ain't having no more game-plays, I
ain't."

Smoke drifted into the air in a thin, curling stream,
hiding part of Terrible's face behind it, hiding his expression and thoughts in a fragrant, ever-moving veil.

Chess knew what he was thinking anyway; she could still feel it throbbing in the air.

Lex lifted his beer. The smirk had left his face, at least. "Aye, seein you dig. Could use me someone worth trusting, gimme the help-out. Someone make heself more on the money side than he getting now, guessing. Like bein a partner, takin he own piece."

Oh no. No, he couldn't be saying that, could he? How in the hell could he honestly think Terrible would go to work for him—with him?

Terrible looked as if he had the same thought. His eyes narrowed; his head tilted to the left. Waiting. Watching, that dead-eye glare like a snake about to strike.

"Thinkin you come on over, do you work for me, aye? What you do now, only my side. With me. Make it all worth up, I will."

"No."

"Aw, now, why ain't you giving it a thought, leastaways? Make Tulip happy, ain't you thinkin? Us not tryna make each others dead, be a cheer-up for her."

Just what she wanted. Bring her into the discussion. Remind Terrible that she'd betrayed him, that while he'd thought something was starting between them—while something *was* starting between them—she'd been running off to spend long sweaty nights in Lex's bed.

Not that Terrible would or could ever forget, but still.

"All knowing nobody beats you, aye? Need me a man like that, make things tight up. Needs a brain, too, which you know you got. You name me a price. True thing, Terrible. Makes me happy, makes you happy, makes Tulip happy. Ain't that the juice?"

"No."

Lex's expression didn't change. He stubbed out his smoke, took another swig from his beer, and set it on the table. "You have you a think on it, aye? Ain't needing the answer on the now, you gimme the tell on the morrow."

Terrible shrugged. "Answer ain't changin."

"Aye? Whyn't you get the thoughts, anyway, we chatter again." Lex stood up and started toward the door. Chess and Terrible moved back a few steps into the kitchen so he could get past, but he stopped a foot or so away from them. Almost—but not quite—too close.

"Oughta give one more thing the mentions here. You ain't wanna come on with me . . . means I get on finding one who will, dig, get me a steel-man of my owns. Ain't sure Downside got size enough for two, aye? Rather not be fighting you causen of Tulip, but . . . got plans, I do, an I ain't losing em."

Chess closed her eyes. Fuck. This couldn't be happening. There was no way she was standing in her own kitchen, listening to Lex threaten Terrible while Terrible's hand twitched on the back of her neck and anger rolled off him in thick waves.

When she opened her eyes again, Lex stood by the door. "On the laters, Tulip. Give you a ring-up, I will."

What was she supposed to say? Great? Awesome, you do that? She managed to raise her hand in a weak sort of wave before the door closed behind him, leaving Chess alone with Terrible and his rage.

She didn't want to look at him. The thought of what she might see in his eyes scared her, and that made her even angrier because she wasn't supposed to be scared of him, and that scared her even more, and four Cepts had totally not been enough. She'd have to grab another one. Immediately. Five was pushing it, but not beyond the boundary of acceptable.

But first . . . time to pay the piper, or take her punishment, or whatever the hell. She glanced up at him, found him staring at the door like he expected it to fly back open and reveal Lex with a loaded gun.

"Hey, I'm sorry," she managed. "I didn't— He was waiting here when I got home, and he said he wanted to talk to you, he wanted me to ask you to talk to him. He didn't tell me why or what he wanted."

His hand left her neck, leaving her skin cold and oddly light, missing its warm weight. She watched him pull his bottle of bourbon out of the cabinet and down a couple of swigs. Watched him grab a beer out of the fridge, stride past her to the couch—the other side from where Lex had sat—and chase the shots with almost half the bottle. Shit. Of course he drank—who the fuck didn't?—but not like that, not usually. Not like he was trying to drown something out, forget it, get rid of it, hide it under an ocean of booze until no one even knew it had been there.

Not like . . . well, not like her.

What was she supposed to do? She'd already apologized. She'd explained. He wasn't responding. Damn it, she wasn't good at this, didn't have any experience with this. She'd never even dated someone for more than a single night, at least not before Lex came along, and they'd never really gotten mad at each other because their relationship didn't matter enough to bother getting mad over. So what the hell was her reaction supposed to be?

Whatever it was, she guessed standing there staring at him wasn't it. She dug in her bag for another pill and forced it down without water while she sat next to him. Not touching him—that might not be a good idea—but close to him, so the heat from his leg brushed against hers.

"So I know that probably wasn't what you wanted to deal with right when you walked—"

"He got the truth?"

"What?"

He lit another cigarette off the butt of the first one.

His eyes stayed focused on the stained-glass window. "He got the truth. That what you're wanting? Me with him?"

"What—no, no, I mean, I wouldn't ask you to do that."

Even as she said it, a sneaky, selfish part of her wondered if it was entirely true. Oh, who was she kidding? Pretty much all of her was sneaky and selfish, but it was still just a small part of her that wondered.

She couldn't ask Terrible to do that. Not ever. But she couldn't deny it would be so much easier. For Terrible to stop hating Lex, to stop gritting his teeth and clenching his fists every time Lex's name came up—which wasn't often—and to not get mad if she wanted to get something to eat with Lex. To not get mad when she went shopping or whatever with Lex's sister Blue—Beulah, actually, but she preferred Blue, and in that Chess supposed she didn't blame her—who had become her friend, weird as that was.

Even weirder was how she was more willing to give up Lex than Blue, if she really thought about it. It was kind of cool having a female friend, even if they didn't do girlie-type things. No manicures or pink cocktails, and no chatting about sex—at least, not on Chess's part. Blue was more open, but then Blue was dating some married guy so didn't have anyone else to talk to about him. But it was . . . well, it was fun. She couldn't help it. It was.

Chess didn't want to think about it, didn't want to dream about it, but she couldn't help the images that bounced through her head in the few seconds before she managed to shut them down. The four of them hanging out at Lex's place, drinking beer on her roof, her not feeling guilty and shitty anymore when Lex called or she went somewhere with Blue. Terrible could just smile and give her a kiss and tell her to have fun . . .

Right, sure. And then they could all go for a frolic in the sparkly diamond rain.

Besides, the thought of Lex and Terrible together all the time—that would never work. Could never work. Even without the whole business rivalry, Terrible hated Lex. Hated Lex because of her, hated Lex because he knew she'd been leaving him after an evening of hanging out—after many evenings of hanging out—and heading over to Lex's place to spend the night in his bed. She'd betrayed him with Lex, over and over again, and even if she could expect him to put his loyalty to Bump aside she knew he couldn't possibly ever forget that.

Hell, even if he tried, Lex wouldn't let him, would he?

Terrible watched her, watched her tight so she felt like she couldn't escape. She wanted to rest her head against his shoulder, wrap her arms around him, but something told her she should hang back. "No. I don't want that."

His eyes searched hers. "Aye?"

"Aye." She smiled.

He smiled back, a brief flash of a smile across his face before his mouth twisted down again. "He ain't lyin on havin plans. Two street men dead in the last week, dig. Right onna corners, just left there."

"Lex killed them?"

"Ain't can see who else done it. Watchers said dudes pull theyselves up in a car, jump out, stab em up an take off again. Ain't even dipped them pockets, dig."

Shit. "So . . . what are you guys doing?"

"Do what we gotta, aye? Ain't can have that shit. Wonder on he not sayin on it, but guessing he ain't with you here."

"Or he didn't mention it because he wants you to work with him."

Terrible shrugged and leaned forward to stub out his smoke. As he did, his glance fell on her arm. "What's on there?"

"Huh? Oh." Damn, she'd almost managed to forget about the Darnells. "Remember my case, the people who broke the mirrors? I busted them today. They weren't very happy about it."

"They hit you?"

"Yeah. Well, they had a witch there who tried to kill me, then they had a gun, but it was fine. I'm fine, no biggie."

He opened his mouth, but she cut him off. "How about you, how was your day?"

She could practically see him trying to decide if it was worth pushing or not; thankfully, he didn't. Even better, he lifted her arm and kissed the smudgy dark spot forming there, sending a shiver down her spine.

"Hey." She reached up to trail her fingers down his thick sideburns, unable to keep herself from grinning. "I might have a few more bruises, too."

His eyebrows rose, his own smile transforming his face the way she loved so much. "Aye? Where?"

"Oh, all over. It's really bad. There are tons of them."

He shook his head. "Damn. Thinkin you oughta show me, aye? So's I can be all certain you ain't hurt much."

"I think you're right." She grabbed the hem of her T-shirt and lifted it off, shivering harder when his warm hands found her bare skin, reached behind her to unfasten her bra and slip that off, too. "I definitely need your help."

Love wasn't one emotion, she didn't think. It was a combination of a whole bunch of them, and each one had a slightly different formula. Like how if she mixed black powder with an equal amount of blood salt and powdered cat's skull, she'd have a nice little hex-shield that would bounce curses back to the caster, but the same ingredients in different proportions would induce people to admit the truth if it got on their skin.

Love was like that, and the formulas were always

changing. It never sat still and let her get used to it; she didn't feel as if she ever quite had her balance.

And there was the formula changing again, going from light and warm to tingly and hot. Hot and getting hotter when his mouth took hers, his fingertips on her jaw and then sliding into her hair. His body urged hers back, so she lay on the couch with his warm solid weight above her and her hands already finding bare skin under his shirt, spreading her fingers apart as wide as she could so she could feel more of him at once.

He took his time, inching his palm up her rib cage to barely skim her breast, sliding it down over the curve of her hip and thigh. His teeth caught her tongue and held it for a second, just long enough to send a flash of heat through her entire body. Still he didn't speed up, but that heat did, racing through her, screaming it was going so fast, and she felt as if she glowed in the ever-darker room as the sun set over Downside.

Then Terrible stopped, and she realized it wasn't her body screaming—well, her body was screaming, like it always did when he touched her, but the sound she heard wasn't her body. Wasn't her voice. It was a voice of terror, a voice of pain and despair, and it sent a shiver that had nothing to do with sex or love or anything even remotely pleasant up her spine.

It was coming from the street outside, and more voices joined it every second.

Chapter Three

> You must always be ready.
> —*Debunking: A Practical Guide*, by Elder Morgenstern

Quite a crowd had gathered by the time Chess and Terrible burst through the tall, heavy wooden doors of her building, down the steps and across the patch of scrub grass and pebbles to the street, where dozens of backs obscured her view of whatever was happening.

Too bad they didn't obscure the screams, those awful wails. Why were people standing there watching if they were so scared—

"Fuck!" Terrible was gone before the word even registered in her head, shoving his way through the crowd. Of course, he could see over them. He knew what was happening.

So whatever it was probably wasn't a good thing. But then she hadn't imagined it would be.

And what the hell was she doing, standing there in the back while Terrible did whatever it was he was doing in the center? Fuck that.

People didn't move as fast for her as they had for him, but the ink on her shoulders, arms, and chest carried enough weight to get them going. Most people thought witches had a lot more power than they actually did, and Chess didn't do anything to disabuse them of that notion. It had kept her safer in Downside than she had any right to be for almost four years, especially since everyone learned that Downside's Churchwitch worked for Bump.

They might have taken their chances with the Church, but no way would they do that with Bump. Fucking with Bump meant fucking with Terrible, and the only people who did that had death wishes even more serious than Chess's. If that were possible.

Through the tiny spaces between people, she caught glimpses of . . . something . . . what the fuck? The street red with blood, a shoe lying in a glistening puddle of it . . .

She reached the center just as Terrible pulled back his fist and slammed it into the face of a man in the circle. That man stood over another man—a dead body—and was swinging the corpse's disembodied left arm like a bat.

The man stumbled and fell onto the bloody cement, the arm in his hand waving as he went down. Chess automatically glanced at Terrible, only to see his eyes close, see him waver on his feet for a second before shaking his head and straightening up.

Her tattoos tingled and burned. A ghost. A ghost and magic and—oh shit. Dark magic, and just punching that man was enough to cause a reaction in Terrible. She had to find a solution to that. No more fucking around. Nothing had worked so far, and she hated being reminded of her failures, but seriously.

Bad enough that Lex knew about it. If the rest of Downside found out . . . she couldn't even imagine how awful that would be.

This wasn't the time to picture it, either, because the killer—she assumed he was the killer—started to stand up. His buzz-cut hair and the back of his dirty white shirt dripped with blood, vibrant and horrible in the darkening air.

Terrible knocked him down again with a savage kick to the throat, using the sole of his boot to shove him to the pavement.

Chess tensed. If the magic affected him that badly from a momentary touch . . .

Nothing. Her sigh was so deep it made her weak. The sole of Terrible's boot—what was it made of? Did it matter, or was it simply having a barrier that made the difference?

Whatever it was, the killer didn't like it very much. He writhed on the cement, grunting, his fingers slipping uselessly off Terrible's boot and his other hand slapping the arm against Terrible's leg. Gross. The sight of that limp hand flapping, as if it was trying to grab back the life that had been stolen from it, made her stomach lurch.

Someone else came out of the crowd and grabbed the killer's legs, holding them down. And still that awful, sly sensation crawled up and down her arms, across her chest and shoulders. Still the black fog of magic intended to hurt and kill oozed into her chest, into her soul, to connect to the filth already there. It countered her high, stole it from her, made sadness and misery and hatred fall on her in a hellish downpour of pain.

At least she could do something about that. She started to turn, intending to run back to her apartment and get her bag, when something struck her.

The killer still lay on the cement. Still fighting against Terrible, still waving that gruesome appendage around like a Church flag at Festival time, still struggling against the other man—Burnjack, Chess thought his name was, one of Bump's lieutenants—holding down his legs.

How long had he been like that? Why hadn't he passed out yet, with Terrible's foot crushing his windpipe?

Terrible wasn't holding back, either. He was putting

weight on that foot, and his weight was considerable, considering he was about six foot four and packed with muscle. She'd estimated it at two-seventy once, and while that had been a bit too heavy, he wasn't exactly light.

So how was the killer still moving, still breathing?

Terrible must have had the same thought. His eyes searched the crowd for her; when they caught hers he raised his eyebrows, gave her a small tip of his head she understood. She nodded in reply. Yes, something magic-related was going on, and whatever it was, it wasn't good.

She jerked her own head back toward her building, letting him know where she was going, and he nodded.

She'd run that fast before, but not very often. Her chest ached by the time she reached her bedroom and grabbed the stack of hardcover books she used as a step stool when she needed one. Usually she didn't anymore, because Terrible got things down for her, but she figured he was pretty well occupied in keeping down a homicidal maniac who seemingly refused to die and radiated black magic and ghost energy like blood spreading through clear water.

She kept all the standard stuff in her bag—iron filings, graveyard dirt, asafetida, iron-ring water, and blood salt; the sort of all-purpose things she used a lot. The box on the top shelf of her closet was where the other stuff was, supplies she'd bought just because, or in case she ever needed them. Always good to be prepared, and almost everything in that box would be helpful in break-ing curses or hexes, weakening dark magics, crossing the Evil Eye.

Okay. Powdered crow's bone, of course. She had some dried chunks of snake, some goat's blood, tormentil, ground rat tails, a handful of lizard eyes and cat claws.

Hell, she should just take the whole box, except some-one would steal it.

Her hands shook as she tossed everything she thought might be useful into her bag, catching the silver glint of her pillbox in its pocket. If only . . . Too bad all the adrenaline in her system made it totally useless to even think about taking more. Maybe after all of it was done she'd take an Oozer or two. If she could; if she was still alive to do so.

Maybe that was being dramatic, but if there was one thing her life had taught her—one lesson it had rammed down her throat until she choked on it—it was that nothing was ever safe. Positive expectations were for idiots.

The crowd had grown in the short time she'd been upstairs. It spread out into the yard of the building across the street, into the corner itself. Some people had brought chairs to stand on or rickety ladders; others sat on the walls edging the staircase to her front door. It was a hell of a show, after all. Nobody wanted to miss it.

Nobody except her, anyway. Too bad she didn't have a choice. She fought her way through the forest of bodies, pushing as hard as she could. What were they going to do, attack her? Fuck them. They needed to get the hell out of her way, and they needed to do it immediately.

With every step—with every person she shoved to the side—the buzzing of her tattoos, the creeping sensation through her body, the cloud of despair and horror, grew, until she wondered how she managed to stay upright.

Luckily she did, and so did Terrible, although he defi-nitely looked paler than he should. Whatever that was, it was clearly starting to get to him, to infect him, and she didn't have much time.

The killer still struggled to get up, still waved that arm around like a fucking winning lottery ticket. No way was that guy alive by normal means; she could see his throat almost crushed under Terrible's foot.

So how was he alive at all?

First things first. She grabbed the iron-ring water—clean water with iron rings in the bottle, left to purify under a full moon—and watched Terrible take a swig. Some of his color returned. At least that was some weight off. For the moment, anyway.

More of that heaviness lightened when she took a drink herself. Excellent. Start with the iron filings, then; clearly iron had some power over whatever the spell was—it usually did—and what she needed most was to neutralize it enough to think.

"*Arkrandia bellarum dishager.*" Her hand swung in an arc over the supine killer, spreading a fine dust of iron. The power lessened again.

But the killer hadn't blinked. He hadn't blinked and he hadn't choked. Chess bent down, trying not to get too close but needing to see it anyway.

Holy shit. Either she was in the presence of some unbelievably fucked-up magic or this guy was out of his mind on Burn—a drug even *she* wouldn't go near—or both, because he hadn't blinked, and tiny shards of iron dug into his eyeballs. As she watched, blood welled around one of the largest pieces, started trickling down to the outer corner.

He could certainly see, though. His free hand—the one not clutching its grisly souvenir—shot out and grabbed for her, caught her ankle in a grip so strong she cried out. Horrible cold magic, death magic, ghost magic, flew up her leg, spread through her body and darkened her vision.

Terrible's foot smashed into the killer's head; blood sprayed from his nose and mouth. Still the killer's hand clutched her ankle; still he pulled harder than she would have imagined he could.

Chess went down. Lukewarm blood soaked into her clothes, her hair. Her stomach lurched. She was covered with it, it was all over her, on her skin. . . .

Terrible's foot slammed down again, and again. The killer's face broke. He still didn't let go, started yanking her closer. What the fuck was going on? He couldn't be alive, no way could he be alive.

One more heavy stomp. The killer's head . . . "exploded" was the only word that seemed to fit, although it wasn't quite as dramatic as that. It looked like . . . like a smashed M&M, oozing blood and spilling pulpy tissue from its hard candy shell.

His grip didn't loosen.

She shoved her blood-slick hand into her pocket to pull out the switchblade Terrible had given her a couple of months before, but Terrible was faster. He crouched down, dug the point of his own knife down into the killer's arm, hard enough that it scraped the pavement beneath.

The killer started to babble, syllables falling from his misshapen mouth dying-fish-like against the pool of blood.

Terrible dragged his knife to the left, slicing through the killer's arm; Chess did the same on the other side. Oh, that was so fucking gross, and the magic kept spreading through her body, thicker and heavier every minute like cold crawling slime, making her vision blur further and her head buzz.

Terrible's eyelids fluttered again. His hand had come in contact with the killer's wrist as he finished cutting through the skin. Chess reached out to grab him, pushing as much energy as she could into him. Please, please let it work. If he passed out that man-thing was going to get up, she knew it, and no one else would have a hope of defeating it.

Not to mention what it would do to Terrible to pass

out in front of everyone, how that would affect him. She couldn't even think of that.

His head dipped for a second, his face paling further. He started to fall forward. No, no damn it, that couldn't— She gripped his arm harder, dug her nails in and shoved everything she had into it, as much energy as she could summon.

That, at least, worked. Too bad when he slipped, his foot left the killer's head, and the killer was moving again. Would that thing never die— No. No, it wouldn't, would it? It snapped together in her head, a disgusting idea, but the only one she could think of.

The man was possessed by a ghost. Or worse, it was a corpse re-animated by a ghost.

Okay. It was a ghost, and she could Banish it. She just had to disconnect it from that body first, and while that wouldn't be easy, it was something she knew how to do.

Terrible straightened, kicking out at the killer and shoving it back to the ground, while Chess threw a handful of graveyard dirt and asafetida at it.

It froze.

Her shoulders had started to sag in relief when it moved again. Shit! It must be getting some sort of extra protection from the body it was in, either the body or the magic or both.

Okay. Try something else. She popped the cap of her salt canister and started walking a circle, focusing on the energy. People stepped out of her way and stayed outside the circle, something she hadn't expected but was grateful for.

But, then, of course they stayed outside it; Downsiders weren't quite as afraid of magic as they were of Terrible, but probably close. At least of this kind of magic.

She reached the end. Fuck. She needed to use her blood to set the circle, but her knife had just been buried in a dead man's muscles. The thought of cutting her own flesh with it was just . . . No.

Oh, this sucked. It fucking sucked. She wiped her knife on her jeans, set down the salt canister, and gritted her teeth. The second this was done, she was going to soak her hand in antiseptic.

"With blood I bind." The stinging pain of the cut in her left pinkie faded when the circle set in place, strong and pure, giving her that little rush of energy that never grew old.

That was all well and good, but whether or not the circle would hold a ghost possessing a corpse was another question entirely.

Terrible glanced at her, his expression a question. She nodded and he turned to Burnjack, still holding down the killer's legs inside the circle. "Go on, now, only don't step on that salt, aye? Don't fuck it up."

Burnjack nodded. The second he let go of the killer's legs they started moving again, kicking and jerking like a toddler having a fit. At almost the same moment Terrible crossed the salt line himself and stood near Chess.

Not too near, of course, but at moments like this she almost didn't give a shit that they'd decided to keep their relationship secret, that Terrible thought it would keep her safer if people didn't know they could get to him through her. It made sense, and she agreed most of the time, but right then . . . right then she was freaked out and covered with cold blood, and she wanted nothing more than to have him wrap those strong arms around her and make her feel safe.

But he couldn't, so she focused on the killer dragging himself to his feet, his upper body wavering, his flattened head sagging forward praying-mantis-like, too much for the crushed neck to support. She didn't know how she managed to keep from throwing up; blood drooled from the sick ruin of his face, dripped on his shirt, flew through the air in a vile rain when he shook his deflated head.

He stumbled toward her, arms outstretched. Did he see her—could he see anything through those eyes anymore? Or, no, he probably felt her, felt the power in her blood. Ghosts always did.

She held her breath when he reached the circle. The entire crowd held its breath when he reached the circle, all of them waiting to see what would happen. He reached out—

The energy of the spell on him, of the ghost and the practitioner, slammed into her and knocked the air out of her chest. So cold, so fucking cold, and so dark. The circle was connected to her and the magic probed the circle, finding her, sticking sneaky inquisitive fingers into her, poking and prodding to see where it hurt the most, finding the weak spots. There were so many for it to find.

She tried to push back against it but she didn't have the strength, not if she wanted to keep the circle in place. It was holding; she would call it a miracle if she didn't know those didn't exist, didn't know it was the Church—the magic the Church had taught her to use— keeping that barrier in place.

How long it would stay in place, she didn't know. The spell on the corpse was so fucking strong.

She clenched her fists and struggled. Not the time to think about it. Thinking wasn't going to help anything. What she needed to do was find a way to separate ghost and body.

She could do it with her psychopomp, but there was no way she could get into that circle to summon it, not without Terrible, and she couldn't take the chance of him collapsing again. No, she'd need to break or weaken the spell first, and that wasn't going to be easy.

What else was new?

Chapter Four

Murder is a crime. Murder by psychopomp is an evil.
—*Psychopomps: The Key to Church Ritual and Mystery*,
by Elder Brisson

No point in setting up a firedish inside the circle; that thing would either kick it over or smash it. But she could set one up just outside, and the smoke would drift into it. The faint breeze came from the west, so that's where she set up, on the broken curb by the sewer grate.

Asafetida and ajenjible went in first, followed by corrideira—all she had—and some melidia. Whatever the hell that thing inside the body had once been, it was now a murderer, and sending it to one of the spirit prisons would be one of the best things—no, would be *the* best thing—that had happened to her that day.

Thick smoke started drifting from the dish, barely visible in the darkness settling over the street. The smell of it filled the air, filled Chess, and chased some of her fear away. That was the smell of Church, the smell of magic, the smell of things she knew how to do. Things she *could* do, and do well. She might not be worth much as a person, but she was a fucking good witch, and she could do this.

Iron had lessened the spell's power before, so that was the first thing she grabbed, gritting her teeth against the sensation of alien hands scrambling her innards. Iron had lessened it and salt had held it, and the two of them together were pretty fucking strong. Stronger than the spell, she hoped.

She filled her palm with them, held them over the hot, fragrant smoke. "Power to power, these powers bind."

Energy warmed her skin; she could practically see it glowing. Good. She took a deep breath and threw the iron and salt at the animated body still fighting against her circle.

"Cadeskia regontu balaktor!"

Blowback like a brick flung at her chest knocked her over. Her head hit the sidewalk with a thud she barely felt. The power was too strong, too dark, for her to feel anything else. It surged over her, buried her beneath it. She struggled for air.

Through her slitted eyelids she saw the body in the circle wavering, saw the ethereal glow of the ghost emanating from it. She'd done something, she'd managed to start separating them somehow, but not enough. Fuck.

Okay. Crow's bone and wolfsbane, some black powder and blood salt. Ignore the throbbing pain in her head and get to work. Again she placed her hand in the smoke; again she said the words of power and flung the charged herbs.

This time she was ready for the backlash. It hit her, but not as hard, and she was able to keep watching.

The body—the killer, the ghost, the animated corpse, whatever she should call it—started to weave, its movements slow and staggering like a drunk looking for a place to vomit. What the fuck did it take to separate that thing? Usually the corrideira and ajenjible were enough, more than enough.

She tossed a chunk of snake onto the fire in the dish, gathered more salt in her hand, and scooped up some cobwebs to go with it. The cobwebs might trap the spell; that worked with some hexes, so why not try it here.

Without much real hope, she powered it over the smoke—purplish now from the burning snake flesh—and threw it. No. Just as she'd thought. This was bullshit. Anger rose higher in her chest every second, anger and a kind of frustrated determination. She should be upstairs with Terrible, warm and safe and high from Cepts and his body. Instead, she was on the street, looking more stupid every minute that she failed to break that spell.

Should she go ahead and summon her psychopomp? Yeah, the ghost-thing would probably hit her while she did the summoning, but it wasn't as if she'd never been hit before. And her psychopomp could tear the ghost from the body—if she could get a passport on it.

The thought of touching that stump of an arm, ragged from where she and Terrible had sliced it in two and still dripping dark blood, made her want to be sick. But if she couldn't separate them any other way . . . what else could she do?

Nothing she could think of, unless she wanted to be there all night. Which she didn't.

Right, then. She dug into her bag, pulled out the silk-shrouded dog's skull, and unwrapped it. Her psychopomp. In her right hand she grabbed her Ectoplasmarker and tugged the cap off with her teeth. She had no idea who that ghost was, so no way to design a proper passport for it even if she had time, but whatever. If she marked it the psychopomp would sense the marking, and hopefully take it instead of her.

She tucked more wolfsbane into her pocket to help hide the scent of asafetida on her skin from the psychopomp, and stepped into the circle.

It felt so awful in there, so awful, like stepping into a pool of cold murky water. A pool brimming with dead things, with sea beasts full of teeth.

The body sensed her, or heard her, or something. She didn't know. What she did know was that it turned and walked toward her, waving that fucking disembodied arm—what the fuck, was it some kind of security blanket or something?—and making horrible grunting noises.

Out of the corner of her eye she saw Terrible move. She shook her head, held up her hand. No. As much as she wanted him to, no. Too risky.

She braced herself and waited for it to come. Once it got close enough, she could scrawl something on it and duck away. At some point she'd have to fight the thing off her; she didn't have a choice. But not yet.

It lunged. She managed to grab its arm above the wrist, avoiding the gruesome prize it brandished but not able to avoid touching it at all. Under her palm its flesh was warm and solid, as if it were alive. What the fuck did that mean, then? Because the thing felt like a ghost and she couldn't imagine a living person was in there, so how the hell did its body still feel normal?

She guessed she'd find out later. She hoped she'd be alive to find out later, anyway.

Three circles would do for a passport. She scrawled them on quickly, tossed the Ectoplasmarker toward Terrible, who caught it, just as she knew he would.

Okay. Time for the psychopomp.

She let go of the body, ducked around it, and set the skull on the ground. Her left pinkie had stopped bleeding from setting the salt circle; she squeezed it hard to get the blood flowing again. Kept squeezing until her blood fell on the skull.

This wasn't the ideal place or situation for a ritual—she didn't have her stang, didn't have her cauldron, didn't have candles—but oh fucking well. "I call on the escorts of the land of the dead. I offer an appeasement for their aid."

The skull started to rock. Something hard slapped into the side of her head, knocked her over. Her arm scraped

the sidewalk. What the—shit, eeww. It had slapped her
with the dead hand; her cheek felt as if someone had
thrown an ice pack at it.

Ignore it. She lifted her right hand, pressed it against
the body's stomach to keep it away.

Then had to swallow, hard, three or four times, before
she could speak without gagging. "I call on the escorts.
Take this spirit back to its place of silence."

The skull erupted into life, rising from the cement as
blue light sparked in its eyes. Bones formed behind it,
the dog's skeleton flowing into being, skin and shaggy
black hair growing over it. Her psychopomp. It would
take the soul back to the City of Eternity under the
earth—the hole had already formed, blurry shapes behind a thin place in the air—and it would stay there.
Forever.

The psychopomp lunged. Chess ducked.

The killer beat at the dog with the arm in its hand,
its grunts turning to howls. No. No fucking way was it
going to defeat her psychopomp, no *way*. Psychopomps
were— They always won; it was their job to win.

She had to get that arm out of its hand, and she had
to do it without getting in front of the psychopomp, because it would give up on the embodied ghost any second and hunt for a soul it could catch. Like hers. The
only other soul in the circle.

Hers might have been worthless—well, no "might
have" about it, her soul wasn't worth shit—but she still
wanted to hold on to it for a while longer.

She needed something that would distract the killer,
make it drop the arm, but not hurt the psychopomp.

Fire. She needed fire.

The killer's grunts had turned into wails, loud angry
moans in the silence as it beat the dog with its gruesome weapon. The crowd had stepped back. Everyone
stood there watching, with their arms wrapped around

themselves and fear in their eyes. Ha. They could join the fucking club.

She held out her hand to Terrible. "Lighter."

He set it in her palm a second later, the black steel warm from being in his breast pocket, warm from his energy. She clutched it for a second, wishing she could do the same to him, then opened it and spun the wheel.

Flame burst from the top, six inches high and pale at the base, just like always. Good. How flammable the body would be she didn't know, but maybe at least that shirt would catch fire. She only needed a distraction, not a full-on cremation.

The psychopomp appeared on the verge of giving up; its tail had ducked between its legs. It turned to look at her. Fuck.

No time like the present. Especially not if she had any chance of surviving. She jumped forward, fisted the shirt, and touched it with the flame.

As she did, the killer swung that arm at her again, hitting her in the back of the head. She ignored it, fought through it.

Thank fuck, the shirt burst into flame, and she scrambled away as the killer roared again and started to beat at its chest with the arm.

Chess gathered her breath. "Take this spirit back to its place of silence!"

The psychopomp obeyed. The killer still waved the arm around, but its eyes—what was left of them— focused on the fire eating its clothing. It didn't see the psychopomp lunge.

One last howl from the killer, which turned into a squeal as the psychopomp grabbed its soul. The hole in the world behind it rippled again, like water running over glass; the psychopomp leapt through it, dragging the soul in its teeth.

The hole snapped shut, the skull hit the ground and

shattered as the body fell on top of it, and Chess sank to her knees in the now-empty circle, wondering what the fuck was going on this time.

The corpse's ruined head didn't look any better under the dull glow of the refrigerated warehouse's fluorescent lights. Its blood had dried a sticky brownish-red; the skin was pale, marked with the tread of Terrible's boot and various scrapes from hitting the pavement. Even the six Cepts in her system didn't help it look any better.

Chess held her hand over it for a second. She hadn't touched the body at all since drawing the passport on it back in the circle. She didn't particularly want to touch it now, but she had a feeling she was going to have to.

This time she wouldn't forget her gloves.

Energy slammed into her palm, anyway, thick dark energy that set off a horrible ringing sound in her head, as if her ears had been boxed. Whatever the spell on the body was, it wasn't pleasant.

But, then, she hadn't expected it would be.

"What you think, Ladybird?" Bump drawled from behind a fur scarf. "What kinda fuckin witchy shit be this time?"

She hated to admit it in front of him. "I don't know."

Silence.

"I can feel the spell, whatever spell it is, and I can feel that it's male—the spell caster is male, I mean—but I have no idea what the spell is. It feels like ghosts, too."

"Be him soul inside him fuckin body do the magic, yay? Like him gone an died, then give a fuckin try to coming back."

"Ghosts can't cast spells," she said, only half paying attention. "Do you know who he is? Who the body is, I mean."

Bump dug something out of one of the pockets in his floor-length white fur coat. "Got us him fuckin wallet here, dig. Be Gordon Samms, it tell. Ain't knowing him, I ain't."

"Had some owes," Terrible said. He stood at her side with his arm around her shoulders, helping to keep her warm. "Lost he some lashers on the card games, were payin slow."

Bump's thin reddish eyebrows rose. "Yay? How much?"

"Six hundred, now. Won heself a game on the other night, paid he a hundred then. At the tables all the time, dig, ain't could stay away."

Gambling. That was one thing she'd never seen the point of, one addiction she'd never picked up. Good thing, too. She'd really be broke if she had.

Terrible glanced at her, then back at Bump. "Burnjack say him were yellin when him come onto the street, just jumped him on Yellow Pete, started beatin him."

"Yellow Pete was the dead guy? The dead guy killed by this one, I mean."

He nodded. "Were a street dealer, dig, down Seventieth."

"So why was he near my apartment?"

"Ain't knowing on that one. Could be him live there, maybe gotta dame there, family, ain't know."

Right. It didn't matter anyway, did it? "Does Burnjack know what the ghost was saying? Did he catch any of it?"

"Asked he on that one, too. Said him only caught a word or two, thinkin be a name. Agneta. Agneta Katina. Be a dame, he said."

Hmm. "Girlfriend? Wife? Daughter?"

"Naw. Ain't married. Ain't sure he likes the dames, dig. Never seen him with any."

"Oughta give Berta the fuckin ask, yay." Bump poked at the body with the tip of his cane, for no good reason Chess could fathom. "Do her got one onna street that fuckin name? Maybe her got some fuckin knowledge on it."

Terrible nodded.

Okay, this wasn't getting them anywhere. She hated to do it, didn't want to do it, but she didn't think she had a choice, either. "I need to get his clothes off."

Bump snorted. "Ain't had the thinking you into the fuckin dead ones, Ladybird."

Chess gave that remark the response it deserved—which was none—and reached for the tattered, singed remnants of the shirt on the body.

Terrible was faster. He always was. "Ain't you do it, Chess. Lemme, aye?"

His eyes caught hers. Warmth rose in her chest, spread through her whole body. Looking into his eyes—into him—was a high she could never get tired of. Bump disappeared, the mutilated corpse on the table before them disappeared, the icy air around them disappeared. It was just the two of them, standing so close the warmth of his body caressed hers.

She reached up to touch his face, meaning to pull it down to hers so she could kiss him, when Bump cleared his throat. Loudly. The moment ended.

"Thinkin we fuckin get on the move this fuckin night? Maybe you quit on the cuddle-ups, get some attention on the fuckin job, yay?"

Asshole.

Terrible reached out for the buttons on the shirt. And fell.

Chess was already moving when his eyes started to roll back in his head, thrusting her arm in front of him over the body. She couldn't catch him, couldn't stop him from falling, but she could at least keep him from face-planting into a corpse.

Or she could quit fucking playing around and figure out a way to make it stop happening. Another good idea might be to get her damn head together; she'd felt the magic, she should have known it would affect him. She'd been so busy getting mushy she hadn't been focusing, and that was a Bad Thing.

He was out for only a second. That was usually the case when he touched something— Wait. What the fuck?

The body on the table—Gordon Samms's—was empty. The soul inside it was gone. So there shouldn't be much for the magic to work on, it shouldn't still feel as strong as it did. Yes, she should feel it, of course, but not that much. And it shouldn't be strong enough to do that to Terrible.

Nobody spoke as Terrible stood up. He didn't look at her. She didn't need him to. The color rising up his neck, the stiffness of his movements, spoke clearly enough, even if she didn't already have a pretty good idea what he would say.

"Okay," she said finally, tossing the word into the silence as if it didn't matter. "So I'm not just feeling residual magic, I guess. Whatever the spell is, it's still—there's still a bag on him or something, there'll be something there. Bump, you have his wallet, did anyone search his other pockets?"

Bump shook his head. "Figured on letting you have the fuckin job, dig, you the one got the handle on it."

It was so cool the way he was always thinking of her. She suppressed the eye-roll and dug around in Gordon's front pockets, stopping at the left one when she pulled out a spell bag about the size of a walnut. Darkness rolled up her arm in waves. Not good; of course it wasn't, what did she expect?

She set the bag on the table near his feet, to check when they were done, and kept searching. Nothing else. Just the spell.

So why did his body still radiate magic, why did it still make her tattoos itch and sting the way ghosts did?

Terrible started to reach for Gordon's shirt buttons again, then stopped. "All cool now?"

"No." Her first instinct was to grab his hand and pull it back, but not only would he really not like that one bit—how childish did she want to make him look? She didn't see it that way, but she knew he would—but she didn't want to touch his skin with anything that had touched that spell. Like her gloves. "There's something in the body, still."

His face darkened; he pulled a cigarette out of his pocket and lit it, still not meeting her eyes.

For a second she considered asking Bump to help her, but . . . yeah, like that was going to happen. No, lucky Chess got to strip the corpse all by herself.

Naked, it was even more pitiful—and gross, but she'd expected that.

What she hadn't expected was the faint teeth marks—dog teeth marks, psychopomp teeth marks—on Gordon's upper thigh. What she hadn't expected was the familiar milky-blue cast on his skin, the coloring she hadn't seen on his face and hands because they were mutilated or dirty.

"Oh fuck." She jerked back, her hand automatically going to cover her mouth; she caught it just in time. "Shit."

"What?"

Her stomach roiled and shifted. It didn't matter, she tried to tell herself. Gordon Samms had to die, she'd had no choice, there'd been nothing else she could do. . . .

That was Fact, and Truth, and she knew it. But her throat still ached as she forced herself to speak. "He was alive. He— I thought it was a ghost stuffed into his body, that he was dead before he attacked Pete, even, but he wasn't. He was alive. He was still alive."

Bump and Terrible watched her: Bump with impatience, Terrible with concern, but neither with understanding. Right, of course they wouldn't know.

"I killed him," she said. "My psychopomp killed him. He was alive, and my psychopomp ripped out his soul and killed him."

She would not throw up. She would not cry, either. She hadn't had a choice. And, as she recovered from her initial panic, she realized that she *really* hadn't had a choice. If he was still alive and moving—or at least, if his soul was still in his body and he was moving, what the fuck—after Terrible crushed his throat and head, then there hadn't been any other way to kill him, and there hadn't been any way to subdue him, and she'd done the only thing that could be done save for literally chopping him into pieces while he watched.

That made her feel better. Some. But still . . . she'd used magic to kill someone. She'd used her psychopomp to kill someone, and that was different from using a real weapon to save her life when she was being attacked. Using magic to commit a murder . . . that was an automatic death sentence.

Of course, so was killing a psychopomp and carving an illegal sigil into someone's chest to prevent them from dying, and she'd already done those, so what the hell.

The thought almost made her smile—not quite, but almost. At least it loosened her chest enough for her to take a deep breath.

"You right, Chess?"

She nodded. "Yeah. Um, yeah, I'm okay. Come on, let's see if we can figure out what's inside him or whatever."

Bump raised his eyebrows. "Any fuckin place I gots the thinking of where some shit maybe got stuffed into, I ain't for fuck wanting get my fuckin look-see in."

Eeww. She hadn't thought of that. "Yeah, I'm not really, either."

Terrible shifted his weight beside her, his arm touching hers. "I cut he all open, aye? Straight down, we get a look inside."

"I'll check his mouth first," she said, moving to do exactly that. What there was of his mouth; his teeth wobbled at odd angles—the few still remaining did, though she had no idea how many of them he'd had before Terrible used his skull as a footrest—and beneath the skin his jaw felt like gravel in a sack.

It made her job easier. His lips stretched open wide enough for her to fit her latex-covered hand inside; she wiggled her fingers in his throat, swallowing the sympathy gag threatening to rise in her own. The man was dead, after all. She could shove her hand all the way down into his stomach and he wouldn't feel it or care.

"I don't feel anything." Except tonsils. Ugh.

Terrible pulled out his knife. "Straight down, aye?"

"I guess so."

The point of the blade slid into Gordon's flesh and disappeared, moving like a zipper's tongue from the base of his throat to his groin. Terrible glanced at her. She shook her head.

"Yay, let he have the keeping on he fuckin cock." Bump grinned. "Ain't fuckin wanna see that come off nowheres."

Ah, Bump. Polite as ever.

Silence reigned as Terrible made another cut perpendicular to the first across Gordon's abdomen. He kept his left hand above the skin, making sure not to touch, but Chess wondered how strongly he felt it, how hard he was fighting against that horrible darkness rising like steam from Gordon's innards.

He stepped back. "Cool?"

"Yeah, I—yeah." What was she supposed to do, reach in and start pulling stuff out? Shit, what was she doing, why was she doing this? How the hell had she ended up there, in a freezer, about to shove her hand into a corpse like it was a cereal box and she was looking for a prize?

Did it matter? Addiction led to working for Bump, working for Bump led to falling in love with Terrible, and it would take weeks spent pawing around inside dead bodies to even come close to making her wish she didn't have him. She guessed all things considered, messing around with body parts was a small price to pay.

That didn't stop her insides from jerking a warning when her fingers closed around something she was pretty certain was Gordon Samms's stomach.

"How's it feelin, Chessie?"

"Really fucking gross," she managed. "And yeah, still powerful. Can you cut this open?"

That was what did it. When Terrible cut the stomach open so she could see what remained of Gordon's last meal . . . she barely made it to the wall before throwing up, humiliated to be doing it in front of Bump, humiliated to be doing it at all, but unable to stop herself.

Terrible's hand in her hair, gathering it behind her and holding it out of the way. His other hand on her back, rubbing it in slow circles until she finally managed to get herself under control. " 'Sall cool, baby, aye? No worryin on it, 'sall cool here."

She started to raise her hands to her streaming eyes and nose but he stopped her, turning her instead to face him while he wiped her face with a rag he'd gotten from somewhere. It was smudged with motor oil on one side but clean elsewhere. Even if it wasn't, she would have been grateful. "Thanks."

"Aye."

Bump nodded when she returned to the table. "Ain't fuckin put the blame on you, Ladybird. Fuckin sick, yay."

What? Had Bump—had Bump just been *nice* to her? How the hell was she supposed to feel about that?

Ugh. Who cared. She had way more important things to worry about.

Like the fact that as the pile of internal organs—ugh, ugh, ugh—grew, she wasn't finding any other spell bag, no spell ingredients. But everything felt like ghosts and magic, every part of him she touched. As if the spell was part of him. How could that happen?

"Ain't finding shit, yay, Ladybird?" Bump shook his head. "Got he all fuckin emptied up, what you fuckin do on the now?"

"I don't know." She eased the gloves off, trying but failing to keep the blood off her skin. When she got home, she was going to spend an hour or so in a very hot shower, and maybe Terrible could pour bleach over her every couple of minutes. "I don't know. Let's see what's in the spell bag, I guess."

She slipped on a fresh pair of gloves and jerked the tip of the iron blade she kept in her pick case through the black stitches at the top of the bag.

The rough edges of the fabric fell open, revealing a— well, damn. The spell was about the size of a walnut because it *was* a walnut—a large one, but a walnut all the same.

She dug the point of her knife into the crack in the shell and pried it open. Blood oozed out. Thick dark blood, so clotted that for a second it looked like some sort of rotted fruit inside the shell.

Her stomach gave another heave, but she ignored it. Not just because she didn't want to go through that again but because part of her was honestly fascinated. How the hell had he—the same spell caster, the same man—done that? What the hell was that spell?

"Ain't lookin so fuckin bad." Bump leaned over the table, peering down. "Fuckin small, yay?"

"But really strong." Were those clots in the blood, or was something else in there? "Blood . . . I think it might be corpse blood, like from a murder victim, or maybe menstrual blood. When someone's using blood like that in a spell, they're not fucking around."

Of all the things she could have done without that day, having to say "menstrual" to Bump was—okay, not the biggest or the most important, no, but it was certainly on the list. Not because she was embarrassed; she wasn't. She just didn't want to have to discuss anything remotely related to the female reproductive system with him.

Sure enough, he grinned. "Yay, seen me some of that blood fuckin turn dames into—"

"There's hair in there," she interrupted, holding one of the hairs up with her gloved index finger and thumb. "See? It's been tied in knots, too. I wonder if it's his."

It probably was. The fingernail clipping she found might have been, too. But the rat's eye, the three sharply bent pins, the tiny pieces of eggshell and feather, the ball of cobwebs and wax—and were those fish scales?— definitely were not.

By the time she'd finished laying it all out in an orderly if grisly row, her neck ached. As did her head, because she had a pretty good idea what those ingredients were for, what the spell did. "I think that's it."

"Aye?" Terrible reached over, offering her a drag off his smoke. She took it. "What's on with the blood, then?"

"I don't know. I guess it's clotted, old, you know?"

"Naw, that ain't it." He folded his arms across his chest. "Too thick, leastaways what I'm thinkin. Old blood don't get . . . rough like that, dig? Gets thicker, aye, an darker, but not like that."

Well, she guessed he would know. Yeah, she'd seen lots of spilled blood in her life, but she probably hadn't paid as much attention to it, had a chance to observe it as time passed, the way he had. "Yeah? You think something's mixed into it?"

He shrugged. "Ain't can say on that one. But that ain't usual blood."

"It feels kind of grainy." She rubbed it between her fingers.

"Ain't should."

"Shit. I have no idea how to analyze it or whatever."

"Ain't you got you a fuckin lab, up you Church? They got the fuckin skills run it all through, yay?"

She stared at him for a second. "Sure, Bump, how about if I head on in there and ask if they'll test the blood from a spell I found on the body of a man I killed with my psychopomp? That'll be no problem at all."

He hunched his shoulders a little, rolled his eyes toward the ceiling. "Were only giving the fuckin ask, yay, no needing to get all fuckin rumbly-sharp on it."

She glanced at Terrible, whose features were arranged into the carefully blank look he always had when she bickered with Bump. He'd been wearing that look more and more lately, hadn't he?

Something to worry about later. "It might be some sort of powdered herb in there, or . . . well, almost anything can be powdered. Bones, animal parts—I don't know how to figure it out, really. But whatever it is, this is a fuck of a spell."

"Know what the purpose is?"

"Yeah, I think so. The hair, the fingernail clippings— it's a binding spell. A control spell. I don't know for sure how it works or how magic got inside him like that, but I think the spell is the reason why he killed Yellow Pete and attacked us. The spell made him do it."

Terrible considered that for a second. "Be why he ain't died, too?"

She nodded, the realization taking shape in her mind as she spoke. "His soul—if the soul is under that much control, I mean, if it's been so strongly ordered to carry out a particular task, it'll force the body to keep going. Like, you know how under hypnosis, people can be injured without feeling it?"

"Aye."

"That's kind of like what this is. His soul isn't his own, it's powered by someone else, which means his body is powered by someone else. So it doesn't matter what happens to his body. As long as it *can* move, it will."

They were silent for a minute, absorbing that. With every passing second the implications grew worse; with every passing second the blood on her gloves looked darker, more threatening.

Terrible finally spoke. "So whoever made that spell got heself a killer ain't can be killed, aye? Got heself a weapon can be used anyplace."

She nodded.

Bump raised his eyebrows, tilted his head. "Damn, then, Ladybird. Lookin like you got some fuckin tough work coming, catchin em all."

Chapter Five

> And they had laws to cover all sorts of unnecessary things, because they did not have Truth to keep the peace.
> —*A History of the Old Government, Volume V: 1950–1997*

She'd just tucked her new psychopomp into her bag and headed through the vast dark-wood hallway when Elder Griffin stepped out of his office and smiled. "Ah, good morrow, Cesaria. I trust you are well?"

She gave him a quick curtsy. "Very well, sir." Aside from the scrapes and the bump on her head and the fear a decent night's sleep hadn't chased away completely, of course, but that wasn't something she could tell Elder Griffin about. Sure, she liked him a lot, and sure, he liked her, too, but some things were best kept to herself. "And you? Nervous?"

"I confess I am, a bit." His face colored slightly, almost pinkish beneath his pale hair. "It seems to be coming up awfully fast. You are still— That reminds me. Come in, please?"

Elder Griffin's office soothed her; it always did. The smell of herbs, the shelves stuffed with books and jars of spell ingredients and skulls and bones . . . Those shelves were empty today, of course, since he'd be moving to a new position after his wedding, and boxes sat everywhere on the carpet, but it was still his office. His heavy desk before the window, and his antique globe on a stand near the small easy chair. Chess especially loved the globe. Seeing where the countries had divided in the days BT—Before Truth, when people still believed in gods and the dead hadn't risen to kill so many people—fascinated her.

She sat down in the wooden chair before his desk. "Yes, sir? Is everything okay?"

He smiled, that peaceful smile that made him look so kind. He *was* kind. He was, in fact, one of the only—no, *the* only—truly, completely kind person she'd ever met in her life. "Perfectly well, my dear. I simply forgot to have you sign for your bonus yesterday. And I confess I am a bit at loose ends today. So much happening . . ."

"Of course." She signed the form he handed her, acknowledgment of receipt for the bonus check attached. Nine grand, the standard amount. And she could use it. Yeah, she'd gotten a pretty good chunk of change back when the whole Maguinness/Baldarel thing had gone down, but after her new car, new couch, and various other expenses—days at the pipes, a couple of nights here and there with Terrible at a hotel in Northside . . . she was doing okay, but it was always good to have more.

Especially since, if things were heating up between Lex and Bump—which it appeared they were—she wouldn't be getting her pills at a big discount from Lex anymore.

Paying full price again. Before Chester Airport, before her deal with Lex, she'd been spending a few hundred a week. She somehow suspected it would be more now. She'd been stepping on it some, the last few months: a few extra here or there, two instead of one or three instead of two, or the couple right before bed that she'd learned meant she felt human still when she woke up in the morning . . . whatever. They cost what they cost, and she needed them, so she'd pay it.

Elder Griffin slipped the form into the Darnell file

and set it down. "You are still attending, correct? Along with your—your young man? You are bringing him to the wedding?"

"Of course. I wouldn't miss that." She wouldn't, either. Every Church employee in Triumph City was invited—that was standard protocol—but he'd made a point of asking her, and of asking her to bring Terrible.

Or, well, he hadn't exactly said "Terrible," because he still didn't know his name. She wasn't quite sure how to bring that one up.

Of course, she could bring it up as the answer to his question. "What is his name, again?"

Shit.

She kept forgetting to talk to Terrible about it and ask what he thought. He had several forms of ID with different names on them, she knew; they were never used but were there just in case. Did he want to use one of those names? Did he want to be called "Terry," as his daughter, Katie, called him? No, he hated that—she didn't blame him. Katie's mother had started that one.

Elder Griffin watched her, his eyebrows a little higher than usual over his blue eyes. Right. It really shouldn't take so long to give him a piece of basic information.

Shit again. "Well, see, sir, he . . . he grew up in Downside, you know, and he never had any family or anything. . . ."

The eyebrows rose higher. "Indeed? I had no idea."

Shit, he was right, wasn't he? Stupid that she hadn't thought of it before, but she'd never specifically told Elder Griffin that the man she was "seeing" was from Downside. She had no idea if he'd assumed so or what, but his expression—well, his expression and the fact that he'd just fucking said he didn't know, duh—told her he hadn't.

But she didn't want to lie to him, either. She wasn't going to lie and she wasn't going to try to hide Terrible or who he was. She loved him and he was hers, and that made her so proud her chest hurt, and if anybody didn't like it they could go fuck themselves.

"Yeah, I mean, yes. So he never actually—nobody ever named him. But he used to get into fights a lot, and people started to call him Terrible. So that's what he's called."

Pause. "I see."

Did he? She scanned his face for signs of disapproval or criticism but found none. A weight she hadn't realized was there lifted from her chest. No, of course Elder Griffin wouldn't do that; he wasn't like that.

He nodded. "I shall look forward to meeting him, indeed. I take it things have gone well, since your . . . disagreement?"

Her face warmed. "Um, yes. And he's, he's looking forward to meeting you, too."

"Excellent," he said. "Well, I should get back to trying to work, I suppose, while I am still in this position. Have you heard from the Elder Triumvirate, to schedule your interview?"

"Wednesday." She hesitated. "I've never done an interview like this before. Is there anything specific you want me to say, or . . . ?"

" 'Tis nothing to be nervous about. They shall only ask about me and how you feel I handle my position here. Please say whatever you feel is best."

"Do you know yet where they're going to send you?"

"I do have some suspicions, indeed, but your interview is part of the process, as they want to determine where I will best fit."

"Should I tell them you'd be a great warden in the spirit prisons?"

His smile widened. "I confess that is not a position I mentioned as one I should like to fill."

The light from the window behind him faded as a

cloud covered the sun, adding to the unexpected solemnity of his next words. "I find myself growing weary of being reminded so often of the depths to which people will sink, Cesaria. Debunking . . . 'tis so important, but I would like, perhaps, to work in an area where there is more hope. More proof of the good in humanity, rather than the bad. Does that make sense?"

She nodded, trying to smile, trying to look as optimistic as he did. A place, or a job, where the negative aspects of humanity weren't readily apparent? Where there was goodness and kindness everywhere?

It sounded great, yeah. Too bad it didn't exist.

Gordon Samms lived—had lived—at Eighty-eighth and Wood, almost in Cross Town. Still Downside, of course—windows devoid of glass, walls and streets thick with graffiti, litter, and grime made that clear—but close enough that a few of the buildings they drove past appeared almost decent.

More than a few, in fact. Chess noticed a SOLD sign outside one and fresh paint on a few others.

Terrible nodded when she pointed them out. "Some parts here got new ones movin in, fixin em up. Still cheaper'n Cross Town, dig."

"Gentrification."

He glanced around. "Aye. Bump gave me the tell on the other day, gots people askin on a few him places. Them all lookin for cheap."

"But he'd never sell."

"Fuck, no. Glad on it, too. Don't even wanna think on living any elsewhere, aye? Be all bored up."

"Me, too."

He smiled at her, the kind of smile that made her breath freeze in her chest for a second because happiness had exploded there and squeezed out everything else. "Aye. Know that one."

He did, too. She remembered him saying it—sizing her up so neatly—in her bathroom one night, only a couple of days after they'd started investigating at Chester Airport. *Some of us needs an edge on things make us feel right,* he'd said, and she'd blushed and fidgeted and got all weird and uncomfortable, because it sucked to think someone could figure her out so easily, that someone could understand her so quickly.

But he had. He still did. And despite the tiny prickle of nerves in her stomach—if he could figure that out so fast, if he knew so much about her, sooner or later he'd know all the bad stuff, too, and how could he understand then, how could he stay with her?—it made her feel good.

What didn't make her feel good was thinking of what he'd just said about not wanting to live anywhere else, and thinking about the sigil, and where they were headed at that very moment. Terrible had touched Gordon Samms and passed out. Dark magics did that to him. And if word got out, if news of that spread . . . how could he stay in Downside, even if someone didn't take advantage of that weakness and kill him outright?

What would he do if he had to leave Downside? What would he do if he couldn't fight anymore—if he couldn't do the one thing he was proud of being able to do.

And she'd stolen that from him.

Well, she'd just have to fucking fix it, then, wouldn't she? He pulled up against the curb, taking his hand off her thigh to shift into neutral. "Hey, Chess. Maybe— I been thinkin, maybe I ain't should go along with you. To that wedding, dig. Might be—"

"What? Why?"

"Just—you don't need me there, aye? Thinkin they all give you the squint-eyes iffen they see me."

Her first thought was to wonder where this had come from, why he was bringing it up now, but then, she knew, didn't she? A look at how regular people lived, a bit of thought about the difference between Downside and the rest of Triumph City, between Downside and Church headquarters, and it was clear enough. Or at least why he was talking about it at that moment; he'd probably been thinking it already. Shit. "I don't care what they think."

"You oughta, though. 'Speople you workin with, it matters."

"No." Damn it. They were out in public, where she couldn't touch his face or climb into his lap or whatever else to change his mind. She grabbed his hand instead, low, where no one would see. "What they think doesn't matter. They don't have any effect on how I do my job or what cases I get or anything else, and even if they did I don't care. I want you there with me. I want you to meet Elder Griffin."

"Have he thinkin you lost yon mind."

"No, he won't. And you know what, even if he does, I still don't care." She squeezed his hand to make him look at her, so she could look in his eyes. Or where his eyes were, because his sunglasses were on. "I care what I think, and I want you there."

He hesitated. "Don't wanna fuck things up for you—"

"You won't. You're not." She clenched her jaw so hard it hurt. It wasn't that big a deal, really, it was just . . . just that she finally had a chance to be with him in public, to show everyone that she belonged to someone, that she mattered to someone, and that she was proud of that. Because she was. "I want you to be there."

"Maybe you—"

"It's—it's important to me, okay? Please come with me."

"Don't think you need—"

"Terrible. You are coming. And if anybody doesn't like it they can fuck off. That includes you."

His lips twitched. "You givin me the orders now, aye?"

"Yes. So cut it out."

Another pause; she could see him trying to come up with another argument and plastered a don't-even-fucking-try-it look on her face.

Finally he sighed. "Aye, right, then. But iffen you wanna change yon mind, you just say."

"I won't."

They'd parked near the dull industrial-green façade of Gordon's building, peeling and dusty in the afternoon sunlight. He opened her door and led the way up the semi-intact sidewalk. Hopefully they'd get some information in there.

Or not. The second she picked the lock and Terrible swung open the door to Gordon's apartment, she knew they wouldn't find anything of use—or, to be more exact, they wouldn't find anything magic-related. No energy beckoned them farther into the room, no dark power set her tattoos on fire.

A good thing, yeah, but not helpful.

Searching through Gordon's things wasn't much better. Playing cards were everywhere—scattered over the carpet and furniture, decks tidy on shelves and the kitchen counter. Chess stopped counting them when she hit twenty-three.

More signs of Gordon's habit showed up in other places. Books on poker and blackjack strategy by the bed, in the bathroom, lying with their spines bent on the floor. Racing forms. Sports pages from four different newspapers. Sports magazines. Poker chips made bright circles all over the dirty brown shag carpeting; torn lottery tickets and betting slips covered them, confetti for a loser's parade.

"Lots of boxes around," she commented as they entered the dim, stale-smelling bedroom. Gordon hadn't been too worried about personal cleanliness; a dark sort of coffin-shaped smudge on the right side of the bed indicated both where he slept and that he didn't change his sheets much. "Was he moving or something?"

"Ain't got any on that." Terrible shifted a few of the boxes so he could get to the closet doors, then stopped. "Hold up. Check this."

She crossed the dirty carpet to take the paper—no, the photograph—from his hand. Two men sitting at a table covered with beer bottles, their arms around each other, drunken grins plastered across their faces. "What? Who's that?"

"'sGordon there, aye? An Yellow Pete there."

Gordon and the man he'd killed. The man he'd been magically directed to kill. "They were friends?"

"Guessing so. Never seen em together what I recall, but ain't like I seen either much, ceptin when Pete checked in, handed over he lashers an whatany else. Pete weren't a gambler, neither."

She started to sit on the bed, then reconsidered. "So somebody didn't just kill Pete, they made his friend kill him?"

"Aye. Guessing they figure makes it easier, dig? Pete ain't be scared on Gordon, he sees him comin."

"Did Pete have reason to be scared of someone?"

He shook his head once, a quick twitch. "Aw, Chess. Always reason to, aye? Ain't can trust on nobody you see."

Yeah. She knew that.

He opened the closet doors to reveal the emptiness within. "Guessing—"

"Wait." Okay, that could be something. That might get them somewhere. Right? "Gordon and Pete knew each other. They were friends."

"Lookin so, aye."

"So someone—whoever did this—knew that, right? Because it's too weird to think they just happened to pick Gordon to kill Pete, and they just happened to be friends. The sorcerer knew."

The approval in his eyes made her feel warm all over. "So the spell maker, he knew em too, aye? Knew em both."

"Looks like it, huh."

He nodded. "Maybe be good talkin to some at the card games. Ain't guessin he neighbors be much for knowledge on him."

Terrible's phone rang. Shit. Lately it seemed like it was never good news, and this time didn't seem to be an exception. He hung up—slammed the phone shut, would be a better term—and rubbed his forehead. "Gotta go. Gots us another man down."

"What? Another—Lex, you mean. Another street guy dead."

He nodded, already pulling his keys out of his pocket and heading for the door. "By the docks, this one. Lemme get you home."

"Why? Why?"

"Gettin late, baby, ain't wanting you up there—"

"And taking me home is going to cost you at least another twenty minutes or so. No. I'm going with you."

"Ain't safe there, an I don't—"

"But you'll be there. There are people there, right? I'll be fine. Come on, take me with you."

Another dealer killed by Lex—another man killed by Lex or at Lex's order. At least so Terrible and Bump thought. But maybe it wasn't him; maybe someone else was doing it. Maybe if Chess saw it, she could find out.

Maybe she just needed to see it. To see that Lex really had done it, that he really was doing his best to fuck up her life.

Whatever the reason, relief blossomed in her chest when Terrible nodded. "Aye, right, then. Only you do what I say, dig? I say get in the car, you do. Aye?"

"Don't I always do what you say?" She raised her eyebrows, grinning at the little flash of memory—memories—the words invoked and the accompanying heat in her veins.

"Aye, guessin you do." His hand brushed her behind when he stepped back to let her in the car, and her temperature kicked up another degree or two. Probably not the most appropriate response right after getting news of a murder, but it wasn't as if they were detouring to her place for a quickie, so what the hell. A second or two of inappropriate thinking was fine.

They were in the Chevelle and speeding up Eightieth before she thought to ask. "By the docks? I thought Bump didn't put men up there."

He shook his head. "Naw, gots a few locals do some selling, only in the day, dig. This ain't one, though. Greenback, he name. Works—worked—round Fiftieth. Only found by the docks."

"So what was he doing up there?"

He sighed and nosed the Chevelle around the corner. "Guessin we gonna find out."

Chapter Six

A crowd of wrong people is still wrong; numbers do not make Right.

—*The Book of Truth*, Veraxis Article 1549

She'd never been this close to the docks before. Terrible had refused to take her—not that she was desperate to see them or anything.

But it was still . . . interesting.

She'd seen a neighborhood like it once before, out by the Nightsedge Market on Lex's side of town, up near the Crematorium. A neighborhood where the few remaining intact buildings almost seemed ashamed of themselves for being so, where crumbling walls and roofless rooms open to the sky were the norm.

And it smelled, the dank rotten scent of the bay mixed with oil and human waste and filth, a horrible fugue that made her wish she had a surgical mask or something to put on. All those germs in the air, bacteria dancing on dust motes and searching for a nice warm body to invade and set up home in.

Terrible noticed her shudder. "Can wait in the car, if you're wanting."

"No." Whatever the reason she wanted—needed—to see the body, she still did.

"Told you were shitty here."

"Yeah, but—look, the water is kind of pretty."

He followed her gaze across the pitted cement to the water, which gleamed with the sunset's reflection between the looming hulks of boats. Under that glow, she knew, lurked filth and muck and death, but the surface . . . the surface was beautiful. Just as with so many things.

He shrugged and took the few steps that brought him to the small circle of people in the middle of the intersection. They moved aside for him without speaking; Chess wondered if a few of them were able to speak. They looked barely human, like evolutionary throwbacks to the period when tiny dark creatures discovered fire. Masses of dirty hair tangled from the tops of their heads to midway down their backs; what appeared to be burlap sacks covered their bodies, and their feet were bare. Even Chess had never seen anything like it. Downside was poor, yes, but these people weren't poor, they had *nothing*. And people who had nothing developed their own world to compensate, and now she'd walked into it.

They knew Terrible, though, backing away from him without looking into his face.

"Who find him?" he asked, and when he stepped to the side Chess saw the body.

Greenback lay on his stomach in a pool of blood on the tar-streaked concrete, his pale face staring at the street beyond. It took Chess a second to realize what had happened, how that was possible; he should have been facedown, but his neck had been cut with so much force it had almost been severed, and his chin rested on the concrete.

Terrible crouched beside the body. Chess tried not to see his boots making dents in the sticky blood puddle. "Who find him?" he asked again.

Someone stepped forward, a dirty, skinny wraith of a woman with long thin scratches on the outsides of her arms and track marks on the insides. "Were me. Seen it, I done. I done seen it."

Mutters ran through the crowd at this; a few people edged away from her. She didn't appear to notice. "Were two mens. Jumped outen a car an cut he. Lay he out like so an drive off."

"What kinda car, you knowing?"

The nest of hair on her head—it had once been blond—shook, like a leafy branch moving with the breeze. "Black one. All I know."

"You seen the men, them faces or aught you could know iffen you see em again?"

Another shake. "Black car. Black clothes."

"You touch he? Got him wallet?"

Yet another shake, faster, so fast Chess knew—even if she hadn't already—that it was a lie.

Terrible glanced at the body, then back at the woman. "Any lashers in it you keep, dig? Drugs, too. Ain't give a fuck on it. But needing to see he wallet, iffen you got it."

She didn't respond.

Terrible stood up slowly. Chess never could figure out how he managed to make himself look even bigger when he wanted to—a particular furrow of his brow, a slight hunch to his shoulders, his arms held just an inch or so farther out from his body—but he did it then, staring at the woman with a calm intensity Chess felt even from a few feet away.

The woman hiked up her dress in the back and produced a leather wallet. Shit, had she been keeping that thing in her underwear?

Yes, she had. Chess hoped to see some sort of thigh holster or garter, but lifting the excuse for a dress showed the woman's spindly bruise-covered legs, and they were bare.

Terrible wasn't coming anywhere near touching Chess

with those hands again until they'd been washed. Twice. At least.

He didn't look any happier about where the wallet had been kept, but he opened it anyway. "Got any else? Needing to see all it, dig?"

Greenback had apparently also had a watch, several small bags of pills and powders, an earring, and a few scraps of paper. That was a lot to keep in a pair of underwear; Chess had to hand it to the woman for that.

Terrible set the items on the ground at his feet and kept digging through the wallet.

He glanced at Chess. "No lashers taken, dig, still all in here. Adds up, too, for what bags there is missing."

"They didn't steal anything, then."

"Naw, ain't lookin like." He turned to the woman. "You see him before the car come? Were he standin here?"

The woman licked her lips, her gaze flicking from the wallet in Terrible's hands to the drugs on the ground and back again in constant restless motion. "Were in the car."

"What? Greenback were?"

"Greenback dead one?"

"Aye."

She nodded. "Him get outen car. Other two followed. Killed he."

Terrible's expression didn't change, but Chess could imagine what he was thinking. Probably it was the same as what she was thinking, which was: What was Greenback doing in the car? If those were Lex's men, why was he in the car with them, and why hadn't they stolen his money and drugs?

"He look like him wantin get out the car, you see?" Terrible pulled a couple of things out of the wallet—papers, she thought—and tucked them in his pocket before handing the wallet back. "Or like them pushed he out?"

"Said I keep the lashers, you did."

He shrugged. "An you keeping em. Weren't lashers I took. Papers, an you don't need em, dig?"

The woman glared at him. He stared back at her, with that same deadly patience.

The woman gave up. "Look like him got pushed. Them follow right on he, cut him throat. Lay him out. Drive on off."

Terrible nodded, then scooped up the bags at his feet. "Any else seen? Heard aught? Got any knowledge?"

A hand raised at the back, a skinny pole with fingers jutting above the crowd of matted hair. "Mr. Terrible? Gots trouble. Mine friend, gots him trouble."

"Aye? What's on?"

The man pushed through the crowd, his bright orange hair—spray-painted, it looked like—glowing as the last rays of sunlight hit it. Seeing it reminded Chess that the sun had almost set, and with that realization came another, an unpleasant one: The crowd around them had grown, and at the end of the street, mist rolled off the bay and started inching toward them.

The man stopped in front of Terrible. Ribs showed through holes in his thin T-shirt like the bones had cut the fabric, and his ashy ankles protruded from the bottom of tight, gaudy striped pants. He wore mismatched flip-flops on his feet. "Mine friend, him taken the speed. Bangin it. Him gone all fluffcutty, ain't won't leave him room, screamin them after he, screamin on ghosts in him head."

"Aye? Maybe him oughten quit the bangin a day or two, get he some sleepin."

"Nay, ain't like it. Ain't like it. Him . . ." The man glanced around, took a step closer to Terrible. "Him done gone out on the morn, come back with blood on he. All wet blood. Fucked in crazy, him bein. Talkin to he, ain't like he, ain't in he eyes. Then him come back, start screamin. Then go all silent on the again."

Terrible looked at Chess, then at the street. The mist had advanced another quarter block or so; it had almost reached them, and the streets darkened by the second.

The crowd grew closer by the second, too. Chess took a step closer to Terrible—easy, because he was moving closer to her—before realizing the crowd wasn't looking at her. They were looking at the body on the street, and she did not want to know what they had planned for it.

"Just keep he locked in, dig? He sobers up, he be right then, aye?"

The man shook his head again, his eyes huge in his dark face. "Been like this three days gone. Please comin have you a see. Be the speed, gotta be. Got he a bad batch, thinkin."

Another glance at her. Another glance at the mist, at the fading glow of the sun dying behind the buildings. "Come back on morrow, dig? I come down see he—"

The scream, so loud and shrill, so full of darkness and horror that it made Chess cringe, cut Terrible off—cut everything off. For a long minute, all there was in the world was that horrible banshee-like shriek, tinged with madness and death and unholy glee.

They all turned—everyone—to see the figure emerge from one of the intact buildings a few doors down and start running toward them.

He was naked. At least from the waist down. A tattered T-shirt stretched across his chest, stained with ever-darkening sweat-rings of gray, like gathering storm clouds. Black shoes covered his feet. The crowd parted; shit, she was looking at a man even Downside dock-dwellers were afraid of.

He stopped screaming. The silence slapped her, made

her body sigh in relief for a split second before he started again.

The closer he got, the weirder he was. Before Terrible stepped in front of her she could see the man's body crisscrossed with scratches and marks, all up and down his skinny legs and arms. Track marks, some of them, but not all of them.

He kept wailing, his voice cutting in and out as it cracked. He stumbled in a pothole and fell; when he stood, blood ran down his knees.

For a second she thought maybe he'd keep running, that he'd be just another freaky-ass thing to see near the docks, but no such luck. He fell again, with an ugly *crack*. Had he broken a bone? He didn't seem to be in any particular pain, but she had a distinct feeling that he wasn't exactly dealing with reality at that moment.

Terrible's hand closed over her arm; she could feel him wanting to drag her back to the Chevelle and throw her in. No fucking way. She let him stay in front of her though, so she was partially hidden by his broad frame but still able to see. The man remained on his hands and knees on the street, wretched hoarse sobs coming from his throat.

"Please," he said. "Please, don' lettem get me. Don' lettem get me."

"Be my friend," the man with the orange hair murmured. "Told you, he fucked in crazy."

Terrible glanced down the street from where the man had appeared. Chess did, too. Emptiness. No one chasing him. Hell, no one even followed him, at least not that Chess could see.

But he kept turning back, his eyes wide and terrified. "Look. Look, they coming."

"Ain't nobody there."

"I see em." He tried to stand up. Oh, fuck, he tried to stand, and he'd snapped his leg. When he stood the bone broke the skin, popping out of his shin like a flipped lever. He tumbled back to the pavement.

Terrible's hand touched hers in warning, and he took a step forward. "Nobody comin. None there."

"Be the truth, Creaseman," said the orange-haired man. "Be me here, be DV. You friend DV, aye? Nobody comin, nobody there, you—"

"They see me." Creaseman kept dragging himself along the street, leaving a trail of blood behind him. His voice shook; it was barely a whisper. "They see me."

He moved his hand to pull himself farther along and collapsed.

It took Chess a second to realize what was happening. At first she thought maybe he was crying, but then she realized his entire body was shaking and horrible foam started dripping from his open mouth. A seizure.

She jerked forward. Terrible's hand stopped her. Right. Nothing she could do, really, and who knew what he might do to her if she got near him. No point in trying to help. She knew that.

It still made her feel sick, though, as he kept seizing. It didn't last long, she didn't think; thirty seconds, tops. But long enough for the image to embed itself in her brain and join the other horrible things in there. Another member for the club, something else to taunt her in her dreams.

He stopped. Started again. Stopped. His hands stretched over his head. He flipped onto his back.

And died.

Chapter Seven

You must always look beneath the surface. The real solutions are always hidden. So are the real mysteries.
—*The Example Is You*, the guidebook for Church employees

Without realizing it, she'd been pressing herself against Terrible, fisting his shirt. His arm slid around her and gave her a quick squeeze before releasing her. Right. She ought to let go, needed to let go, because they weren't alone on the street, and while she wasn't the only woman grabbing the nearest man—or vice versa— even by the docks it wouldn't be a good idea to look too comfortable touching him like that.

Terrible took a few cautious steps forward, his knife still ready. Chess grabbed hers, too. Not so much because she thought she'd need it—although it certainly wasn't out of the realm of possibility—but because she felt safer with it. That man was dead. She knew he was dead. She knew it because she'd seen him die, and she knew it because when she glanced up she saw the bird swooping overhead, limned in the last rays of sun. The psychopomp taking his soul.

"Somethin in him hand." Without taking his eyes off the man, Terrible waved her forward. He crouched beside the body, reached out—

And fell.

Thankfully he was only a couple of feet away; she'd

already been approaching him. Still it seemed to take forever to reach him. She threw herself to her knees, ignoring the pain streaking up her thighs, and clutched at him. He was so fucking heavy. What had he touched, what the hell was—

A little plastic packet was what he'd touched. It lay on the dead man's palm, still half in it, with Terrible's fingers barely making contact.

She grabbed his hand, pulled it away from the packet. Pulled his head into her lap. He'd come around fast, he usually did, shit, people were watching and he'd just— he'd be furious. He'd be furious and he'd be humiliated, and the fear already building inside her grew sharper, colder, when she thought what that might mean. How it was her fault, and how her attempts at fixing it thus far had failed. How if she were Terrible she'd be giving up on the idea that she could fix it. Would have already given up, in fact.

His eyes opened. For a second they scanned her face, the sky, the crumbling buildings edging the street, before consciousness snapped back into them. "Fuck."

"I don't—"

"Fuck." He pulled away from her, his gaze still wandering up and down the street. The crowd around them watched. Double fuck.

She didn't bother to glare at them. Didn't dare to react at all. The last thing she wanted to do was make him angrier, more upset. Already his neck and jaw flushed darker every second, color creeping up over his face. He could control his expression, could make himself look like a forbidding statue, but he couldn't stop that. Never had been able to.

A minute passed. Two. He pulled two cigarettes out of his pocket, lit them and handed her one. He cleared his throat. "Guessing whatever he got there ain't just drugs, aye?"

"Yeah. It looks like it, anyway."

His chin jerked. "Oughta call some others out here, have em pick it up, pick him up, too. Ain't wanna be—"

"Why?"

He glanced at her, his eyebrows raised, but didn't speak.

"Let me at least have a look at it. I know Bump has all those chemicals and stuff that can analyze it or whatever, but—"

"Ain't want you touchin it."

"But I won't—I mean, I'll put on some gloves, okay, and now we know something's there, right, so I'm prepared for it." Damn it. Of all the fucking things to happen.

He didn't meet her eyes as he nodded.

Well, shit. The least she could do was get it over with quickly so they could get the fuck out of there. She wanted to go home. She wanted *him* to go home, and she wanted to go with him. She wanted to forget this whole horrible day.

No chance of that. Forgetting wasn't as easy as it seemed; life had taught her that, if nothing else. But it had also taught her that where there was a will there was a way, and she had a pillbox full of ways in her bag.

She took four of them and slipped on a pair of latex gloves for the second time in as many days. "Okay. Let's see what he had."

It was a little packet, exactly like the one in Chess's bag at that very moment. Not quite an inch square, with a Ziploc top, filled about a third of the way with whitish powder. Just like any one of dozens, hundreds, she'd held or seen or used in her lifetime.

But none of them had ever sent energy roaring up her arm to explode in her chest, so much of it and so thick that there wasn't enough room for breath. None of them had made a stinging, screaming screen of red wash over her vision, made her head ring so loud she thought for a second she might have gone deaf. No wonder Terrible had collapsed. What the fuck was in that packet?

For a few seconds she struggled with it, forcing it down into something she could handle, pushing against it with all her might, until it finally started to ease up. She sucked in a deep, shuddering breath. Her vision cleared.

Terrible turned to DV. "Where he buy this?"

DV shrugged. "Offen Rickride, same as always, what I got. Buy he three bags, dig, only one's left there."

Terrible's face darkened. Rickride must be Bump's dealer, then, the one who lived in the area.

She'd ask him about it later. Discussing it on the street probably wasn't the best idea. Time to focus, so they could get the fuck out of there.

Up close the body before her looked even worse. His skin hadn't yet taken on the artificial pallor of death, that sort of waxy flatness, but the scratches and marks on his skin already stood out more sharply, looked angrier and more vivid.

Terrible edged closer to her, grabbed her arm. "Getting you outta here. Now."

"But—"

"Take you some pictures, iffen you need a better look. That body ain't gonna be here much longer."

"What?"

He glanced at the growing crowd, at the mist now tickling their legs, gripping his knife tighter as he did. Chess felt his unease; it didn't show, wasn't apparent to any of the people standing a few feet away—at least she hoped not—but she knew it was there. Felt it the same way she felt darkness in that fog like angry whispers, and the power created by the edges of the earth by the jointure of three elements. The mist was hungry; it wasn't magic in itself but it had its own power, as everything did, and that power made the hairs on her neck tingle and shift.

Was it her imagination, or had the crowd gotten a little closer than it was before?

"C'mon."

He stared at the crowd while she pulled out her camera and snapped four or five pictures. They probably wouldn't be important at all; just scratches, not runes or sigils or anything like that, but still. She needed them, and, if she was lucky, enough respect remained for Terrible that the crowd of hungry faces watching her wouldn't decide to try to take the camera from her. Terrible could handle a lot of things, but the crowd looked too big now even for him.

She'd barely lowered the camera when Terrible started hauling her to her feet. She tucked the little plastic packet into her pocket. When she got home she'd toss it straight into the African Blackwood box she kept for magical items of dubious origin.

Assuming she got home. The crowd stepped closer still.

Terrible didn't look scared, but she knew he was—or, well, not scared but uneasy. And she knew all that unease was for her, as if she'd heard him say it out loud. He wasn't worried about protecting himself or being attacked, he was worried about it happening to her, and she knew it not only because she knew him but because he took her hand as they started to walk.

"Push yon sleeves up."

"Wha—oh." Of course, dumbass. She did it as quickly as she could, hoping the people staring at them with blood in their eyes knew what the tattoos on her arms meant. Hoping they even knew what the Church was, for that matter.

She couldn't tell if they saw her ink or not, or if they cared. But a woman with long brown dreads who smelled like a sewer stepped out of their way as they neared her.

Terrible didn't seem to be moving quickly, but he was, and she tried to keep up without appearing to speed herself.

The hardest part was not looking back. They'd passed the edge of the crowd, into the mouth of the street beyond, into the fog. It should have been a relief, being out of the way of them, but it wasn't. It made her feel even more naked, made her feel as if at any second someone would hit her over the head or she'd fall before she heard the bullet coming. She tightened her grip on Terrible's hand.

He squeezed back but didn't look at her until he had her in the Chevelle, with the doors locked. The crowd outside inched closer to the car; Chess couldn't see the bodies anymore. All she saw was people, those ramshackle dock-dwellers standing in ragged lines, with the mist moving up behind them.

Terrible started the car and put it in gear. "Told you, ain't a good place to be."

"No." She rubbed the back of her head, trying to brush off the stares she imagined she could still feel. "No, I guess not. And I guess we have to go back tomorrow, huh?"

"Aye. Talk to DV again, try to find Rickride see where that speed come from."

"Great." One last glance back at the shadowy shapes in the mist. "I can't wait."

Half an hour later they trudged up the stairs to her apartment. Neither of them spoke, just as they hadn't in the car on the way there, every foot they drove a reminder that they'd have to do it in reverse the next day. Every foot a reminder of what they'd left behind. Chess couldn't stop seeing bone exploding from skin, couldn't stop seeing foam in the corners of a dying mouth or Terrible's head sinking when he touched the speed.

There were too many things to say to pick one, so all of them bottlenecked in her throat, forming a horrible lump that writhed and stung and felt like it was trying to break through her skin. She had no idea if Terrible felt the same.

What she did know was that if there was a worse possible time for Lex to show up, she couldn't imagine what it could be.

Terrible stiffened. She did the same. Oh fuck, please, no, don't let him be there to try to push Terrible again about working for him; Terrible was pissed off enough already. And probably pissed off at her; it was her fault he kept passing out, after all.

That the alternative was being dead didn't seem to matter so much. Didn't matter, to some degree, because she knew that if he couldn't do his job he'd probably rather *be* dead.

Lex watched them walk down the hall, his nose wrinkling. "Been having you two a time in the sewers? Look like you done rolled around in a dust pile, you do."

At least she had some words for him. "This really isn't a good time, Lex."

"Aye, tell me on it," he replied, shifting himself out of the way so she could unlock her door. "Ain't a good time for nobody, Tulip. Thinking it be just the opposite, dig. Crazy shit going down my side of town."

She felt what he carried in his pocket before he pulled it out and gave it to her, before she even knew he carried anything at all.

"Where did you get that?"

He folded his arms, gave the ceiling an exasperated glance. "Ain't you even gimme the invite in? Got some knowledge for you."

She pushed the door open. The wards on it stung her

skin as they reacted to the energy from the powder in her pocket and in her hand.

Terrible shoved past Lex to follow her into her apartment. The first thing she did was grab the African Blackwood box from its spot on the bottom shelf in her living room, toss both packets into it, and slam the lid. The weight of heavy clotted magic lifted from her shoulders. Much, much better.

Too bad she couldn't put Lex in there, too. For that matter, too bad she couldn't put the whole fucking day in there.

Terrible crossed to the fridge, gave her a questioning glance. Beer would be good, wouldn't it, a cold— No. No, because she wanted to get a couple of Oozers down her throat immediately. No fucking way was she going to process what had happened sober. "Water."

He grabbed a bottle of that and a beer, and walked to the counter at the edge of the kitchen.

"Could use me a beer, too, I could," Lex said.

Terrible glared at him. "Fridge's there."

A long moment passed before Lex shrugged and crossed the floor. The silence was ugly.

Chess spoke a little too loudly in her haste to break it. "So where did that come from, Lex? What is it, where did you get it?"

"Took it offen some jaxers." He twisted the cap off the beer. "Always got such cheap beer, you do. Why you ain't buy better?"

"Because I want to piss you off, that's why. Who did you take it off of? How did you find it?"

He acknowledged her sarcasm with a twist of his lips. "Four of em, dig, having theyselves a wander down the street on the yesterday. Seemed wrong, they did. Too spaced, like them bodies all stringy-loose. An scared as shit, they was, too, all balled together like tryna hide under theyselves, but having them some freaky-ass laughing. Were mighty fucked up, Tulip. Never seen any so bumberjaxed, I ain't. Never seen powder like that, neither."

He'd plunked himself down on the couch, right in the center so if either she or Terrible wanted to sit they'd be cozying up next to him.

She sat on the arm with her feet on the cushion, so she could face Terrible, still standing at the kitchen counter. "Do you know what it is?"

"Nay, but this ain't the first time we got these, dig. Third time, seen two like it in the last week. So brought it here, aye. Figured on you giving me the help."

"Why?"

He rolled his eyes. "Like you ain't gonna."

"No, I mean, why me? What can I do?"

"Thinkin you know what. 'Sall magic and ghost shit, it is."

Yeah, she knew that. But how the hell did he know that? Lex had about as much magical ability as a plastic cup.

He must have seen the question in her eyes—well, she wasn't exactly trying to hide it—because he tipped his head in the direction of the Blackwood box. "Take that box off in the dark, dig, an give it an open. Shit's all glowing, it is. Damn freaky."

Glowing? Fuck. That didn't sound good, not at all.

Terrible followed her into the bathroom—the only room in the apartment without windows. It wasn't light outside, no, but she wanted utter darkness for this.

She set the box on the toilet lid, hit the light switch, and opened it.

First the wave of dark magic rolled over her; she kept some unpleasant shit in that box, not just the packets but some curse items, a few things she'd found and a few she'd bought for security's sake.

All of which she could see, because Lex had told the

truth. The packets glowed. She shot a quick glance at Terrible. "You okay?"

He nodded. " 'Sget he outta here, aye?"

That was probably for the best, huh. But first . . . "That guy, DV, he said his friend bought the speed off what's-his-name—"

"Rickride."

"Right. He's one of yours, right? One of Bump's?"

He nodded, his face white in the pale blue light from the open box.

"And now I guess one of Lex's people sold the same bad speed. Do you guys get your stuff from the same—"

"Naw. Not what I got, anyroad. Don't deal with the same supply."

"So how is this happening, then? How—"

"Ain't knowin that one, neither." He glanced away from the box, his eyes glittering in the semi-darkness. "Guessin we got us a connection, though, like the speed and them bespelled dudes—Samms an he just now. The same, aye?"

"I guess so, but I don't know—well, I don't know how, or why. The speed doesn't feel so much like that spell Samms had on him, the nut spell."

"Be the same ones doin it? You got that from it?"

Damn it. She'd hoped he wouldn't ask that. "I don't know for sure. This feels male, like that did, but . . . there's something different about it. I don't know what it is, but something's different."

He nodded. "Dude back there ain't had a nut on he, though. For bein controlled, like Samms."

"No, he didn't have much on him, did he?"

The eerie glow cast by the tainted speed illuminated his faint smile, the little tilt of his head. "Naw, that he ain't."

She saw his hand rising to touch her face, saw the look in his eye start to change, and tried to stop herself from saying the words already formed in her head, in her mouth. Too late. They popped out anyway. "I'm sorry. About the speed—about what happened when—I should have—"

"Ain't yon fault." She didn't think he meant it, though. His eyes left hers, his shoulders lifted like a pair of scissor blades snapping the moment-that-might-have-been in half.

"It is my fault. And I should have found a— I'll visit the church. I'll do some more research and—"

"Aw, shit. Don't know why you still botherin on it, ain't gonna find—"

"I will." She reached up and pressed her palms to the sides of his face, his thick muttonchops dense and rough-soft against her palms. "I will. I promise. I just—"

"Oughta give it the leave-out, Chessie, ain't can—"

"No, I can. I will."

He still didn't look at her. Shit. She inched forward, raised herself on her tiptoes so she could be closer to him—so her face could be closer to his, so she could put everything into her eyes and force him to see it. "I know you don't really like talking about—I don't like it, either. But you have to let me try this stuff, okay? I know it's not fun. I know that one time it made you sick, but it was only the—"

He pulled away. "Aye, right. Right, then."

He didn't mean that, either. She knew that "Right, then." It meant *I'll agree so we can stop talking about this*.

Too bad knowing what it meant didn't give her any way to counter it. She stood there for a minute, a long uncomfortable one, before finally managing, "It's important, Terrible. I'm sorry. I'm—but I'm not going to let this keep happening. You have to let me fix it. I know I can fix it."

Finally he nodded. "Aye. Guessin us might as well keep givin it the try."

The bathroom wasn't a big room at all, especially not with him in it, but she still had to reach out to grab him and pull him close enough to press her forehead into his chest. "I'm so fucking sorry about this. I'll fix it. I'll find a way to fix it, I swear. It's all my—"

Lex's voice intruded through the closed door, ruining the moment as effectively as—well, as effectively as he ruined so many other things. "You two forgotting on me?"

Shit.

"Tryin to," Terrible muttered, but he opened the door and walked into the short hall after her.

Lex twisted his upper body on the couch to watch them return. Chess steeled herself for some kind of dirty joke, but he said, "Ain't good, aye?"

"No." She set the now-closed box back down on its shelf. "No, not good at all."

"Ghosty shit, aye?"

"Yeah, but—" Oh, damn, that was fucked up. She sat down beside Lex, barely noticing she was doing it. She hadn't made the connection in the bathroom, hadn't really thought about it because their discussion hadn't gone that way. But now that she did . . .

"But?"

"It isn't ghost magic that glows," she said, still trying to get her head around it. "Ghosts themselves glow. But the reason they glow, what glows about them . . . How is that even possible?"

"Wanna spit it out, Tulip? Pretend like some of us ain't witches got the same knowledge as you."

That at least snapped her out of her daze, just in time for her to catch Terrible's eyes narrowing at Lex. She wondered what parts of Lex's body Terrible was removing in his head. Not that she really wanted to know. "Ectoplasm."

"What?"

"Ectoplasm." She looked at both of them, Lex on the couch beside her and Terrible standing against her bookshelves glowering at Lex. "Ectoplasm is what glows. It's what they're made of— I mean, ghosts are souls but it's ectoplasm that's visible. That's what enables them to solidify, why they can only solidify around things that are already solid, because of the way it reacts to— Never mind. The point is, the only thing that feels like a ghost and glows is ectoplasm."

They stared at her for a second. Not as if they were waiting for her to go on—both of their expressions told her they knew very well what she was saying—but as if they were having the same problem she was.

Terrible said it first. "Why the fuck anybody snort a ghost?"

"I don't know. I don't think it'll—I can't see it giving some kind of high. I mean, I've never heard of somebody getting high off it."

Thankfully neither of them mentioned that if it were possible to do so, she probably would have done it.

And now she probably should. A heavy gong struck somewhere in her stomach. "I'll try it."

Terrible's brows lowered farther. Oh, here it came. "No fuckin way."

"No, listen. I'm the only one who can. Lex wouldn't feel any magic, so he wouldn't know what the effect was, and you'd—you'd need to be there in case something went wrong, so—"

"Naw, don't give a fuck, Chessie. Some else gives it the try. Not you."

"Aye, thinking he got it right, I do, you ain't should be giving—"

"Shut up, both of you." Like it wasn't bad enough

having one person worry about her like that, in that tight way that made her feel obligated, as if something was expected from her. No matter how much she loved Terrible, it still grated, and that was only one person. She didn't need to have two. "How are we going to know why people are doing it if we don't know— No, that doesn't make sense."

Thinking about it made her reach for her pillbox. "Lex, you didn't feel anything when you touched it. So you would have done it, right? If you'd bought it. You would have chopped a line like normal."

"Aye, guessing so. Them two days past were shooting it, too."

"And it feels like magic, too." She washed three Cepts down with water from her bottle and grabbed a cigarette. "It's not just ectoplasm, it's magic."

"You get high on that?"

"Not that kind of high, no. And especially not magic like that." Yes, there was a little high in it: the rush of power, the lifting feeling of magic in the pit of her stomach, and the way it could force a smile onto her face like a drag off the pipes. It was a weak high, usually, not one she chased, but still there.

The men waited for her to continue. "It's dark magic. Someone who can feel it will know that. It feels . . . well, it feels bad. It feels unhappy and sick. Nobody who could actually feel the energy coming off that shit would snort it, seriously. But if you can't feel it when you touch it, I don't think you'd feel it after you did it, you know?"

Terrible nodded. "So you thinkin it ain't the ectoplasm they tryna get high from, an not the magic neither. Them buyin it ain't know—'sall hid in there."

"Right."

Lex put his empty beer bottle on the rickety table. "Aye, sounding all on the sensibles, but where the hell it coming from, then? Ain't thinking we got no troubles in our supplies, iffen you dig. Ain't can say the same on Bump, but guessing Terrible knows."

"No trouble, not what I got."

"Guess you guys need to start asking some questions, then," Chess said.

Lex lit up a cigarette, leaning back on her couch and propping his feet on the table. "Talkin on questions, when you coming on over, Terrible, start working with me?"

"I ain't."

Silence. Lex blew smoke slowly into the air. "Really thinking you wanna have you a mind-change on that one, I do. Ain't tryna pull no shit with you here."

Terrible didn't respond; his face didn't move, not a blink, not a twitch. Any normal man would have been extremely uncomfortable right about then, with that cold blank look aimed right at him.

Lex wasn't a normal man. Or, he wasn't abnormal, he was just . . . normal with a few extra shots of arrogance, like a cocky blended coffee drink. And Chess knew that Lex didn't believe deep down that Terrible would seriously injure him. Didn't believe Terrible would kill him.

Because of her. She'd stopped Terrible from continuing to attack Lex after he'd broken his jaw that night, and she guessed in doing so she'd proven to Lex that she wouldn't let Terrible kill him and—worse—that Terrible would listen to her and let him live.

She couldn't feel bad about saving Lex's life, but damn, she didn't feel good knowing Lex sat there with confidence wrapped around his shoulders like a king's ermine because of her. "Making the offer causen of Tulip, dig, but making the offer causen I got a need for my own muscle. Getting that one whether it's you or some else."

Terrible shook his head. "Guessin you find some else, then."

"Aye, I dig it." Lex stood up and took a few steps

toward the kitchen, stopping just beyond where Terrible stood so he could face both of them. "Ain't can say I ain't gave it the try, though. You remember that one, aye? On the later. Gave it the try, I did."

He was talking to Terrible—it seemed as if he was, anyway. But as he finished he looked directly at Chess, right into her eyes, and cold spread through her chest because she knew what he meant. What he was really saying to her, to them both.

He was planning to have Terrible killed.

Chapter Eight

Home décor says so much about a person, after all.
—*Mrs. Increase's Advice for Ladies,* by Mrs. Increase

"Here." She held out her hand, waiting for him to put his arm into it. Was her hand shaking? Not surprising. Despite the fact that her high was kicking in, nerves still jittered up and down her spine. They were probably going to find some of that powder at Rickride's place, and what she was about to try would probably not work.

Admitting she couldn't fix a problem she'd caused—yeah. Not really the best start to her day.

Seeing the doubt in Terrible's eyes while she scrawled the new sigil on his skin didn't help. Even the tingle of magic sliding through her to him didn't help. The only thing that would help would be if it worked, and she didn't think the odds were great. Maybe it would, sure, but . . . maybe not.

"Okay." She put the chalk back in her bag. "We'll see what that does."

He nodded and got out of the car.

Rickride lived on Eighty-seventh, far enough from the docks that the crooked skyline of ships wasn't visible but close enough that the sour undercurrent of brine and dead fish clung to the air. A fairly typical Downside street, made grubbier by its proximity to the docks; more boarded windows and garbage on the pockmarked sidewalks, more crumbling walls. And a—was that a SOLD sign attached to a porch six or seven doors down? How old was that? She didn't get a good look; Terrible was moving too quickly for her to see. Had to have been fairly old, though. Or maybe stolen and stuck up to repair a hole?

No time to ask. They'd reached the top of Rickride's steps, and before Terrible's fist hit the wood she knew something was wrong. That smell creeping out from under the door, the shabby curtains over the front windows, visible from where they stood, spattered with darkish spots and splotches. Shit.

Terrible pulled his knife. Chess did the same, and he pushed the door open.

Yeah. Someone had gotten to Rickride. Maybe the same person who'd hauled Greenback into and out of a car the day before. Probably the same one who'd put Gordon Samms under magical control and gotten him to rip up Yellow Pete. Almost definitely the same one, in fact, because Rickride was in pieces all over the place and the floor under her boots was sticky, and death invaded her nostrils.

Not just Rickride's death, either. As they wandered through the rooms, they found more: another couple of men, torn up and discarded as if a giant psychotic child had grown tired of trying to find the prize inside.

Terrible nodded at her questioning look. His skin had flushed darker with almost every step they took, his eyes narrowing with anger. "Aye. Bump's, too."

"So . . ." She didn't want to ask. She knew she had to ask. "You think this could have been Lex? Someone he hired?"

His head tilted. "I . . . Shit. This ain't like Greenback yesterday, just got sliced. Or them others, them street-men. Shot, stabbed, dig? Like normal. This ain't normal."

"No." She switched on her flashlight, slipped on a glove. "Let's see what we can find. Maybe one of those walnuts or something."

He nodded and started to turn away, but she grabbed him. "Wait. Here, put one of these on, okay? Just—it's pretty gross in here, you don't want to get any blood or whatever else on you."

His slightly raised eyebrows told her he wasn't fooled, but he took the glove anyway and forced his hand into it.

They didn't talk for a few minutes, each picking their way through piles of body parts and blood slicks. Chess felt around underneath the battered couch and ramshackle coffee table, searching for a walnut spell, but didn't find one. Nor did she find one in any of the corners or behind the small television set or stereo. There wasn't one in—

"Terrible. Look here."

"Aye? What?"

She held up the box. A box full of speed packets; a box full of magic. The bad kind, the kind that made her hands and arms go almost numb.

He reached for it but stopped himself at the last second. "All spelled up, aye?"

"Looks like it, yeah. And he was selling this out there, to that guy yesterday at least." She flicked through the packets, the tingles growing worse with every one she touched. "And these didn't come from Bump?"

"Woulda come off Levi, he hands out up here. Don't think he does like that, in boxes, but maybe 'sjust how Rick holds it, dig?"

"Can you ask him?"

"Ain't can find him. Been lookin, but—"

A shuffling noise, like a slow clumsy footstep, on the floor above. Shit.

Terrible shook his head at her as he picked his way silently through the detritus on the floor to stand beside the wall dividing the staircase from the rest of the room. His expression clearly told her to stay put, but fuck that. She got up and crossed to stand at his side.

Another movement up there. Fear trickled down her spine. If the killer was up there, and the killer was another bespelled freak who couldn't be killed by normal means . . .

She guessed they'd find out pretty quickly.

She was right. Her eyes barely registered the presence of the man before he was moving, practically flying down the stairs at them.

Damn, he was fast. Before she could react Terrible had shoved her to the side, banging her shoulder against the wall. His right hand moved, aiming that wicked-looking knife of his with deadly accuracy, or what would have been deadly had the man been able to die. He wasn't, not in the state he was in—the state she thought he was in, was pretty sure he was in.

And now he was a bespelled man with an ugly gap in his throat, like a bloody fucking Pez dispenser.

He turned and swung at Terrible, who ducked and kicked out with his right foot. His boot connected with the man's knee; a horrible loud crack rent the air, and the man stumbled.

Stumbled but didn't fall. Chess realized his knee was broken; his leg bowed the wrong way, as if the joint was on backward, but he was still standing. He didn't feel it.

Worse, if he touched Terrible, Terrible was going to collapse. And she'd be left to deal with the mindless, unfeeling, indestructible killing machine on her own.

Shit. The man swung at Terrible again, almost hitting him. Terrible attacked with the knife, widening the ghastly blood-drooling pseudo-mouth in the throat. The man's head tilted at an angle, not quite hanging off his body but clearly not held on the way it should be.

Would he fall, when his head was removed? Would that make his body still?

Looked like she was going to find out. Terrible darted around him, drew the knife through the air one more time.

The head fell off. It tumbled toward the floor in slow motion, eyes wide and staring, mouth hanging open. It bounced off Terrible's arm as it went, and they hit the ground together. Sure enough, her new sigil had failed.

And sure enough, she was most likely the only woman in the world who knew beyond a shadow of a doubt that the beheaded corpse of a magic-controlled soul would still walk around.

It stumbled around the room for a few seconds, arms outstretched like every stereotypical headless man ever, before a new head popped into place. Well, not a new head. Its ghost's head, luminescent in the dim room.

It saw her. Looked right at her, its translucent features changing as it grinned. It grinned at her like she was a jug of water and it was dying of thirst; grinned at her like she was a pile of money and it was broke.

Grinned at her like she would grin at a free bag of pills.

She started to leap out of the way, only to lose her balance and fall to the disgusting floor. A disembodied arm lay only a foot or so away from her face. She swallowed hard to keep from throwing up.

The ghost—the body, the man, whatever the hell it was—had almost reached her. Well, fuck it, she was already filthy, right? She rolled over, shoved her legs up with all of her might.

This time the man tumbled back, and this time Terrible was up and moving, grabbing her hand and yanking her to her feet. She was already digging into her bag for her salt canister, already trying not to think about what she was about to do with her psychopomp, about the way certain types of magic could stain a person's energy, pollute it, and how she didn't know how many times that magic would need to be performed before it would cause that kind of damage.

She stayed behind Terrible, both of them taking slow, careful steps backward to draw the man away from the wall. Of course, what they were going to do once it got away from the wall she had no idea, but—

Oh. That's what. As the man neared, Terrible threw himself forward, collapsing in a heap with the man trapped beneath him.

She supposed that was one way to do it.

She also supposed she'd better hurry up, because ghosts were strong, and who knew how long the spell would last or what would happen when it ended. Every instinct she had told her to grab Terrible and pull him away from the body wriggling beneath him like an over-turned turtle, but she couldn't. He'd done that for her, so she could create her circle, and she knew without even having to think that he'd be pissed at her if she didn't do what she was supposed to do.

So she did, focusing as much as she could on the circle and trying not to think about just what the hell was going on.

And what the hell it meant.

She was still trying not to think about it five hours later as Terrible turned the Chevelle in to the Church parking lot. Not because she hadn't thought about it in the interim, and not because they hadn't discussed it in the interim, either, but because the sun was about half an hour from setting, and Elder Griffin was getting married.

Terrible slid into a spot and shut off the engine. "Don't

bother me iffen you wanna change yon mind, go in on your alones, aye? I dig it, maybe this ain't—"

"Terrible. Shut up." She leaned over and kissed him, a good, long, hard kiss to let him know how much she wanted him there. Four Cepts and two lines before leaving the house, combined with the fact that he was actually there, actually going with her, made her entire body feel light and cheery, as if she was made of glitter.

Maybe too cheery. His hand slid down her front to cup her breast through the white cherry-patterned dress Blue had gone with her to buy. "Maybe we take a longer while, aye? Be late."

"No, we can't. Come on, let's get in."

His short, quiet laugh heated her throat. " 'Swhat I'm tryna do, Chessiebomb, iffen you—"

"Right." She smiled and put her hands on his cheeks but pulled away just the same. "Come on, seriously. It's getting late."

"Aye, right then."

He came around to her side and opened her door for her, eyeing her up and down as she got out of the car. His hand squeezed hers; a slight twist of his arm turned her to face him, standing not quite a foot away with his face in shadow. "Shit. You so fuckin pretty, Chessie. True thing. So . . . ain't even can breathe sometimes."

Everything stopped. Her breath, her heart, everything, even the breeze making her hair dance over her bare shoulders. It all stopped, leaving her standing there watching herself. As if it wasn't her, because nothing like that could be happening to her. He was talking to some other Chess, some Chess who wasn't filthy and wrong, wasn't a liar and a junkie.

She was stealing him from that Chess, the Chess who deserved the happiness pounding its way through her system like a line of the best speed she'd ever done in her life, the Chess who deserved to have someone love her.

She wasn't that Chess. But she wasn't giving him up, either. No fucking way. No matter what she had to do.

She leaned forward on her tiptoes to kiss him again. His palm cradled her cheek, slid back so his fingers could play in her hair.

"Thanks." With her heels on she was—well, she was still shorter than him, he had her beaten by about a foot normally—but the distance felt so much less. She wrapped her arms around his waist. "I mean . . . thanks."

"Only sayin the truth."

Another car door slammed nearby, ending the moment. Damn. Well, time to go in anyway, really.

Her heels clicked on the cement and her full skirt tickled just above her knees as they headed for the tall, heavy double doors of the Church building. Pale blue light glowed in the row of windows to the right—the chapel windows, where the ceremony itself would take place. Chess held Terrible's hand tighter. She never got to do that in public; it was almost scary.

People filled the entry hall. They leaned against the blue-white walls, sandwiched themselves together on the long low benches, so many of them that they hid the dark wood. They stood in groups, holding glasses, laughing and chatting; their bodies in the requisite black or white made the room look like a checkered flag.

Automatically her eyes sought Elder Griffin, only to realize that of course he wouldn't be there. He'd be getting ready somewhere, doing whatever pre-ceremony rituals he was supposed to do. Another reason—as if she needed one—to be grateful Terrible had come with her. She usually hung around with Elder Griffin during these all-Church-employee things. Or at least she tried to, because when she didn't she ended up doing incredibly stupid things, like she had at the Festival Closing Ceremony the year before when she'd ended up in bed with Agnew Doyle, a fellow Debunker.

What a mistake that had been.

The chapel doors opened. Good. They could go in and sit down, instead of milling around hunting for someone to talk to or an out-of-the-way place to stand. People were looking at Terrible, in his black bowling shirt with the blue stripe down the front, with his DA haircut and thick muttonchops, broken nose and scars. Chess straightened her back further. Fuck them all. If they wanted to judge him—judge her, too, because of him—they could go ahead. The only person she worked with whose opinion she cared about was Elder Griffin's, anyway, and he wouldn't look at Terrible like that. At least she hoped he wouldn't.

They found a seat about five rows from the front; not all the way in the back, but not too close, either. The chairs around them began to fill up, too. Chess caught Doyle—sitting next to Dana Wright, so that was still going on, then—staring at her. Staring at Terrible, actually. Oh, right.

Terrible noticed, too. He caught Doyle's gaze and raised his eyebrow; his left arm slid around her bare shoulders and pressed her to his side. Doyle paled and looked away. Heh. She guessed his last meeting with Terrible, when Doyle had ended up huddled on the ground with broken fingers and wet pants, had made quite an impression.

Two Goodys in their blue ceremonial dresses circled the room, lighting the candles. Someone switched off the overhead lights. The entire atmosphere in the room changed; voices quieted, people shifted into more comfortable positions on the hard wood seats.

Elder Griffin appeared in his blue Church suit, white stockings gleaming below his knees, broad-brimmed hat shielding his face. The candlelight sparked off the gold buckles on the hatband and on his shoes. It took her a second to figure out why he looked wrong to her, what bothered her: Unlike during Holy Day services or when working, he wasn't wearing white makeup or powder, and his eyes weren't blackened. She didn't think she'd ever seen him without either before.

By his side stood a tall man as blond as himself, also wearing blue but a regular suit. Of course. Must be Keith, then. She hadn't had the chance to meet him yet.

They reached their places before the stang set up in the front and stood facing each other. Elder Yao walked a circle around the room, pouring salt, enclosing both them and the guests, dragging silence in his wake. A wedding was a magical ritual; he was creating a magical space.

The room—the room inside the circle—waited. Chess shivered; the warm soft hush of the magic in the air made her skin tingle, made her stomach tingle. Added to how light she already felt inside, to the cheerful heartbeat of speed in her blood, and she felt almost as if she could open her arms and fly.

Terrible's arm tightened around her. Not much, but enough that she felt it. He didn't look pale, but she tilted her head back anyway so she could whisper, "Are you okay?"

He nodded. "Aye, no worryin."

He didn't look as if he was lying. But then it didn't seem to be all magic, any magic, that caused the problem, did it? Only black magic.

Elder Ramos was still acting as Grand Elder, until the Confirmation in a few weeks' time. He stood up from his chair at the far edge of the circle, ending the line of her thoughts. It was starting.

Elder Griffin and Keith joined hands.

Elder Ramos spoke. "Thaddeus Aurelius Griffin, you

have requested to enter into the legal and magical binding known as marriage with this man, Keith Richard Freeling. Is that your wish?"

"Yes."

"Keith Richard Freeling, you have requested to enter into the legal and magical binding known as marriage with this man, Thaddeus Aurelius Griffin. Is that your wish?"

"Yes."

A long chain of specially grown blue roses and two lengths of white silk hung from the crook at the top of the stang. Elder Ramos picked up the rose chain and draped it over Elder Griffin's and Keith's shoulders, so they both stood inside the loop. "Your wishes are Fact. Facts are Truth."

"Facts are Truth," the audience responded.

From an inner pocket in his blue velvet Church suit, Elder Ramos pulled a ritual knife. The blade caught the candlelight and reflected it back, like a sharp piece of flame itself, hovering between the two men. "Marriages are bound by blood. Do you consent to being so bound?"

"We do."

Elder Griffin and Keith let go of each other's hands but kept their arms out, turning them to expose their palms and wrists. One of the Goodys—Goody Martin, who Chess liked—crossed the floor to kneel in front of them, holding the iron ceremonial goblet.

The knife came down, drawing lines of blood on the fleshy parts of each man's palm. Elder Ramos handed the knife to Goody Martin and grabbed the men's hands, pressing them together. *"Paratu lakondia herondia."*

Magic pulsed warm and bright over the crowd. Chess sighed from it; everyone sighed from it, at least all of the witches—all of the Church employees.

She looked up at Terrible again, just to check on him.

He didn't take his eyes off the ceremony but held her hand tighter, pulled it onto his lap.

"As your blood runs in each other's veins, so you are bound. As your blood enters each other's bodies, so you are bound. As your energies combine to create a new energy, so you are bound."

"We are bound."

Just like her Binding, a few months before. Well, not quite: A marriage binding connected the souls, transferred some of each person's energy to the other through blood and magic. The magic wasn't necessary in this case, since Elder Griffin's blood already contained magic, but it was part of the ritual. By giving Keith his blood—even that small amount—he was giving Keith some of his energy, his power. And the magic in his blood reacted to Keith's energy, so Elder Griffin's changed ever so slightly itself. They were one couple with the same energy.

Her Binding hadn't been about sharing, though. It had been about control, and the First Elders—holy shit. That was why. That was why ectoplasm was being put in the speed.

And that ectoplasm was combining with energy to make a new energy. Hot motherfucking damn, that was it. The ectoplasm and the walnuts. Two energies combined to make one new energy; two spells combined to make one complete spell.

It was all she could do not to yank Terrible from his seat and run out of the room with him so she could tell him. But she couldn't do that. Even if she wanted to, she couldn't; that would break the circle and ruin the ceremony.

The second the ceremony ended and the circle was recalled, though . . .

Another thick wave of magic pulled her back into the room. Elder Griffin was drinking from the goblet, wine mixed with a few drops each of his blood and Keith's. She'd missed part of the ritual.

Keith drank next, emptying the goblet. He handed it back to Goody Martin.

Elder Ramos picked up the lengths of white silk from the stang and used them to wrap both men's hands in turn. "So you are bound by magic and blood. So you are bound by law. So your binding is now Fact. Facts are Truth."

"Facts are Truth," the audience echoed again.

"May your union be long and loyal."

Applause broke the air, echoing off the walls. One final burst of magic exploded over their heads, ran through Chess like a shiver, and disappeared. All of the magic disappeared; Elder Griffin and Keith walked to the doors at the left side of the room, breaking the circle together for luck, and Elder Ramos called the energy back.

Black-uniformed waiters and waitresses entered the room to start setting up the bar and buffet, moving empty chairs, doing whatever it was they were supposed to do. Chess had only been to one wedding before, early in her training, and hadn't stayed for the party at that one. She'd never been to a party with servants in her life, for that matter. How the hell was she supposed to know what they were doing?

"Were faster'n I thought," Terrible said. He still sat in his chair.

Chess did the same. "Yeah, it doesn't take long, really. It's just a binding ceremony, I mean, they're legally married when they sign the papers, which they did earlier. But listen, I figured it out." She glanced around them. Too many people still sat or stood nearby for her to be able to talk. Besides, she was starting to come down; she wanted to duck off somewhere private and bump up.

"I figured it out, what's happening. Come on, let's go outside, okay?"

Most of the crowd headed out the front doors to wait for the chapel to be ready. They stood on the wide patio where the Reckonings were held on Holy Day, near the 1997 Haunted Week memorial, their clothing stripes of light and shadow scattered across the dark cement.

Chess avoided them and pulled Terrible in the opposite direction, as far into the shadows as she could without actually looking like she was trying to hide. "It's to control them. The ectoplasm."

Confusion crossed his face for a second, then cleared. "In the speed, meaning?"

"Yeah. Remember how I was Bound before, when the whole Maguinness thing happened? It was the First Elders, and they Bound me to them through the ectoplasm, they put it in my blood during the ceremony. Remember the scars?"

"So them doing it to put ghosts in them bodies?"

"Right. But it's not just ghosts. It's magic, they've bespelled it—ectoplasm will hold a spell, because it's an energy form. It's not a whole spell, either. It's half of one. And the walnut is the other half."

His brow furrowed. "Thought you say not the same ones doin it."

"Yeah, I know, but . . . I was wrong. I mean, I could be wrong now, but I don't think I am. It's why the ones taking the speed— Remember what that guy said at the docks, that it's like his friend wasn't even there sometimes? I think the speed opens them to control, and the walnut is how they're controlled. It's two spells but they combine into one, if you know what I mean."

"Him earlier had one, aye. Only him yesterday didn't."

"It might not be on him, it doesn't have to be. Just close to him, like under his bed, in his house."

"Like them Lamaru left a death curse at you place before."

"Right."

He considered it for a minute. "Be why when them doin the speed they all scared an shit, then like they ain't even in them bodies? Ain't got the walnut controllin em yet."

"Yes. I think so, anyway. We'll go back to my place after this, okay, and I can test it out—shit, I can't believe I didn't do it before, hold both of them at once and see if the energies combine."

He shook his head, a bemused sort of shake while he smiled at her with his eyes. "Can tell just by feelin em both together?"

She nodded, hoping the warmth in her cheeks didn't mean she was blushing but knowing it probably did.

"Damn. Ain't know why you wastin yon time with me, you c'n do all that shit, all—"

She stopped him with her hands on his face, tilting it down so she could look right at him. "Cut it out. I'm not wasting my time, and you know why, anyway."

He raised his eyebrows; she grinned. "It's because you're so good in bed. So, you know, as long as you don't start slacking off—"

"Ain't ever been the type for lazin, aye?" His hands slid down over her hips. "Why we ain't leave now, I show you—"

She pulled away. "We don't have to stay much longer, I promise. But we can't go yet. I want you to meet Elder Griffin."

He nodded and lit cigarettes for them both. "Thinkin Lex come over throw us off? He the one?"

"No." She said it a little too loudly. Oops. "Not after what happened to his father, remember? I can't see Lex trusting any kind of witch with something like that, at least not a witch he didn't know really well. And—you know I don't have anything to do with it, right? I'm not, like, doing—"

His lips cut her off. Not a long kiss, or a deep one, but one that made her cheeks do that tingling have-to-smile thing anyway. "Know you ain't, baby."

People started filing back into the building, or at least most of them did. A few resolute smokers stayed on the patio, talking or looking up at the sky, pale and starless above the city's glow. Chess looked up at it, too, at that blank stretch of cloudy gray covering the world like a sheet pulled over its head. It was watching her, wasn't it? Watching her and Terrible, and for some reason the sight of it—the thought of it—made pain and loneliness twist in her chest.

Pain because she wasn't part of that sky, would never be a part of it, because it looked like a home she could never enter. She'd never know what it was like to be so peaceful. Pain because she was so fucking insignificant, so small, so worthless compared to that incredible expanse. Loneliness because she didn't belong to it, and because she knew one day she'd be alone again, and because some deep part of her still felt alone; would always feel alone. Terrible knew so much about her, knew her so well, but he still didn't know everything—hell, he'd just reminded her of something else she couldn't share with him. He never could know everything; she didn't dare tell him everything. She wouldn't even know how.

Loneliness because no matter how much she loved him, no matter how much he loved her, she was still just herself, and she could never be more than that.

Terrible's fingers brushed her cheek. "You right?"

She snapped her gaze back to him, forced a smile. "Yeah, sure. Right up. Why?"

Instead of answering he leaned forward and kissed her again, this time wrapping his arm around her to pull her close against his warm hard body. A long kiss, a real one, that she felt all the way down to her toes. He kissed her under that wide impassive sky and she kissed him back, and it reminded her that she did have a place in the world, she did have a home, and that home was being built right there where she stood. With him.

He broke the kiss but kept holding her for a long moment, resting his cheek against the top of her head. "Love you, Chess."

Her eyes stung; she squeezed them shut harder, willing it to stop. "I love you, too."

Another minute, and then he let go, took a step back. "Wanna get us in now? Can stay out here the whole time iffen you're wanting."

She grinned. Some of the weight lifted from her chest. "The sooner you meet Elder Griffin, the sooner we can leave . . ."

He jettisoned his almost-finished smoke. She took his hand, and together they walked through the open double doors, back into the party, leaving the sky alone outside.

Chapter Nine

Because what matters is that we bond with those we love, and stay with them, and live in Truth.
—*Families and Truth*, a Church pamphlet by Elder Barrett

The first thing they did was head for the bar set up against the far wall, near the door to the elevators. There was a bathroom back there, too, and she wanted to bump up quickly.

She also wanted people to stop looking at Terrible. He didn't react, but she knew he noticed it; no way he wouldn't, he paid too much attention to his surroundings for that.

Of course, speaking of paying attention, doing a bump had its own problems. She'd never let anyone at Church see her take even an aspirin, much less anything else, so she needed to be extremely careful. Normally she'd let it go, but normally she wasn't about to introduce Terrible to Elder Griffin. Normally she wasn't watching the two separate parts of her life come together with a crash that sounded like murmured gossip.

She needed either more speed or another Cept to take the edge off that. Both would be even better.

She gave him a quick kiss and headed down the hall.

Thankfully the bathroom was empty, so she could flush the toilet while she opened her pillbox, flush it again when she closed it. Much better. One more Cept, and sure, one little bump, too, just a small one, just to keep her from mellowing too much.

She'd have to chug some water, too, which she did. Fuck, she felt good. What a relief.

She continued to feel good while she walked back in to the chapel and saw Terrible holding their drinks. Felt even better when she kissed him and better still when they found a spot near the windows to sit.

"Ain't you wanna chatter with any else?"

"Not really." She shrugged, reached up to flip her hair back from her bare shoulders. The dress was cut straight across the front, with spaghetti straps. She couldn't decide if it was fun or not to wear it; she'd never worn anything like it before. "If you weren't here I'd probably end up standing around by myself or talking to Elder Griffin, anyway."

As if to deliberately prove her wrong, people started approaching them. Of course. Everyone wanted to know who he was, what he was doing there. Well, she figured it was obvious what he was doing there—holding her hand, sitting next to her, kissing her—but it had been fucking dumb of her to think for even a second that people wouldn't be desperate to shove their noses into her business.

Because nothing was more entertaining than other people's lives, right? And nothing would make them feel better about their own than the chance to judge someone else's.

Whatever. She smiled at them all, introduced Terrible to them all, forced herself not to glare at them when they double-taked on his name.

They were coming in from another smoke break when she finally saw Elder Griffin and his new husband coming toward them. "There he is. We can go after we talk to him, okay?"

The relief on Terrible's face would have made her

laugh if she wasn't busy feeling guilty instead. Of course he was uncomfortable; how could he not be?

Elder Griffin's gaze traveled up and down Terrible's body. Chess didn't see disapproval or judgment in his expression, which was nice, but that didn't ease the tension starting to build in her abdomen again. Not a lot of tension, but as much as was possible considering the narcotics in her system. And thank fuck for those.

Elder Griffin took her hand. He'd taken off his hat and stashed it somewhere, so his light hair haloed his head and made his blue eyes seem even darker. "Cesaria. I'm so glad you're here."

"Me, too. It was great, it was a beautiful ceremony." That was the right thing to say, right?

It seemed to be.

He introduced her to Keith, whose eyes were as kind as his. Good. Elder Griffin should have someone kind. Well, she wouldn't have expected him to be with someone who wasn't.

Please, please let them like Terrible, and please let him like them. No, it wasn't as though they'd be spending a lot of time together, but still. "Elder Griffin, this is—"

"Terrible, correct?" Elder Griffin smiled, the kind of smile that made relief wash through Chess's body like the first rush of her pills in the morning, and held out his hand.

Terrible took it. "Aye."

Elder Griffin hesitated. His eyes cut to Chess, so fast she wasn't entirely sure she'd seen it. What was that? It looked like a double take; it looked like some kind of surprise or even disappointment. Shock, really. That was it, shock. Why? Because of the way Terrible talked?

Shit. Disappointment washed over her as quickly as the relief had. She'd thought for sure Elder Griffin wouldn't be like that, that he wouldn't decide Terrible was worthless or whatever for some dumb superficial reason.

But then, he was still smiling. "I'm glad to meet you. Cesaria has seemed quite happy of late."

Shit. Good thing Terrible already knew how happy he made her, or that would have been so embarrassing.

Terrible nodded. "She tells me on you a lot."

"And what do you do?" Keith asked. Maybe she didn't like him so much after all.

And maybe she and Terrible should have come up with an answer for that question, which was fucking inevitable, wasn't it?

But Terrible had apparently done that on his own. "Construction."

Of course. Made sense. It was certainly believable. And, duh, of course this wouldn't be the first time he'd been asked that. He didn't have all those IDs just because he thought they were pretty. How many of those did he have? Six or seven? Different names on his driver's license, his electric bill and water bill and cellphone bill, none of them the same. Bump had a few forgers—well, of course he did—and they took care of all that stuff.

How did someone become a forger, anyway? She'd never really thought about it. Getting all the Church forms and everything—

What? She flipped her head back to their conversation in time to hear Keith say, "And are we going to see you here having a marriage ceremony?"

Oh, for fuck's—

Terrible shrugged. "Aye, if Chessie's wanting."

Her mouth fell open. No, he hadn't— Okay, she was going to pretend she hadn't heard that.

But her cheeks felt hotter than they should.

Keith asked Terrible about his tattoos, taking Terrible's left arm to examine the almost full sleeve he had there. Okay, she definitely liked Keith. And the way he stood, occasionally reaching out to touch Elder Griffin, glancing over to look at him. That was good. That was right.

Elder Griffin sidled up to her, bringing with him the scent of white wine and incense. His eyes were serious, his expression the same. "Cesaria . . . you know I will not be in my office for the next week."

"Right. And you won't be there at all, right, if your— when your promotion comes through." She hoped she managed to sound cheerful and optimistic about it, not dismayed and unhappy that he'd be leaving his position and letting another Elder take over the Debunkers.

"Yes, well. But . . ." He glanced at Terrible. "You know which house we've been given, correct? The one you and I looked at."

Yeah, she remembered. Remembered looking at it with her heart in useless pieces in her chest because she and Terrible had had a fight and she'd thought their relationship was over, and she'd been in so much pain she could barely talk.

Not a good memory. But she did know where the house was. And she should probably say something about that, too. "Oh, that's great! No, you didn't tell me they'd given it to you."

He nodded. "Can you come there, on the morrow? Perhaps for lunch. Half past eleven or so. Can you? I'd like . . . I'd like to talk to you."

He'd stopped looking at Terrible directly, but she saw him peeking out of the corner of his eye, his gaze darting over and back, over and back, fast and sneaky.

Cold crept into her chest and out, spreading through her body like she'd snorted liquid nitrogen. He didn't like Terrible. He was standing there smiling at him and being nice, but he wanted to warn her off, wanted to tell her he didn't approve or whatever.

It shouldn't matter. But it did. It mattered because

they were each one of the main parts of her life, they were both important to her, and bringing them together was ... Well, shit, what did she expect? Wasn't like she didn't already have plenty she needed to keep from the Church.

Elder Griffin was still watching her—or rather, watching her and glancing at Terrible—and waiting for her answer.

"Oh, um, sorry. Yeah, I mean, yes, of course. I'd be happy to come."

"Excellent." One more sideways glance. "Excellent. I look forward to seeing you."

Keith's voice floated into the space between them, still talking to Terrible. "And are you doing a lot of work in Downside? I have some friends thinking about buying property there. The prices are so low and they can fix them up—"

"Ain't such a good idea." Terrible glanced at Chess; she caught the half-amused look in his eye, given the discussion they'd had before about gentrification, but she didn't think Keith saw it. She hoped not, anyway. "Whatany you fix up there just get fu—just get wrecked again, aye? They burn it down afore they see it clean. Ain't safe."

Keith shook his head. "That's what I told them, but they said—oh dear. Thad, my cousin Jill is heading straight for us. . . ."

Chess forced a smile as Elder Griffin's expression turned questioning. "You should be talking to people. I'll see you tomorrow."

Which she would. It made her feel sick, but she would.

Elder Griffin smiled, a real, fond smile. "Trust me, my dear, we'd rather not be talking to Keith's cousin Jill. Keith, perhaps if we make our way to the other side of the room?"

What if he made her move back onto the Church

grounds? He could do that; his approval of the idea had been the main reason she'd been permitted to live off on her own. If he retracted his endorsement . . .

Something else not to think about, to push out of her head the way she pushed out her goodbyes and congratulations and all that shit before Keith and Elder Griffin walked away.

She swallowed the last of her drink and leaned into Terrible's chest, pressing her face to it for a long second so she could breathe him in. "Let's go, okay? Do you want to go now?"

"Sure you ain't wanna chatter on any else, aught like that?"

The smile she'd forced turned genuine when she met his eyes. Funny how just the four inches her platform heels added made such a difference, made her feel so much closer to him.

Whatever. Let Elder Griffin try to force her back onto Church grounds. Nobody ever said she had to work for the Church, right? She was a damn good witch; she could find a way to support herself somehow, right?

Because she loved her job, yeah, but she *needed* Terrible, and if she had to give up one of them, it sure as fuck wouldn't be him. "I'm sure."

Back in the Chevelle, back on 300 toward Downside. Back to where they belonged, and she could breathe easier again as lampposts flew by and Triumph City surrounded them like an ocean of lights. "I'm glad you liked Elder Griffin."

He shrugged. "Seemed aright. Ain't talked to he but minutes, aye?"

Yes, but that was apparently long enough for Elder Griffin to judge him and find him lacking. And that— that was extra disappointing, because she'd thought he was a better judge of character than that.

But, then, he thought *she* was worth something, didn't he, so obviously she'd been wrong. Hardly the first time.

Terrible rested his elbow on the car door. "Hey. When Keith gave me the ask on—"

His phone rang, cutting him off. He hesitated, then looked down at it. Even in the greenish dashboard glow and the rhythmic flow of pale light through the windows she saw his face darken. Uh-oh.

He pressed the button, held it to his ear. "Aye . . . Naw, headin—fuck. On the—aye. Be there fast."

He shoved the phone back into his pocket and downshifted the Chevelle, his face in grim, angry lines. "That powder's showed up again. Four of em at Trickster's, screamin the place down an ain't leavin."

"Shit, seriously?"

He nodded. "Gotta get them outta there, dig, see if we can get some knowledge out of em. Give Cat-Stan what him pay for, too, keep the place safe."

"Right." Funny. She knew very well what he did for a living and what it entailed—she'd seen the evidence of it walking around on crutches or behind bruises for years before she really spent any time with him—but it had never occurred to her that drug or gambling debts weren't the only kinds of debts he'd collect. Of course Downside bars would pay Bump some protection money, like so many of the other businesses did.

The speedometer told her they were doing about a hundred, zipping in and out of traffic and passing slower cars. At that speed they reached the Ace Street exit in a few minutes; the Chevelle's fat black tires left long angry streaks on the cement as Terrible steered it down the curved ramp and jumped the light at the intersection.

"Guessin you head on back yours we get there, dig, an I give you the ring-up—"

"What? Why would—"

"Ain't wanting get yon pretty dress all fucked up, aye?

An them shoes an all? Four dudes out them minds in there, ain't gonna be—"

"Yeah, and? I can't help in a dress?"

He hesitated. "You just, you lookin so—"

"I'm going with you." Not to mention that if there were packets of that powder around, someone needed to be able to touch them. And it wasn't like her attempts at fixing that problem were making one damn bit of difference.

A few pieces of black chalk always laid in one of the little pockets inside her bag, so she could find them easily. Funny. Some people thought addicts were lazy, but it took an enormous amount of work and time. Making sure she put things back exactly where they belonged so she could find them no matter how fucked up she was, making notes on everything so she wouldn't forget, trying to do things in a set routine as much as possible. She devoted a lot of energy to appearing normal, to not giving anyone a reason to suspect; it was a very small price to pay.

"Here. Give me your arm," she said, as she had earlier. And with about as much hope.

He held it out, wrist up. She glanced at him. "Aren't you going to ask what I'm going to do with it?"

"You want me to?"

"No, I just—no, it's fine." Warmth spread through her chest and up to her face, warmth that had nothing to do with pills or booze or anything else. It was trust heating her from the inside, making her feel like a real live person who mattered. The kind of trust she didn't think he gave to anyone else. The thought made something swell inside her, something wonderful and painful all at once.

The kind of trust she didn't deserve.

She glanced out the window to distract herself. They'd reached Fortieth already, ten blocks from Trickster's. She didn't have much time; wasn't like he'd stay in the car waiting for her to finish marking him up when they got there.

One deep steadying breath to gather as much power as she could, and she set the chalk against his skin. First a sigil for strength. He didn't need it, of course, but it made her feel better to give it to him anyway. Then protection. She tried a couple of those. Maybe a few runes, too? The standard ones, a couple of bindrunes to be safe . . . more sigils, a few charm symbols . . . She even added a sigil to protect against the Evil Eye. Some anti-sleep sigils might be good, too, given the passing-out thing. She made up a couple of those on the spot.

When she was finished, his right arm looked more decorated than his left. He examined it without much curiosity. "Figure on that makin a difference?"

"I hope so. I mean, it can't hurt, right?"

He didn't answer.

"Something has to work, Terrible, you know something will. We just—I just haven't been focusing on it like I should. But I'm focused now, and I'll figure it out. Okay?"

He nodded. "Aye, know you will."

But he didn't sound convinced.

She leaned over to give him a quick kiss. "You should. Didn't we already decide I'm the best witch in the whole world?"

His snort of laughter made her spirits rise. "Aye, ain't can forget that one."

His smile—both of their smiles—froze, then shattered, when they got to Trickster's. Or, well, not quite to Trickster's; they couldn't get in, she didn't think, and they couldn't get past on the road, either, not with all the people. A huge crowd of them: kids staring at the spectacle, light-fingers trying to steal a living, people placing bets. The obligatory old woman in a bathrobe and curlers stood at the edge of the rippling mass of humanity;

Chess wondered for one ridiculous second if she rented herself out for shit like that.

She had one last moment to savor that semi-amusing thought as Terrible cut the Chevelle's engine. Before it had fully died, his door was open and he was climbing out, and rather than wait for him she did the same. Time to see what new victims the ghost-and-magic-infused speed had claimed.

Chapter Ten

> You must guard your soul and that of your neighbors. That
> is your responsibility as a living being in possession of a
> soul.
>
> —*The Book of Truth*, Laws Article 2172

The screaming hit her first. High, desperate screams,
ripped from raw throats to sail into the night sky—that
same blank sky, dead but full of life, that had made her
so melancholy before. In the face of those screams the
crowd itself seemed to shrink, the streetlights to recede.

She reached the edge of the crowd in time to push
her way into the gap Terrible left as he plowed through
it. Please, please let those sigils she'd put on him hold.
Please, please let him not be affected by that powder.
She couldn't imagine how he would feel if half of Downside saw him collapse. She didn't want to imagine it.

As she got closer the screams started to separate themselves, to become more than simply desperate wails.
Different voices, forming a barrier in the air, weaving
together. Men's voices, a woman's voice.

Sobs rode beneath them, choking, hopeless sobs. The
kind Chess recognized. The kind she'd learned a long
time ago wouldn't do any good at all.

Only a few backs stood between her and the scream-
ers when she finally saw them. Saw Terrible, too; his fist
hit one of the men in the face.

The man fell. Terrible didn't. She had a second to be

thankful for that before she noticed the rest. Two more men, there were; the lone woman was already down, sobbing and clutching her face and hair. Blood trickled down the backs of her hands and forearms. What the fuck?

One of the men had taken off his shirt. His thin, hairless chest and back glistened with sweat as he ran around the circle with his arms spread out, like a child playing airplane.

A terrified child playing airplane; his face was hideous with fear, his mouth a gaping pit, his eyes bulging. He didn't even seem to notice Terrible.

Terrible saw him, of course. His fist leapt out again. The runner went down.

The third man took about the same amount of time to silence, and only the girl remained. Her sobs were more horrible somehow in the dead quiet. Chess felt her own heart throbbing in time. She knew that sound, those hopeless, helpless sobs. That was the sound she heard inside herself every minute, every day, the sound she took whatever she could to drown out. The sound that hung behind the voices in her head telling her how bad she was, how worthless and wrong, a constant back-drop of pain.

Terrible advanced on the girl slowly, in a pose Chess had seen before: one hand up, the other touching the handle of his knife behind his back. Ready in case she sprang up and attacked him. Who knew what she was hiding behind her hands, beneath her legs, or up her sleeves? Especially in Downside, where the crying child you stopped to help might rob you blind and leave you to die.

The men lay still on the pavement, scattered around the circle, which closed in to examine them. Shit. She was supposed to be doing something too, right? Duh.

The almost empty packets weren't hard to find. What

was hard was touching them. The second her fingers closed around them her arm caught fire, ghost energy and dark magic flying up to make her tattoos scream. She let go, grabbed a latex glove from her bag, and slipped it on. Damn, carrying three or four of those packets—or however many there were—around with her until she could get them home wasn't going to be fun, was it?

Even with the glove on, touching the packets made her squirm. The men, at least, had been having themselves quite a time; hardly any powder remained. Was there a certain level, maybe, where the high turned into hysterics? A place where the victim started to lose control?

Something to talk to Terrible about—something to talk to Lex about, too. Damn it. Lex. Lex and his threat. She'd managed to bury it in her mind all day, tucking it beneath her nerves about Elder Griffin's wedding and having Terrible there with her. But crouching there in the middle of a huge gang of Downsiders, it came flooding back, made her skin prickle even more than those magic-infected drugs already did. Any one of them could be armed, any one of them—any group of them—could be planning to leap out and make good on Lex's warning.

A gasp from the onlookers drew her gaze. The sobbing woman had dropped her hands. Fuck.

Deep scratches ran down her eyelids and cheeks, dark and vicious against her pale skin. She held out her hands. "Help me. Help me, they're coming, they're after me, please, look what they made me do oh please help me . . ."

Just like the man by the docks the day before. Well, of course, right?

But what exactly were they seeing? And had the spell been completed yet, did they have the walnut spell on them?

Terrible crouched beside the woman, talking to her

in that low, soothing voice Chess knew well. Could the woman even see him—see anything?

Maybe. At least her eyes were still in her head.

The litany of terror continued as Chess approached her. Where the hell should she— Damn. She tucked the packets into her black-chalk pouch, not liking the idea of them possibly contaminating some of her magic tools but with nowhere else to stow them quickly. She could buy more chalk the next day.

She didn't even need to make a special trip. She could buy it from the Church storeroom when she went to listen to Elder Griffin condemn the only person who'd ever really mattered to her. Well, that was a lucky break.

Terrible glanced up at her, edged over so she could crouch down beside him, and scanned the crowd. "Any know her? Got she name?"

No one did.

Okay. The drugs were probably still on her, and Chess needed to get them. She wanted to make sure they were all the same—well, she knew they were, but she wanted to make sure—and get them off the streets.

Where the fuck was it coming from?

She could only hope one of the freaked-out victims on the street saned up enough to say.

"Where are the drugs?" She reached out, gave the girl's arm the briefest touch. Refusing to go home and change was the right decision, no question about it, but she had to admit she wished she had a pair of jeans or something. Crouching on the street in heels, letting her bare skin touch the concrete, wasn't exactly fun. "Where did you put them?"

"No . . . no more . . ."

Chess exchanged glances with Terrible. They weren't going to get anything from her this way, were they?

Movement behind them; some of Bump's men picking up the unconscious bodies and putting them in the rusty bed of a pickup splotched with Bondo. They watched Chess and Terrible, obviously waiting to take the girl if necessary, waiting to be told what to do next.

Good. The sobs were starting to grate on her, aural sandpaper scraping at the filth inside her.

"I'm going to look for them, okay?"

Was that a nod? She thought it was a nod. She hoped it was a nod, because either way she was going to find those drugs. It occurred to her that she was stealing drugs off someone too high to notice what she was doing; sure, it was because she was helping, but still. It didn't make her feel good.

Nor did the girl's reaction when Chess slipped her hand into the girl's jeans pocket. She screamed and lashed out, her hand bent like a claw aiming at Chess's face.

Chess started to duck, her own arm rising instinctively, but Terrible was faster. The girl's hand fell just short of its target; the girl's torso fell back onto Terrible's left arm. He'd knocked her out.

Well, what else was he supposed to do, she guessed. She shot him a quick glance of thanks and started checking pockets.

Mother lode. Four packets hid in the girl's front pocket, and when Chess held her hand a few inches over the girl's legs she felt more. Ten in each of her socks. No way was this girl just a user. Who the hell could even afford that much at one time? Even crap speed was twenty a gram; Chess only paid twenty for the good stuff, but she got it wholesale, as it were. This girl was—had been—walking around with at least five hundred bucks' worth of speed on her.

Hell, not even Chess could do that much in such a short time that she'd need to carry it with her.

Of course, the girl might not have a home, but ... No. She didn't look particularly dirty—not under all the blood, at least—and she didn't smell. Her clothes were clean, too, and didn't appear worn out; not secondhand, at least not that Chess could see. She didn't know much about fashion, but she'd sure as fuck seen and worn a lot of thrift-store and free charity clothing in her life.

Terrible gave her one last glance, then said something to the men standing there, Chess didn't hear exactly what. The crowd had begun to dissipate, bored now that the spectacle was over. Music broke over their heads as the sound system started back up inside Trickster's.

Two of the men picked up the girl and carried her to the truck; Chess picked up all of the packets, grabbed the three from her bag. Twenty-four full grams, not counting the tiny bits left in the men's bags. All that speed—could she despell it somehow, or . . . ?

No. And even if she could, she couldn't remove the ectoplasm. Damn. That sucked. But not as much as doing a line of it probably did.

She kept holding as many packets as she could while she peeled off the glove, so they ended up caught inside it like a latex bag, and stuffed the others in after. Not great; she could still feel them. But not as much, and when she tied the glove shut at the open end it lessened a bit more.

Light flared across the pavement; Terrible's lighter snapped shut and he held a cigarette out to her. He hadn't lit it for her—not in public—but she still appreciated it.

He glanced at the bar, which was rapidly filling back up. "Get a beer?"

Well, they could talk just as easily in there, couldn't they?

Looked like everyone else had had the same idea. Trickster's might have been empty while everyone watched the show, but when Chess and Terrible walked through the door, it was crowded and hot like the inside of a sauna in the spirit prisons; red gels over the black lights furthered the impression.

And of course there were the people, shouting at one another over Blitz's "Someone's Gonna Die Tonight," lurching around the floor or slouching against the walls in a stupor. Something inside her relaxed. It might be pitiful, it might be gross, but it was where she belonged.

Of course, what that said about her . . . yeah.

Terrible got them both beers—Trickster's didn't serve anything else, which kind of sucked because she was thirsty—and led her to a table near the back. Three people sat around it on cracked leather chairs tiger-striped with gouges and scratches in the dark wood. They glanced up when Terrible reached them.

He waited.

He didn't wait long. They gave him kind of dirty looks—at least it seemed like that to her—but didn't argue. Of course they didn't. And there was that wrong but undeniable pride again, followed inevitably by the knowledge that she didn't deserve any of it. That was followed by the expression on Elder Griffin's face, and she needed to forget it all as soon as possible.

Bleh. She sat down next to Terrible, wishing she could touch him. Instead she played with the label on her beer, which was already peeling as condensation built up on the bottle.

He lit her smoke and leaned closer. Not too close, but close enough that he didn't have to shout. "She ain't work for Bump. Not what I know, leastaways."

"I don't think she works for Lex, either. She wasn't marked." She lifted her left hand and showed him the back of it to illustrate her words. Slobag's—oops, Lex's, since his father, Slobag, was dead—men were all marked, a Chinese character inked onto the backs of their left hands.

"Them ain't all inked, always."

"True, yeah, but . . . if she worked for him, why would she be over here?"

He shrugged.

"I'll ask him, if you want. I just still can't see Lex involved in this. But . . . if she wasn't working for Bump or Lex, who's she working for?"

He smiled, holding her gaze for a second longer than he normally did in public. Warmth started to spread slowly through her veins. "Aye. Wonderin that one myself."

"Where did they take them?"

"One of Bump's houses. Let em sleep it off, dig, see iffen we get some knowledge from em on the morrow. Be good we do, aye. Ain't likin this shit."

"Me either."

Under the table his hand reached over to touch her thigh. Just the faintest, fastest touch; nothing anyone would see or notice. Nothing that looked deliberate. But she felt it, and it spread through her entire body anyway.

"Gimme a favor, aye?"

"Sure, what?"

His eyes met hers again, but this time he didn't smile. This time something serious rested in them, something that looked a lot like the kind of concern that set her teeth on edge. "Know you don't buy offen the street much, but . . . don't buy off nobody, aye? Off any else."

Wow. She had not expected that. "I don't buy off the street, no, I—Lex brings me most—"

"Aye." He averted his eyes from her, scanning the crowd. Was he wondering if someone was out there planning to kill him, too? "Don't— Let me bring it you, dig. Don't want chances."

No. Fuck. She didn't want that; she'd never wanted that. Never wanted any connection between the two things she needed. She'd done that before, and unfortunately, no matter what the intent was, sleeping with someone who brought her drugs looked and felt too much like sleeping with someone for drugs. "No, you don't have to—"

"Know I ain't. Gonna, though."

"But—"

He shook his head, slowly but emphatically. "Ain't chatterin on this one."

"I can feel whatever it is they've done to that speed, you know, the ectoplasm and the magic, so—"

"Aye. But some out there spreadin bad shit could put all kinds in it, dig. Not just magic. Could be any else in there, an iffen we got our ones handin it out too . . . No chances on it, Chess. Mean it. From me, or straight offen Bump. Aye?"

Shit. He did have a point there. She nodded.

His shoulders relaxed; she hadn't realized he'd been tensing them. "Right, then. Got any thoughts who them is doin it? Ain't see no touch-back between that dame and him yesterday down the docks, or Samms or Rickride neither. Just random."

"No. I wish I did, but no."

"Got any thoughts on who? From the energy, meaning."

She thought about it for a second, taking a slow, contemplative sip of her beer. "I'm not sure if it's the same caster for the speed and the walnuts, but it's similar. Both men. And—" She stopped.

"Aye? And what?"

"I don't . . . I don't know." She shook her head. "I thought there was something else about it, but it slipped out of my head before I could pin it down. You know what I mean?"

"On the feeling? Aye. Maybe got to do with feelin like you Church? Or like with them hookers afore, the sex magic."

It shouldn't have—it was totally wrong—but just

hearing the word "sex" come out of his mouth sent a little thrill up her spine. "No. It definitely wasn't sex magic."

His lips curved the faintest bit, so subtle she doubted anyone else would be able to see it. "Aye? You certain? Maybe you ain't recognize it, is all, needs you a reminder."

Damn, it was so hard pretending she didn't really care about him, pretending she didn't feel as if someone had poured her out of a jug to puddle all over everything, so turned on she could hardly breathe.

Part of her was absolutely sure it didn't matter, anyway. Even the drunkest Downside alley rat would see the smile fighting to spread across her face, the way her skin flushed.

"Why we ain't go on home," he went on. He still didn't look at her, but heat radiated off his body to caress her skin; she imagined if she touched him he'd jump. She knew she'd jump if he touched her. "Thinkin maybe there's more to chatter on that one."

Her nod felt jerky, too eager, but she couldn't help it. Her muscles didn't seem to be entirely under her control. "Maybe you're right. I think—I think I need some help with that."

"Been thinkin on givin you the help all night, Chessie-bomb. Every minute."

Her mouth was too dry to speak. She swallowed the rest of her beer in one hasty gulp and stood up.

She folded her arms over her chest to keep from reaching for him as they pushed themselves through the crowd. At least, *he* pushed through the crowd. She followed in his wake, her heart jumping up and down in her chest like a puppy begging to be fed.

Well, some part of her body was begging, anyway.

Past a few more stumblers clutching empty bottles and out the door. The stretch of road under the streetlamp was blank, like a hole full of light. The crowd had blocked it, so Terrible had parked partway on the sidewalk, farther down past the edge of the building to the left, almost into the strangled-looking lawn used as a combination parking lot, bathroom, campsite, and dump.

Music followed them, quieter now because the bar's door had closed but still in the air around them. The faint breeze smelled of rain, whispering across Chess's oversensitive skin to make her shudder, and Terrible stopped short.

Chess knocked into his shoulder. "What?"

He didn't reply for a long moment, then shook his head. "Nothin. Come on, let's us get you in the car."

She started to move, but he muscled himself half in front of her, nudging her closer to the street itself and farther from the bar's wall. That— He didn't usually do that. That seemed kind of weird.

He slowed down for a second when they hit the alley on the side of the building, leaning forward and glancing to his left. A spark of fear ignited in her chest.

"Is—"

"Naw, no worryin," he replied, but something in his tone made her eyebrows quirk. That sounded too casual, didn't it?

She knew he'd be cautious with the Chevelle where it was—he usually parked under the light for a reason, not because he thought it looked cool—but she hadn't expected him to be uneasy. He didn't *look* uneasy, but she felt it, knew it was there.

His hand hit her arm, a quick tap telling her to start walking again. Faster. His keys jingled in his left hand as he lifted it to the car door.

She started to cross around him to get in once he'd opened it, but before she could he pivoted, shoving her back with his left elbow so her hip slammed against the Chevelle's front quarter panel.

She managed to bite back a cry of surprise and pain, instinctively ducking farther down, trying to get out of the way as she heard him gasp, heard footsteps. A shadow crossed over her face, fast, moving with the whispering hiss of fabric rubbing against itself.

Three seconds? Five? She didn't know. What she knew was that Terrible grabbed her and hauled her off the ground, practically throwing her into the car.

"Lock it." He slammed the door behind her and was gone, chasing the shadow into the alley next to Trickster's.

She looked at the door, looked around. A smattering of people stood on the street, brushy Mohawks and tattooed bald heads catching the light, but no one paid attention to her.

She got out of the car and headed up the alley.

Weeds scratched at her legs. She didn't think they drew blood but didn't care enough to check. Couldn't stop to check, because Terrible's back had disappeared into the darkness, been swallowed by it.

She kept going, fighting the uneven ground in her cherry-red peep-toe platforms—damn it—even though she knew it was useless. They were gone by the time she reached the dingy empty space behind the bar, its incompetent fence still vibrating in the back corner around a torn-out hole.

She paused to grab her knife from her bag and headed for that hole. Too late for her to do anything, yes; it had been too late the second she opened the car door and Terrible was already gone. But she wasn't going to just stand there waiting, either. Who the hell knew what was happening?

Not far off, an engine roared. The street screamed in protest as a car took off; she picked her way across the empty cement lot of the abandoned building behind the bar, holding the knife at the ready and straining her eyes at the space around her.

It wasn't that it was so dark, really. She could see the cracked pavement, the fence posts gleaming dully and the various rubbish strewn around.

The problem was what she couldn't see. The abandoned building in whose back lot she stood was full of blank windows; shadows shifted and moved in the small spaces, in the little corners and areas overhung with broken roofs. Anything could be in those places. Anyone could be.

Movement at the corner. She pulled her knife hand back, waiting.

It was Terrible. Walking slow, rage transmitting itself in his every move, the set of his shoulders. She took an involuntary step back. Fuck.

What should she say? What could she say, really. Obviously he hadn't caught their attacker. Or rather, their would-be attacker, since he hadn't stuck around long enough to actually attack. What the hell had been the point of that, anyway? To jump out and run away? Had he—she assumed their attacker was a he, she thought the figure she'd seen, that moving shadow, was big and solid—planned to attack them but run away when Terrible saw him and started to fight?

Somehow she didn't think that was the time to ask Terrible about it.

He caught her eye, shook his head. "Had he a fuckin car on the wait."

"You saw it?"

"Ain't matter. Weren't theirs, guessing. Somethin they took for this one. Told you to gimme the wait."

He'd reached her at that point. His fingers brushed her arm as he passed, urging her to follow, which she did again.

She wasn't going to comment on the waiting-in-the-car thing. "You want to go back inside? Get another beer or something?"

"Naw, let's just get us gone. Back mine, aye?"

She hesitated. "We wanted to check those spells together—"

"Can wait on that one."

It wasn't until he'd put her in his car, sat down himself, that she noticed his right leg and his shirt down that side were wet, clinging to his skin. Her fingers hovered over the fabric for a second, not wanting to touch it, not wanting to be sure.

Stupid. She already knew. But like an ass she reached out anyway, gritting her teeth, and felt absolutely no surprise at all when the fingertips she lifted off his thigh were red.

Chapter Eleven

Vigilance is important. Work is important. But intuition
and instinct are important, also.
— *Debunking: A Practical Guide*, by Elder Morgenstern

"I don't get it," she said again, peeling open his bowling shirt as he sat on the toilet lid. Her voice wanted to crack when she saw the T-shirt beneath, dark with blood already drying at the edges. "What was the point? Jump out, stab, and run away? Why do that?"

He shrugged the shirt off without answering and let it drop to the cold white tile floor, then started to pull up the hem of the T-shirt; the muscle under his right eye twitched at the movement.

"Here." She helped him, her mind whirring. "That's what he did, right?"

He didn't nod, really, just gave her a sort of quick chin-tip that let her know she was right. Anger still filled the austere bathroom and made her shiver.

"But so why—" Oh.

Lex. Lex had to be behind this; Lex had threatened to have Terrible killed, and she'd—well, not at that moment outside Trickster's, her mind had been on other things—been expecting something. But not . . . not this.

It didn't seem like a very effective attempt on someone's life, did it, to pop out of the shadows, slice a knife across their ribs a few times, and then run away. The wounds weren't even that serious; the scratches were deep but not fatal. Not a very good assassin, then. Or maybe—oh, shit.

Her eyes met his; his changed when they saw the knowledge in hers. "Aye. Were givin me the hello. So I got it him out there."

"That was only the first time."

"Figured on it comin soon. Ain't thought for sure be this night, but had the knowledge be seein him soon."

Cold spread through her body. Where was her bag, where were her pills? The ones she'd taken at the wedding, almost four hours ago—shit, it felt like it had been weeks—might as well have been vitamins for all the effect she was getting from them, and the realizations piggybacking over one another to fill her head made her stomach churn.

He knew it was coming. He'd been expecting it. They'd gotten the drop on him, and nobody got the drop on him, except . . . "It was me, right? Because I was there. You had to get me out of the way, and that gave him his opening. You had to get me into the car, and that gave him time to get away."

"Don't matter, Chess, ain't like—"

"It matters." Damn him. Damn him, damn him, damn him. Of course. Lex knew Terrible. Lex knew exactly what Terrible would and wouldn't do, and what he would and wouldn't do when she was there. Knew that the only time Terrible was vulnerable was when he was with her.

The bathroom around her started to spin. Where the fuck was her fucking bag?

She slumped on the edge of the tub and grabbed it with hands that didn't want to work. Too damn bad, she'd make them. That conversation could not continue until she'd gotten her pills. She couldn't even let herself think about it anymore until she'd gotten her pills.

Terrible kept undressing while she gave four Cepts a nasty, bitter crunch between her teeth and washed them down with a grimace. Her eyes closed. Only a minute now. Just having that taste in her mouth made her feel better, just knowing they'd start working in a few minutes made her feel lighter, easier.

It didn't change the fact that this was all her fucking fault, of course, but then what would?

"Oh, hey." Duh. She offered the box up. "Do you want one, does it hurt?"

He shook his head. Right.

He kept a first-aid kit under his sink, as she did; it was open on the floor, and she dug around in it to give herself something else to look at. Not that she didn't want to see his bare chest, of course she did, but having to see those wounds and knowing they existed because she'd been there, knowing that had he not needed to protect her, he either wouldn't have been injured or would have caught the motherfucker . . . that really wasn't something she wanted to do.

But she had to. So she closed her eyes for another second, sighed, and stood up, setting the kit on the edge of the sink.

His breath hissed when she dabbed a warm, wet cloth over the cuts. She looked up. "Sorry."

Another nonreaction, a shrug of his eyebrows while everything else stayed still.

It only took a few minutes to wipe away the drying blood and pat the scratches dry. Four of them, thin horizontal slices across the bottom of his rib cage. Not deep, but not shallow either. Not shallow enough to make her breath come easier. "Maybe we should go to the—"

"No."

"These could probably use stitch—"

"No." His glare left no room for further argument, and honestly she didn't want to argue anyway.

Okay, then. No stitches. In the kit were some of those butterfly-bandage things. They'd have to do. Should they go on before the— No, that was dumb, the ointment went on first, then the bandages. What the fuck was wrong with her? She'd done this shit for herself dozens of times—Debunkers got injured fairly often, crawling around in attics and reaching into crevices and whatever else—and she'd never had this much trouble, never found her hands shaking as she smeared antibacterial goo over her wounds.

But then, she'd never done it with the expectation that there would be more. She'd never done it knowing it was because someone had been hired to cause the wounds.

And shit, she just didn't fucking care that much about herself. But this wasn't her, this was Terrible, and someone was out there with cash riding on his death, someone who knew what they were doing.

So her hands shook, and even as the first swirls of tingly relief started in her stomach she knew they weren't going to stop.

"Can see right down yon dress, Chessiebomb."

Her gasp of laughter echoed in the room. More relief. Relief and something else, too, because all that furious energy in the room was changing in a very familiar way, one she'd half expected. She wasn't the only one who looked for ways to distract herself from things she didn't want to think about. "Oh?"

"Aye."

That tone in his voice didn't help calm her down. Nor did the fact that as she smeared the wound with ointment his hand rested on her hip.

She ignored it. Ignored it while she closed the scratches as best as she could, while she placed a clean gauze pad over them, and while his hand moved, sliding under her skirt to skim the back of her thigh.

When his fingertips slipped under the edge of her panties, she spoke. "Stop it. I need to get this taped on."

"Thinkin it's on there all right up. Whyn't you come with me, we finish cleanin up later."

"No, I'm almost— You shouldn't be moving around a lot, anyway."

"You do all the work, then, aye? C'mon. Look, you got me all fixed up." The dress's bodice loosened around her ribs; he'd pulled the zipper down, and his fingers found the hooks of her strapless bra.

"Just let me take these shoes off."

The bra opened. He stood up, a smile she knew very well crossing his face, and grabbed her hips to start urging her out of the room. "Naw, naw, leave em on."

His mouth broke her laugh, broke her feeble attempts to protest. Feeble because she didn't want to protest, especially not when his hands spread heat over her bare back, down over her bottom and thighs.

There was still stuff to talk about. He knew it; she knew it. But as her dress fell to the floor she stopped protesting, took his face in her hands and let him walk her out of the bathroom and across the wide cement floor of his apartment to the big gray bed. Those subjects weren't going away because they got distracted for half an hour or so. And even if she hadn't needed him she would have needed him, because those images of what could have happened refused to leave her alone and somewhere inside her, down where all of the other filth hid, she knew just how possible it was for them to become reality.

What she would do if that happened she couldn't even imagine; of all the thoughts and fears she locked away, that was the one she didn't think she could handle.

So she didn't. Instead she fell back on the bed shoes and all, and let him make her forget.

* * *

She was still trying to forget those things the next morning, as she trudged across the Church grounds to Elder Griffin's house. Unfortunately, when she did manage to push those thoughts away, they were immediately replaced by thoughts of the woman and the three men from the night before, whom she was going to see when she left the Church grounds.

Or of course, by fears of what Elder Griffin was going to say to her and what she would say back, and those weren't pleasant, either, though not quite as worrisome. He at least wasn't trying to kill her, or Terrible, or anyone else. He was probably just going to offer an opinion, and would hopefully—would most likely—listen to her response and not rescind her permission to live off-grounds.

She'd taken four Cepts in her car, done a little bump for luck. Probably wouldn't work, but at least it all meant she felt okay instead of terrified and sick, so that was something, anyway.

A black bird-shaped wind chime tinkled at her as she opened the iron porch door and crossed the few feet to the house itself. Flat stacks of cardboard sat outside the door and under the wooden swing seat, empty boxes broken down and waiting to be dumped or recycled or whatever else would be done with them. The wedding had only been the night before, so Elder Griffin and Keith couldn't have been sleeping there before that, but they'd been moving things in for a few days.

The door opened almost before she finished knocking. Keith, with a broad smile on his face and his feet bare beneath faded jeans and a blue-striped shirt. "Cesaria! Great to see you again, come on in."

They shared a slightly awkward cheek-kiss and he stepped aside, gesturing with his arm at the open hallway: pale-wood floors and pale-brown walls, the baseboards and moldings painted a bright teal blue. Sunlight poured in through wide-open windows, the white curtains shifting and twisting in the summer-scented breeze.

Summer and magic. They'd done a house dedication that morning, she figured from the lingering fragrance of coal smoke and incense.

Elder Griffin stood off to her right, surrounded by a living room full of modular furniture and bright art prints. Her gaze swept it all as she curtsied and exchanged greetings. Funny, she'd never been in his house before, but it was exactly what she would have imagined.

What she hadn't imagined was the sight of him dressed similarly to Keith, in jeans and a button-down shirt. For a moment she stared; it was almost as bizarre as seeing him naked. Well, maybe not that bizarre, but weird nonetheless.

So weird it took her a minute to realize Keith had spoken. "Sorry, what?"

"Just apologizing for the mess. We're still trying to get organized. You know, moving."

"Sure."

"But next time you come we'll be all set. And maybe you'll bring Terrible? We could have dinner."

"Sure," she said again. Discomfort wound itself around her, squeezing hard. Why would he be inviting Terrible if Elder Griffin didn't like him? What was she there to discuss? "That'd be great."

"Please sit down." Elder Griffin gestured toward a dark-brown armchair, which faced a matching sofa over a long slim coffee table. "Thank you for coming."

She nodded, sinking into the chair with her bag in her lap. It didn't need to be in her lap, no, but the weight comforted her for some odd reason; holding it gave her something to do with her hands.

"Coffee? Tea, soda? Wine? We have plenty of everything." Keith stood in the open archway of the room.

"No, thanks."

Elder Griffin and Keith exchanged glances. Keith clapped his hands together. "Well, okay, then. I have some errands to run, so I'm going to go. I'll be back in a couple of hours or so."

What the hell was going on?

Saying goodbye to Keith didn't provide any answers. Nor did watching Elder Griffin get up and close every window on the bottom floor of the house. That discomfort wasn't just squeezing her anymore; it was choking her, making it harder and harder to breathe, and she was trapped in that cushy chair watching the space around her shrink and grow more silent with every slam of frame into sill.

Finally, Elder Griffin sat down on the couch across from her, leaning forward with his forearms on his knees. "Cesaria."

"Yes?"

"Cesaria, I hardly know . . . I . . ." He shook his head. "I have been trying all morning to decide how best to begin this discussion, and I fear I am no closer to an answer than I was when I awoke."

How was she supposed to reply to that?

He sighed, reached for the wineglass on the coffee table. Did he usually drink during the day, or was he trying to get himself drunk to have this conversation?

What the fuck was going on?

"Let me say this first. I have closed all of the windows. We are the only people in this house. I tell you this because I want you to understand that this is a private conversation. You may speak freely. I hope you will speak freely, as I am about to do."

He seemed to expect an answer to that, so she gave him one. "Of course, sir."

"I do not believe it will be a surprise to you—I hope it will not—if I tell you I have always felt . . . I have always been very fond of you, my dear. I have always felt I perhaps understood you better than the others, and you—well, I cannot speak for you. But I don't believe I am incorrect to say that you and I have . . . a good relationship. A closer relationship than others."

"Of course, sir," she said again. "I mean, yes. I, I feel that way, too." The strap of her bag was the same dull olive-green color as the bag itself, military green; she watched it as she twisted it around her fingers then untwisted it, twisted and untwisted, pulling it tight so her fingers turned bluish-red at the tips. The same color she imagined her face was. It was everything she could do not to get up and run.

"I say this not to make you uncomfortable," he said after a few seconds, "but to make certain you know it before we continue. I care very much for you, Cesaria. And I want to help you."

Fuck. Time to brace for the storm. "I'm fine. I mean, I don't know what you're worried about, but—"

"Oh, dear. No. I fear I've said this all wrong. Your young man. Terrible."

"No, he's, I know what you're thinking. I know he might look—but really, Elder Griffin, you don't have to worry about me. He would never hurt me, never, and—"

"Oh no." Elder Griffin shook his head. His eyes when they met hers were so full of sadness that she felt it like a hand around her throat. "No. I do not suspect for a moment that he would. That was clear to me. My fear is not for you. It is for him."

Her hands fell still. "What?"

"My dear . . ." He leaned forward farther. "What did you do to him?"

Chapter Twelve

Holy fuck.

The world stopped; for a moment she thought her heart was going to follow suit. What had she done? He was going to want an explanation and she couldn't give him one, how was she supposed to give him one?

I don't know what you mean was on the tip of her tongue; deny. Deny, deny, deny, deny everything. She even began to say it, her mouth opening to form the words, but when she met his eyes again she couldn't.

He knew. He'd shaken Terrible's hand and he'd felt something—those sidelong glances at the wedding, the surprise on his face when his skin touched Terrible's, made sense now—and if she lied she'd only make it worse.

But how the hell was she supposed to even start to explain? Much less admit to him what she'd done.

She'd killed a psychopomp. She could be executed for that. And there she sat in front of an Elder. An Elder who, no matter how fond of her he might be, had both the authority and the obligation under Church law to report her crime.

Would he believe sex magic? Or maybe that she'd

done something, some sort of ritual to make Terrible stronger? Something like that? She couldn't say that she'd let him come into intimate contact with her blood in an unlicensed marriage; he'd know it was a lie, because her own energy hadn't changed. What could she tell him, what could she say, what the hell was she going to do?

She'd have to leave the Church. She'd have to go immediately, she'd have to run, assuming Elder Griffin let her leave his house after she confessed. She'd go straight to Terrible's place and stay there, and he'd help her figure out what to do.

Leave the Church . . . leave her home. Her palms felt sticky and hot. Her entire body felt sticky and hot, the space behind her eyes tingling and aching.

"Please tell me. He felt . . . I felt your magic in him."

Still she said nothing. That was that, then. Time to do what she'd hoped she would never have to do, time to act on the choice she'd already made in her heart—the choice she'd made the second she pulled Terrible's gun from his waistband that night to shoot the hawk coming for his soul.

"It will stay between us. I ask you to trust me. Let me help you. Let me help him."

"Why?" It came out in such a dry sort of whisper, she wasn't even sure at first that it was audible.

He shook his head, a sad kind of shake like a man hearing news of a tragedy in another part of the world. "Because I care. Let me help you because I want to."

Her cheeks itched; when she raised her hand to rub them she realized they were wet. Great. Crying. It would have pissed her off if she'd been able to feel anything but fear, anything but pain, so strong it pushed right through her high and refused to let her escape.

Elder Griffin sighed. "Cesaria . . . I know what soul-binding magic feels like."

A fresh packet of tissues sat in a pocket of her bag; she pulled one out, wiped at her eyes. Not that it mattered. The tears weren't stopping, weren't slowing. It was too late to stop them.

And it was too late to lie, or to hide. It was the end. The end, and she could at least face it with some dignity, and with Truth. "You remember the night, that night when I got shot? When Kemp shot me, you remember."

Elder Griffin nodded. And kept nodding while she told the story, each word scraping at her throat as it came out, making it hurt even more. The ghost whores, the house, the psychopomp birds she'd managed to bring under her control. Kemp, naked, his skin covered with magical tattoos, coming out from the darkness with a loaded gun and shooting. All of that, Elder Griffin basically knew.

What he didn't know . . .

When she got to the part about killing the psychopomp, he gasped. His face paled, almost as if he still wore the white Church makeup designed to make the Elders look like spirits, to emphasize their dominion over them.

Might as well finish the story. She didn't think she could stop at that point, anyway, not when the images kept coming, not when she saw Terrible on the pavement with his eyes closed and his blood spreading in a dark pool around him, as if it was all happening again.

Her voice shook, a low dry rasp cracking the still air between them. "I used my knife. The sigil, the one they used to use, the one you told me about. Not the changes Oliver Fletcher made, just the original one, the Church one. I carved it into his chest and I activated it. I couldn't—I couldn't let him die, I couldn't stand it, and, and I can't even say I'm sorry because I *am* sorry but I'd do it again. I need him. I can't . . . I *need* him."

He sat without moving, without speaking, for a long

time. Chess didn't say anything, either; what more was there to say? She'd confessed. They said it was good for the soul, but hers was so covered in shit she didn't think anything would make a difference, and she sure as fuck didn't feel any better for having told him.

What she felt was sick, and scared, and what she felt most was the desire to go home, to climb into bed with Terrible and lie there while he kept her safe. Or to visit the pipe room, to claim a section of sofa and smoke Dream until the world faded away, became a not-very-interesting TV show with the volume turned way down.

"I see," he said finally. "I see."

Another pause.

"Have there been any . . . effects from this? Has anything changed about him?"

"No. He's . . . well, no, not his personality or anything. But dark magic—if he gets near it, touches something made with it, he passes out."

"I see," he said again.

That package of tissues wasn't going to last much longer. She'd already used up about two-thirds of them.

He stood up. Shit. He was going to pick up the phone, he was going to turn her in. And she couldn't blame him for it, because she'd killed a psychopomp to keep it from performing its duty. She deserved to be punished for that.

She deserved to be punished for a lot of things.

"I am getting a drink. Would you care for one?"

She shook her head.

He left the room, heading into what she guessed was the kitchen; she used the opportunity to crunch up two more Cepts, fast, swirling water from her bottle in her mouth to try to cut the horrible bitterness on her tongue.

It didn't help. Nothing would help. But it soothed her, at least a little, and at that moment she could use whatever she could get.

What she should probably be doing was throwing herself out the door, tearing across the grounds to her car, and hauling ass back to her apartment or Terrible's, but she couldn't bring herself to move. The Church was her home, the Church had rescued her, given her a future, made her something real. And before Terrible had come along, the Church had been everything she had; well, the Church and her pills had been everything she had.

The thought of leaving it made her heart feel as if it were made of wet sand, sluggish and heavy. She wouldn't do that until she had absolutely no other choice; she wouldn't do that until all hope was gone.

She should have known better than to hope, yeah. But it kept happening, anyway.

Elder Griffin reappeared, holding two cans of Coke. He opened one and set the other on the table in front of her. On a coaster on the table, rather. Any other time she would have smiled.

"So," he said. "I confess I have very little idea what to say. What you have done . . . It is a grave crime, Cesaria. Grave indeed."

How was it possible that her entire body was numb but the sharp cold ache in her heart grew worse with every second?

Not just because he could turn her in, not just because she could be executed. She realized, looking into his sad blue eyes, his serious face, that ever since Terrible had found out about her sleeping with Lex, Elder Griffin was the only man she cared about—the only *person* she cared about—in the entire world who didn't know about a bad choice she'd made, a bad thing she'd done. The only one who didn't know who she really was, that she was a junkie, that she was a slut, that she was a failure, that she was worthless and disloyal.

Elder Griffin had believed she was special. He'd believed she was good. The disappointment in his eyes hurt.

" 'Twas a selfish thing you did." His gaze left hers; he stared at the ceiling. "I am . . . I am shocked to hear this. I am disappointed to hear it."

Fuck. She was crying in earnest now, crying from shame, crying because she'd lost something valuable. Something she'd always known was valuable but hadn't realized how much she counted on. He was right to call her selfish. He was right to be shocked and disappointed in her. Aside from everything else, what she'd done had broken the oaths she took when she was officially inducted into the Church.

And she still couldn't say she was sorry. Because it would be a lie.

"I never would have expected such a thing from you."

Enough. Death would almost be preferable to hearing more, to hearing how badly she'd fucked up again.

Another tissue. "I know you have to turn me in. It's okay, I understand. I just . . . maybe you could let me go, and I'll, I'll leave Triumph City or something."

"No."

He wasn't even going to let her run away. He didn't even care enough for her anymore that he'd let her live. "Um, okay, can you, can I call Terrible and tell him—"

"I have no intention of repeating this to anyone."

"I know it's your— What?"

He looked down at his hands clasped together in front of him, like in pictures she'd seen of people praying when they still believed the old religions. "I have no intention of turning you in, Cesaria. You know what the penalty is for killing a psychopomp. I cannot . . . I cannot do that, though I know I should."

Relief made her dizzy—relief or the first flush of happiness from her pills, or both. She didn't know and she didn't care. Instead she sat there, her tears starting afresh, faster than before, feeling relieved and slimy to be feeling relieved. Sleazy.

"Thank you," she managed. Shame. More shame, piling on what already lurked in her heart and soul. Shame because he was going against something he believed— she knew he was—and shame because he was doing it for her. "Thanks."

He acknowledged her gratitude with a dip of his head, gave her another minute to stop sniffling before he spoke again. "You do know what that sigil could do? Why it's making him vulnerable to dark magics?"

"It could— It makes him more vulnerable to possession, right?"

Anger flashed across his face. "How could you be so— You knew what the consequences could be, I told you the story and—" He stopped himself, pressed his hand to his forehead for a minute and sighed.

She'd never seen him angry, aside from one moment in the battle in the City of Eternity months before. She'd never heard him yell. Maybe he would yell. He certainly should.

He didn't. Small cabinets flanked the couch; Elder Griffin leaned over to open one of those, from which he pulled a large blue ashtray and set it on the table. "Feel free to smoke. Keith does on occasion."

It hadn't occurred to her before, but suddenly she was dying for a smoke. She could use a line, too, but she didn't think she'd get one until she got home. Yeah, she could bump up in the car if she had to, but she had a feeling that wouldn't be enough.

He watched in silence as she lit up, then he spoke. "The sigil broadens his own magical powers slightly, and, of course, because you activated it with your blood it gives him a minute amount of your power. But it weakens his natural defenses, because it uses his energy to bind his soul to his body. So when he comes in contact with magic, it affects that energy and changes it, because he is not powerful enough to handle it. He doesn't know how."

"It changes the energy that's holding his—it changes that energy?"

He nodded.

Her hand shook as she dragged off her cigarette. "That means the energy isn't effective, right? When it changes. It's not doing its job, binding his soul to his body. That's what you're saying, right?"

Another nod.

"So that means he's not passing out. He's— His soul is . . ."

"Escaping, yes. The sigil prevents it from leaving entirely, but there is an extremely brief time period—I would guess the merest fraction of a second—when the bond breaks. Cesaria . . . he's not fainting. He's dying."

Her stomach churned. She was going to be sick, she was going to be sick, she couldn't stop it.

But at least she made it. At least she managed to choke out the word "Bathroom," and at least she was able to hear and understand his response over the ringing—the *screaming*—in her ears. And at least she made it.

Dying. Dying every time. Would his soul always come back, what if one day it didn't? How could his body take that, how long would it be able to—did his heart stop when it happened, was his fucking heart stopping, was his breath stopping, what if one day it didn't start again, how long could he go without oxygen? Was his body dying when his soul left it?

Her stomach was empty. That didn't stop it from trying to empty itself further, over and over. She stayed there, her knees aching from the tile floor, her forehead sweaty under her bangs.

One thing she knew, anyway. They could never remove that sigil from him. If they removed that sigil he'd die. They had to find something new to add to it—to him—something protective, some sort of shield. She had to find something, had to do something. Immediately.

Finally her stomach settled. She managed to stand, to splash cold water on her face—she avoided looking in the mirror—and make it back into the living room. Her body felt like a slack rubber band.

Elder Griffin handed her a cold damp cloth. It almost set her crying again. He was being so nice to her, and she didn't deserve it.

Not just nice in handing her the cloth, either. Nice in pretending she was perfectly fine and resuming the conversation without a bunch of hovery questions. "I take it you have attempted to rectify the situation?"

"I've—I've marked some other runes and stuff on him, and a couple of those helped, but not enough, and I don't know which one works best. We keep meaning to try them individually but whenever we get started on it . . . um, we get distracted or something."

Mercifully he didn't ask by what, but she assumed he knew, anyway. Her flaming face was probably as good as a blinking sign over her head.

"There is no way to completely destroy the risk associated with that sigil." He stood up, walked past her to the far end of the room where the built-in bookshelves had already been filled. "It will always be a danger for him. I take it he had some mild ability before that happened?"

"Not a lot, but yeah, it was there."

He grabbed several books, handing two of them to her as he walked back to the couch. "All right, then. Let us see what we can find, shall we?"

Her phone rang when she was about halfway home. The code MSB came up on the screen: Blue. Lex's sister. "Yeah?"

"This is why I like calling you. You're so friendly."

"Good."

An edge crept into Blue's voice. "What's wrong, Chess?"

What's wrong is that your brother is trying—no, not trying, is actively pursuing, has paid someone—to kill my boyfriend. What's wrong is that once again some-one who trusted me has learned how fucking stupid that was.

But she didn't say that. "Sorry. Sorry, I just— I'm not having a great day."

"Want to meet up for lunch or something? I kind of wanted to talk to you. About that speed. We found six more people out of their heads from it last night."

A gaggle of girls in a blue convertible cut Chess off; she swerved to avoid them. Bitches. "Shit. That— Wait, how do you know about that, why are *you* the one call-ing me?"

"What?"

"Why isn't Lex calling me? He's the one who talked to me about this before, he brought some of it to my apart-ment so I could check on it."

She could hear the shrug in Blue's voice. "I don't know. Lex asked me to call and tell you about it, and I was going to call anyway to see how your dress went over last night. It was last night, wasn't it?"

Right. Lex asked her to call. Lex asked her to call be-cause Lex knew damn well Chess wouldn't want to talk to him, that she'd be furious with him.

If she had any doubt at all that he was behind the attack the night before—which she didn't—that would have put an end to it. Bastard.

But Blue didn't get involved in that side of Lex's busi-ness; in any side of it, actually. Which meant Chess couldn't take her anger out on her.

Nor did she particularly want to. What good would telling Blue about Lex's contract on Terrible do?

"Chess?"

"Huh? Oh yeah, it was last night. It was fine."

"Did you have a good time? What about the dress, did Terrible—"

"Yeah, it was okay. You said six more last night? Do you know where they bought the speed, did anyone find out?"

Pause. "Um, yeah, actually. There was a guy with them who hadn't done any of it. He said they got it up off Baxter, Baxter and Seventeenth."

That was north. That was way north. It was also definitely Lex's side of town. "Is he still around? Did you guys keep him or something?"

"Lex found out where he lives."

Right. Chess flashed her blinker, pulled into the right-hand lane in preparation to exit. Lex. He'd want to be there if and when she questioned someone. If he even told her who it was and let her be there. "I want to talk to him."

"He's not here right now, he's—"

"Not Lex. The guy."

Another pause. "What the fuck is going on?"

"What do you mean?"

"You know what I mean. You're right, Lex doesn't have me talk to you about this stuff. He hardly talks to me about it at all. Why do you sound so cagey when you say his name?"

The light at the bottom of the exit was red. Chess paused, glanced around, and kept moving. "Nothing's going on. I'm just worried about this speed thing."

"Right. I assume you don't mind calling Lex and asking him to tell you where the guy is, then?"

It was Chess's turn to pause. Shit. She really didn't want to put Blue in the middle of anything; bad enough she was anyway just because she was who she was. Lex's sister, who lived on the wrong side of town.

Lex was all Blue had left. "Yeah. I'll call him."

Relief came through the phone loud and clear. "Okay, good. Now tell me about last night."

Chapter Thirteen

Anyone can do magic, and everyone should! You just have to be careful what *kind* of magic.
—*You Can Do This! A Guide for Beginners*,
by Molly Brooks-Cahill

She expected the Market to be packed on an afternoon as sunny as that one, but it . . . wasn't. It was busy, sure, but only busy, certainly nowhere near the standing-room-only levels it usually reached on hot sunny days.

But then, it was early afternoon, and it *was* hot out—already in the nineties—so that might account for it. She bet once the sun started to set, it would be a zoo.

Damn that stupid promise she'd made to Terrible the night before. The pipes were across the Market, but she really didn't have time, and she couldn't score anything else because she'd said she would ask him for it.

Unless . . . she could ask Bump, couldn't she? Terrible said she could get it straight from Bump.

Bump's "private stock" kicked ass, too.

She headed down the center aisle, past the booth selling cheap vinyl tie-back tops and miniskirts, past the blue-velvet-draped booth laid out with jewelry made from bolts and scraps of tin, past the booth with oil lamps and broken appliances sold for the parts, until she reached Edsel's, almost at the end.

"Hey, baby." Edsel's deep, smooth voice poured over her like syrup; his pigmentless skin was hidden under a black wide-brimmed hat and his pigmentless eyes behind black lenses. Edsel had to be careful of the sun. "Ain't seen you in a week, you right?"

"Yeah, sure. Right up." It wasn't as hard to smile as she thought it'd be. Seeing him really did make her feel better. Once he'd been the only person she could call a friend. He still was her friend, and one of the few people who knew about her relationship with Terrible—not because she'd told him, but because he'd followed the whole story as it happened. "How's Galena?"

His ice-blue eyes sparkled over the frames of his glasses for a second, the way they always did when he talked about his wife. "Gettin big now, she is, feelin some kicks an all."

"How much longer?"

"Bout four months."

Chess ran her fingers over some of Edsel's merchandise, not paying much attention but enjoying the shivers of power floating up her arm. That high was even legal, and Galena's pregnancy imbued everything she made with extra power. A few defense-charm bags made of shed snakeskin, bird-bone scrying sticks, insects in wax for hexes. All vibrated with that energy.

Not to mention the regular items: spiderwebs, bones, herbs, mirrors, animal bloods, various types of salt, black powder, iron in all different forms. The basics.

She took her almost empty iron sack from her bag and started scooping filings into it. She could get them cheaper from the Church, but not only did she like buying from Edsel—not only could Edsel use the money—but she didn't particularly want to go back there.

Ever.

"Business good?"

"Aye. Been meanin to give you a touch on the phone, dig. Somethin I got the thinking you ought should see."

He turned to the back of his booth and opened an

African Blackwood box like hers; in fact, she'd bought hers from him when she first moved to Downside four years earlier. The African Blackwood blocked negative energy and dark magic, which meant if he was keeping something in there, it was not good news.

Fuck. The second he lifted the lid her tattoos reacted, tingling and itching, a burning on the surface of her skin. Whatever he had, it wasn't just touched with dark magic; only ghost magic, ghost energy, would elicit that particular reaction.

What he held out to her was a key.

She didn't want to take it. She took it anyway. The irritating pin-scratched feeling of her ink intensified. The key didn't feel like a key somehow, like an inanimate object. It felt alive, warm and heavy, slightly damp as if from sweat; it was repugnant. Like holding a boiled earthworm.

It was one of those old-fashioned keys with a round bar and big crooked teeth. The kind the Church used for doors within the building, the kind that had magical powers anyway. All keys had a touch of magic simply by virtue of their existence; keys were gateways.

Thick black paint coated it, but a chipped spot revealed what lay underneath. She looked up at Edsel. "It's iron."

He nodded. That explained the warmth of it, then. When iron and ghost energy mixed, the iron heated.

It still made no sense at all, but at least she knew why it was warm.

"But—how can it take ghost energy if it's iron? Iron repels ghost energy. How can that work?"

The thing in her hand was an impossibility. Something that could not, should not, exist.

But, then, Terrible should be free to not pass out when he touched dark magic. Elder Griffin should still be proud of her. Theoretically she should be living on

Church grounds, normal and happy like everyone else. "Should be" was another term for "bullshit."

Besides, she'd answered her own question. "They've infused the paint."

"Aye, that's how I got it figured on, also. Be some kinda controller, that do, with the iron an ghost, and just bein what it be, dig."

"You can control ghosts with it."

He shrugged. "You got that knowledge better'n me, baby. Got me some knowin on them dark magics an all, but not the ghosts. You Church teaching you all it, aye?"

She barely heard him. A key that could be used to control ghosts or have power over them. Could the key open the City of Eternity somehow? It shouldn't be able to, but who the fuck knew for sure what something like that could do, something that wasn't supposed to exist?

Or . . . well, damn, she knew of at least one person out there who liked to mix ectoplasm with other shit and bespell it. Did the key have something to do with that?

Yep. Of course it fucking did. When she closed her eyes and focused for a second, she could feel the energy, that same miserable energy as from the walnut—at least she was pretty sure that was it. It was definitely familiar.

So how the hell did the key fit in to that?

Man, people were shit, with their games and plans and endless quest to hurt and control.

She held the key horizontal in front of her eyes, seeing if there were any markings on it. "Are . . . are those initials?"

"Thought em were, aye. Lookin like 'R' an 'A' to myself, how bout you?"

"Yeah, I think you're right." Was it an "R" or a "K"? A "P," maybe? It must have been scratched into the key before the key was painted. Well, duh, of course it was, since the scratches weren't in the paint itself. If they were, they would have been easier to read. "Where did you find this?"

"Ain't were me on the find. Sharp-eye Ben—be a cutpurse, speed-banger too—brung it on me, thinkin maybe I hand over some lashers for it."

"Did you?" She was already reaching into the cash pocket in her bag. Yeah, if Sharp-eye Ben was into the speed-needle, she bet he could use as much cash as he could get. The needle was always the end, she knew. The needle meant giving up, not even trying to live the lie anymore. She hoped to fuck she never found herself there.

"Aye, gave he five. Only to make he happy, dig."

She handed him a twenty. At least that was something she could do; Edsel wouldn't take money from her unless she was actually buying something, but this way she could pay him back and add a bit of a reward, and that let him keep his dignity, too.

He dipped his head toward her iron sack. "Be included, aye?"

"That's at least ten bucks' worth."

"Aye. An ten an five, still fits under."

Pride was such a funny thing. People would starve for it; they'd kill to keep it or kill because it had been injured.

Pride wasn't something she'd ever had a lot of. Her pride came from things beyond her control. She was proud of her magical abilities, but those had just happened, an accident of birth. She was proud of Terrible, proud to be with him, but that was because he was who *he* was.

She'd been proud knowing that Elder Griffin liked her best, considered her the best Debunker he had. . . . Shit, she needed to get to Bump's.

First, she scrawled "Sharp-eye Ben" in her notebook.

She could ask Terrible about him. She could ask Bump about him, but Terrible was more likely to know. Bump didn't give personal attention to many of his customers.

"Anything on with that bad speed been hearin on? Galena brother gave me the tell last night, had a batch of em outside Trickster's. An more all over, actin off."

More? How many more? "Off how?"

"Just . . . like they ain't got a hearin on when them talked to. Like them got somethin else them hearing. An like what them hearin ain't good."

"And Galena's brother said it's affecting a lot of people?"

"What he say, aye." Edsel looked past her, nodded to someone passing by. "Livin by the slaughterhouse like him do, guessin him see all sorts."

She didn't doubt that. All of Downside was too close to the newly rebuilt slaughterhouse; when the wind blew right the stench of fear, raw meat, and rancid blood floated across the empty remnants of offices and homes, over broken streets, hanging there like a warning. But the area directly around the death-house always carried that smell; the building marked its territory.

It wasn't as bad a neighborhood as the docks, no, but those living around the slaughterhouse generally weren't the most upwardly mobile people in the world.

As if she could talk. As if anyone in Downside could talk, but especially her, now that her superior at work knew she was a selfish criminal, that she'd betrayed him and the Church and everyone else.

She chatted with Edsel for another minute or two, but her head was already at Bump's place, in that awful red nightmare of a living room, cutting lines on the table, making herself feel like a person and not something slithering in the mud.

She made that a reality a few minutes later. One of Bump's interchangeable blondes answered the door in response to her knock; this one wore a black leather dominatrix outfit complete with thigh-high boots, and had hot-pink eye shadow up to her eyebrows. She looked like some sort of kinky child experimenting with makeup.

"What you wanting?" she asked finally, after giving Chess a good long up-and-down look.

Chess pushed past her. "I need to talk to Bump. He in the living room?"

No reply. Chess glanced back; the girl stood there gaping at her. Well, whatever. Brains had never been high on Bump's list of desirable attributes in women, at least not that Chess had seen.

Bump's place never changed, and never failed to make her eyes dilate in shock when she entered it. Clashing reds screamed at her from the walls, reds and Bump's collection of "art," which consisted either of paintings or photographs of weapons or paintings or photographs of female genitalia. Or both. Walking down the hall was like walking through said genitalia, emerging into a crimson womb that made her claustrophobic.

He'd added some new porn and some gold-painted crown moldings. Like a bordello decorated by a blind man.

Bump wasn't blind, though. He sat on the red couch, his bare feet on the glass top of the low red steel coffee table, his gold toe ring catching the light from the gold-and-crystal chandelier. His gold-tipped cane rested against the arm of the couch. In his be-ringed hand was a financial magazine.

It would have surprised her if she hadn't already known him. Or hell, if she hadn't known how things worked. Bump hadn't gotten to be lord of the streets west of Forty-third by being stupid.

"Ladybird," he said. His gaze drifted past her. "Terrible ain't come on with you?"

She shook her head. Shit. She'd been so focused on getting there, she hadn't thought of how to ask for it. Bump wasn't a street dealer; she couldn't just walk up and ask. She wanted him to give her some of his personal supply, too, and that was tricky.

So she said, "I wondered if you had any news about that bad speed. Did you get it analyzed or whatever, and find out how much of it is speed and how much is ectoplasm?"

He closed the magazine and tilted his head, not speaking for a long moment. "Why come you ain't fuckin bring Terrible on the alongs?"

"I came from work, that's all. I was in the Market and thought I'd come by and ask about it." All at once she realized she was still standing, and felt stupid for it. The urge to lay down a cloth or something on the couch before she sat on it never went away, but she ignored it—as she had all of the other times—and plunked herself down.

"Got you a special fuckin interest, then, yay?"

She narrowed her eyes. "I can go if you want."

If he made her leave, she'd just ask. That's what she should do, anyway. So why didn't she? Because of Terrible. Because for some reason she didn't want to tell Bump that Terrible made her promise not to cop anywhere else.

Bump waved a lazy hand. "You got you fuckin here now, yay, might as well havin yourself a stay. I give you some fuckin knowledge, you give me some. How's that for dealins?"

"I don't know much, really. How are those people from last night, the people from outside Trickster's?"

"Them fuckers hangin on, yay. Bad shape, you dig me, specially the fuckin dame. An what her deserves, playin fuckin dealer onna streets here."

"So you know she was dealing?" All those packets the

woman had—yeah, they'd suspected, but it was good to have confirmation. Would be good to have it, at least.

"Hear on it. One a them fuckin dudes gave the tell, gots another, a fuckin onlooker, yay, saw her onna corner."

"She didn't work for you, then."

He gave her a disgusted look, his thin reddish brows gathering together over his eyes. "The fuck you thinkin on, workin for Bump? No fuckin way her gettin the work from me, sellin that spooked-up shit her all bagged with."

She ignored the insulting tone. As usual. "You found out what else it was cut with? Was it cut with anything but ectoplasm?"

"Nay, Ladybird, pure fuckin snow mix in the spook juice. Some fuckin dollars behind it, you dig, causen the fuckin pure ain't so cheap. Like mine."

There was her opening. "Oh, right. Can I get some of that? I'm running low."

He watched her for a second too long; she kept her eyes wide, innocent—as innocent as she could be in that position—as if there was nothing unusual at all in her request.

Which there kind of wasn't, because he usually gave her some when she was there, but that was because she was giving him information instead of getting it.

And Terrible was usually there. In fact . . . had she ever been alone in a room with Bump? No. Weird.

He stood up, the faint curl of his lip letting her know exactly what he thought of her request. She ignored it, instead examining the cover of the magazine he'd been reading: some smug rich asshole leering at her over a headline about real estate moguls.

He pulled out the little black-lacquered wood box and set it down on the table before her. When he passed her on his way back to his seat she caught a nose-itching waft of whatever shitty cologne he was wearing. "Have you a fuckin time, there, ain't worry on where Bump get his after you fuckin do it all up."

As if she would.

As if she even cared what he said. The box had barely hit the table before she reached for it, her thumb catching the clasp and opening it up. There had to be at least three or four grams in there, all packed into one bag. Fuck yes. She scooped some out onto the mirror set in the box, chopped herself a nice solid line. "So you think she was working for Lex? Trying to grab some territory?"

She'd just thrown the question out there to make it seem as if she was still invested in the conversation, so his answer surprised her enough that she almost dropped the short gold straw. "Ain't thinkin Lex use the fuckin dames do he street deals, yay. Him ain't can keeping he nose out the fuckin panties, dig."

He shrugged; as with everything Bump did, it took a long time, was dramatic, and made it seem as if he had ball bearings instead of joints. "Had me the fuckin thought back on the when we get you out there, fuckin hook you up with he, maybe fuckin get us some knowledge. Only you fuckin took on up with Terrible steadaways."

He sounded disappointed. But then he pulled out a cigarette and lit it, rocking his head back and forth in an either-or sort of movement. "Lessin maybe you wanna fuckin change-up, have a go? Bettin Terrible ain't fuckin mind, be for the positive on we all, yay?"

Just when she'd started to think maybe somewhere under the sleazy exterior lurked a real human being, he pulled some shit like that.

And the idea that Terrible wouldn't mind if she headed on over to the other side of Downside to get into bed with Lex? Yeah. So wrong she didn't even know how to describe it.

So she didn't. Instead, she bent over and sucked up that line, let the delicious numbness spread from her nostril to her sinuses and the back of her throat to her brain, let her heart give a cheerful jump and start beating faster, pumping light and happiness through her veins. Shit, she'd needed that so bad.

"So she wasn't working for Lex."

"Bettin he gots he some fuckin knowledge on it, though. Ain't buyin the fuckin thought he all fuckin innocent or whatany shit, yay. Scum all the way through, him fuckin is."

That wasn't right—well, she didn't agree with the bit about Lex being scum all the way through—but she wasn't going to argue that with Bump. No, the part about him knowing what was happening wasn't right. Couldn't be, because Blue had called about more deaths, and Lex had brought the shit over for her to— Right. Blue, who didn't know the business, and Lex, who was trying to kill the most important—the only important— person in her life.

Lex would totally bring it over to throw her off. Lex would totally pull any kind of sneaky shit to get one over on Bump, and especially to get one over on Terrible.

She didn't want to believe it. But she'd learned very young that the thing that sounded the worst was probably the way things would end up being; she'd learned that the thing she didn't want to believe was always the one she should, because it would come true.

Speaking of worst things . . . Bump spoke again. "You got him hired he fuckin self a man kill Terrible, yay? Been fuckin told on it, dig, dude came out fuckin nowheres. Devil, he fuckin name, dig, only ain't even fuckin named in English. Devil in them fuckin language, yay, what the meaning is."

He snorted. "Thinkin he make Terrible dead. Fuckin dumb."

Devil. That was his name. She couldn't decide if it was better or worse that she at least had a name to give him; probably worse, really, because now he wasn't just a phantom, a shadow in the night. He was an actual person.

Terrible could beat him. She knew he could. But . . . shit. Time for another line, because she didn't even want to consider letting her thoughts go down that road. Maybe Terrible couldn't die with the sigil on him, but that didn't mean he couldn't be injured. Maimed. Put into a coma for life. Severely brain damaged.

No. No more of that, no more of those thoughts. Her hands shook as she chopped out another line, a thicker one, and sucked it up. That was better. And while she was at it . . .

She pulled one of her own gram-sized plastic-bag packets from her pillbox and tried to keep her voice steady. "Hey, you don't mind if I take some of this, right?"

Bump's lips went very thin. He didn't answer. If she hadn't been so high she might have felt guilty, but as it was, nothing could make her feel guilty. She was awesome, the world was awesome, it sparkled and shone and revolved around her, and none of the bad stuff lurking in her memories had ever happened. That had been a dream. This was reality.

Besides, fuck Bump. He'd wanted to prostitute her out to Lex as if she was property to trade.

Whatever. She didn't want to think about that, either. What she did want to do was knock back three more Cepts, close her eyes, and give herself thirty seconds—or a full minute—of feeling good. Feeling like other people felt. Feeling clean and right.

When she opened her eyes, Terrible was standing in front of her.

Chapter Fourteen

Is it a burden? Yes, it can be. But it is also a privilege, to be a Church employee and to demonstrate to the public the kind of obedience required.

—*The Example Is You*, the guidebook for Church employees

"Hey, hi!" was all she could think of to say, as her smile widened and her heart gave another leap.

His hand found the back of her neck, rested there for a second while he bent down to kiss her forehead, and shifted position when he sat down next to her.

She wrapped her arm around his, rested her head against him. "I'm glad you're here."

"Waited for you, your place."

She lifted her head to look him in the eyes. "You— Why didn't you call or something?"

"Thought you was meetin with that Elder. Got bored of doin the wait, figured on comin here see iffen we got any new knowledge on them last night."

Right. Elder Griffin. Thankfully the speed kept the memory from crashing into her too hard; thankfully it helped her remember that one good thing had come from that meeting—aside from the realization that Terrible was dying, that every time he touched dark magic he *died*. She swallowed. "I did meet with him. And we have some stuff to talk about later, okay?"

He nodded, then turned back to Bump. "So what we got?"

Bump gave him a quick rundown of the conversation so far—at least that's what she assumed; her mind drifted a little bit, watching Terrible's face outlined sharp against the shrieking walls—ending with the idea that Lex knew something and their curiosity over where the girl had come from.

He did not, she noticed, suggest to Terrible that she climb into Lex's bed to learn some secrets.

"Got knowledge that last one, leastaways." The couch cushion moved beneath Chess as Terrible shifted his weight, reaching into the left back pocket of his jeans and producing what looked like a wallet. It *was* a wallet, a pink one. Chess fought the urge to giggle.

At least until she remembered that horrible key in her bag and pulled it out.

Bump looked from one of them to the other. "What we fuckin got here, you playin a fuckin show-an-tell? I ought should go get me somethin for holding up, an join the fuck in?"

"No, this—"

"Naw, taken—"

They both stopped. When his eyes met hers, she saw amusement in them and let her own show through, too. She pressed her lips together and nodded for him to continue.

"Aye, well. Taken this off she. Weren't me taken it, but Clincher Tink got it when they get em all in that house on the last night. She ain't livin down here at all, dig. Northside."

He produced a driver's license in the name of Marietta Blake. The girl they'd seen the night before.

"Why come her fuckin down here dealin, got all them ghosted-up speed on she, then?"

Terrible shrugged. "Maybe we give her the ask, she come on around. Maybe Chess head on to her address, see what knowledge she get?"

She met his questioning glance and nodded. No one needed to say the obvious: A Northside family or whatever would be a lot more inclined to give her some solid information than they would if Terrible showed up at their door. Or, well, maybe not more inclined, but they wouldn't run to call the Squad.

At that particular moment, though, using her authority as a Church employee—misrepresenting her reason for asking questions—appealed to her about as much as de-fleshing her own body did. "Let's try talking to her first. Did they find a walnut on her?"

"Naw, not what they gave me anyroad." He glanced at the ornate clock on the wall next to yet another pornographic photo. "Oughta get us over now, aye?"

"Right." It was close to three o'clock. An hour, hour and a half tops for that, then maybe she'd call Lex. Maybe. If she could keep herself from screaming at him when she did.

Both men were looking at the key in her hand. She'd dropped it into an inert plastic bag and sealed up the top; that helped, but she still felt as if her skin was rippling as she held it out to them. "Edsel gave it to me. He said"—she checked her notes—"Sharp-eye Ben brought it to him. You know him?"

Terrible nodded. "Got some heavy owes, Ben do. He gave Edsel the tell where he finding it?"

"No."

"Thinkin it got aught to do with all this shit?"

She nodded. "It feels like the walnut."

He shook his head. "Fuck. Guessin we off to see Ben too, aye? An got he a place up Seventieth and Baxter."

"By the docks," she said, and found no satisfaction of being right in his grim nod.

* * *

Chess was starting to feel edgy. That might have been comedown, but she didn't think so. She should have another few hours on that speed.

She popped another Cept to be sure. She popped it because she had things she had to say, and none of them were going to be pleasant. She popped it because there was something she couldn't say, not ever.

"So, I met with Elder Griffin this morning," she started. Where the hell did she go from there? How could she tell him— Well, the part about him was good, right? Was more cheerful. Would make him feel better, anyway.

"Aye?" He glanced at her. Several times.

She dawdled with her water bottle, dawdled lighting herself a smoke, dawdled until she couldn't dawdle anymore. "He thinks he knows—he's pretty sure he knows—a sigil that's going to keep you from passing out."

She should tell him what was really happening, that his soul was leaving his body every time. She couldn't. Was that a lie or an omission? Were omissions lies?

Did it matter? Neither of them was Truth, the entire Truth, and that meant both were wrong.

But what good would it do him to know? Just as Blue never, ever needed to know whose gun had killed her father. That it had been Blue's was Fact and Truth. That it would be torture for her to know, that it would destroy her, was also Truth. That Chess had to carry that burden for her . . . Truth again.

And the Truth about what happened when Terrible touched dark magic?

If all went as planned, it would stop happening. And there was no reason why it wouldn't, because Elder Griffin had designed the sigil and she hadn't. Without her to fuck it up, it had to work, right?

Tension zinged through the car. "What?"

"Elder Griffin, he thinks he has—"

"How's he knowin on it? Thought you ain't s'posed to do what— How's he know?"

Another Truth she didn't want to share, but she didn't have a choice about this one. He'd never believe she'd confessed to Elder Griffin because she was just in the fucking mood to or something. "He . . . Last night at the wedding, when you shook his hand. Um, he felt my magic on you. He felt that I'd done something, some soul-binding magic, and . . . he made me tell him what it was. I didn't have a choice, really."

"Fuck. What he done to you, he doin aught? You needing to get out, what's—"

"No. No, he's not going to turn me in. He helped me find a sigil that might help, well, we found some sigils that might help and designed a new one from those." It was getting harder to talk; her throat wanted to close up, as if she'd swallowed a large cold steel ball and it was lodged under her jaw.

"So he all good then? Ain't turning you in, he cool on it?"

There it was. "No."

Silence. She could feel him glancing at her, waiting for her to continue. She couldn't. She wanted to; she wanted to tell him the way she wanted to throw up when she'd taken too much, when she was hung over or whatever. But that same sick knowledge that the process itself would be painful and disgusting, the knowledge that whatever relief may come from the purge would be short-lived and that next time the junk coming up would be from further down in the depths, made her want to hold off as long as possible.

"He's not turning me in, but he's . . . he's disappointed in me, and what I did was selfish and a serious crime and he thought I was better than that. He, um . . . I betrayed the Church and he never thought I would do something like that."

Silence. Long silence, while they passed tumbledown buildings decorated with graffiti and people sitting on front steps. She broke it once or twice, pulling air through her sinuses, drinking her water.

"Sorry," he said. "Shit. Knew I ain't shoulda gone along. Never woulda happened iffen I ain't been there. Never would—"

"No." Damn, she hadn't even thought he'd think that, but of course he did. "No. I wanted you to go, and I'm glad you did, and no matter what happened I'm still glad you went."

"Aye, but—"

"No. I wanted you to go. I'm glad you went."

He nodded, staring at the street in front of them. "An . . . you right? Meaning . . . know you an he was—know you liked he an all."

The lump threatened to rise again; she swallowed it hard, sniffled even harder. "I'm okay, it just . . . yeah, it kind of sucks. But I'm fine, really. It's no big deal."

He reached over and touched her hair, a faint caress, like a light breeze blowing through it. It made her entire body tingle. Worth it. It was worth it. She'd never realized how important Elder Griffin was to her, no, and now he knew the truth about her and that hurt so bad. But it was worth it.

"You wanting— Us can wait an talk on the later, aye? Don't worry me, neitherways."

"No, no, it's fine. He came up with some things, and we designed a sigil that we're pretty sure will work. He figured we'd be drawing the sigil on—well, I don't know, maybe he knows exactly what we'd do—but we can go down to Flip's and get it inked."

He pulled out a cigarette of his own and lit it up. "Cool. Meanin get down there anyways."

They'd hit Baxter, far enough north that none of the buildings had intact windows and the rotten-fish-and-chemical scent of the bay drifted on the air. Not too close; they were still four or five blocks east, and a dozen or so blocks south. But close enough.

"So this guy we're going to see—Ben. He lives up here? I didn't think anybody lived up here."

"Aye, some do. Mostly them work the docks. Some of em thinkin it safer, less people around. Ain't, though."

He slowed down when they hit Sixty-fifth. "Ben black dude, aye? Bald, got he a mustache an beard. Always wearin one a them trench coats. Might be onna street."

"And if he's not? Do you know where he lives?"

"Aye. Been there." Color washed over his neck.

Right. He'd said Ben had some heavy debts, so of course he'd been there.

And it looked like he was going there again. He made a U-turn at Seventy-fourth and parked in front of a skeletal building on Seventieth. Steel beams showed through gaps in the walls, especially at the corners; the whole thing looked as though it would collapse if someone slammed a door too hard.

She waited for Terrible to turn off the car and open his door, but he didn't. He sat there with his hand on the keys, his brow furrowed. Once he opened his mouth and closed it again, glancing at her.

"Are you okay? What's wrong?"

He rubbed his forehead and the back of his neck, shooting her quick sidelong glances. What the hell? What were they going to see inside this building that he felt so . . . embarrassed about? That was how he looked, embarrassed—nervous—and the faint color already on his skin deepened as he blew out smoke, staring straight ahead. "Been—been wanting to have a chatter on somethin."

"Okay, what—"

"That . . . Keith, at the wedding. You recall him givin me the ask on me an you, on—"

Oh. Shit. The temperature in the car suddenly seemed a few degrees colder. Did he really have to . . . She wasn't going to try to hold him to it, didn't think it was necessary, and the whole discussion was fraught with problems. "Hey, it's okay. I mean, I know he put you on the spot. Don't worry about it. I'm sorry he did that to you, what a thing to—"

"Naw." He shook his head. "That weren't— Been thinkin on it since before then, too. An had the thought, maybe you oughta give up you place, dig?"

"What? But if I move back on Church grounds I can't—"

He sneaked another glance at her, fast, then returned to staring at the empty street before them. "Naw, ain't my meaning. Meaning to say . . . come live at mine, dig. With me."

She had no idea what to say.

He didn't give her a chance to come up with something, either. After barely a pause he continued, "Always there anyroad, aye? We ain't slept at yours in weeks. Seem like a waste, you keep payin rent an all. . . . Already got you stuff at mine. An mine's safer, dig. Ain't as many people got the knowledge where it is."

As many people, or one particular person? She knew he really hadn't liked coming to hers and finding Lex there, having Lex show up after they'd come back from the docks.

Not that she thought that was the main reason. At least she was trying not to think it. She was trusting him, for real, and trusting him for real meant not looking for ulterior motives or doubting his intentions. But she knew it was there, no matter how small.

The rest of his reasoning, though . . . Shit, what should she say? Panic—a deep gulping panic she hated feeling—wrapped around her chest and made it hard for her to take a drag off her smoke. Living together . . . that was something serious people did. Something people who knew how to make real commitments did. Something people who weren't confused as hell about who they were, or scared as hell about who they were becoming—happy people—did.

And even without that . . . Her brain seized an answer, the only one she could truly give. "I can't."

His face reddened further. "Oh aye, knew it were—no worryin, just—"

"No, it's not that, it's not because— I'm not allowed to. The Church won't let me. Well, they won't let any of us. Employees, I mean. Without being married we're not allowed to live with someone like that."

Silence.

"Especially me, because of where I live. I have to submit proof that I actually live there, remember? A few months ago, when I had to get those bills together for their records? And they can inspect me anytime, to make sure I'm following the law. It's not— That's all, I just honestly can't."

Did he believe her? She hoped so, because it was Truth.

She hated that part of her was relieved about that. Only a tiny part, sure. But part, nonetheless. A part she hoped to fuck he wasn't aware of, because if he was he'd think it meant she wasn't sure about him, that she didn't love him. Which was so far from Truth it wasn't even funny; she loved him so much she could hardly breathe, as if there was some sort of Terrible-shaped growth in her chest that squeezed out everything else, reached up into her brain and twisted it so she could think only about him.

Maybe thinking of him as some sort of parasite wasn't the best or most romantic analogy in the world, no. But she couldn't help that. It was how it felt, how she felt.

And most of the time it was awesome, the most incredible feeling in the world.

It only terrified her once in a while, because how was she supposed to handle that sort of feeling? Happiness always came with a price tag, and she couldn't read the one attached to him; some privacy, yes, some freedom, yes, but . . . there was something else, a responsibility it meant she had to him, an obligation. A change from the person she'd always been and the way she'd always lived, and reaching for something she didn't know if she could hold on to.

"Gotta be married," he echoed, still staring out the windshield.

"Right. And that's— I'm happy the way things are, honest. Don't worry about that, okay? We can still stay at yours most of the time, I just need to keep the address. I need to go over there often enough and keep enough stuff there so they can't tell, that's all. Don't—don't feel like you have to do this. I'm fine."

When he didn't respond she reached out and set her hand on his thigh. She squeezed it. "Hey. I love you, okay? I really, really do. You know that, right?"

A nod. "Aye."

Relief loosened the tense knot that had formed in her chest. "Good. Because I do. So let's not worry about it. As . . . as long as I get to be with you, I don't care where, you know?"

Shit, that was too much, wasn't it? She still couldn't get the hang of the whole I-love-you thing, the romantic stuff. It always felt like she either sounded as though she was having a little joke or writing a greeting card, like there was a fine line in between that was just right but she couldn't quite balance on it. At least not very often.

But he nodded again and let his hand fall on hers. "Aye. Aye, me too."

Too bad they weren't somewhere private, where she

could kiss him. She settled for wrapping her fingers tight around his. "I wish it was different, though."

"No worryin on it." He pulled his hand away and turned off the engine, ending the conversation in that one swift movement. "C'mon, let's get this done."

He took her arm when he opened the door for her, leaned down to look her in the eyes. "Let me talk, aye?"

She nodded. It felt good to agree to something he wanted; even if it hadn't she would have nodded, because he was right, but still.

The stairs to the porch creaked when they stepped on them. The front door appeared to be fastened by nothing but wires and stubbornness. Terrible pushed that open slowly, one hand on the knife tucked behind his back, peering around in the relative gloom.

Relative because a hole in the ceiling allowed sunlight to bleach a patch about two feet by two feet on the dark-wood floor. Enough light flowed in and reflected from it to allow her to see a staircase in front of them, a couple more doors along the hall past it.

Those stairs, too, protested as they climbed them. Terrible didn't seem to be making any effort to be quiet, which reassured her. Of course, he was almost silent when he walked—force of habit, she always imagined—but when he didn't try, he didn't try.

Sharp-eye Ben's door was the third on the right along the narrow upstairs hallway. The house itself had never been one of the grander ones; most of those were farther south. But it appeared to predate those, too. Chess guessed it had been built in the nineteenth century, maybe even earlier. It was a piece of history, fading and disintegrating like a memory no one cared enough to keep alive.

Ben didn't answer Terrible's first knock, or his second, louder one. "Ben! Got some asks for you, open up!"

"He ain't comin out two days past," a sharp high voice

piped up. Chess and Terrible both turned to see that the door catty-corner to Ben's had opened. In the doorway stood a woman with blue braids erupting from her head in an odd patchy pattern, as if she'd grabbed clumps of hair and braided them, then tied them off with scraps of red T-shirt.

A hole-filled jersey dress about five sizes too big covered her from neck to mid-calf. Well, covered most of her; one of her breasts poked out of a hole. She didn't seem to notice it or care.

She shuffled her dirty bare feet. "Seened him two days past, I did, an he actin all secret-scared, you see what I say? An ain't hardly said a speak, neither. Ain't like himself, causen he a chattery talker, had the guessing causen he speedy always, see. But he coming on home two days past, an ain't even said not a speak to me, hardly, just closing himself in there an ain't coming out."

She paused. Terrible opened his mouth, but the woman started another torrent of words before he could make a sound. "I knows he ain't had a come-out, see, causen I'd a hear on it. He door broke. It making noise like a cat getting skin ripped off it, anywhen gets opened."

Ben must have come there directly from selling the key to Edsel, and he'd probably scored then, too. Which meant it was very likely that he was locked in there with his eyes about to fly out of his skull, convinced ghosts or murderers or, hell, human-sized insects or something were banging on his door. Speed-bangers on a run didn't tend to be tight with reality.

"Somebody's coming visit himself, though, on that same day, sunset time, right about. Hearing voices in the hall, see, so's I had myself a peeping through the hole the door's got, an saw who them was."

This time neither Terrible nor Chess tried to speak. Chess wondered how much this woman would tell them if they let her keep going. Wondered, too, how it was that none of her neighbors had beaten her up or killed her yet. Most people in Downside didn't appreciate having their private business blabbed.

"Were himself ladygirl, an guessin be some friends she got. She an them went on in there, see, an I hearing themselfs coming out on a fifteen minutes later, thinking it were. All they left, then, heading out to them car onna street, see, but ain't seed Sharp-eye coming out never since, an that were on two days past long now."

"Ladygirl?" Terrible glanced at Chess. "Gotta name for she?"

The woman grinned, showing gaps in her crooked teeth. "Only callin her Ree, on sometimes, an hearing him say lovey-like names, see, them lovey-like names like sweetness an all."

Ree. Rianna? Ria? Luria? Maria?

Marietta.

Terrible must have had the same thought. He pulled the pink wallet from his pocket again, slipped Marietta's driver's license out of it, and crossed the hall. "This she?"

"Aye! Were she, that one. Knowing that, seed her many times, she the lovey one two-three months going on now. Ain't knowing where themselfs had the meeting-up, see, only one day she were around the place alla time, making the noises. Only themselfs be having the fightings onna last weeks or so, screamin yells. Ain't got the knowledge on what they fightings on, but Yellow Pete stopping coming."

Yellow Pete again. So Yellow Pete had been friends with Sharp-eye Ben, too? As well as with Gordon Samms. His murderer.

Or, the man who'd been magically forced to become his murderer.

Chess fought the urge to grab the woman and take her home. What else did she know? What else could she see? Maybe if she lived near Chess, she could figure out what the hell was wrong with Chess's life, explain it all.

Ha, like Chess needed that. She knew exactly what was wrong with her life: her. And everything she touched turned to shit, and everyone she touched ended up bleeding, at least on the inside. Some of the cheer the woman's babbling had created left her.

"Yellow Pete be a friend to Ben? Or to she?"

"Aye, oh aye. To Sharp-eye, Pete was. Here on a lot, see, an when Ree coming along themselfs having three togethers. Only on the weeks past Pete ain't having himself coming over no more, causen all they three having some big screaming fight on one day."

"Fight on what?"

"Dunno. Only hear a speak or two, see. Sounding like they argue on who they gots loyalty to, who's makin deal better. Ain't had the hearing all, though, causen my man were wanting himself fed an bedded up, see."

Terrible handed the woman a twenty. "Got any else for us?"

"Got plenny." The gap-toothed grin showed again; one of the few remaining teeth hung at an angle, as if it was trying to escape. She reached up to scratch her exposed breast. Obviously she knew it wasn't covered, then. Chess had no idea what to think of that. "Ree looking all clean-like, she not being from here, see, not around here. Ain't never could have the figuring why she wanting Ben, he all skinny-like an big ears, only she do, guessing, causen she here alla time an they making the noises."

That one Chess could figure out on her own, and when Terrible glanced over at her, she saw he could, too. Marietta was a Northside girl wanting to live on the edge, and she'd found herself a boyfriend who was already there to give her what she wanted.

Talking to her family—assuming she had one—might not be such a bad idea.

Or it might be completely irrelevant, of course. What was relevant was that they talk to Ben immediately. Maybe he'd crashed?

Terrible nodded at the woman. "Be a help, aye? Thanks on it."

"You coming back anytime, I helping more. You telling Bump? Telling himself I were helping?"

Terrible nodded, then crossed back to Chess and tried the doorknob. Locked. "What you thinkin I oughta do? Break it open?"

"Let me try first." The lock looked pickable, at least, and if it was pickable she'd be able to pick it. If it was chained Terrible would need to kick it in, but best not to do that unless they had to. She could picture Ben hiding inside, paranoid, with sweat dripping off his body. The last thing they wanted to do was burst in and give him a heart attack.

It took her a minute or so to pick the lock. No chain. Blue-braids over there—still watching them—hadn't lied. The door did sound like a cat being skinned when Terrible pushed it open, a hideous screeching sound that raked up Chess's spine.

The second the door parted from the jamb, power hit her, the deep slithering power of dark magic, of ghost magic. Of a particular kind of ghost magic.

Ben had scored, all right. But what he'd bought himself wasn't very good.

The apartment stank, a smell she tried to ignore even though she knew what it meant. They crept into it, the grimy floor trying to grab their shoes. To the right a kitchen, dirty take-out boxes and containers on the counters creating a buffet for the flies buzzing around. Ugh.

To the left the living room. Someone had made an effort to tidy up in there. A warped slab of wood sat on two stacks of old water-bloated magazines to form a makeshift coffee table, on which three loaded syringes were lined up with military precision. Beside them a rubber catheter coiled neatly, and beside that a notebook with its cover closed and an empty ashtray.

Behind the table, against the wall, was the sofa, a hulking shape under a dirty sheet. Someone had put a vase of now-dead flowers on the windowsill, taped a picture of Triumph City at night to one bare-plaster wall. An ancient TV sat on cinder blocks in the corner.

But the feel of it, the feel of that magic, the skin-itching feel of ghosts, refused to let her fully process the room itself.

She followed Terrible down the short hallway, past a bathroom she didn't even want to consider looking into. At the end of it, on the left-hand side, stood a door, and beyond that Ben's bedroom waited for them.

Ben waited for them, too, torn into pieces and strewn around, scattered on the blood-soaked bed, surrounded by flies.

Chapter Fifteen

Living in Truth does not mean living in innocence. The man who does not take precautions to safeguard his family and possessions is not holy. He is a fool.
　　　　　—From a speech by Grand Elder Wickens, Jan. 2010

"Just ramblings, it looks like," she said, flipping through the pages of the notebook they'd taken from Ben's. Her throat still ached from being sick; her stomach still threatened to twist again every time she failed to keep the memory of Ben's body from flashing back into her mind. "Shopping lists, shit like that."

Terrible swung the Chevelle up onto the curb and came to a stop, leaving the engine running so its throaty rumble echoed off the houses around them. "Now he gone, Pete's gone, Samms's gone. An all of em friends."

"He must have known something. Him and Pete."

"An them fightin with the dame." He lit a smoke. They sat outside one of Bump's safe houses, the one where Marietta and the men she was with had been taken the night before.

It looked exactly like any other shell house in Downside, covered with peeling paint and filth, its gutters stuffed with years' worth of rotting leaves against the cracked and missing shingles on the roof. Anyone on a casual pass-by would have no idea what it was.

Only someone with experience would see the signs. The shadows of the upstairs windows almost hid the bars across them on the inside. The downstairs windows were blocked by old furniture and junk. The door was intact, and closed; not unusual, no, but another clue. Chess knew there would be plenty more inside.

"And she was dealing," she said.

"Guessin a bunch of em is. Gave it to Rickride, maybe Levi, too, an now the dame. An whoever sellin on Lex's side, iffen he gave us the truth. Got us seven, eight street men dead, all over."

"When Edsel gave me that key, he said it's up by the slaughterhouse, too. Galena's brother said there's been a lot of people acting crazy around there." But no murders that she knew of; did that mean something? "Oh, maybe Bump could kick some cash his way for that?"

"I'll take care of it." He looked around them, looked at the house. "Guessin we oughta get us in, aye? See if she still alive so we can give her some asks."

More signs of the house's true purpose inside, as Chess had expected. Especially the heavy steel door at the foot of the staircase. Bump never used the first floor; too difficult to keep the presence of his people hidden.

Terrible knocked on that steel door, a set pattern of knocks: three, then one, then two. No reply.

He glanced at her and tried again. Still no reply.

"Ain't right," he said. "Oughta be answerin."

Uh-oh. Chess shifted on her feet. Marietta had been up there, along with the men and probably more of that speed. Her guardians—guardians, jailers, watchers, whatever—hadn't tried any of it, had they? And gone crazy?

Terrible shook his head when she asked. "Naw, them ain't so stupid. Know them ain't s'posed to tank while them workin, 'specially not that shit."

Sunlight poured through the empty windows. In its glow, the empty house with its bare patchy walls and dusty floorboards looked almost cheerful. Now a shadow passed overhead; it passed over Chess's heart, too, making it cold. "Do you think . . . something happened to them?"

He reached for the doorknob. It turned in his hand. "Fuck."

Chess didn't need him to tell her to pull out her knife and flick the blade out. Nor did she need him to tell her to stay close as she followed him up the stairs, silent step by silent step. No chances of a creak giving them away; the stairs, like the floors upstairs, had been reinforced with steel when Bump decided to use the place.

She didn't like the smell in the air. Not one bit.

Terrible glanced back at her just before his head cleared the upper floor, a questioning look she understood very well. Not a sound came from the floor above. Not the faintest indication of movement, of any kind of life up there.

Terrible's eyes told her he felt it too, knew it too. The sensation of . . . emptiness. Stillness, the heavy unnatural stillness of a room empty not because there were no bodies in it but because life had left those bodies.

Two of them. Bump's men, propped up against the wall like passed-out drunks, their heads leaning toward each other and their legs straight out in front of them. They'd been dragged there; trails of blood from their feet to deeper pools indicated the spots where they'd died.

Where they'd died messily. Red exploded at her, assaulting her eyes at the same time the smell hit her nose. It wasn't that there was so much of it, it was that what there was had gone everywhere. It sprayed across the walls in horrible arcs; it spattered the ceiling like a rash.

Terrible took her arm and shifted her so her back was against one of the non-bloody spots on the wall. "Stay here."

Fuck that. There was nobody in the place; they both

knew it. She followed him while he checked the small bathroom, the two other rooms used for storage or whatever else—Chess didn't think she wanted to know too much about what went on in there, really.

But only emptiness greeted them. Emptiness and that silence growing louder and louder every second, until it beat against her eardrums. She spun around, certain someone stood right behind her, but no one was there.

When they returned to the main room—the death room—Terrible bent down and placed his fingers on the forehead of one of the dead men. "Ain't warm. Been dead awhile."

"When was the last time you talked to them?"

"I ain't since last night, afore we got sleepin. Dipper Bob say he checked with em on the morn an they right up then, bout ten maybe? So seven hours, leastaways."

Seven hours. She'd been in the shower, getting ready to head to Elder Griffin's place. She'd been drying her hair, putting on some makeup, getting ready for her day, and these men had been dying. Not just dying; being killed.

"Hey, wait. They were shot."

"Aye, just—aw, damn, aye. Weren't torn up, like them under that spell do. Some else done this, aye? Some not under the spell. Came an took them who'd been doin the speed."

They stood there for a few seconds, letting the implications sink in. How had the killers found Marietta and the men? They wouldn't have had their—

"Their phones. Where were their cells? Did they have them?"

"Ought not to. Shoulda been taken first thing, put inna— Hold on."

Chess headed for the windows while Terrible ducked back into one of the empty rooms they'd inspected. Outside, the street looked completely still, completely empty, but she knew people lurked inside the other houses. People squatted in those buildings, slept under those leaky roofs, set fires in them when the weather was cold.

Had any of them seen anything?

"Chess. C'mere."

She'd taken about three steps toward the open doorway when she felt it: the shiver of magic—of dark magic, a very familiar dark magic—over her skin. What—how had that happened, how had it— Oh.

Terrible stood beside an open safe set into the floorboards. Every step closer to it brought an increase in the energy; it didn't surprise her one bit to see a walnut sitting by itself on the rough steel bottom of the safe.

"Bump's men took it off one of them?"

"Guessin so." He glanced at the doorway. "Ain't can ask em, aye?"

Well, actually, she probably could, if she wanted to. Trouble was, she didn't. Making the long cold trip down to the City of Eternity—most people stayed aboveground and went through a Church Liaiser, but she was a witch herself so she'd get to go it alone, yay—stripping down, letting a spirit use her body . . . no fucking way. Enough people had already done that in her life.

She'd go down to the City if she had no other options. She didn't think they were quite there yet. "It had to be one of the men. I would have felt it on Marietta."

He nodded. "Figured so."

Damn. If she'd searched the men—well, really, what difference would it have made?

It might have meant more guards assigned. It might have meant the two out there would still be alive.

Or more likely it would have meant more guards died. Not a damn thing she could do about it now, either way. Fuck.

"Got them phones here." Terrible held up two of them,

a sparkly pink one that had obviously been Marietta's—well, probably had been, anyway; for all she knew, one of the men had liked sparkly pink phones—and a black one. He tossed her the pink one and started pressing buttons on the other. "Fuck. Dead battery. Any luck you got there?"

Marietta's phone still had juice, yeah, but that didn't do any good. It required a pass code, and Chess had no idea how to figure that one out. "It's locked."

"Give it me. Take it over one a Bump's brainmen, aye? He get it cracked."

She handed it over.

He made his way around the room, inspecting the walls. "Ain't can see how them mighta touched up whoever came to get em, dig. No phones an all. How they get found? Got any thoughts?"

"Only . . . only that maybe somebody told them where Marietta and the guys would be. Maybe somebody knows where this place is, knew they'd be coming here?"

He nodded, the frown on his face sending a chill up her spine. "Aye. What thought I had, too. Got us a traitor."

"Working for—"

"Works for whoever pushin that bad shit around, aye? Tryin build theyselves an army, I'm thinkin. Start them a war here."

It was after six by the time they sat down at Dunk's Diner to eat. Or they sat down so Terrible could eat and Chess could pick at food; several more pills meant she didn't want anything else, but she knew he'd insist that she at least have something.

So she did, nibbling at fries and a burger while they talked, looking out the wide windows at the streets full of people. The setting sun cast long warm streaks of light across Downside, red and gold-orange across the sky.

"Ain't them Lamaru, aye?"

She blinked; it hadn't even occurred to her that it might be them again. Or, rather, another group like them; as far as she knew, they'd been essentially wiped out. Three months now and she hadn't heard a word about them re-forming. But they certainly hadn't been the only anti-Church group. "No. Doesn't feel like them at all. And it's not group magic."

He nodded. "Good. Ain't got that trouble, then."

She looked at him, moved her foot under the table to brush against his, then pulled it away. The touch reflected in his eyes, in that spark deep inside them that was just hers, just for her, and despite everything she started tingling.

Finally he averted his eyes, glancing around the diner to make sure no one had seen them. "So ain't them Lamaru. Only one mighty fucked-up dude, aye?"

"Right. After this we'll go back to my place and see how the energies combine—the walnut and the speed, I mean, since we didn't get to last night."

"On morrow you head over Marietta's place? See iffen you get some knowledge there we can use."

"You want to come with me?"

He shrugged. "If you're wanting. Ain't sure havin me there's the best idea, dig, I ain't look too much like Church."

She glanced around the diner. No one appeared to be paying them any attention. "I think you look perfect."

He cocked an eyebrow at her; his mouth opened, then closed again when his phone beeped. "Fuck."

He scowled at the screen and stood up, already moving.

"What? What's wrong?"

Whatever it was, it was serious enough for Terrible to run out of the diner.

Chess went after him. She worried for a second that someone would grab her and make her pay the bill before she got out the door, but no one did. That made sense, really; what were the owners going to do, go after Terrible for the money?

He disappeared around the corner; she followed, down the block and across the street, her lungs aching, to where a small raggedy crowd of people stood on the corner. Shit, not another one, please not—

It was over by the time she got close enough to see. A man was down, out cold with cash and drug packets spilling from the front pocket of his hoodie. The onlookers stepped out of her way as Terrible crouched beside him, grabbed the cash, and shoved it into his pocket. What was— Oh. Oh, fuck.

Chess reached out to catch Terrible's arm before he picked up one of the packets, but he stopped himself before she touched him. Relief flooded her chest.

Short-lived relief, because the look in his eyes when they met hers would have scared her if she didn't know him as well as she did. "Ain't one of Bump's."

"Yeah, I guessed that."

He twisted his lips in what would have been a smile if he hadn't been so obviously furious and pushed a button on his phone, while Chess tried to absorb what had just happened. A dealer who wasn't one of Bump's, selling ectoplasm-cut speed on the corner in Bump's territory. They'd caught one of them, they'd actually fucking caught one of them. Whoever sent Terrible that text would certainly be eating well for the next couple of weeks.

But, shit, he'd been selling. He had cash on him, how much had he sold, and who— Right. She left Terrible there with the still-unmoving body of the dealer and chased after his last customer. "Hey. Hey, stop."

The woman turned around when Chess touched her shoulder. "Aye? The fuck you wanting?"

"That speed. Give it to me."

Cracked lips stretched into a disbelieving grin. "Fuck you."

"No, listen—you have to give it to me. You can't do it, it's poisoned."

They'd attracted a little crowd themselves. Shit. Because nothing was more fun than an audience.

"Fuck you, poisoned. Know who you is, Churchwitch. Why you ain't buy you fuckin own, you wanting some?"

Chess pointed back at Terrible, who was standing over the dealer with his arms folded across his chest. "Why would Terrible knock that guy out if he wasn't doing something wrong? Ask him, okay? He'll tell you. He'll get somebody to give you a new bag. Just let me have that one."

The woman hesitated. The golden sunset light managed to make even her wizened face look almost smooth and delicate, blurring the harsh lines and drooping eyebrows.

Chess held out her hand, palm up. "Come on. If you know who I am, you know I'm not lying about being able to get you more. Give it to me. Okay?"

The speed landed in her palm. Fuck, that magic, that dark nasty slither of it up her arm, over her skin.

Who the hell was that dealer, and who was he working for?

Chapter Sixteen

In Debunking—as in so many other things—one mistake can ruin everything.
—*Debunking: A Practical Guide*, by Elder Morgenstern

Terrible opened the back door of the storage space and nodded at Chess. "He's talkin now."

Damn. The dealer had lasted—she checked her watch again—almost half an hour. Not bad.

It was even more impressive when she saw him, almost unrecognizable under the angry glare of the single naked lightbulb hanging from the stained ceiling. Blood covered his face, drying in thick sticky lines from his pulped nose and mouth. One of his cheeks had a horrible caved-in sort of look, like a dented fender. Broken fingers crumpled uselessly at the end of his arms, tied to those of the chair. She was glad the pills she'd taken would kick in soon; viewing that without help was not pleasant.

Terrible wouldn't quite meet her gaze. She turned from him, giving him what privacy she could, and tried to see the whites of the dealer's swollen eyes. Sympathy crept unbidden into her heart; it wasn't just blood running down his face, but tears, too.

Sympathy until she remembered what he'd been selling, what it would do to people. Sympathy until she remembered Yellow Pete's arm flailing around in the hand of a body controlled by magic, Sharp-eye Ben torn up on his bed, Rickride strewn across his floor. Sympathy until she thought of living people trapped inside bodies compelled by another person, their souls crying out but unable to escape, their freedom stolen.

Flesh was a hell of a prison.

She walked closer to him, keeping her eyes as steady and cold as she could, and reached out to touch his hair—the only spot she could see that wasn't soaked in blood.

No magic. Even when she opened herself up a little more, she got nothing from him. "Who's doing the magic?"

He just looked at her.

At least, he just looked at her until Terrible's fist snapped his head back. Chess forced herself not to react, not to cringe as more blood flew from his mouth. If he saw weakness he'd take advantage of it. If he saw weakness he'd try to form some kind of bond with her, and she definitely didn't want that.

So instead of wincing, she set her jaw and repeated her question. "Who's doing the magic?"

His lips were so swollen—and she suspected he was missing a few teeth—that at first she thought he was speaking some sort of foreign language. It wasn't until the words sunk in that she realized what he'd said. "Don't know shit about magic."

Terrible hit him again.

"Ey! Said I don't know, I don't know. I ain't no witch, don't know any witch."

Chess and Terrible looked at each other. Terrible shrugged. The guy had been talking before she walked in, so . . . maybe that was the truth?

Or maybe he was more afraid of what a witch—the witch he apparently worked for—would do to him than what Terrible would do. Kind of hard to believe, really.

Witches who liked to play on the nasty side of magic could do a hell of a lot of damage, but Terrible could do as much if not more in the course of a day's work.

"Told you everythin, told you all I know, what else you wanna know? Tell you what you wanna know."

"Where are you from?" Chess asked, more out of curiosity than anything else. He wasn't from Downside, that was for sure. Not only did he not sound like it, he didn't look like it. Underneath the bruises and swelling and blood there was . . . something that didn't look like Downside. Didn't look like Triumph City.

"What the fuck you wanna— Okay, okay, don't hit me again! Come from Baltimore. Ain't from here, from there."

"Why?"

"Why you ask? You wanna go out on a date with me or—"

The chair rocked back when Terrible hit him again. For the space of a heartbeat, the chair leaned there on two legs before righting itself with a thud.

It took another few seconds for the guy to come around.

Chess tried again once his eyes cleared. "Why did you come here? Why are you in Triumph City, in Downside? Who are you working for?"

He tried to move his fingers but winced instead. "Southpaws—true 'til death."

"That's a gang or something?"

"You fuckin stup— Okay, hey, hey, sorry. Just can't believe some chick ain't heard of us. Everybody knows the Southpaws."

Terrible folded his arms over his chest, raised one eyebrow. "This ain't Baltimore, aye? Ain't give a fuck who down there. Care who's here, an you ain't s'posed to be."

He shrugged. "Free country."

"No, it isn't."

"I don't see no Church down here. No law says a man can't move house."

She imagined how much fun it would be to push up the sleeves of the long-sleeved shirt she wore under an old Crumbs T-shirt and show him that the Church was standing right in front of him. Probably not a good idea, no, but fun.

Terrible's slight smile showed her he was thinking the same thing. Now was probably not the time to do what that smile made her think of, either; maybe later. It would be nice to have something go right that day.

It would be even nicer if they could get some good information from this guy. What the fuck was his name, anyway?

"Tagger," he said when she asked. At least, that was what she thought he said. Close enough, anyway.

"Right. So what are you doing here, really? Why are you here?"

He moved a bit in his chair; Chess thought it was supposed to be a nonchalant shrug, but it looked more like a nervous twitch. "Searchin for some new play, is all."

"Did you bring the speed with you?"

"What?"

Another punch. No more obfuscation or game-playing, not anymore. This was the big question: where he'd got the speed, who he was working for. And he could play the "what?" game to delay as long as he liked—as long as he could stand it, anyway—but he wasn't leaving until they knew.

Terrible leaned forward, bracing himself with his hands on Tagger's wrists—his weight pressing them into the hard arms of the chair—so he loomed over Tagger, blocked his vision of everything else. "Can keep you livin a long time, dig? Still lots of places I ain't touched on you yet."

The little stare-down didn't last long. They never did with Terrible. Not the sort of thing she should be proud of, again, but . . . well, what was she supposed to do? Be upset that no one in the world would ever be able to touch her again as long as he was there? Feel bad because the man she was firmly convinced was the best, strongest one in the world loved her? Fuck that.

"He called up Janko. My man Janko, he's in charge. Called Janko, said got room up here, send some dudes. Said got a takeover plan."

"Who?"

Tagger hesitated, but started talking when Terrible pulled his fist back. "Ain't met the dude. Got the powder from a chick. Had me meet her up . . . up off Baxter, think it was? By the docks, there, right at em."

Marietta? "What was her name?"

"Ain't caught a name. Ain't asked. Guess she work for Raz— Fuck."

"Who?"

Tagger looked at her, looked at Terrible. Looked at Terrible's clenched fist for a long moment, then sighed. "Razor be the name I was told. He the one running it all, the one moving in. Come from someplace else, don't know where. Don't know him, only met him once."

"The boss, his name is Razor? That's what he calls himself?"

Tagger nodded. "'Swhat he said to call him."

"He alone? Got partners? Where he came from?"

They were finally getting somewhere now, and she only hoped they could get something stronger, something more, out of Tagger before one of Bump's men slipped an employee at the Crematorium an extra fifty to add his body to the pile, no questions asked.

Tagger screamed, cutting into her thoughts. Terrible had grabbed the fingers of his right hand and twisted them. Damn, what had the man said to bring that on?

Something insulting, whatever it was, because when the scream ended, the apologies began.

Terrible interrupted them. "Where you met him? Where he stay?"

"Don't know. Met him where I met the chick, up off Baxter like I said. An alley off it, by a building used to be a taxidermist. Walked down it, he was there."

"Who else you meet here? Any you pals come up from Baltimore too? You got any more? Better knowledge you give, better chance you stayin alive, dig?"

Tagger's eyes were as wide as they could get, which wasn't wide at all given how puffy they were. "Not a snitch, okay? But two Southies come up with me. Three of us. Razor, he said money here and he gonna take it. Said . . ." He looked down. The next words were a mumble, made even more unintelligible by his ruined mouth. "Said the two gangs runnin Downside at war, be a good time to get his feet in."

It was all Lex's fault. Lex and his stupid war, Lex and his big plans, turning Downside into a beacon for every criminal in five states. Lex and his fucking explosions and— Okay, technically the explosions had been Slobag, but Lex had been behind it and she knew it. Shit, he'd even gone hunting for some new muscle of his own, hired some asshole to kill Terrible, hadn't he? She couldn't imagine what the grapevine must be saying about that one.

It shouldn't have surprised her; they'd already figured out that some outside gang was trying to make Downside its new home. But it still did.

Worse than that, though, it scared her. Looking at the latest crop of torn-up bodies tossed around the shabby apartment building on Fifty-sixth in which they now stood scared her, with her entire body going cold and her mind adding to those new images a few old non-favorites she'd never wanted to see again. Terrible on the street, the hawk swooping down . . .

Lex's man wouldn't be the only one wanting Terrible out of the way, if a new gang was trying to muscle in.

Hell, some of them might even be looking for her.

They were obviously looking for somebody. Unless they just liked setting their human-attack-dog zombies loose to see what they would do, which was entirely possible. She didn't know which of those options sounded worse, but she sent a few more pills down her throat to muffle them. When had she taken the last ones? While she waited, and they'd been with Tagger for about forty-five minutes, and she'd had something to eat . . . Whatever. She hadn't taken that many. And she wouldn't take more, because losing count was never a good idea.

Zimmer—one of Bump's men, whose phone call was the reason they were there—shuffled his feet as he indicated the bodies; the scraggly dreads and spikes of his hair jiggled with the movement. "All of em lived here. Only them two's bought offen me, though."

"You come make a drop-off, aye?"

Zimmer nodded. "Always, once in the week this same night. Them bought steady."

"Speed?"

"Nay, them buyin keshes for most, some pills. Sizzle on sometimes, but mostly just the light shit. Never no straight powders."

Chess glanced around the room; she couldn't bear to do more than that. All that blood everywhere . . . like footprints marking a path on a map, showing who the killers had reached first, where they'd dragged the bodies, how they'd used the parts they tore off to kill the others.

It looked as if at least a dozen people had been in that building. "So . . ." Her voice cracked.

She cleared her throat and tried again. "So no one else in the building bought from you? They were all clean?"

"Aye, 'sfar's I got knowin, leastaways."

Fuck, that was bad. That was *bad*. "So, why, then? Why just kill them all?"

"Could be maybe them worrying on getting theyselfs identified an all, were the thought—"

"Naw," Terrible interrupted. He'd been wandering around the hallway—the entryway to the building, where they stood at the foot of the stairs—peering out the windows, ducking his head into the other apartments on that floor. "Weren't thinkin on theyselves. Weren't thinkin at all, dig? Some else wanted all dead here."

"Ain't had the feelin on any them knowin each t'other much, dig?" Zimmer darted his gaze back and forth between Chess and Terrible, as if he expected one of them to attack him or blame him. But then, Chess imagined that in his position she'd be pretty nervous, too; hell, she *was* pretty nervous. "Weren't like I seed em all chatterin much or any like that stuff, when I come. They ain't mentioned none of t'others to me, neither."

Terrible came back to her side. "So they come in, kill you men, aye? Then head through the rest of em."

Zimmer burst into tears. What the fuck?

For a minute they just stood there, staring at him. How the hell was— How close had he been to those customers of his? Sure, walking into that mansion of manslaughter couldn't have been fun—wasn't fun, she wasn't exactly enjoying herself—but Zimmer seemed barely to have the strength to stand. His skinny arms were wrapped so tight around himself that she wondered if he could cut off his own circulation, and tears and snot ran down his face to dribble off with every quavering shake of his body.

That, at least, she could do something about. She

reached into her bag and grabbed a couple of tissues, handed them to him as unobtrusively as possible.

"Sorry," he mumbled, swiping at his face with them; he used the whole handful, like he'd never been introduced to the concept of Kleenex before. Or had no idea how big his own face was.

Not really the time to be a bitch, she reminded herself. And she didn't feel like being bitchy, either, not in the face of what was obviously serious pain on Zimmer's behalf. He looked like he was ready to explode from it; she wondered if she should try to help him find a place to sit down.

"Ain't can believe it happening on agains," Zimmer said. Or sobbed, actually. "Two days past, my friends, they been torn—"

"*What?*"

Zimmer gave a little shriek and jumped back; Chess would have laughed if it hadn't been so pitiful and if the anger and confusion in Terrible's voice wasn't so understandable. If she didn't share that anger and frustration, rising harder in her chest with every second.

"My—my friends, some friends I got, kilt two days past an like this, had the thinking be my fault, all on me or—"

Terrible held up his hand, ending Zimmer's stammered sentence with the gesture like an orchestra conductor ending a performance. "Hold up, now, aye? You sayin you seen bodies like this—you got friends died like this, an you ain't said shit on it?"

Oh fuck. How many were there, how many more? They'd been so focused on street men—on dealers being killed, on dead customers—well, of course they had been, because it was business. Because it was a war over territory, everyone fighting for the same however-many square miles of earth and the same customer base.

Wasn't it?

She glanced at Terrible, but he wasn't looking at her. It didn't matter. He didn't need to; she knew what he was thinking, that he had the same questions running on a what-the-fuck loop in his brain.

Whether Zimmer knew exactly what they were thinking or not—she bet he didn't—he obviously knew something was wrong. "Thought—ain't none tell me I oughten say on it, them weren't workin for Bump an don't use, them worked down the slaughterhouse or on the garbage truck, maybe played them some cards onna Friday nights, an—"

This time Chess interrupted him. "Cards?"

"Aye, well, sometimes them do—them did, only ain't knowing why them dead now, an torn up, figured them got hit by dogs or some like it. . . ."

He seemed to realize how lame that sounded; his already pink face reddened further. "Only sayin, ain't seed no reason to give Bump the knowledge on it, were all, them families had it, an called them the body wagon and all, so . . . Guessin I shoulda said on it?"

All those houses. In her mind she pictured Downside from an aerial viewpoint, all those buildings: squats and barely-hanging-on-with-rent-paid apartments and duplexes and rooms-by-the-hour and doorways and, shit, all those buildings, and most of them had bodies inside them eking out whatever living could be eked.

All those Downsiders, all anonymous, maybe known by sight on their streets or blocks but not two over. All those faces she'd never seen and names she'd never heard. Why would she?

All those people in all those houses, and how many of them could die and have their deaths make not the slightest impact on the people around them? How many of them could even say their neighbors would notice? As she'd thought while they stood and listened to Sharp-eye's blue-haired neighbor with her exposed breast, most people didn't appreciate having neighbors who paid attention to their comings and goings. Most people wanted their private business to be just that, their own private business, and people trying to get involved could very well find themselves getting dead instead.

So how many people could at that moment be lying in pieces on floors in small dingy rooms, while the people next door resolutely kept their heads down and their gazes focused straight ahead?

Shit, until a few months before—well, nine months or so before—she could easily have been one of them, living her solitary life in her small apartment and never speaking to anyone unless she was scoring.

She needed air; the room had started to rock around her, sliding back and forth, and her face felt hot and sticky. "I'll be right back."

Not that it helped much. Night had fallen but it was so hot outside still; it was like stepping out of a sauna into—well, into another sauna. The heat made her feel weak and itchy, made her think of all those people crowded together on the baked, foot-searing concrete, all those people closing their blinds during the day or tacking blankets over their windows to keep out the blazing sun, vain attempts to make it a little cooler inside . . . all those people invisible to passersby. The insides of all those houses, silent rooms no one could see.

How many of them still felt the heat?

What the hell was going on?

She slipped a few more pills into her mouth while she stood there watching the street, hoping to calm herself down and settle her stomach. Was it her paranoid imagination or were there a lot fewer people out than usual?

Not that she would know, though. This wasn't her neighborhood. For all she knew, empty streets were the norm. But still.

Terrible walked onto the small crumbling stoop after a couple of minutes. "You right, Chess?"

"It's just so hot in there," she said, knowing he wouldn't believe that was why she'd gone outside but knowing he'd let it go, at least for now.

Which he did, thankfully. He lit a smoke, offered her one. She shook her head. "So, I was thinking. What Zimmer said. Maybe you should—"

"Aye, had the same thought. Find out iffen anybody seen people disappearin, noticed people not bein around." He shook his head. "Ain't even thought them might be goin after . . . people, dig? Just anybody them stumbles across. Ain't can figure on why, neither. Why kill them got nothing to do with Bump or me or any else?"

"Cutting off Bump's income?"

He considered it. "Naw. Not iffen them wanting move in, make themselves money here. Who buys off them, iffen nobody alive to do it? An them bein killed ain't customers, neither."

"Doesn't make any sense."

"Aye, well, guessin it do to them." He shifted his weight, folded his arms. "Oughta get us outta here, aye? Got more coming in a few, pick up the bodies. Maybe you wanna get home now, dig, you don't need to watch."

"What about Zimmer?"

"Tell him go on home, too, once them get here. He can wait out front 'til then."

"Think he'll be okay?"

"Aye, won't be long some comes on to meet him. No worryin on it. C'mon."

They didn't speak again until they were in the car, heading toward his place— No, probably toward Bump's place, she figured, to tell him what their new twisted theory was. Now, there was something to look forward to.

Terrible's hand touched her thigh, rested there warm and heavy. "You right, baby? What's troublin?"

"Something doesn't make sense," she said, trying to figure out how to word it. Shit, she was tired. What a long-ass day it had been. Maybe a few Nips would help; she grabbed a couple from her pillbox and downed them. "I mean, none of it makes sense. But this Razor guy, he wants to take over Downside? Aside from killing innocent people . . . why do it like that?"

"The magic, meaning?"

She nodded.

"Aye. Had the wonder on that myself. Guessin he figures he turn em all into slaves or whatany it is he doin, they turn on Bump, Bump's men. Fucked-up way of doin it, though."

"Right. Couldn't— I mean, I don't know, but wouldn't moving in and selling regular drugs work just as well, if he's importing people from other cities to work for him? Why not take over that way?"

Terrible parked in the small private lot behind his building. They sat in silence for a minute or two in the closed car before he spoke. "Maybe takin over the business here ain't all him wanting, aye? Got he some other plans for he slaves."

She didn't want to nod. Nodding would be agreeing, and agreeing would be opening her mind to all kinds of conjectures, the kind that woke her up in the middle of the night with cold sweat sticking her bangs to her forehead and her heart pounding. The kind that made her reach for her pillbox so fast she hardly knew what she was doing.

The kind that were almost as bad as her memories, because she didn't have to imagine the kind of shit that sick power-mad psychos did to the small and defenseless. She already knew.

But she did nod, because yeah, there was a very good

chance that their new friend Razor had more in mind
than just taking over Downside's criminal industries.

Triumph City was Church headquarters. The nation's
capital. Building a secret unkillable army in Downside,
only half an hour or so from the Church grounds, from
the City of Eternity . . . Holy shit. If that's what Razor
had in mind, they were all pretty fucked; if that's what
Razor had in mind, she needed to find proof of that immediately so she could take it to the Elders and—

Yeah. And hope they'd listen, because she'd lost her
advocate with the Elders, hadn't she? A week before,
she could have walked in with a bugnuts theory like that
and he would have listened to her, would have made the
others listen. Now . . .

They might still listen thanks to her track record, but
it would take a fuck of a lot longer and require a fuck
of a lot more proof, as well as requiring some seriously
imaginative explanations for how she'd found out about
it. Before, Elder Griffin wouldn't have asked, would
have assumed she'd come by the knowledge honorably.

She'd really made the fuckup that kept on fucking up,
hadn't she?

"Maybe got he a gang like that, too, aye? Thinkin
them all witches, not just him?"

"Maybe, yeah. Well, probably."

He smiled, that slow smile she loved. And even then,
when she was fighting to keep herself from crying, fighting to keep her mind from having a fucking picnic with
the creepy and awful possibilities implied by the phrase
"a gang of necromantic witches taking over Triumph
City," she still loved it.

"Ain't ever a bore, leastaways, aye?"

She smiled back, happy to smile at him, happy the
speed was starting to hit. "No, I guess not."

"Chess! Shit, fuck, Chessie—Chess!"

What? What the hell, why was he— What was going

on? Where was she? What was that— Terrible's face was only inches from hers, his eyes frantic and wide. Behind him she caught a glimpse of ceiling, a— What was in her nose, why was there something in her nose? She'd been in the car, where was— Fuck, what—

A wave of thick greasy nausea overtook her; without even being fully aware of it, without quite knowing what was happening, she rolled onto her side and threw up. Everywhere. On the tile floor, on her hands . . . Where the hell was she, what had happened?

She was in Terrible's bathroom, she realized after a second. And shit, she had no memory at all of how she'd gotten there.

Which meant whatever had happened was not good.

Chapter Seventeen

> The dead never stopped or hesitated. Their motive was only to kill, and all attempts to stop them failed.
> —*The Book of Truth*, Origins Article 167

"I'm sorry," she managed—"choked out" would be a better phrase—as he wiped off her hands and face for her. "I didn't mean to make a mess, I'm sorry, I didn't—"

"Ain't give a fuck on that." He grabbed more toilet paper and wiped around her nose, around whatever the hell was hanging out of it. She wanted to ask. Something in his reddened eyes, something in the growing sense of certainty creeping up her spine, told her not to. "Gonna be sick again? Wantin try getting into bed?"

"I don't—" Well, no, she did have an answer, which was that she was not done being sick. She managed to lean over the toilet, at least, while Terrible held her hair back. "I'm sorry."

"Aye, well." He stood up, handed her a wad of tissues, and grabbed the trash can. She watched his back as he left the room. Fuck. This was bad. It had happened, hadn't it? The thing she thought would never happen, the thing she was always so careful not to have happen. She'd lost count, she'd lost track of what exactly she'd taken, and it had happened.

She reached up to touch her clammy face, to feel the thing in her nose.

" 'San opiate inhibitor," Terrible said, returning to the room. His hands curled around her upper arms, urging her to her feet. "Leave it in, aye? C'mon, let's us try putting you in bed."

He scooped her into his arms—slowly, carefully—and carried her into the big main room, where he set her on the soft gray bed. Her stomach rumbled a warning but stayed put.

So did Terrible. Standing there, looking at her. In the faint light from the open bathroom door she couldn't read his expression, but she had a pretty good idea what it was. "I'm sorry, shit, Terrible, I'm so sorry, I just— I lost count, I guess, I wasn't paying attention and—"

"Aye, guessing so."

He unfastened her jeans and stripped them off her with impersonal efficiency, and fear blossomed in her stomach and chest. Fear that gurgled and rose and made her grab blindly for the trash can beside the bed so she could be sick again. Fuck, what a disgusting process. No wonder he didn't want to talk to her or look at her— well, on top of everything else, of what she'd just done to him. And to herself, yeah, but she couldn't have cared less about that.

When she was done he pulled the covers over her, took the trash can and walked away.

Shit, that was it. She'd fucked up, and he'd reached his limit; she'd known the line was somewhere, known that one day he'd realize he didn't want to babysit a junkie, and she'd gone and grabbed that brass ring her very own self and pushed him into it. She'd forced his hand. She'd forced the other shoe to drop.

His shadow moved in the kitchen for a few minutes and he came back again, holding a glass of something clear with a straw poking out of it. "Here. Try this, see iffen it helps yon stomach."

Sprite. It did help her stomach. Too bad it couldn't do

anything for the terror and misery pounding through her body, the shame so thick and strong she was half afraid she'd explode from it. How could she have fucked up like that? "Terrible, please . . . I'm sorry, I'm so sorry. . . . I love you, please don't be mad at me."

Pause. A long pause, and then he turned and started to walk away. Or she thought that's what he was doing; in fact, he walked around to the other side of the bed, stripped off his clothes, and climbed in next to her. Warmth radiated from him, from his chest so close to her back. It spread over her, through her, and she managed to relax. A little.

"Ain't mad at you," he said finally. "I ain't. Just . . . shit, Chessie, don't know what to say. Scared the shit outta me, aye? All the sudden you just fuckin fell, dig, straight onto me, out cold and weren't wakin up."

"I'm sorry."

He pulled her closer to him, so close she almost couldn't breathe, and his stubble made the skin of her cheek and throat itch. She wasn't about to complain. "Just . . . damn, baby, don't ever do that one again, aye? Not ever."

"I won't. I don't want to." And that was definitely true. She never wanted to do that again. She didn't even want to think about doing it again; hell, she didn't want to think about the fact that she'd done it. She'd lost control, and she . . . she was the one in control, she'd always been the one in control. She'd always been so careful. Yes, she let the pills control her—somewhat— but ultimately she was in charge of how many she took, how often, and she'd always been able to handle it.

Right?

She cleared her throat. "When can I take this thing out of my nose?"

"Morning. Still workin now, keeps you from bein sicker an all."

She nodded. An opiate inhibitor. "Why did you have it?"

"Never know, aye? Keep em in the car."

Had he always kept them in the car? Or had he started when they got together? No way in hell was she going to ask that one.

But she still wondered as she looked up at him in the semi-darkness. Had he planned for this? She knew he paid attention to her pills and how many she took; if she hadn't taken the ones that led to her little accident— fuck it, be honest and call it an overdose—outside where he couldn't see, would he have said something, would he have stopped her? Would he have suggested she not take the speed in the car if he'd known?

None of those were questions she could ask him. But she knew no matter what the answers were before, they were certainly in the affirmative now, and she knew that not only because she knew him but because when she opened her eyes—every time she opened her eyes—he was still awake.

Watching her. All night.

She waited for him to bring it up in the morning—well, technically the afternoon, because she couldn't seem to get her eyes open until then—but he didn't. Not unless she counted his typical wake-up greetings to be bringing it up, which she didn't. Nor had he said a word when she took two Cepts—hell, OD or not, this wasn't the time to deal with withdrawals—and did a little bump to get her still-a-bit-sluggish mind and body going. Nobody said she had to stop, she just had to remember not to drop the ball again. She had to remember to be careful, to pay attention, that was all.

He didn't try to convince her to stay in bed a little longer, though, either, which was generally code for staying in bed *naked* for a while longer. He didn't even hint at it. She tried not to be worried by that.

And it wasn't the time to worry about that, either, because they were in the Chevelle advancing up a long curved driveway that wound through some trees before it stopped in front of the Tudor-style mansion in Northside where Marietta Blake had lived. It was time to focus on other things. Like on how they probably wouldn't get any information at all, and this would end up being a totally wasted trip.

But they had to make it, because they'd officially reached the grasping-at-straws part of the investigation, hadn't they? They had a name: Razor. Who could be anyone from anywhere, and who could *be* anywhere. They had—she'd confirmed it only an hour or so ago when they stopped at her place—speed cut with ectoplasm and blood in walnuts that worked with the ectoplasm-cut speed to control the user.

And they had way too many dead people, and pretty good odds that more people would be joining them, and she really didn't want one of those people to be her. Or him.

Terrible opened the car door for her, and they made their way across the manicured stretch of green lawn, striped by late-afternoon shadows, to the front door. The sound of blue jays in the trees sent an uncomfortable twinge through her body; jays weren't the strongest of psychopomps, no, but they weren't lucky birds, and it was difficult for her to hear any birds without being made nervous by them. Especially in situations where she very well might be in danger, like this one. Exclusive wealthy neighborhood or not, Marietta was or had been up to her neck in whatever was going on, and nothing said her family was innocent.

Yeah, being with Terrible meant she was safe if people were all they were dealing with, but there sure as fuck wasn't a guarantee, was there? Not with some crazy sorcerer wanting to see them all dead.

The door opened on her third knock to reveal a tall lean man in an impeccable gray suit, with thick glasses covering half his face. "Can I help you?"

Chess flashed her Church ID, sleazy as it felt to do so. "I'm looking for Kyle or Lindsay Blake? It's about Marietta."

He dipped his head, low enough that she saw light reflected in his bald spot. "One moment, please."

He wandered off but left the door open, so . . . Chess and Terrible exchanged glances and entered, standing on the shiny dark-wood floor of what Chess thought the Blakes would call an entry hall. Pale high ceilings rose over their heads, with black beams crossing them; a wide staircase hugged the wall, leaving a bare expanse of gleaming floor to its side. Serious money, yes indeed. She hadn't bothered to investigate the Blakes—aside from anything else, she'd need an Elder to pull their financial files—but who knew, maybe it would end up being worth doing.

The man returned after a few minutes. "Follow me."

Something in his voice . . . bothered her. Or it sort of felt like it bothered her. The whole house sort of bothered her, though. For a second she wondered if maybe it was just too big, too ostentatious, but then she remembered Roger Pyle's place. She'd never had any serious problems with that, so no, that wasn't it.

The house felt so *cold*, though. There was something dark and watchful about it, something she didn't like. It made her uncomfortable.

Terrible didn't look any more relaxed than she felt as they entered some sort of living room off the hall. More ceiling beams, more dark wood. The place made Chess long to light up a smoke, do a few lines, and start making out with Terrible on the low leather sofa.

Of course, she pretty much always wanted to do that, but damn that house was stuffy.

She reached out to brush Terrible's arm, mouthed, "Are you okay?"

He gave her a shrug and a nod. But the way he glanced around the room, checking all the entrances and exits, made it clear he noticed what was bothering her, too.

The man bowed again. "They'll be with you in a moment."

He left, closing the door behind him. Chess didn't know whether she should be impressed or amused by the fact that he'd left a couple of strangers alone in a room full of expensive items—the candlesticks on the mantel had to be worth a few grand alone—but she had shown a Church ID. And not everyone mistrusted the Church.

And it didn't matter, anyway, because almost immediately the door opened again to admit a woman who had to be Marietta's mother. Her face darkened when she saw them. "My daughter isn't here. I don't want you people—"

Out came the Church ID again. "Mrs. Blake? I'm Cesaria Putnam, from the Church. We wanted to ask you some questions about Marietta."

Mrs. Blake looked her up and down suspiciously, and examined Terrible even more closely. She snatched Chess's ID from her hand to inspect it.

"You can call the Church to verify it." Not that Chess wanted Mrs. Blake to do that, but experience had taught her that making the offer usually meant the person wouldn't bother.

"My daughter isn't here," the woman said finally, and handed the ID back.

"That's fine. We just have a few questions."

Mrs. Blake sniffed, but she stepped back and motioned for them to sit.

"Is Marietta's father available?"

Mr. Blake entered at that point. He shook Chess's hand in that firm businessman way, as if he'd had tons of practice, and she focused on that touch as he did. Did he feel like magic, like he had any talent at all?

No. Not a drop, really. He looked vaguely familiar, but then he looked a bit like Marietta, so why wouldn't he?

He crossed the floor to sit in an overstuffed chair that creaked when he moved. He appeared to be part of a matched set with Mrs. Blake; oh-so-tasteful graying hair, casually expensive khaki trousers, and a tucked-in white shirt. Growing up in this house must have been tons of fun.

Of course, somehow Chess didn't get the feeling that either Blake parent had been fucking Marietta or beating the shit out of her, so she had an advantage over Chess, but whatever. It still struck her as a horrible, stultifying place to live, not so much because of the old-money ooze or the dull furnishings but because of the coldness that permeated the entire house and seemed to emanate from the walls.

"Kyle, dear, these people want to talk about Marietta."

Mr. Blake nodded. "Carmichael told me, of course. Marietta's not here. Don't know where she is."

"Yes, so Mrs. Blake said." Were they protesting a little too much? They didn't seem like protect-the-kid types, but they did seem very much the what-would-the-neighbors-say types. And they seemed very much like they'd have the money to send Marietta somewhere far away to hide out until things blew over.

Also, Chess hadn't yet said why she was there, other than "to talk about" Marietta. Which implied some sort of guilty knowledge on the Blakes' behalf, didn't it, even if it wasn't the kind that was really "guilty." So who knew where the conversation could go? "But I was wondering if you could tell me anything about her? Her associates. What happened. How . . . how things started."

Mrs. Blake gestured at the couch. "Sit down. Care for a drink?"

Chess and Terrible shook their heads and took seats on the cold squeaky leather. Mrs. Blake poured herself a hefty glassful of amber-colored liquid; Mr. Blake, Chess noticed, already had a smudgy glass half full of the same in front of him. Damn. Did these people just spend their days half drunk? She had to respect that—or at least understand it.

And, hey, maybe it would make them more inclined to slip up and say something worthwhile.

"Marietta was always . . . difficult. She wasn't a happy child." Mrs. Blake took a mammoth swallow of whatever it was in her glass—bourbon or scotch, Chess wasn't sure—and settled into the other armchair. "She didn't fit in with the other kids. When she was fourteen she disappeared. She was gone for three days before we found her in the community center. She'd been sleeping in the laundry bins."

Mr. Blake grunted.

"The last few years, ever since we bought her a car, she'd be gone for days. We never knew where she was. She took up with those people. . . . Miss Jessel would talk to her—"

"Miss Jessel?"

"Miss Jessel is—was—the nanny, but she stayed in touch after she left us when Marietta turned sixteen. She'd talk to Marietta, and Marietta would insist she was fine, and Miss Jessel would let it go. But I don't think she was fine. I never thought she was fine."

"Could I get in touch with Miss Jessel?" Not that she'd need to, but it fit the ruse to ask.

Mrs. Blake paused long enough to drain her glass. "I

suppose I could find Miss Jessel's number for you—she hasn't called in six months or so. Stopped right around the time Marietta got involved with that man, that Ben person."

Sharp-eye Ben? "That started six months ago? Do you know anything more about him?"

Mr. Blake cut in. "Only that he was scum."

"Kyle!" It wasn't shock in Mrs. Blake's voice; it was a warning, and Chess's face grew hot when she realized why: Mrs. Blake was warning him to watch what he said because of Terrible. Because of how Terrible looked. Bitch.

Mr. Blake didn't seem to have any of the same compunction, though. "He is scum. Living in that filthy ghetto, involved with those people, if you can even call them people. That whole Downside slum should be razed to the ground. It's an eyesore. It's disgusting."

This was her job, Chess reminded herself. Wasn't even actually her job; she'd misrepresented her reason for being there, which meant confronting Blake on his shitty views and shitty words and general shittiness was not a good idea. It was not something she could do.

Mrs. Blake stood up into the silence. "Would anyone care for another drink?"

"Well, that was basically a waste of time, huh?" Chess said as the Chevelle nosed back onto the street.

"Were guessin it would be though, aye?"

"Yeah, it just . . . I still hoped, you know? Like that we could walk in and the Blakes would give us a list of names and dates or something."

His eyebrow quirked in amusement. "That kinda shit ever happen for you?"

"Well, no, but I can still hope."

"Aye." His hand landed on her thigh and gave it a rub. "Aye, you do that, Chessiebomb."

She slid her hand over his. "So . . . what are we doing now?"

"Ain't know. Figured on you maybe bein tired, headin back yours let you rest. I gotta head over Bump's, dig, give him what's on."

Oh. The smile left her face. Kind of silly of her, really; of course he needed to talk to Bump, and it wasn't as if he'd think taking her with him would be some kind of treat for her. Yay, hanging out with Bump, her favorite thing.

But she'd hoped . . . well, she'd hoped he'd want to spend some time with her now that she wasn't sweaty and puking, with a chunk of plastic hanging out of her nose. Some *alone* time. So much was going on, so many things that frankly terrified her, and she wanted to forget them, even if it was only for a little while.

She gave his hand a squeeze. "You don't have to go to Bump's right away, though, right? You could come up to mine for a bit first."

"Aye." He squeezed back, sending shivers of excitement and happiness through her. "Needin make sure you get to sleep all right, aye? An nothin happen or whatany."

"I definitely think that's a good idea."

They rode on in comfortable silence, hands still clasped, until he slid the Chevelle up to the curb across the street from her building. The sun was setting, leaving that peculiar fuzzy dusk-light where nothing looked clear or real. But then, very little of the last few days felt real. Horrible magic and destroyed bodies and Lex and Elder Griffin turning his back on her—it all felt like some kind of bizarre Dream hallucination, and she wished it would end.

"C'mon." Terrible opened his door, came around to open hers, and she stepped out, glad for the break in her thoughts, glad to be focusing elsewhere.

Warm breeze, faintly scented of garbage and exhaust but still pleasant, shifted her hair and sent a few strands of it to tickle her cheeks. She tucked it behind her ear as they crossed the street, heading for the wide front steps of her building together. Not close enough to touch even accidentally, but close enough that they almost could. Close enough that she could peek at him sideways and watch the way he held his head, the way his shoulders moved when he walked.

The steps to the front doors started about halfway from the curb, with wide ledges along each side. Sometimes people sat on them, climbing the steps part of the way up so they could access the ledges, which were too high to reach at the street end. They were like thick walls along the edges, with scrub grass, gravel, and pale dry dirt forming a border around them.

A black-clad shape—a man—ran out from behind the one on the left and headed straight for them, a knife glinting in his upraised hand.

Chapter Eighteen

> There was nowhere to hide. There was no escape. The dead
> saw all, and no walls could keep them out.
> —*The Book of Truth,* Origins Article 155

Terrible's hand almost knocked the wind out of her,
shoving her back and behind him before she'd even
really registered what was happening. She stumbled and
almost fell to the rough concrete. Damn her heavy bag,
if she'd had a second to brace herself it wouldn't have
knocked her off balance like that.

But it had.

Something small flew through the air; Terrible batted
it away with his hand and went down.

Holy shit. The speed, it was a packet of that speed,
and Terrible's eyes were just opening again when his
attacker—Lex's assassin, Devil, it had to be him—pulled
his foot back and kicked Terrible in the ribs.

Chess was already moving, trying to get up and si-
multaneously trying to attack, trying to push the man or
hit him, trying to do something. She got a look at him,
one that chilled her even more; snub-nosed and heavy-
browed, almost as big as Terrible, with the flat dead eyes
of a man used to doing his job with brutal efficiency.

Flat dead eyes like Terrible's were when he was working.

Terrible jumped up before she could do much more

than launch herself forward, putting himself between her and Devil. His fist connected with Devil's face, but Devil used his knife as he stumbled back, slicing a thin line from Terrible's right elbow to his wrist.

Terrible hit him again, his left fist jabbing forward and up; Devil jerked to the side at the last second so the blow landed on his shoulder instead of his throat.

Another right from Terrible hit his nose. Blood started pouring from it; the man's grin beneath it was horrible, red hiding his lips and staining his teeth. He struck again with the blade, another cut on Terrible's arm. Devil didn't look like he was trying very hard to cut deep; it was as if he was happy to just paper-cut Terrible again and again. What the fuck was he doing?

Running away, that's what he was doing. Terrible hit the man again; as he stumbled sideways a dark-blue car, one of those anonymous modern semi-sedans, hopped the curb with its passenger door open. Chess caught a glimpse of the driver before Devil threw himself into the front seat and the car squealed away.

"What was—" she started, but no one heard. Terrible was tearing across the street with his keys in his hand.

Chess ran after him. "I'm going with you."

She could see the argument he wanted to make plain on his face. But she could also see his impatience, the knowledge that arguing would take more time than unlocking her door.

He barely waited for her to finish sitting down before gunning the Chevelle; they jumped off the curb in a fury of noise and exhaust.

Terrible routinely drove at speeds that made her nervous until she'd gotten used to them, but she'd never seen him really open up the Chevelle before. They tore up Forty-seventh after the blue car, closing the distance. Fast.

And obviously being seen. The blue car turned left,

swerved left again into an alley, jumped onto the on-ramp at Highway 300 with the Chevelle right on its ass. Chess braced herself. It didn't help, didn't make her heart stop pounding like a fucking jackhammer in her chest, but it at least gave her something else to focus on besides the idea that if the driver of that blue car decided to tap his brakes, they'd be picking her up off the high-way in garbage bags.

Together the two cars wove through traffic, from the right lane to the left and back again. The blue car took the interchange exit at Highway 101 and started to run the cloverleaf. Ugh. Driving in tight circles at crazy speeds: just what she needed when nerves were making her stomach twist up on itself in a way that made the few bites of food she'd taken earlier feel like balls of lead.

When they hit the stretch of highway between ramps, Terrible swerved around the sedan and started to nose in front of it. Tires screeched. Chess thought the sedan spun out; she didn't know for sure, though, because the Chevelle definitely did, and for a too-long, too-sickening moment, the world was a blur of light and noise. Then they started to move again, back up the entrance ramp. The wrong way.

She forced her eyes to stay open, forced herself not to cover them up. If he thought she was scared—if he knew she was scared—he'd want to slow down. He might even stop and make her get out. For whatever reason—love? Loyalty? Death wish? Maybe all of the above; probably all of the above—she didn't want to do that. She was in it, and she was staying in.

Horns blasted. Blinding headlights swerved out of their way. The blue car ran over the shoulder and back into traffic, with the Chevelle following.

Terrible started to pass the blue car to cut it off. Again the driver slammed his brakes and spun, then ran into a

parking garage beneath a lonely-looking building off—
Of course. Off Thirtieth, they were on Thirtieth. Lex's
hired killer, in Lex's territory. She hadn't even thought of
it; just the presence of the Chevelle in this area could be
trouble. At least it was getting dark out, more so by the
second. Maybe they wouldn't be so noticeable.

Terrible slowed as they passed into the shadows. The
Chevelle's headlights discovered a few abandoned cars
huddled between faded white lines on the cement, empty
husks of cars hiding from the world.

And, as they turned to pass the ramp to the next
level, as they drove around the elevator bank or office
or whatever it was blocking the center of the garage,
they saw another car. The blue car. Not shrinking back
against the crumbling cement wall, but planted right in
the center of the aisle, doors open. Engine still running.

Empty.

Outside the garage dead weeds reached in a wheat-
colored tangle for the sky, a tangle with streaks of green
as new growth wound its way in, naked in the headlights' glare. The weeds shook slightly. Maybe from the
wind, maybe from Lex's hired killer and the car's driver.
Shit.

Terrible's palm slammed into the steering wheel.
"Fuck!"

"He probably didn't get—"

The greenish dashboard light illuminated his glare.
"Ain't fuckin leavin you here."

His eyes narrowed further when she opened her
mouth again. Right. Suggesting she go with him wasn't
a good idea, either.

Okay, then. She lowered her gaze and saw what she'd
managed somehow to forget in all of the noise and terror of their little joyride. He'd been cut. His arms glistened dully with blood, brackish in the semi-light. She
reached out a tentative hand. "We should—"

He snatched his arm away, throwing the Chevelle into reverse and stabbing the gas without speaking. Yeah. She got the message.

For the second time, Lex's hired muscle had managed to ambush him. For the second time, Lex's hired muscle had managed to injure him. For the second time, Lex's hired muscle had gotten away.

And for the second time, Lex's hired muscle had managed to accomplish all of that because Terrible had been either distracted by her or unwilling to risk her getting injured. Mother*fuck*. Lex had found himself a weapon, all right.

Her.

No tandem showers after they got back to her place. No nothing after they got back to her place, in fact. He'd practically growled at her when she tried to bandage him up, and he headed for Bump's almost immediately.

Which left her with nothing to do. Nothing except drugs, anyway, which was a given.

Putting a thick wall of narcotic peace between herself and the events of the day helped, but not enough. There were still the previous days to deal with. She'd lost something important, something that mattered. She'd lost Elder Griffin's friendship and approval.

Now she was in danger of losing something even more important, and fury thrummed through her body as she set the alarm on her car and pounded on the side door— the hidden door—at Lex's house.

The guard who opened it for her started to step aside. She didn't wait for him to finish, shoving herself past him and storming up the stairs. Lex was probably in his room. As far as she knew, he hadn't moved into another one.

And if he had? She'd just fucking check them all.

His door was closed but not locked. Not that it mattered. She had her pick case, although she didn't think she needed it. Even with her pills making her insides fizz with fake cheer, she was pissed enough that she thought she could kick the damn thing off its hinges if she had to.

She threw it open instead, stalked halfway into the room before she realized Lex wasn't alone. He had a girl with him, next to him on the low blue couch.

Oh well. "Call him off, Lex."

"Hey there, Tulip, ain't this a sweet—"

"Call him *off*, Lex. Now."

Lex glanced at the girl—a curvy little blonde; Chess didn't pay any more attention than that—and jerked his chin. "Gimme a few, aye? Head you down on the other room, dig, watch you some TV."

The girl glanced at Chess, then back at Lex, before standing up. "Aye. Be there, I will."

Chess felt her long up-and-down gaze as she passed, and ignored it. Fuck her.

The door closed. Chess gave it a five count—not that it mattered, since the girl was probably standing right outside with her ear to the door frame—before she spoke again. "I mean it."

"Ain't know what you talking on there, Tulip."

"Don't fucking— Yes, you do. Now call him off."

Lex leaned back and lit a cigarette. With his feet up on the low coffee table, he looked like he was having a pleasant chat with a friend, perfectly relaxed. Maybe not just relaxed, either; a few feet away, a vodka bottle missing its cap sat next to a couple of shot glasses, one of which had a semicircle of burgundy lipstick on the edge. "Why'd I do that?"

Shit. She hadn't expected that. "What— Because, that's why. Because this is bullshit, and—"

"And? And what? Causen you asking me to? Damn, girl, had the knowledge you got some selfish shit in that head you got, but ain't—"

"Self— What?"

"*What* what?" His eyes narrowed. "What the fuck thinking you got there, I give up causen you run over here and gimme the asking to? Ain't some fuckin game, this ain't."

"You don't need him dead. You know you—"

"Aye? You gimme the tell, then, what it is I'm needing. Seems to me I recall makin the offer he come on working for me, I did, and he gave me the nay on that one. Knew what were on when he done it, too. Maybe oughta be givin the chatter to he now, aye?"

"Don't fucking pass—"

"Aw, fuck this." He stabbed out his smoke and stood up, crossed the few steps to stand in front of her. "Ain't having this chatter with you, I ain't. An ain't callin no shit off, neither. Told you an he both I got plans, I do."

She met his glare with one of her own. "Right. Such great fucking plans you need to use me to carry them out."

She had him with that one. She had him, and she knew she had him because he smiled a too-casual smile. "Aw, I dig it. You all on the angry side causen it you putting the danger on, Tulip. Ain't me. Be you. An ain't that a low-bone?"

So much for having him. "This is not me doing this."

"Oh? You sure on that one?" His smile changed, just enough so her heart gave a tiny jerk in her chest. She knew that smile. Knew the look in his eyes, too.

The urge to take a step back was almost overwhelming. She refused to do it. No. No fucking way would she let him see that he was affecting her, even the tiniest bit. She would stand her ground. "I didn't hire somebody to kill him."

"Oh nay, nay, you sure ain't done that one. But what was it you did? Aw, right, I gots the memory now, I do. You was spending you nights over on here with me, aye, an playin like you wasn't to he. Aye? That one were it, weren't it?"

Had he gotten closer to her? "That's not—"

"Thinkin it is, I am. Thinkin all them nights we had ourselves a damn good time over here—ain't we, Tulip?—you letting Terrible have himself the belief you all alone in you own little bed, aye?"

His eyes loomed over her, bigger than they should be. Yeah, he was definitely getting closer; she smelled the faint spiciness of his skin and the alcohol on his breath. People said you couldn't smell vodka. They were wrong.

Looking like a pussy sucked, but her only other option was to stand there and let him kiss her. Because that was definitely what he looked like he was getting ready to do, and knowing she wasn't exactly available for kissing didn't matter a damn bit to him. If anything it would make it more fun for him; it always had, hadn't it?

So she took a step backward, then another, subtle steps that she hoped seemed casual. Mistake. It only seemed to egg him on, and somehow she'd let him maneuver her so her back was almost to the wall.

"Guessing he thought something on between you and him—maybe even there was, aye? Seems to me he playing awful damn mad in that death-yard he finding us on that night. Like maybe thinking had heself the right to be so mad."

This was not good. Not good, really not fucking good. Her heart hammered in her chest as if it was trying to take flight. As if it was trying to escape. She'd never seen Lex like this before.

Well, no, that wasn't entirely true. She'd seen Lex like this before. More times than she cared to count, she'd seen Lex like this.

She just didn't remember him being this . . . "insolent" was the only word she could think of. Insolent. He was trying to get to her, not just because he wanted to turn her on but because there was some kind of point to be made by doing so. Because he had some kind of point to make to her. *About* her.

And, shit, she was afraid he was making it, because her eyes stung and her chest ached, and because no matter how much she didn't want it to, her stomach was tingling—her stomach and everything below it—and her lungs refused to expand enough to let her take a deep breath. No. What he was saying wasn't . . . It was true but he wasn't getting it right, he—

No. He had it exactly right. He had *her* exactly right.

"So now . . . now you here all pissed up at me, aye, only maybe I ain't the one deserving it. Maybe you gots youself all meaned up causen you the one sold him out at the start, aye? An causen you know you keep on doing it."

"Fuck you, Lex."

"Ain't that why you here, Tulip?" His fingers touched her hair; she was flat against the wall now, with her only option for escape being to duck down and spin away. She wouldn't give him the satisfaction.

At least, fuck, she wanted to believe that was why she wasn't moving. Please, please let that be it and not because she wanted him to do what he was about to do, not because she saw the flames and wanted to shove her hand into them because she deserved to burn. Not because all she was really doing with Terrible was destroying him right along with herself, and whatever sick fucking part of her it was that enjoyed that shit saw a way to do it even faster.

"Giving me the tell you here causen you want me leaving Terrible alone. Coulda called me with that one, you could. Coulda told Blue on me—you ain't done that, noticing. Why come?"

"I—"

"You here causen you got the thought you oughta be,

Tulip, and causen you like it. Causen you wanting pretend you ain't who you is, wanting pretend you got it in you be all straight and solid an all. Aye? Only you ain't can be."

How was it possible for her mouth to be bone-dry but watering at the same time? She swallowed; it seemed like her voice went down her throat, too, because when she spoke it barely made a dent in the thick silence. "That's—"

"Iffen you could be, you ain't woulda come here. Ain't even woulda kept me on you speed dial. Never had the thought you the kinda girl tells herself lies, I ain't. Maybe all them others, but not youself. So why you keep tryin it now?"

He had her. He had her, and he knew it. And yeah, he was enjoying it but maybe not as much as she'd originally thought. Something lurked there behind the pleasure in his eyes—the pleasure and that other thing drowning her with every breath she took. Frustration, maybe. Anger. Curiosity?

She tried one more time, tried in the most pitiful way she could. "I love him, Lex."

"Aye, sure you do." His fingers brushed her cheek, slid into her hair to curl around the back of her neck. "Too bad it ain't in you to make that mean shit."

And his mouth fell on hers.

She didn't want to respond. Especially not when his words, when that fucking cruelty he'd handed to her as casually as a fucking cigarette, reverberated in her head and her chest, vibrated through her body.

But she did respond. She responded because he was right, because she wasn't good enough, because her presence in that room was evidence enough of that even before she grabbed him with arms that hurt—even before she grabbed the flame and yanked it closer to her because that pain wasn't enough.

He was right. He was right, he was right, she couldn't do it. Who the fuck had she been kidding, thinking she could have a real relationship, that she could be true to someone, that she could not fuck someone over, not destroy them. Who the fuck had she been kidding, thinking loving someone with every fucking thing she had, with every . . . every part of her, her entire soul, was enough?

Everything she had and everything she was didn't equal shit. Even if her soul was quadrupled on top of the pile. And that hurt so much she couldn't stand it.

So she let Lex slide his hands down her back so one could slip between her legs from behind while the other grabbed her hip and pulled her closer. So she squeezed her eyes shut in a vain attempt to stop the stinging and fought back the sounds that wanted to escape from her throat as she kissed him harder; she didn't know for sure what they were, if they were sobs or gasps or what, and she didn't care.

So she let him use her.

Maybe at least if Lex was using her—if she was using him—she would finally stop hurting Terrible. Maybe she could finally stop waiting; not for him to leave her but for her to admit she couldn't do it, that the Chess he saw wasn't the one that really existed. That she'd almost died the night before and only cared because of what that would have done to him, and part of her hated him for that obligation. That she couldn't stand having him love her, because it forced her to try to be better than she was.

It was so hot in that room, so hot and small, the walls shrinking around them to press them closer together. She'd suffocate. She'd suffocate and she'd die, and that would be fine because she couldn't do it. She couldn't be good. She couldn't be the person Terrible needed her to be. The person he deserved. Fuck, Lex was right, wasn't he? Why else was she there, why else was she letting him kiss her neck, why else was she letting him open the top button of her jeans and pull her toward his bed?

She didn't want him. Well, no, she *wanted* him, she couldn't help wanting him, because every inch of her skin remembered those nights they'd spent together. She wanted him but she didn't want to want him, and her body warred with itself, and that felt right because that was what she knew, that confusion between knowing something was wrong, knowing it was awful, but knowing that it felt good and she wanted it when she shouldn't. Trapped.

Trapped like she always had been by her weak body and her weak soul and the fact that she was filthy and sick and wrong. Terrible loved her and she didn't deserve that, and now she was proving how little she deserved it, because she couldn't stand expecting better from herself.

Lex's fingertips slipped below the waistband of her jeans, opening the fly further so he could start pushing them down, and something snapped. No. No, this was wrong, not just wrong because it was wrong but wrong because it was *wrong*. The body against hers was smooth instead of hairy, wiry instead of brawny; it smelled wrong and it felt wrong, and it wasn't what she wanted—wasn't who she wanted. It wasn't Terrible's. And she could choose not to do this.

She could try to be what she should be.

"No," she mumbled. It was harder to do than it should have been with her tongue wrapped around his. "Lex, wait. . . ."

"Shit, Tulip." He had her jeans halfway down over her ass now, his fingers digging into her flesh. "Ain't matter, we ain't never gotta say on it, be our secret, aye? Ain't—"

"No!" Somehow she found the strength to push him away, to force the words out. "No, Lex, I don't, I don't want to. I don't want to do this."

The haze in his eyes cleared slightly; his chest heaved as badly as hers did. "Aye, you do."

She guessed she couldn't argue that one. "But I'm not going to."

He stood there staring at her, with his jeans hanging open at the waist and his Crimpshrine T-shirt bunched up and caught on the button. She tried not to notice, especially not when cool air touched her bare hips because her own jeans were still halfway down them. So close. She'd come so fucking close to throwing everything away.

Maybe she had, anyway. What the fuck was she going to do? Tell Terrible she'd let Lex kiss her because she knew Terrible was wasting his time with her? Fuck.

She fastened her jeans with shaking hands. "I meant what I said. About calling him off."

He shrugged. "An I did, too."

Great. Just fucking great. So what had she done, what had she accomplished? She'd gone to Lex's place to make some kind of fucking stand and had succeeded in not only failing to get him to agree to do anything she wanted but in almost letting him get her into his bed again.

Chess Putnam, ace problem solver. For fuck's sake. She needed to get out of there immediately. She needed to get *high* immediately. She needed— Well, she needed a lot of things. At least two of them she could have right away, although she couldn't imagine how willing Terrible would be to even look at her after he heard what had happened.

Of course, she could just not tell him. . . .

"Got any else you wanting to give me, or what?"

As if she hadn't given him more than enough.

The thought popped into her head that he might agree to do what she wanted if she did what he wanted. That she could offer him that deal, and he might very well take it. It would make her a whore, yeah, but . . . but it would be worth it if it meant Terrible lived.

He'd hate her for it when he found out. And he would find out; he would know. She wouldn't be able to hide it.

But that might be worth it, too.

Lex shook his head. "Ain't changin my thoughts, Tulip. Not even for that one."

She blinked. "I didn't—"

"Nay, you ain't, but you was having the thought, you was. You forgetting, got me some knowledge of you, aye?"

What could she say to that? Nothing. Shit. Not only had she made herself a whore by even contemplating that deal but he'd turned her down, thus making her an unsuccessful whore.

Cold spread through her chest, through her body. Such awful cold, the kind of cold so deep it hurt. The kind she didn't think anything would warm. That was it, then.

She didn't say anything else. There wasn't anything else to say. She grabbed her bag from the floor and left— ran, really. The sounds of the TV blaring in the other room, reminding her that Lex hadn't even been alone when she got there, got louder and louder until she wanted to scream from the noise echoing in her head. All those old familiar voices and a new one: *Too bad it ain't in you to make that mean shit.*

She barely managed to make it back to her car before she started to cry.

Chapter Nineteen

Everyone has secrets.
—*Families and Truth*, a Church pamphlet by Elder Barrett

She needed to see him. It probably wasn't a good idea to see him, not when her hands still shook as she lit herself a cigarette and even after her second shower of the night she felt deception clinging to her skin, a stain she couldn't wash off.

No, she hadn't gone to Lex's place hoping he'd kiss her. She didn't think so. She hadn't been aware of wanting him to do it, at least. But what the fuck did that matter?

It didn't, not really. It had happened. She couldn't make it un-happen. She had to live with it, shove it down deep inside her where all the shit went, that place so overflowing with it that she thought one of these days she'd die choking on it. And if it weren't for the fact that death meant the cold, merciless horror of the City of Eternity, that wouldn't be such a bad damn thing, either.

It was too hot outside, even at midnight when the streets were starting to fill with people. She threw on a denim skirt, shoved her bare feet into her Chucks, and headed for the Market. Terrible would be there; he hadn't replied yet to her text but she knew he'd be around there somewhere, probably at Bump's place right off it, maybe closer to the pipe room, but there, collecting debts and keeping an eye on things.

She stopped at Edsel's booth first, as the pills she'd taken before leaving her place started to hit. He was breaking down his booth early, his skin an almost eerie luminescent orange in the torchlight providing the only illumination; he'd already switched off the string of little bulbs he hooked up with an oil generator to show off his products.

"Hey, baby," he said. Was it the light, or did his smile not seem as wide as usual? Did his eyes dart from side to side as if he expected her to have someone lurking behind her? Terrible, maybe?

Which meant she probably already knew the answer to her question, but she asked it anyway. "Seen Terrible?"

Sure enough, he shook his head. "Were hopin he'd be on there behind you. Heard he around breakin heself some bones, sure, but he ain't come by say hiya or nothin."

That might explain why he hadn't texted her back yet, at least, if he was busy. "Okay, well— Wait, you were hoping?"

Yeah, something was definitely wrong. Edsel's ice-blue eyes shifted again. "Got some knowledge for him, thinkin. You call him up, tell him bring heself over here?"

"Yeah, sure, I—I can pass the message on, you know, if you want to—"

Someone stepped up to his counter, cutting her off as if she wasn't even there. "Got any cat bones?"

Edsel looked at her, looked at his new customer. Or customer-to-be, at least. Exhaustion and the necessity for income warred on his face for a few seconds before he nodded. "Aye, gots em here."

Chess turned to glance around the Market, looking

for Terrible. No, she wouldn't see him over some of the booths, but they weren't all that tall. He had to be around somewhere, if Edsel had been told he was, if Edsel had been asking around.

People walked past her and it felt like they were staring, accusing her; she felt naked in front of them, sick and sad and all those feelings the pills were supposed to chase away. Their casual glances made her itch; their imagined hostility—or, hell, some of them were genuinely hostile, this was Downside, after all—made her tattoos tingle, because she was sure they knew what she'd done.

Another check of her phone showed no reply. Shit. Had he— He couldn't have heard she'd gone to see Lex, couldn't know what had happened already, could he? And decided to dump her without another word?

She bit her lip, bit back the panic threatening to build. No. Not unless Lex had called him the minute she left, sent an emissary over to find him and tell him. And Lex wouldn't be that cruel. Or stupid. He knew the only reason Terrible hadn't killed him was her; because he'd helped save her life the night the Lamaru had gotten hold of her, and because she'd asked Terrible not to. Lex had to know that if Terrible was done with her, he himself would be done living very soon after. Lex wasn't that damn hard to find; he couldn't hide from Terrible forever. No one could. No one ever had.

Of course, if Terrible had found out about her going to see Lex, on top of what happened the night before . . . Yeah, she could see him deciding that was enough. If she wasn't almost dying on him, she was sneaking over to his enemy's house the second he left her place. Great. She was terrific at this whole girlfriend thing, wasn't she?

Shit. If she were Terrible, she would have gotten sick of herself already. But then if she were Terrible, she never would have given herself another chance to begin with. Never would have fallen in love with herself to begin with, not if she could help it.

That was the problem with love, though, wasn't it. It couldn't be helped, couldn't be controlled. It just roared in and took whatever it wanted, destroyed whatever it wanted; the most dangerous addiction of all, because nobody survived it intact.

But an addiction that was impossible to let go, because even through her misery and the awful certainty that the right thing to do would be to end it before she caused him any more pain, she couldn't. Even as she stood there feeling guilty and sick, even as she still felt Lex's hands on her no matter how hard she'd tried to scrub the sensation away, the rest of her begged for Terrible's arms around her, to hear his voice, to be near him so he could make everything okay, the way only he could. It was like magic, being with him, and she couldn't give it up no matter how much she knew she should.

So where was he?

She'd check Bump's quickly. Maybe he hadn't gotten her text. Yeah. That's what she'd do, and then maybe she'd send him another text or give him a call.

Edsel was still busy showing his potential customer an array of different animal bones, but he looked up and nodded when she told him she'd be back in a minute.

More people seemed to be pouring into the Market every minute, and with every one her nervousness increased, although once she was away from Edsel's booth and actually doing something she felt better.

He appeared beside her just as she reached Bump's front door. "Hey, Chess."

Relief sagged her shoulders, relief and warmth combined with the drugs making their smooth, sweet way through her bloodstream so she could smile instead of crying. "Hey! You didn't answer my text."

"Said you was comin here."

Something was wrong. Wasn't it? He didn't meet her eyes, no, but they didn't do that in public: too easy to get lost. He didn't stand very close to her or touch her, but they didn't do that in public, either. And his voice rolled over her skin like always.

But something was wrong just the same. She felt it.

Of course, that could be the fact that he'd been in a fuck of a bad mood over Lex's little friend when he'd left her earlier, and she didn't think the few hours that had passed in the interim would have changed that. It could also be her guilt and the knowledge that she'd have to tell him where she'd been. Maybe that was it, actually. Maybe it was her.

Or maybe not. He twitched his head to the side, indicating she should follow him into Bump's place. The door opened under his hand; he must have just come from there. Had he been waiting for her?

Instead of heading to the right, toward Bump's uterine living room, he turned left, led her around a corner and back down another hall. She'd never been in that part of Bump's house before. Maybe it was where he slept when he stayed there?

Probably. Almost definitely, because he opened a door on the right-hand side and ushered her into a small room, barely big enough to hold the sofa and TV in the middle of the floor. Another door connected to it; she guessed that was the bedroom—if there was one—but he didn't open it.

Instead he closed the door behind them, casting the room into almost total darkness; a thin line of light came from under the door and the one of the adjoining room, but that was it. Fuck. Something was definitely wrong.

She waited for him to turn on a light. He didn't. Didn't move, either. Didn't kiss her, didn't reach for her. He just stood there, his body a large black shape looming against the fuzzy pale outline of the door behind him.

A thought occurred to her, something she could say to fill up the space growing wider between them by the second. Something to keep him from saying what she knew he was about to say, what she deserved to have him say. "Hey . . . were there more people tonight? With that speed, I mean, did we have more—"

"Went over Lex's place, aye?"

Well, shit.

At least she'd already planned to tell him where she'd been. At least she could remind herself of that as she tried to hide her surprise. And at least she could give him the respect of not trying to deny it or of asking how he found out about it. "I guess you know I did. I was going to tell you. I came here to tell you."

"Ain't gotta tell me. Knew it soon's I drive by you place an yon car gone."

"I just wanted to—"

"Gave him the ask pull he man, aye?"

She hadn't even finished opening her mouth before he continued. "What the fuck, Chess?"

"I didn't—I'm—"

"You don't think I can beat him." He leaned against the wall. For a moment the high wild flame from his lighter cast his face into bright relief. When he clicked it shut, the image remained, his outline dull red on the backs of her eyelids as she blinked to try to clear it. "Aye? Thinkin he's got me."

"What? No, fuck no, I—"

"Don't fuckin lie to me, Chess. You—"

"He's—he's *cheating*. That's why I went there, that's why I told him to stop. He's using me. He's putting me into—"

"Aw, I dig. Thinkin I ain't can keep you safe. Ain't smart enough to catch him, an—"

"Damn it, will you— That's not true, you know that's not true." Didn't he? Her hands twisted at her waist,

wanting to touch him but afraid to try. "He's not playing fair, Terrible. He's playing this fucking bullshit game
and he's using me to play it, and—"

"What offer you gave him?"

"What?"

Another flash of his profile as he dragged off his
smoke; the cherry flared, then dropped to his side again.
"What offer you gave him. To call off he man, dig. Ain't
had the thought he do it just causen you ask, aye? Guessin you offer he a trade. So wonderin what it were."

It wasn't a lie to say *nothing*. Technically. Technically
it wasn't a lie. "Nothing."

Disbelief came off him in waves. Not only disbelief,
either. She'd been right that his mood hadn't improved
much since earlier—of course it hadn't—and Edsel had
been right, too. Terrible had been collecting while she
was at Lex's, breaking bones, bruising flesh. Violence
and aggression, some of it leftover and some of it not,
filled the small space in which they stood. "Aye?"

"I didn't make him any offers. I didn't. I didn't offer
him anything."

He didn't answer. Fuck. What should she . . . How the
hell was she supposed to handle this, what should she
do, what did people in relationships do?

The fact that she didn't know, had no idea how to deal
with relationships—at least, not in ways that didn't in-
volve trampling them under her feet like discarded party
decorations on a hangover morning—was no excuse, either. No, she didn't know how to do that, not really. But
she knew Terrible. She *knew* him.

Which was even worse. How could she have been so
fucking thoughtless? Of course he'd see it as her doubting him. Of course he'd think she believed—fuck, Lex
was right. *She* was right, to doubt herself. She didn't
know how to love him, didn't know how to make it
mean something.

But she stepped closer to him, anyway, lifting her hand to touch him, because the space between them hurt, and the only way to make it hurt less was to make it smaller. She stepped closer because she had to try.

His fist snapped shut around her wrist, yanked her arm to the side so she spun, off balance, stopping only when her back slammed against the plaster. It happened so fast only the jolt of pain told her it happened at all, the pain and the heat of his body in front of hers, his rage vibrating against her skin.

"Gimme the tell." His grip on her tightened even more, hard enough that she felt the bruise threatening to form under her skin. His cigarette was gone—she didn't know where, but she knew it because his other hand grabbed her other wrist and pinned it to the wall behind her, too. "What happened. All of it. Look so fuckin guilty, you tell me why."

Her brain felt numb. Her hands were definitely numb. For the second time in as many hours, she was pinned to a wall with her heart trying to smash itself into pieces against her ribs, and she couldn't fight it—couldn't fight him—even if she wanted to. "I told him to quit using me. I told him to—"

"What fucking happened."

"I told him I—"

His grip switched from her wrist to her throat, forcing her to look at him. Her eyes had adjusted enough for her to see how close he was to losing control. "Did you—did you fuck him? Just fuckin tell me, did you—"

"No!" The fact that she could answer that one with Truth should have made her feel better. It didn't. "No, I didn't, I swear I—"

"No—no fuckin more, Chess, can't fuckin take it more. Tryin give you trust, but—"

"No, you're—"

"Ain't—just fuck this, fuckin thinkin on him touchin

you. He shows up you place like he fuckin belongs there, an I gotta *see* it again, you an he, an you still fuckin—still let he show up, still getting you needs off him, letting he—"

"I'm sorry," she said. Shit, she'd never . . . It had never occurred to her that she wasn't the only one who remembered that night in the graveyard, who remembered the way Terrible had found her with her hand stuffed into Lex's jeans, trying to convince him to take them off right there on the cold hard ground. Of course she knew he *remembered* it, but she hadn't realized—she'd never even thought—that he would still see it in his head, keep replaying that moment, keep hearing her trying to talk Lex into fucking her on the frozen dirt, talking about how they'd had sex two nights before, the night Terrible had opened his soul to her. How fucking dumb was she?

But then . . . no one had ever been jealous over her like that. No one had ever wanted her like that, as more than just an available and willing body, and seen the fact of her sharing that body with them as more than a few hours' entertainment. And jealousy from her had never been part of the game, either; what did she care what they did when she was done with them? "I didn't—"

"The fuck I gotta do? How the fuck I can stop, stop *seein* that, get him out my fuckin head, outta yours, him tryin kill me an you ain't even— How? How can I fuckin stop it?"

"I don't—I love—"

"You make you a choice. Now. Me or him, aye? Me or—"

"You." The word flew out of her mouth, propelled by her panting breaths. He was so close to her and he buzzed with energy, with power and anguish and the deep burning anger of lust, and she burned along with him because just having his hands on her skin, holding her in place in that familiar way, made her temperature soar. Because just then he was in pain and so was she, desperate furious pain, because she was killing them both and couldn't stop. Didn't want to stop. She wanted to jump on that death-train and ride it harder, faster, all the way into whatever damnation awaited her, and if she had to pay for it later she'd get everything she could from it now. "You, I swear, I never—I love you, I—"

His grip didn't change. He still held her throat, his fingers digging into the back of her neck, but he raised his hand, forcing her to her tiptoes while his mouth took hers. While his mouth *attacked* hers, hurting her, cutting off her breath.

He let go of her other wrist; she only realized it because her hand—both of her hands—found his neck, his head, twining into his hair, pulling it. Had she thought earlier that Lex was a flame, that she could burn herself? She'd been wrong. This was a flame. This was throwing herself into the inferno and letting the pain of it, the roaring heat, sear every cell in her body. "I—"

"*Mine*, Chessie." Cold plaster hit her ass, quickly replaced by his palms; he'd shoved her skirt to her waist. Her panties were gone, she didn't know where. She didn't care. Couldn't think when he kept kissing her like that and making the world spin. He gripped her hips to pull her to him even harder, grinding against her so she could feel the thick outline of his erection through his jeans. "Aye? Fuckin—mine. Not his."

"I'm not his, I wasn't—"

"Shut up." His teeth sank into her neck. He twisted her hair while his other hand kept moving, up under her shirt, over her breasts. "You—fuckin done, done with this, seein him. Done takin pills offen him, him pushin you down—no fuckin more."

"Yes. Never, never, I won't—"

"*Mine*." It was a snarl, low and harsh in her ears as he spun her around, his hand on the back of her neck forcing her to bend at the waist while she tried in vain to grip the wall.

"Yes." It was true, and she knew it was true. And thank fuck it was, because at that point she would have said anything he wanted, done anything he wanted. She *would* do anything he wanted, as long as it meant he didn't stop, as long as it meant the fingers now slipping between her legs stayed where they were. "I lo—"

"Shut *up*," he said again. She didn't know when he'd gotten his jeans open, but he had, and he slammed into her so hard that her knees buckled and only his hand on her hip and his pelvis flush against her behind kept her from falling.

Again. And again, and again, while she bit her lip to keep from screaming. He fisted her hair and yanked it down, arching her back so it hurt, so it shook. Every muscle in her body shook. She couldn't help it, couldn't stop it, especially not when he kept driving himself into her harder and faster and his fingers kept moving, doing exactly what he knew she wanted him to do, exactly the way he knew she needed him to do it. His voice, harsh gasps filling the room, his hands on her bare skin, his body forcing hers to his will . . . It was too much, all too much. Her legs almost stopped supporting her weight. Her fingers scratched uselessly at the faint ridges in the plaster.

His fingers disappeared; she couldn't hold back the sob bursting from her lips. Was that too loud? Like she fucking cared. Anyone could be standing right outside the door, anyone could walk in and see them any second, Bump or one of his women or anyone, and she couldn't bring herself to give a shit.

He left her then, his hand in her hair the only contact between them as he wrestled her farther into the room, into the darkness. She stumbled, banging her toe, but fear dwarfed the pain. Fear and arousal; her body still throbbed, still shivered and clenched and twisted inside from wanting his back so bad.

He spun her around again, practically throwing her down onto the couch and landing half on top of her, taking her mouth with as much violence as before. "You . . . so guilty . . . Shows up all the fuckin time and you letting him, keeping you place—an how many pills, Chessie, how many you took, hidin em from me, shit—just . . . fuckin . . . can't, I can't—"

"It won't happen again," she managed. Her voice broke. That made sense, didn't it, because everything was broken, *she* was broken, he'd crushed her beneath his heel so all the empty places showed, and she knew he saw them. And she needed him to fill them again. Needed him to fill them because he was the only one who could, the only one who ever had. She clutched at him as if he were a raft in a stormy sea, twisting the fabric of his shirts between her fingers so he couldn't suddenly slip away. "I'm sorry, so fucking sorry, it—"

"Not sharin no more. An not— No more fuckin hiding. No more lockin out."

His weight lifted from her. His hands gripped her thighs. What was— Oh. Oh no, he wasn't, he couldn't, not—

She didn't finish the thought. It came too late, anyway, because that was exactly what he was doing, something that scared her, that felt too much like yanking out her soul and handing it to him. Something too intimate to share with the nameless one-nighters who filled her past, something she hadn't been able to share with him despite his attempts.

Her bare skin scraped the rough fabric of the sofa as he shifted her, muscling her thighs onto his shoulders. She grabbed his hair and tried to pull his head away; he twisted her wrist, hard, and smacked it against the back of the couch. This time she felt the pain shooting up her arm, felt above it all the thrill of panic and fear and something else, something dark and greedy that blossomed when his mouth started moving against her, so slowly, so gently, so . . . careful.

He paused. Paused just long enough that she understood what it was, what it meant. One last chance. He'd let her say no if she really wanted to.

It might mean losing him, but he'd let her.

But somehow knowing that—having that chance, that pause—made something else rise in her chest, over the frantic need, the love and the anger and the panic and fear and shame and everything else. It gave her strength. It reminded her of trust. Yes, she was scared. But no, she didn't have to be. She never had to be, not when he was there. So she could let him keep going, she could. She could do that for him. For herself.

So she did.

Oh . . . *fuck*. She'd been right to be uncomfortable, to think it was too intimate. Right to have her only memories of that—her only knowledge of it—be of violations and humiliation, of vulnerability and shame. It *was* intimate. It *was* vulnerable. It was as if he was looking all the way into her, all the way down where the hidden things were, so he could see them all, could see *her*.

But . . . it was also as if that didn't matter to him. Because he kept going, his breath hot on her sensitive skin, his fingers curling into her thighs and sliding up her rib cage under her T-shirt to caress her breasts, and he found her hand fisted at her side and forced his into it, forced her to entwine her fingers with his and squeezed, and suddenly it didn't feel scary anymore. It felt right.

It felt like he loved her.

It didn't stop feeling that way when he shifted her again so her hips had room to move and her head fell back over the arm of the couch. The dizzy grayish ceiling above them shook as she shook, looked farther and farther away with every second as her vision blurred when he kept going, teasing her, caressing her, delving into all of her hidden places until she could hardly breathe.

Panic roared back into her chest, into her head, panic and pressure and heat. Panic *from* the pressure and heat, and her hips were moving on their own, and the high walls around her twisted and turned when she tried to focus on them.

She was going to scream. She was going to scream, she was going to cry, white heat spread through her body and she couldn't control it, couldn't control either of them. This was too much, it was too much and she was too scared, she couldn't do this.

Then he tightened his grip on her hand, stroked her rib cage as he sped up his movements just a little, and something crashed inside her. *She* crashed. She broke open above him, broke apart, and the world around her broke, too, so only Terrible was left. Terrible, who she trusted. Terrible, who she loved, who loved her.

Who kept doing it, pushing her over the edge again, and then again, until finally he changed his grip and straightened up, still holding her thighs so he could drive himself back into her with a force that sent a scream flying from her mouth. "Gimme it again," he said, leaning over as he knelt on the floor in front of her, his eyes so close to hers they blocked everything else. "No more with him. No more. Not ever."

The words wouldn't form. Not because she didn't want them to but because she couldn't breathe. For a second she stared at him, her mouth moving without sound, before her voice finally came to her rescue. "No. No more."

His mouth on her neck, his arms under her thighs almost folding her in half while his hands gripped her rib cage to hold her in place, and he started moving again, still angry, still rough. Her eyes had adjusted enough for her to see his face, the way the light from under the door caught his jaw and chin when his head fell back, the way it caught the muscles in his bare arms as he squeezed her tighter, grabbed her shoulders to pull her down to meet his thrusts. It showed her his expression when he looked down at her, his emotions naked on his face, in his eyes.

Her heart couldn't take it. Her oversensitive flesh couldn't take it; it exploded, and somewhere in the distance she felt his head on her chest as he shuddered above her, his breath coming in hot, loud gasps until they both stopped shaking.

Chapter Twenty

> What we do affects others. All actions have consequences. A good homekeeper and spouse makes sure her actions create positive effects. A poor or lazy one may find herself alone.
> —*Mrs. Increase's Advice for Ladies*, by Mrs. Increase

He eased himself away from her, his head down. For a few seconds, silence reigned, broken only by the sounds of his zipper and belt buckle. She had no idea what to say as she rearranged her skirt—where the hell had her panties gone, anyway? She'd have to find them—and apparently neither did he, because he kept his face turned away while he lit cigarettes for them both and handed her one.

A few drags later, he finally spoke. "Ain't gonna give you a sorry."

Great. That was an opening. Except it totally wasn't. "I— You don't have to. I do. I mean, I'm sorry. I didn't think—I'm sorry."

"Just ain't can fuckin stand it no more. Gave it the try, true thing, but—can't."

"I know. I'm sorry." She let her fingers brush his arm, a quick touch she wasn't brave enough to extend. "But it's not— It wasn't because I don't think you can beat him. I know you can. I know it. He just pissed me off so much, I didn't think. I'm sorry."

His head dipped, his profile outlined in pale gold. A quick nod, one that to anyone else might have looked like not much at all, but she knew better. The nod was the end of it. Relief washed over her, so strong and sharp she was certain that she'd have fallen if she'd been standing.

Relief and a fresh flood of shame, exactly the way she'd felt at Elder Griffin's house. She'd gotten away with it.

It made her sick.

But to tell him wouldn't mean she felt better; it would only hurt him all over again, destroy everything he'd tried to do, ruin the real Truth she'd given him. So she swallowed it, and—what the hell—grabbed the packet of speed from her pillbox and did a couple of quick bumps to make sure it stayed down where it belonged.

Down where his comments about Lex bringing her drugs, about the OD, down where the fact that he'd started to say something about her not giving up her apartment, would go, too, at least until she knew a good time to bring them up—if there ever was one. The OD, yeah, she'd been expecting that one, understood that one. But she hadn't thought— Well, why would he care about Lex bringing her drugs? It wasn't as if he wanted to do it or she wanted him to. And, yeah, it would be great if they didn't each have stuff scattered all over both apartments, but they still spent just about every night together, they still saw each other just about every day, so what difference did it make?

And she'd told him why she couldn't; she'd told him it was against the rules. Did he think she'd lied about that, or . . .

Or did he think if she really wanted to she would have done it no matter what.

She hoped to fuck he was wrong about that.

Somehow she suspected he wasn't, not entirely. But what was— Everything was changing so fast, and how could she keep up with it? What else would have to change, if Lex wasn't supplying her anymore, if she was never alone, watched all the time . . . Fuck.

She cleared her numbed-out throat, grabbed her water bottle from her bag, and took a drink. More important things to think about, to discuss, than her emotional weirdness and panic. She'd think about all of that later. "So . . . were there more tonight? Any—"

The words ended up buried in his chest; he'd grabbed her and yanked her to him, his arms hard around her shoulders, his hand on the back of her head holding her tight and his breath stirring her hair. "Sorry. Sorry, Chessie, aye? Shit, ain't meant to— Sorry."

"I love you." Her throat felt too tight as she spoke. Destroying him, destroying them both . . . please let her be able to stop doing it. "I do, fuck, I love you so much, Terrible."

Another minute, maybe, and he pulled away from her, looking around behind them to the closed door with his hand braced on the back of his neck.

When he turned back to her, his voice was steady. "Aye. More of em this night. More'n ten I had sight of, an heard on more, all of them got locked up another house of Bump's. Hearin on more dead, too, more ripped-up bodies. Ain't good, aye."

"Fuck. No, that isn't—"

Screams cut into her sentence, sliced it neatly apart so the rest of it stayed caught in her throat. That didn't sound— Shit, was that coming from outside? There were so many of them, what was— Fuck. "Edsel."

Terrible's brows drew together. "Edsel?"

"Shit, he wanted to talk to you, he said he had knowledge for you. He seemed really nervous. I told him I'd bring you to him when I saw you."

Terrible started running. The screaming hadn't stopped. Fuck fuck fuck. That wasn't good, wasn't the sort of scream that became part of the general street noise in Downside: fights, cackles, screams just for the hell of it, which rang out at all hours of the day and night so she didn't even notice them if she wasn't paying attention.

Please let it not be Edsel. They burst out of the front door of Bump's place and into the Market, where the screams were louder. And more numerous. Her feet hit the ground in a rhythm, running after Terrible, every slap of sole against cement a jarring reminder of her own forgetfulness. Please, please, because if something had happened to Edsel it was her fault; she was supposed to bring Terrible to him, that would have kept him safe, what the fuck was wrong with her? She'd even wondered at his booth if he'd been asking around and been overheard. Someone could have overheard him telling her he knew something.

But she'd forgotten. She'd forgotten because she'd been so busy thinking of her own fucking feelings. As if she fucking mattered.

People scattered as Terrible plowed down the aisle of the Market and pushed through the crowd gathered around Edsel's booth. It was Edsel's booth. Oh no, oh fuck no—

Terrible emerged from the shadows a second later, his gaze scanning the crowd for a second until it fell on her, pausing before moving on. His lips moved—she had some vague idea of what was being said, that he'd found some people to pack up Edsel's stuff. She could barely hear it over the loud tinny ringing noise in her ears that had replaced the screams.

What she couldn't do was look down, look below Terrible's face. She couldn't. Couldn't see what he carried, didn't want to see that fall of white-blond hair over his arm, that pale motionless face turned to the sky beneath its mask of horrible blood.

Terrible met her eyes again. Right. Follow him. He

rushed toward the Chevelle—so she assumed, she hadn't seen where he parked—and she sped after him, trying to stay close enough that his nearness would comfort her but not so close that she had to see Edsel's silent body in his arms.

"Still breathin, Chessie," Terrible said, as soon as they'd pulled away from the crowd far enough for her to hear him. "Ain't dead, aye? Still breathin."

She really, really wanted that to make her feel better, but it didn't. Not when it was clear in his voice and his eyes, clear from the way Edsel didn't regain consciousness, that the "ain't dead" part could change any second.

She didn't find her voice until they were in the Chevelle, racing onto the highway toward the nearest hospital, in Cross Town. *If* it was her voice; it sounded like someone else, someone panicked and sick and guilty, so fucking guilty. "This is my fault. It's my fault, I told him I'd send you to— Fuck!"

"What?"

More speed, that was what. She'd taken . . . shit, she'd taken four Cepts before she went to Lex's, right, then two more before she got to the Market? The last two had barely been an hour ago. Damn it, she couldn't have any more. Shouldn't have any more.

But she had speed—she probably shouldn't take too much of it, either, but she could have some.

Two more bumps, bigger ones, and she could keep talking. Two more bumps and Terrible's hand holding hers on his warm thigh when she was done. "When I was talking to him, a customer walked up. He claimed to be a customer, at least. He said he wanted cat bones and . . . all kinds of shit, whatever. But he didn't feel right. I just—damn it, I didn't notice it, I didn't think about it, I was so—I was looking for you."

His hand tightened around hers.

"I felt better when I got farther away, but I thought it

was because I was, I don't know, actively searching or something. I was worried because you hadn't answered my text and I just . . . Fuck."

Because it was all about her, right? All about her and her stupid fucking feelings.

"Ain't yon fault. How you was s'posed to—"

"I was *supposed* to be fucking paying attention when something suddenly felt wrong in the air. I was *supposed* to be doing my fucking job and thinking about what that shit meant, and don't tell me you don't know exactly what I mean."

Yeah. That was great. Why not piss off and upset him, when he'd just forgiven her for pissing off and upsetting him?

Fuck.

The road brightened as they got farther from Downside: more lights, better ones. Unbroken ones. The Chevelle zoomed under those lights, fast enough to almost turn them into a solid streak, and Edsel remained silent and unmoving.

He wasn't the only one.

Two hours later she'd lost count. Lost count of how many cigarettes she'd smoked, how many bumps she'd sneaked in the bathroom, how many times she'd reminded herself it was all her fault. Two hours later and she finally took a couple more Cepts while she and Terrible stood outside the emergency-room doors, watching nothing much happen in the parking lot.

Two hours until Edsel's wife, Galena, finally came outside.

He'd been stabbed a dozen times. He was concussed. His ribs were broken. They knew that. What they didn't know was whether or not he'd live, and the weight of that question looked heavy on Galena's curly head, slowed her steps even more than her pregnant belly had when Chess saw her a few weeks before.

Oh right. Her friend, the one she'd totally let down and allowed to almost be killed, the one she'd practically handed over to the people who wanted to kill him because she was too busy worrying about her love life to focus on everyone around her? He had a wife and a baby on the way.

What was the record for number of people fucked over in a single day, because she was pretty fucking sure nobody could beat her at that one.

Galena's skin shone dark in the flat yellow glow of the bug lights outside the entrance as she made her way to where Chess stood against the wall with Terrible's arms around her. At least there was that; they weren't in Downside so they didn't have to be so careful, and if the hospital Goodys and the doctors and Elder-Doctors looked at them strangely, she didn't give a fuck.

"Were woken up he a time," she said, her sweet high voice barely a whisper. "Gave you name, he done. An some other name I ain't knowing, maybe you do?"

Chess shifted position, careful not to break contact with Terrible. Not then, when she needed him—well, she always needed him, but at that moment the strength of his body against hers was pretty much all that kept her from having a total fucking fit. Especially not when she heard that Edsel had come around and said her name. He probably blamed her.

She hoped he did, anyway, because if he didn't, that was just further proof that he was someone whose friendship she didn't deserve.

"What name he gave you?"

"Agneta Katina. You know she? Ain't—ain't like some other dame he got, aye? He ain't—"

"Naw, naw." Terrible's grip tightened on Chess's hand. "Ed ain't pull that, you knowin that one. Heard that name before, we did. Thinkin that what knowledge he wanted to give, aye, Chess? Be what Gordon Samms were sayin, you recall?"

Shit, that was right. She'd made a note on it, even, and then hadn't asked Terrible about following it up. Stupid. "Has he ever said it before, Galena?"

"Never hearin it."

Chess glanced at Terrible. He shook his head. "Ain't got shit back on it yet. Not one of Bump's, not one Berta knowin."

"Did he say anything else, Galena? Anything at all?"

"Just you name, an that one."

Okay, then. At last they had somewhere to start— well, not start, but somewhere to go next. Chess guessed that as much as she hated to leave Galena there, they were going to have to.

But first . . . "Did he talk to anyone in particular today, do you know? Or go somewhere he doesn't usually, anything like that?"

Galena considered it for a minute. "Went he lookin for stuff on the morn, see, stuff I can make up for the booth or what he can sell right off the booth, bones an such an all, if you diggin me?"

"Where did he go?"

"Ain't said. Just that him were headin out, had he some guesses on some animal teeths to find."

"He— Where? I mean, I know he didn't say, but did he say anything that might give you a clue, or did—"

"Fuck." Terrible held up his phone. "All gone again. Sent one over to give the house a check, dig, the three watchin em dead and all them gone."

"All—the ones you just told me about at Bump's, the ones who took the speed?"

He nodded.

Damn it! "How the fuck is that happening? How are they being found, how are they being taken?"

His face was grim as he pulled his keys from his pocket. " 'Sgo have us a look."

Not that it made a difference. They'd found exactly what they'd found at the other safe house: a building empty of everything but corpses. No clues. No nothing.

But they'd gotten a name. So after spending a sleepless night doing lines and berating herself, Chess went to the only place she could think of to get some information: the Church library.

The name "Agneta Katina" turned up a few hits in the system, the most recent being a woman who'd died in Sweden during Haunted Week. Chess wrote down the information but without much hope. Sure, it was entirely possible some dead Swedish ghost was working with the person infiltrating Downside with ghost-cut speed, but it seemed like a long shot.

The search results indicated another page available, though, so she clicked on the link. Probably nothing, a follow-up on the dead Swedish woman, or maybe a—

A ship.

Holy fuck, it was a boat. Not just any boat, either; a privately owned ex-military ship, converted into a freighter/transport ship for a shipping company. KVB Shipping, it was called.

She scribbled it down and started a new search, aware of her heart pounding faster in her chest but ignoring it. It could be nothing, it could still be nothing. Drug dealing wasn't usually something corporations got involved in.

But drug *smuggling* was definitely something shipping companies got involved in, and if they could find someone, if they could find some of the sailors from the ship who might talk to them, who might give them some names . . . She knew enough from Bump to know that it was pretty easy to bribe some dockworkers and shipworkers to look the other way while a couple of cases were loaded or unloaded.

KVB Shipping wasn't just a corporation, it seemed. It was a division of a larger corporation. Shit, she should have paid more attention to this stuff in school, because figuring out what all those initials and titles meant wasn't easy. Stockholders, yes, she knew what those were, and she knew what a CEO was, but CEOs weren't usually doing a lot of work on-site with ships, right?

And KVB had like a dozen different divisions. Shipping. Media and Entertainment. Housewares. Technology—that's right, they'd introduced some new kind of cellphone or something, hadn't they? She had some vague memory of seeing a news story about it one day while she smoked a kesh and watched one of those mindless TV shows about how the latest gadget was the only road to real happiness.

KVB Chemical. She jotted that one down, along with KVB— Oh, KVB owned part of Triumph City's major-league baseball team, the Elders. Did that mean— No, because different divisions also owned part of several other cities' teams.

So who the hell owned the company to begin with? The actual business records on the mainframe were dull stuff, annual reports in incomprehensible business-ese, but . . . Hold on. She might be able to get the information a lot more easily elsewhere, right?

She logged out of the Church database and opened an Internet window. Funny, she'd never really used the Net for case research before, but why would she? Her cases usually involved private rather than public information, and either way the Church's Computer and Data department—sometimes referred to as the Code Squad—kept as tight a grip on the cyberworld as the Church did on the real one; every page, every website, every bit of information available online, had been cleared through them first.

Hell, C&D brought in almost as much money as tithing taxes did, what with the fee to license and register a computer, the fee to license and register an Internet access line, the annual fee to keep that access and the identifying permanent browsing address active, the fees to build a website, the fees to have C&D clear it, the monthly charges to have them recheck the site to make sure it was acceptable . . . millions of dollars in income every month.

But a large company like KVB might very well pay the fees, probably would pay them. And she might— Yes. Hell yes, there was a website, and there was an "About Us" page, and there was a company history that told her exactly who owned KVB, who'd started the company back in 2000.

Kyle Victor Blake, born in the Midwest, raised in the South, and a resident of Triumph City according to his last Church identification—his driver's license—issued in the last year.

Kyle Victor Blake. Marietta Blake's father.

What the *fuck*.

She started to head for Elder Griffin's office, her mind already whirring to think of a good explanation for why she wanted Kyle Blake's financial records and private files. The idea died in her head before it was even fully formed. Right. Elder Griffin wasn't about to be doing her any favors anytime soon, was he?

No. In fact, the best idea was to leave. She knew where Blake lived; she could go back and talk to him again about the *Agneta Katina* and about his daughter. And about his comments about Downside, for that matter, which took on a new and very interesting tone in retrospect, didn't they? Why was he doing business in

Downside when he hated it so much? Or was that just a front?

She'd go home, grab Terrible, and head for the Blake house, and it would be almost as if she hadn't been at the Church that morning at all.

Or she'd end up seeing Elder Griffin anyway, because when she stopped by her memo box outside Goody Tremmell's office, she found a notice from the Elder Triumvirate. Probably confirming her— Wait. What the hell?

Okay. It could mean anything. It could mean nothing. There was no reason to panic, none at all.

Yeah. Maybe if she told herself that enough she might one day manage to believe it, but she doubted it. She sure as fuck didn't believe it then, when she stopped in the open doorway of Elder Griffin's office with the Triumvirate's notice clutched in her fist and her entire body filling with dread.

What she saw through the doorway didn't help calm her down.

The office had been almost empty the last time she'd seen it, all of his things in boxes as he prepared to move to his new position, whatever position that would be, and make way for whoever would be overseeing the Debunkers next.

It was still almost empty, but growing less so by the minute, because Elder Griffin stood in front of his bookcase, unpacking his boxes.

She must have gasped or something, because he looked up. Their eyes met; that hurt. He looked almost as if he didn't know her. He looked exactly as if he didn't care about her or like her. "Good morrow, Cesaria."

She curtsied. "Good morrow, sir. I . . ."

He turned away and kept moving, pulling skulls from a box and setting them back on the shelves.

She swallowed. Swallowed the panic, the tears threatening to clog her throat, the gorge threatening to rise. Swallowed it all and tried again. "Sir . . . there was a letter in my box, a notice from the Elder Triumvirate canceling my interview with them on Wednesday. The one to discuss you and your new position? I don't— They don't say I should contact them to reschedule, so . . . um, I just wondered if something happened."

How fucking stupid. Of course something had happened. Please, please let her be wrong about what she thought it might be. Please, she didn't deserve to have things work out for her but Elder Griffin did. Shit, please let her not have ruined his life, too.

Another glance. "Come in. Close the door."

She'd never thought his office—his presence—would feel so cold and uncomfortable. She should have; life had certainly taught her that nobody stayed happy with her for long. Why would they? She was a fucking junkie who ruined lives every time she opened her mouth.

But it still sucked. A lot.

The door *snick*ed shut behind her. A few cautious steps took her not to his side, of course, because she didn't dare, but close enough. "Did something happen?"

"Yes." He set an empty box on the floor and picked up a full one. "Something has happened. I shall no longer be leaving my position."

"What? But your promotion, you were—" She needed to stop. It wasn't her business.

But she couldn't help it. "You were looking forward to that, sir, I don't understand."

He stopped. "I am no longer deserving."

"I don't—"

"Cesaria." He shook his head and looked at her, taking a step closer so he could lower his voice. "Surely you don't believe I can still accept a position of higher authority? After our discussion?"

No. Oh shit, no, this couldn't be happening. "I don't—"

"I've agreed to lie for you. I've agreed to hide your crime from the Church. In doing so, I condone your behavior and I prove myself disloyal and unworthy of further promotion. I prove myself weak."

"But that's bullshit!" Oops. That probably wasn't good, the way his mouth tightened. "Sorry. I'm sorry, but—that's not fair, you shouldn't—"

"I cannot lie, Cesaria. I cannot swear an oath that I have always upheld the Church's sacred laws when I have not. I cannot allow you to lie to the Triumvirate when they ask you to swear the same. I cannot ask you to lie because of my own failure."

The words felt like a fucking choke hold around her throat. She'd failed him, and now she was forcing him to give up something he wanted, to give up everything he wanted—all of his dreams of advancing in the Church, dreams she knew he had. All because of her.

"Actions have consequences," he said. "I made a decision, and now I must live with it."

"I'll tell them." She swiped at her eyes and forced them to meet his. "I'll tell them what I did. I can't let you do—"

For the first time, his expression softened. Not a lot. Nowhere near enough. But it was there just the same, and it sent a fresh wave of nauseated misery up her throat. "No, you will not. You cannot. You *will* be executed, and your soul *will* be sent to the spirit prisons if you tell. And I will be—at the very least—released from my position entirely for even considering hiding your crime and for not reporting it immediately."

He turned away and reached back into the box for another bone, a cat spine it looked like, which he placed on the shelf. "Whether intended or not, I have become an accomplice. And that, Cesaria, is something we shall both have to live with."

This couldn't be happening. Elder Griffin giving up his promotion for her, the one she knew he'd been so excited about. Elder Griffin being so cold to her, so obviously regretting ever being . . . being friends with her, or whatever he'd been. She didn't have a word for it; she'd never known a word that would fit. But she knew it was important.

"Elder Griffin . . . I know you don't want to hear it again, but I never meant to— I never wanted this to happen, I never wanted you to—"

"I'm aware of that." A flash of anger came from him, one that made her take a half step back without meaning to. Not because she was scared, but because it made her feel so much worse. "I take my own responsibility in this. That is my burden."

He walked around her then, to stand with his hand on the doorknob. "Unfortunately, you must also take your own, and I cannot help you with that."

She opened her mouth, wanting to say something, but there didn't seem to be anything more to say.

He opened the door, his entire demeanor changing with the movement, a smile she knew was fake plastered across his face. "Goodbye, Cesaria. Facts are Truth."

She nodded, pausing as she walked past him to not quite meet his eyes. "Facts are Truth, sir."

The door closed behind her with a decisive bang, leaving her alone in the pale hallway with its echoes.

Chapter Twenty-one

Appearances can fool. Only behavior is Fact, and Facts are Truth.

—*Church Wisdom*, a pamphlet by Elder Bryar

It didn't stop echoing, either. Not after she turned up Bikini Kill so loud her windows shook, and not after she stopped at a gas station a block away to throw four Cepts into her mouth and do a hard bump. Not enough, but all she could chance at that moment. Besides, nothing would be enough. Nothing was going to chase that sound out of her head, or make her stop seeing that plastic smile on Elder Griffin's face and the disappointment in his eyes.

He'd turned his back on her. She'd let him down, and he'd turned his back on her. And there was absolutely nothing she could do about it.

Just like she couldn't do anything about letting Terrible down—the OD; those frantic, shameful seconds in Lex's bedroom that sent a stab of pain through her chest the second she thought of them; the way she pushed him away even as she grabbed him. Or Edsel, still clinging to life in the hospital because of her carelessness. Or everyone else, really, everyone she'd ever met, everyone who'd ever been unlucky or stupid enough to depend on her.

She clenched her fists a few times, tensed her shoulders in an effort to calm down and let the speed give her a little cheer. It was sort of effective; at least she could work her phone enough to send a text to Terrible asking where he was, because wherever he was, that's where she was going. It would be okay if she could see him, so she could remember that yeah, maybe she'd fucked up as far as the Church and its rules were concerned, but she hadn't had a choice. At least not one worth making.

Her phone beeped a few seconds later. He was at Bump's. Good. Not that she wanted to see Bump, but at least at Bump's she didn't have to pretend. At Bump's she could touch him.

The drive took forever, and her body started to relax from her pills just before she took the exit toward the Market. Finally. She hadn't slept much the night before, so the speed was making her edgy, and essentially she was a total fucked-up bundle of nerves and pain at the moment—or, well, always, but especially then.

She crossed the Market as fast as she could, ignoring the smells of cooking meats from the firecans across the way. When had she eaten last?

Didn't matter. Terrible was going to make her eat at some point, so no need to worry about it.

Also to be ignored was the seller of tin wind chimes and luck charms who'd set up in the spot Edsel usually took. With effort, she sped past him.

Yet another of Bump's women responded to her knock. A brunette this time—that made a change—with breasts that looked as if they needed special engineering to keep from tipping her over face-first and a pair of shiny hot-pink spandex pants showcasing every swell and crease. Typical. Chess could just imagine how the woman must look in the middle of Bump's crimson horror of a living room.

Lucky for her, she was spared the sight. The woman plunked herself down on a stool at the bar along the back wall and left Chess to head down the blood-colored hallway on her own.

As always, it took her eyes a minute to adjust to the horrible room. And as always, something she thought was real happiness rose in her chest when she saw Terrible sitting on the couch, something that grew even more when she sat down next to him and he slid his arm around her. "Hey, Chess. You right?"

She kissed his neck and lied. "Right up, yeah. You? Anything going on?"

"Thinkin we maybe got us a line where Edsel were yesterday. Lookin for teeth an all, dig, thought sounded like it might be an easy one hunt down."

"Yeah? How?"

"Hey to you too, Ladybird. Nice way you fuckin giving Bump the hellos."

Oh, right. With Bump's place came Bump. "Hey."

He snorted. "Ain't should fuckin give youself the stretch-out, there."

Should she bother to answer? On the one hand, fuck him. On the other . . . he was still her dealer. And Terrible's boss. And on the other, he was a sleazy, annoying asshole.

But, yeah, that dealer thing . . . Damn it. "Sorry. Lot on my mind."

"Yay, fuckin betting you do."

Whatever. She had more important things to do than worry about Bump's precious little feelings. "I found *Agneta Katina*."

"Aye? Where?"

"At the docks." She smiled. "She's a boat."

"Damn." Terrible shook his head. "So fuckin obvious, you say it."

"I know, I thought the same thing. But yeah, she's a ship. A freighter—well, a military ship converted into a freighter."

Terrible's eyebrows rose. "Aye? What kinda ship it were?"

"Don't know. I just know it was bought from the Church in 2002 and converted for shipping and passengers. Like a private yacht with a fuck of a lot of storage space."

"Who done it? Converted it, meaning. Who owns it, you know? Gotta head the docks anyway, we check it out—"

"Yeah, wait 'til— What? Why are we heading to the docks?"

"Remember Galena sayin on Edsel lookin for teeth? Thinkin we know whereabouts he were." Terrible nodded toward the far wall, the one where another bar broke the red ocean below a stag head mounted on a slab of gold plate. A stag head like the kind people bought from taxidermists . . .

The realization must have been all over her face, because he nodded again, this time at her. "Aye. You got the recall, him the other night say he met Razor up on Baxter. Gotta building up there, Eightieth an Baxter, used to be—"

"A taxidermist," she finished. Fucking duh.

"Had the thought maybe iffen we got people movin around up there—them from outside, dig, not from the docks—maybe word got back onto Edsel on shit worth pickin up."

She smiled at him, and didn't have to work hard to force that smile into her eyes, too, where he would see it and know it was for him. "I think that's a great idea."

"Aye?" He smiled, too, color finding his cheeks as it always did.

"Yeah."

"Aw, ain't that fuckin sweet." Bump poured himself a shot of something from a black bottle and downed it.

"Maybe Bump oughta fuckin leave, yay, givin you the private here?"

Chess glared at him, but Terrible spoke before she could say anything. Not that she really would, but she liked to think she would. "Oughta get us out there, have a look, aye?"

"Yeah, we will, but I haven't told you the best part yet. You know who owns the *Agneta Katina,* the ship? Kyle Blake."

Terrible looked about as surprised as she thought it was possible for him to look. "Him before? Marietta's father?"

"Yep." Grinning made her feel so fucking good, almost as good as the look in his eyes made her feel. "So he's behind this somehow, I guess. I don't know why he'd be doing anything down here or why he'd—"

"Kyle Blake?" Bump cut in. "He that stupid dame's father? You gimme the joke, yay? Ain't you knowing he?"

Wouldn't she have fucking said if she'd known?

She didn't say that either, though, just waited with her eyebrows raised.

Bump sighed and stood up, heading for the bar. Heading past the bar, actually, through the doorway on the left to what had to be his bedroom, because a woman's voice drifted out of it, too low for Chess to make out the words but with the tone unmistakable.

Bump gave her some kind of reply and appeared again in the doorway, holding something. A magazine. The financial magazine he'd been reading earlier, the one with the smug rich bastard on the cover. He tossed it at her. "Oughta pay you some fuckin attention on the world outside Terrible's bed, yay? Thought you had you a fuckin brain."

She ignored the insult—she barely heard the insult—because the rich bastard smirking at her from the cover wasn't just any rich bastard. It was Kyle Victor Blake:

millionaire real estate developer, afternoon drinker, khaki wearer, Downside hater, and father of Marietta.

She'd thought he looked familiar.

Terrible leaned closer to her, peering at the magazine. "He own the ship?"

"Yeah. He owns the company that owns the ship, so— I don't get it, though. Why would he— His corporation is huge, like almost a billion dollars huge. And it's legit. He's not laundering money or anything, at least not according to the Church."

"Maybe you Church ain't got they the fuckin knowledge on he, yay?"

"No. I mean, I guess it's possible, but the business records I could see are all intact, and because of its size the company is audited annually, the books gone through and everything."

Bump snorted. "Like anyall ain't can fuckin lie easy to you fuckin Church."

She glared at him. She shouldn't let him get away with that, she should say something. Tell him to fuck off. Ask him why, if Church employees were so fucking stupid, he kept forcing her to work for him. That would be a good start. Then she could tell him what an asshole he was, how much she—

Terrible lit a cigarette, closing his lighter with a decisive *click*. He didn't speak.

But Chess got the message. Right. "The point is," she said, still glaring at Bump, "he makes plenty of money on his legal stuff. There's no indication that he's ever been involved in drugs before. He seemed viciously anti-drug when we met him. So why would he start with this ghost-infected speed, using drugs to magically control people?"

"He a witch?" Terrible asked.

"No. No talent, either. After Haunted Week he was one of the adults—he was nineteen—who volunteered to be tested to see if they qualified for Church training, but he failed. Pretty badly, too. So he can't be the one doing the magic itself. And I didn't feel any on him when I shook his hand."

Bump shrugged. "Only meaning he had the fuckin hire-on, got he someself can fuckin do magic. Like me, yay, got you, Ladybird." His oily grin—half proud, half sarcastic—set her teeth on edge.

Terrible spoke before she could, cutting off the sharp reply she'd been ready to make. "Could be him ain't knowing on the magic, though, aye? Thinkin he just buyin straight-up speed, ain't got the knowledge it cut with ghost and shit?"

"Could be," she said.

Bump shook his head. "Nay, nay. Thinkin him got all the fuckin knowledge what him people sell, yay, got all the fuckin plan on why, too. Ain't fuckin stupid, him ain't. Bump got what him up on, too, what him fuckin plans be."

He waited, his eyebrows raised, giving his next statement the dramatic weight she guessed he thought it deserved. "Blake come to Bump, see, four, five weeks past, he done, looking for a fuckin deal. Wanting me fuckin sell Downside on, dig, sell him all I fuckin got, wanting fuckin take over, make he some fuckin developments and wha-the-fuck."

She was pretty sure her mouth literally dropped open. No. No way. Yeah, people were scummy and selfish and heartless, and yeah, people would generally crush their own mother's skull under their feet if it meant they could be rich or famous or whatever other bullshit people were raised to believe actually mattered. But if she was understanding Bump, what he was getting at, that couldn't . . .

Couldn't what? Right. There was nothing people couldn't or wouldn't do.

"He's doing it deliberately," she said. "He's turning them into zombies, he's controlling them so completely, he's getting them to kill each other. Or themselves. He's getting rid of all your customers to drive you out of business, to take over your territory."

Bump shook his head. "Ain't fuckin all, Ladybird. Ain't just me, neitherways. Bettin him gave Lex the fuckin chatter, too."

"Gettin em out of Downside all over," Terrible finished. "Ain't gotta worry on finding dead ones new homes, dig? Ain't gotta worry on em fuckin up you new building, squattin inside an all. Just clean the place out, tear it down, build all new on it. Like over a death-yard, aye? Him tryin turn Downside into some fuckin suburb, an he kill any tries stoppin him."

"So what you thinking, on that dude Blake? Got a thought why him wanting Downside so bad?"

They were in the Chevelle, Black Sabbath coming quiet through the speakers and the high afternoon sun in her eyes, heading for the building on Eightieth where Marietta Blake had apparently met Tagger. Whether they'd find anything there was another issue—and she doubted they would—but they'd be close enough to the docks to check out the *Agneta Katina,* as well, so that might be something.

"I don't know. He's done it before, I guess. Looks like this is the way he likes to work. Actually . . . listen to this."

She shifted in her seat, angled her body to face him more as she read from the magazine Bump had given her. " 'Blake's first major urban-rehabilitation project was in the former Wainwright area of Baltimore. After the 2013 riots he bought whole blocks of abandoned and empty buildings, converting them to modern housing and a now-thriving shopping district.' "

"Aye, got some recall on that. Thinkin he caused them riots?"

"I don't know. Maybe. Maybe it was just what gave him the idea. Easier to buy all that property when the people who should live there are gone. This is all about money. Who cares who dies, as long as Kyle Blake gets rich."

Terrible's mouth twisted: a half smile, half frown. " 'Salways all about money, baby. Everything."

She sighed and glanced around. The streets were even emptier than they had been before. From Sixty-fifth and Wallace onward she hadn't seen a single person.

Terrible said it before she could. "Awful fuckin empty up here. Ain't good, aye."

"It's not just me, then."

"Naw. Oughta be lots on the street, it bein hot out an all, too. Should see more."

"So they're . . . Do you think they're . . . ?" She couldn't finish the sentence. It didn't matter. He shook his head, the downward tilt of his lips and the look in his eye telling her he knew exactly what she was thinking. And thought she was right.

"Ain't thinkin them somewhere good. Don't like this one, Chessiebomb. Don't got the right feel to me." He hesitated. "Thinkin maybe oughta take you on ho—"

"No."

He glanced at her, then sighed. "Aye, right. Guessin you needing to see, anyroad."

"If there are any people on the ship who don't know what's going on—if any are honest, you know—I can get us on board with my Church ID, too."

"Wish we had us some other way find that dude Razor."

"I wish we had some other way to do all of this," she said, and immediately wished she hadn't when his brows drew together and his hands tightened on the wheel. Quickly she added, "I mean, I wish we had more information about Blake. I wish the Church could help us out."

He had to realize how lame she sounded, but thankfully he let it go. With the way he seemed to be feeling the last few days—at least since her little near-death fuckup—the last thing she wanted to do was give him another reason to keep an extra eye on her or worry about her.

"Any knowledge you can get on him, up you Church? Maybe get he records or whatany, like you get in you cases?"

"No. Um, I saw Elder Griffin earlier, but . . . he wasn't really in the mood to talk. I don't think he'd pull the records for me."

She felt him glance over at her while she kept her gaze pinned to the emptiness outside the window. She didn't want to talk about it. Didn't want to tell him. Damn it, wasn't it enough that he knew she'd had to tell Elder Griffin, that he knew Elder Griffin was angry at her, that he knew she'd fucked up and lost someone who mattered?

Why couldn't she just look . . . *good* to him? Like a good person, a worthwhile one?

He broke the silence. "Still ain't happy with you, aye?"

"No." They'd reached Baxter; she watched the ruined building on the corner swing on its axis as he turned the Chevelle. "No, he's not."

"Ain't turning you in, though?"

"No." She needed another subject. And more speed, right there in her bag at her feet, waiting for her. Beckoning her. Something to give the pills in her system a needed kick, because thinking about Elder Griffin was not exactly letting her relax into her high.

Of course, speed also fucked with her ability to feel

ghosts. Maybe not such a good idea. Damn it, what the hell was she supposed to do? Didn't she have enough shit in her head without all the extra baggage of the last couple of days?

Fuck that. She needed something, whatever it was. And she couldn't have it, and the whole thing sucked.

Terrible cleared his throat. "Ain't . . . Maybe not such a good time for pills, dig, might be—"

"I'm not— I know." Her face felt as if someone had poured gasoline over it and lit a match. Was she that fucking obvious? Shit, how much babysitting did he think she needed? "I'm not stupid, okay, I know where we are."

"Ain't sayin you is, baby, just—"

"I didn't even reach for my bag."

For a second she thought he was going to push it. No matter what she said, she sure as fuck had been thinking of grabbing her pillbox, and she knew he knew it; he knew her too well to doubt it. And if he pushed it, she'd— Damn it, what did he want from her? She'd already promised to be more careful, she'd apologized so many times already. She'd promised before not to get too fucked up when they were alone together. She'd already let him so far into her life, let him see so much . . .

Right. And he'd wanted in because he loved her. He'd asked her not to jump too far off the bridge, he'd been upset by the OD because he loved her and wanted to be with her. With *her*. What was the matter with her?

He wasn't trying to make her feel bad, either; this wasn't the time, and he had every fucking right to mention it. His life was in danger, too. Especially so, in fact, because he'd die before he let her get hurt, and that was something *she* knew about *him*. Something she never doubted.

"Sorry," he said, breaking the tense silence. "Sorry, ain't meant—"

"No. No, I'm sorry, I didn't . . . I'm sorry."

Some of the tension lessened. Some.

He pulled the car up onto the curb at Eightieth and Baxter, and when he shut off the engine she remembered something else they needed to do. "Hey, let me get that sigil on you, okay? We should have tried it last night, but I guess now's as good a time as any, right?"

He didn't reply, which she took as assent as she pulled her black chalk and her notebook from her bag and reached for him.

He caught her arm. "Chess . . . what I say afore. Ain't meant—"

"It's okay." She met his eyes and, like always, warmth sparked deep inside her, warmth that turned into some kind of strength. Fuck, she was so lucky. "Really. I shouldn't have snapped at you. I—yeah, I was thinking— it's just been a really shitty day."

"Aye. No worryin on it." His hand squeezed hers for a second before letting go. "C'mon, let's us get movin. Sooner we done here the better."

"Right." Where to put the sigil? His right arm was probably the best place, since he didn't have much empty skin on his left. She turned his hand palm up and slid her fingers from his wrist to the crook of his elbow, over the smooth skin, the hard muscles beneath. His pulse pumped steady under her fingertips.

"Got me some ideas, you thinkin on places you want you a better look at."

She grinned. "I bet you do."

"Only tryin give you the help."

"Uh-huh." But she squeezed his arm, held his gaze a few seconds longer. Unfortunately, the fact that the street looked empty didn't mean it was empty, or she would have kissed him.

Too bad anything—anyone—could be watching, and

chances were that whoever it was, they weren't friendly. They never were.

Instead, she looked into his eyes long enough for him to know what she was thinking, long enough to see she wasn't the only one thinking it. And then she got to work.

She knew the sigil already, of course. She'd helped design it; she'd sweated and worried over every line. That didn't stop her from double-checking it, from making absolutely sure she was putting it on right, throwing as much power as she could summon into it as she inscribed the thick black lines onto his flesh.

He shifted in his seat, and she glanced up. "You okay?"

"Aye. Just . . . Aye, I'm right."

"You sure?"

He nodded. He looked okay, she thought. Not too pale or anything. Was he flushed, maybe, his eyes a little bright?

The first time she'd ever marked him—back at Chester Airport, almost eight months before—he'd reacted, she remembered. And so had she. That same tingle sliding its insidious way up from her pelvis, subtle enough that she barely felt it but strong enough that she couldn't help but notice it.

Yeah. His left hand, resting on her knee, tightened; that was it, all right. And nothing to do about it, at least not for a while.

So she finished. The distant snap of the sigil setting vibrated for a second in her chest. "That should do it."

"Aye?" He inspected the swirling lines she'd scrawled on his arm, halfway between elbow and wrist. "Cool."

Nobody had ever just believed in her like that before. Nobody outside the Church, anyway. That was a high in itself, one that never got old.

Too bad it wouldn't be enough. Not for the experience she thought they were about to have.

Not for the experience Terrible apparently thought they were about to have, either. She stood at his side and watched him load himself up with weapons from his trunk; knives tucked everywhere, brass knuckles and chain in his pockets.

Last was the gun. He inspected the clip, glanced at her, shoved it in. "Here."

"What?"

He held it out to her, low down so the car hid the gesture. "Take it, aye? You only got that blade, oughta have more."

She looked at it, trying to suppress a twinge of superstitious fear but not quite managing it. That was the gun. *The* gun, the one she'd killed the psychopomp with. It sat there in his hand, staring up at her with its impassive steel eye.

When she glanced from it to Terrible she found him watching her just as blandly. Yeah, he knew.

She took the gun. It fit awkwardly into the pocket in her bag where she kept her asafetida and graveyard dirt, the stuff she grabbed most often.

"Guessin you ain't got a better place for it."

"Nope." Not unless she wanted to leave it sticking halfway out of her pocket or she wanted to carry it. Which she didn't.

"Aye, then." He stepped back and slammed the trunk closed. "Let's go."

Chapter Twenty-two

> From the oceans they rose, from the hulks of long-gone ships, from deep beneath the water's surface. And they walked to shore with murderous intent.
>
> —*The Book of Truth*, Origins Article 64

They found the doorway without any trouble, about halfway down the alley. Part of the door itself still tried to cover the empty space; they slipped past it and into what had once—obviously—been a taxidermist's shop. It was now something between a squat and a room for anyone wanting a little privacy—for any number of reasons. It smelled like a dead man's bathroom.

Hardly any light made its way through the holes scattered among the filthy windows just below the ceiling, but it was enough for her to see footsteps in the inch-thick dust on the floor, smears from movement. Lots of movement. Whether it was from their mysterious new pal Razor or Kyle Blake himself or whomever else, she couldn't say, but the few bones and teeth still lying around made it easy to believe Edsel had been there.

She said as much to Terrible, and he nodded as he headed toward another doorway near the back.

No windows beyond the door, which had been some sort of workshop. She could guess what kind, too. More bones there, but recent ones; rodents and scavengers that became trapped after following the scent of death. The scent that still hung in the air and itched her nose.

All of the good stuff had been taken, but that didn't stop her from switching on the flashlight from her bag and peering into the dull plastic bins along the wall. No. Just some unidentifiable bones, no skulls or spines or anything she could consecrate for herself and use. Damn.

"Chess."

"Yeah?"

"C'mere."

She followed the beam of his light to the opposite corner. Hmm. Another door.

In the floor.

"Clean on them edges," he said. "Like been opened some, dig."

She leaned closer. "Yeah. Shit."

"Lemme go, aye? Check it out. Know you ain't like the downs, no—"

"No, I can't—I have to see it anyway, if it's related to the magic or if there are ghosts down there or something."

"It feel like magic in here?"

"No. There isn't any. But who knows what could be down there, you know? They could have iron plates or whatever to block it."

He shrugged.

She knelt by the door—trapdoor, really—to get a closer look. It was locked, but that wasn't a problem; she had her pick case. And, yeah, she definitely needed it, because those marks were fresh. The areas at the edge were free of dirt and dust, and there were signs of movement in what covered the rest of the floor. "Let me just get it open."

He held the light for her while she picked the lock but grabbed her hand before she could lift the handle. Oh, right. He might have to let her go down there, but no way would he let her go first.

Please let it be just a little storage area, a few feet deep, maybe, where they'd scooped out some of the dirt the Church had filled it with, please— No. No, of course not.

It was a tunnel, a tunnel breathing warm foul air at her. It was a damp ladder covered with dirty shoe marks, covered with a faint greenish tinge of mold. "Fuck."

"Aye. Ain't good."

"No, it isn't."

He crouched beside her, leaning over the empty space to shine the light down into it. "Ain't see shit in there, just empty. Tunnel, though, keeps goin."

He didn't wait for a reply; by the time she'd opened her mouth, he was halfway down the ladder. He was going first this time, then. Last time they'd done something like this he'd dropped her down, and she'd hurt herself, and . . . Her body heated at the memory.

Terrible was obviously remembering, too. His hand slid up her thigh as she climbed down. "You wanna get them jeans you got off again, you just gimme the say."

"Ha, no." But she paused long enough to lean over and kiss him, still amazed somewhere deep inside that she could do so, that he let her. That he kissed her back, his hand finding her neck and resting there.

"C'mon," he said. "Lessee what we got waitin for us."

Nothing. At least that was what she thought at first, as they picked their careful way along the rough slimy tunnel floor. And it was a tunnel in the most basic sense of the word, a narrow hallway crudely hacked out of solid earth; not like Lex's tunnels, which had been built for utilities or the train or something back before Haunted Week and had cement walls and floors and fluorescent lighting in places.

This tunnel wasn't flat. It wasn't even. It jogged oddly to the left once or twice before resuming the same trajectory; Chess couldn't figure out why.

"Light posts or some shit, guessing." Terrible shone

the light up and to the side, toward the outcropping of solid dirt. "Thinkin we under the road."

"Oh, right." She looked ahead again as they reached another curve. Probably the last curve, because bright light emanated from it so the end couldn't be much farther. "Shit. That means we're headed straight for the bay, doesn't it?"

"Aye."

"And that means—"

His hand on her arm cut her off. In the same motion he switched off the flashlight, tugging her to the side.

A few seconds of silence. More than a few, really. Enough for her to lose track, enough for her to become aware of her heart hammering in her chest.

Terrible glanced at her, tilted his head to the side. Had he heard something? She hadn't, but, then— Oh. Yes. He had heard something. She leaned forward enough to see a man—one of Razor's, she assumed, one of Kyle Blake's—climbing from the bay into the tunnel, silhouetted by the blank bright blue behind its mouth.

Terrible pressed his palm against her thigh for a second, a "stay here" gesture, before making his silent way up along the rough wall.

The guy looked up. "Hey! What—"

Chess watched him fall. Watched Terrible pull bungee cords out of his pack and hog-tie the guard, stuff a bit of dirty rag into his mouth. "Oughta hold he a bit," he said, shoving the guard farther away from the lip of the tunnel, back into the shadows. Back where the guy probably wouldn't accidentally roll off and drown.

"Are there any more?"

He glanced behind him. "Bettin so. Ain't can see em, but gots us a little boat here, get us onto the *Agneta*, guessing, so . . . were I handlin it, be more men waitin there."

She slid her hand across his back as she stood beside

him, looking down a few feet at the surface of the water, the sunlight glinting off it so bright it felt like an attack. The "little boat" he mentioned—a dinghy? A raft? Some sort of *boatlet*, anyway, something that looked like a toddler's bath toy—bobbed below. "Yes, but they're not as smart as you."

He snorted.

"Hey, if they were smart they wouldn't have come here—against you—in the first place, right?"

He shrugged. Casually, as if it didn't matter, but color started on his neck just the same, so subtle she wouldn't have noticed if she hadn't been watching for it. Expecting it. "C'mon, let's get us over there. Longer we stand here, better odds we get seen."

She squinted up at the pale steel side of the *Agneta Katina* rising skyward and stumbled against the wall, digging in her bag for her sunglasses, ignoring the gun butt rubbing against her arm.

"So this is like a private entrance, huh, for Razor or Blake or whoever?" She glanced back at him. "And how do you always have your sunglasses ready?"

"Don't carry as much shit as you."

"Uh-huh." Found them! She slipped them on, smiling. "I get there in the end, though."

He dipped his head in acknowledgment. "Know you do, Chessiebomb."

With the dark lenses shielding her eyes from the horrible screaming sun, she was able to get a better look at the ship before them, a line of other ships stretching to the left and the right. They were so still, looming over the end of the tunnel, glaring at her—at the world. They were so aggressive, as if any second they were going to start advancing onto land and slicing through it, flattening anything and everything that got in their way.

She'd never been on a boat before. Not ever.

She and Terrible stood right at the end of the docks,

or, rather, right below them; she guessed the tunnel opened about five feet below the ground. Guessed, too, that when night fell it would be full of water, because she thought the tide usually came in around sunset, and the bay wasn't far below the tunnel floor.

That water, dark and murky and smelling of waste. The unblinking cruelty of that sharp sky. And the ships, a long row of steel walls, silent towers rising dead gray against the blue.

They looked abandoned. Not a soul on any of them—not a living soul, at least. Every one of them stood butted up to the docks, as silent and cold as wrapped corpses against a Crematorium wall.

But what might be lurking inside . . . That she didn't know. Wouldn't know until she went inside, and the frown on Terrible's face told her he'd had the same thought.

Terrible hunched his shoulders, touched her arm. "Figure be a private way in or aught like it. Guessin we find out."

"Yeah." One last glance at the boats, menacing her from a sort-of-safe distance, and she shouldered her bag more securely. "Okay, let's go."

They managed to get into the dinghy-thing without too much trouble, except for the splinter digging into her palm from gripping the bare wooden slats that functioned as seats. The boat moved beneath them, shifting when they shifted; it dipped down low when Terrible climbed in, and terror raced up her spine. The water beneath them . . . so dark and murky, stinking of dead fish and slime and sea monsters or whatever the fuck was down there. She eyed it with distaste.

"Witches ain't like the water, neither? Or just you?"

"I don't like it," she said, wishing she had a better excuse. "I mean, I've never been on it before. But I don't think I like it."

"Aye. Neither me." But he picked up the lone oar from the bottom and used it well enough.

At least from what she saw. She closed her eyes after they started moving. Watching the dock recede, even just a few feet—it was horrible, and the water was horrible and boats were horrible, and she'd rather be doing anything, anything, other than sitting in that dinky block of wood being tossed around like a speck of dust in the breeze.

"You right, there, baby?"

"I'm fine," she said, without opening her eyes. Yeah, it sucked looking like a pussy, but she didn't think she could open them. Hard enough feeling as if her insides were tumbling over each other—in a bad way—when she couldn't see. She had some vague suspicion that if she actually saw the horizon jumping around like an old movie, she'd be sick.

"Almost there, dig."

"Great. Then what?"

"Guessin be a door, a ramp or ladder or whatany like that. Them gotta get on someways, aye?"

The boat veered beneath her; she heard him doing something but didn't know what, and she dared to open one eye. Sure enough, the steel wall of the *Agneta* had a hole in it, a small door—what looked like a door—cut into the side. A short rope ladder hung from it, and Terrible was tying the boat to it. "Get you up first, aye? Rather me, only wanna— You know."

She swallowed. Hard. He wanted to be there to catch her if she fell, didn't want to knock her into the water if he did. Man, she wished she were doing something else. "Yeah, okay."

The docks themselves were empty. Not a single person stood on them. Not a single person on dry land saw them sitting in the little boat—at least, if there were people, she didn't see them. No one moved. A ghost town.

Chess focused her gaze on the tower at the edge of the dock, a sort of radio or control tower or something, a steel spire poking the sky. It wasn't very tall, maybe twenty, twenty-five feet or so, but it was a steady point to look at while Terrible finished his knot and helped her stand up.

Climbing from the rocking boat onto the first damp, dirty rope rung was bad. Climbing up the ladder itself, her knuckles scraping the side of the boat while it tried to twist beneath her, was worse. Her hands and feet were numb from fear, although the ladder was only four or five rungs; hardly a ladder at all.

It was tied to some sort of thick bolt or post set in the floor, several feet back from the doorway. The rest of the room was clear. No one stood there, no one watched or waited.

Her feelings came back the second she dragged herself onto the steel floor. A shame, that, because what she felt wasn't good. Not at all. Dark magic, death magic, washing over her in a wave of sorrow and filth, nearly making her already unhappy stomach crawl out of her throat.

She gasped and tried to swallow it, without much success. Or, with success—she wasn't sick everywhere—but she didn't think that was going to last.

Terrible slipped over the edge to stand beside her. "Feelin off, aye?"

"You feel it, too?"

"Feel somethin. Ain't so bad, though." He colored a little. "Ain't like what it were, thinkin. Like maybe be worse afore."

"Before the sigil."

He nodded.

Footsteps came toward them, down the hallway to the right. They stood in a plain room with bare dingy walls and scuffed flooring. Chess imagined this was some sort of loading area; it didn't look like the sort of place the boat's millionaire owner would visit.

Terrible threw himself against the wall, pushing her to the side so he stood between her and the door. His knife shone in his left hand, down low against his thigh, ready to be lifted and used when the door opened.

Which it did. Terrible lunged, his right arm wrapping around their visitor's throat, the knife held just below it so the sharp tip could be felt.

"Where's Razor?" He jerked his arm back, tightening his grip on the man's throat before loosening it again. "Where?"

"I don't—don't know—"

A driblet of blood sprang up under the knife's point. "Ain't bother me iffen I kill you now, go find he myself."

The man gasped; when he looked at Chess, she forced herself to keep her face impassive. "I—think he's in the captain's room. Think he is."

"How we get there?"

"Be all guarded, you ain't getting in, just to say—"

The blood ran faster down the man's throat as Terrible widened the cut. "How we get there?"

"Two—two doorways down this hall, up three floors. First—first door on the left, you—"

He tumbled to the floor, out cold from Terrible's fist to the top of his head. Chess didn't need Terrible to tell her to keep a lookout for more while he tied the man up as he had the one in the tunnel, and shoved him into the corner.

Together they moved down the hall, the power in the air growing stronger with every step, until they reached the first doorway. It opened onto a staircase, its sick energy breathing at her like bellows of evil.

Terrible paled a bit but shook his head when she opened her mouth. "Feelin it, aye, but not so bad."

Something had to be close. The open stairway led

both down and up carpeted steps, and foulness filled the air. Nothing to obstruct whatever magic was happening near the stairs, then, on whichever floor it happened to be. They'd have to look for it—if they couldn't get Razor to talk.

For the first time the idea came to her that this could be it, that the sorcerer could be on the ship and they could catch him and end the whole fucking mess. She didn't have a lot of hope that would be the case, no, but it was possible. And she could really use some kind of positive thought at the moment.

The second doorway—the second staircase—felt as bad as the first. And was just as empty. Terrible leaned close to mutter, "Ain't got the right feel to me. Oughta be more here, dig, more men."

"What do you think is going on?"

He glanced at her, nodded toward her bag. "Thinkin they on the wait, dig. Get ready."

He was right. Her shaking hands found the gun, had just pulled it from her bag when she and Terrible hit the top of the stairs.

And found an army of magic-controlled zombies waiting for them.

The zombies didn't make a sound. They moved en masse, their silence adding to the horror of it. Terrible started shooting; she started shooting, knowing it wouldn't make a difference, that they wouldn't feel it. Realizing, too, as she squeezed the trigger, that she was shooting at innocent people.

A couple of them fell. Blood splattered everywhere, on the walls, on the low ceiling, on the steel floor. None of the bespelled victims noticed it. None of them looked, none of them reacted, and tears in her eyes blurred their faces as she looked at them. They were just people, people who'd made a mistake, people who'd gone chasing a high and found magic and death instead.

Terrible pushed into the crowd of them; they clutched at him with bloody hands, swung at him with slick weapons, pipes and bats and wrenches. She kept squeezing the trigger, knowing the gun was empty, not knowing what else to do, until Terrible reached back to grab her hand and started dragging her along behind him.

Ow! Fuck, they were— A blow glanced off her shoulder, off her leg. Searing pain in her arm; a blade, someone was slashing at her, and blood ran down her hand to the floor. Shit, that wasn't good. Magic in her blood, magic connected to her, and no time to clean it up. No time to even think about it, because stopping to think about it would probably mean dying.

She stumbled and almost fell, only Terrible's grip keeping her semi-upright. The magic around them, the thick choking miasma of it, clogged her lungs, clouded her brain. Thank fuck he was standing, the sigil was working, he was still moving.

Moving well enough to run, in fact. He ran down the hall, his footsteps pounding on the carpeted floor, and she ran with him, trying without success to hold her arm tight enough to stop the bleeding.

The horde followed. Not running as fast, no, but following behind, close enough that fingers touched her back once or twice.

They reached the next staircase. Terrible yanked her into it, pushing the door behind him. It didn't close all the way, of course—they were being chased too closely for that—but she appreciated his attempt. As much as she could appreciate anything, at least, because her stomach churned and her breath came in awful harsh gasps, burning her lungs. She fought to keep going up the stairs, up one flight, then two, and when they reached the top of each more of the bespelled appeared, more followed them, reaching for them with hands controlled by someone else. Fuck, how many of them were there?

Stupid fucking question. Half of Downside was there—or maybe not that many, but there was a reason the streets were so empty.

They'd reached the top of the third staircase. She thought it was the third, assumed it was, because Terrible spun around into the hall and ran to the right, back toward the end of the boat. Back toward the way they came, since they'd gone one stairway too far; back toward—she guessed—the captain's room where Razor was supposed to be.

She was right. The hall outside an open door was stuffed with people, silent blank-faced people standing perfectly still. Waiting for them.

Terrible stopped short, his hand on her wrist. "Got any magic you can do?"

"No, I— Wait." Blood dripped from her arm and trailed behind her. The bare feet of the bespelled were touching that blood, stepping in it. Iron filings and iron-ring water had weakened the spell before, right? Not enough, but a little?

And the key, the one Edsel had given her. The key connected somehow to whatever magic was being done.

She had to separate those bodies from that magic. Had to break the magical connection controlling their souls, the magic-bound ectoplasm, the— Her glance fell on Terrible's arm. Terrible's sigil.

An overload of magic interrupted the energy of the sigil holding his soul in place. Only for a second, yes, and not permanently, but long enough to make him—to make his soul escape.

So maybe, if she could somehow send a jolt of *extra* magic through the bodies, she could disconnect them from the magic holding them?

It probably wouldn't last, just as Terrible's soul always came back because of the sigil. But it might confuse the zombies. It might give her and Terrible the few seconds they needed to get away.

"Maybe," she said. "Maybe I do."

Or maybe she didn't. She probably didn't. But what the hell. She could at least make the attempt, right?

Footsteps on the stairs behind them; they'd managed to put some space between themselves and their attackers, but not much. Not enough.

Or so she thought, until Terrible kicked open a door to her right and pushed her through it, slammed it behind them.

She didn't need him to tell her they didn't have much time. She was already digging in her bag, yanking out everything and anything she could think of. The key, tingling in her palm. Some powdered crow's bone, some sapodilla seeds, some goat's blood—that could work, mixed with her blood.

She needed more than that. She didn't have more. It would have to do.

She set her firedish on the floor, moving as quickly as her shaking hands would allow. The door started vibrating: fists of the bespelled beating it, shaking it in its frame. Shit, shitshitshit, hurryhurryhurry . . .

The herbs went in the firedish. She touched her lighter to them, blew on them gently to make them catch faster, and pulled out her knife. "Power to power, these powers bind."

The door shook harder. Terrible braced his back against it. They were in some kind of storage room, some kind of closet; she had the vague impression of brooms and mops and shit like that, the smell of ammonia and bleach stinging her nose.

Stinging her nose and mixing with the sharp fragrance of the herbs in the firedish. Okay. She set the point of her knife against her left pinkie and sliced. Not enough blood from that; she knew there wouldn't be. She braced herself and set the point of her knife against the wound in her arm and dragged it, widening the cut so blood flowed faster, ignoring the stinging pain. Her blood fell on the burning herbs as she waved her arm over them, droplets sizzling and smoking, billows of smoke rising to make her eyes burn even more than they already did from the pain.

She moved her arm to the side so it dripped on the floor. Shit, she hoped this worked, because if it didn't—

The door cracked in the top corner, big sharp splinters falling to the floor. She looked up at Terrible.

Their eyes met. In them she saw that same confidence she always saw, his confidence in her. Biggest mistake he'd ever made, wasn't it, trusting her? When she had no idea what she was doing—no idea in their relationship, and no idea at that moment, pulling some vague theory for a spell out of her ass and gambling on it saving their lives.

Fuck, please let this work. . . . Please let her know what to do.

The smoke thickened. Her blood covered the floor. She dumped the vial of goat's blood into the puddle, emptied her little packets of herbs, grabbed the key. Time to go.

She looked up at Terrible again, holding out her hand for him to take. Really looked at him, knowing it was a second they couldn't spare but needing it. Needing to say something to him one more time, even if she couldn't say it out loud. Needing to see him do the same thing, needing and getting that second or two when everything stopped around them and his skin was warm against hers, when the strength of his fingers was like strength in her soul and just touching him, knowing he was there, made her feel so *safe*. Even then, even knowing she was very possibly about to die . . . he was there, and she was safe as long as he was.

Her lungs ached from the hot smoky air she sucked into them, one last deep breath, and she nodded.

Terrible opened the door.

He stepped back, yanking her to her feet and to the side as the crowd pushed into the room. The movement sent fresh pain shooting up her arm, sent droplets of blood flying off her arm. Good. The more of it she could get to touch them, the more she could spread around, the better.

Especially better was the sight of the bespelled slipping on her blood, falling, their bodies hazy outlines in the clearing smoke. Her blood, strengthened with energy and herbs, touching them—it might be a start. She hoped it was a start.

In her shaking left hand she still held the key. She didn't really know how to use it, but she had it. Maybe— Yes, worth a try.

The room was full. Terrible tugged her out through the doorway, punching his way through the crowd, kicking at those who fought back. Hands pulled her hair, more hits on her head and limbs, more pain. Twice on the top of the head, fast and hard so her vision jangled and her knees buckled.

It was just the two of them, just her and Terrible in the center of a horde of grasping hands and blank faces. The key burned her skin; it hurt. It burned and hurt because ghost magic and iron didn't mix, and the key was both. It burned her skin because she was pushing her own magic into it, and that didn't mix.

It wasn't safe to do it. It could overload her, could deaden her. Hell, it could kill her. But Terrible had to get out. She couldn't let him die there.

She sucked in a deep breath, hard, wishing to fuck there was something mixed in with it to calm her down. It was all down to her, she had to be the one. He was counting on her.

What words of power should she use? A Banishing spell, a— No. She was supposed to increase the power.

Hard to do with her heart pounding so hard and her chest so tight and her breath coming so fast, but this was her job. The one thing—well, okay, one of two things— she knew she could do. Knew she was good at, damn it.

So she took as deep a breath as she could, feeling her chest—her whole body—fill with every bit of power she could summon, ducked down, and shoved it all into the key. Into the key, into her blood, into the air already thick with smoke and magic. *"Garmarak kedentia ronlo prientardus!"*

The words shot heat, strong raging heat, up her legs, into her head, like a pot boiling over. Words to build and enhance magic, words to make it stronger, com- bined with everything she was pushing into the key— she shook, barely able to keep her fingers closed over the iron as it turned white-hot against the floor.

Power spread from it, though, radiated from it. She felt it racing along the floor, crawling up the walls and the legs of the possessed and into the air. She'd been right. She'd been right about her blood giving it a kick, increasing the power, been right about the smoke and the key.

But she'd also been right about the cost, about what it required, about how mixing magic with iron wasn't a great idea. Well of course she'd been right about that, it was one of the first things they learned in training, and when you considered that the iron in question—the key—was coated with ectoplasm-infused paint, it was worse. Iron and ghosts didn't mix, and by pushing her power through the paint, through the key and into the iron itself, she was trying to make it mix.

The iron rebelled. Her body rebelled. Fuck, it felt like she was dying; her insides twisted and writhed, and the key hurt to hold. Waves of blackness, dizzy and sick, washed over her, through her.

Her legs gave. She slumped to the floor, thankfully sparing her knees but not her forehead, which hit the steel with a painful thud. Her fingers burned. Her bangs stuck to her forehead from sweat; her already itching and tingling body felt sticky and slick from it.

Still she pushed. Still she drew power from everything and everywhere she could. It wasn't enough; it couldn't be enough. The floor weaved in her vision and burned her arm when she fell onto it. She barely noticed. All of her focus was on the key in her fingers, the horrible sick heat of it. She had to give more, there had to be more power somewhere, more power inside her.

Thudding in her ears: her heartbeat, the sound of her blood in her veins like waves crashing against the shore in a hurricane, louder and faster. Her lungs didn't seem to work properly. Dizziness clouded her vision, made her feel as if she clung to the key in the middle of a swirling vortex, a hellish merry-go-round that threatened to fling her off into nothingness at any second. She was weakening, she was losing . . .

The floor beneath her vibrated, but was that from falling bodies or just because she was shaking? Looking up would be a good idea; she should look up, should check and see what was happening, but it seemed like an impossible thing to do.

And she wasn't sure she wanted to, either. She'd been trying to override the spell, trying to override a spell like Terrible's sigil; what if she'd done so and done it so well he'd never come back? Yes, Elder Griffin's sigil had been holding—but for how long?

How long had she even been there? It felt as if she'd been lying on that floor for hours, for days, as if her muscles had frozen in that position and she'd never be able to move again.

But she did. Through the illness, the wavering vision that distorted everything, she saw bodies staggering, falling, and getting back up. Not enough. It wasn't enough, fuck, she wasn't strong enough, she was going to die. She and Terrible were both going to die.

That wasn't good enough.

She turned back to the key, focused on it as much as she could. Words of power came to her choked, dry throat; she croaked them out, not really feeling as if they were helping but doing it anyway.

The City rose before her. The City of Eternity, the malicious dead waiting to sink cold hooks into her flesh. The darkness, the emptiness, the fear she'd never been able to express to anyone. It washed over her, flooded her system with horror.

But Terrible's life was on the line. Well, Terrible could die from the spell itself, if Elder Griffin's sigil failed to hold; was Terrible dying? She couldn't think of it, couldn't not think of it, and he was strong in her mind and her heart as she dug deeper, focused harder.

Somewhere inside her was a wellspring of hate. A small furious ball of it, a ball of rage and pain, the knowledge that she wasn't good enough and never would be, that she deserved all of the pain she'd gotten in her life, all of the abuse. She'd been born bad; she'd been born with something . . . something wrong with her, something she could never make right. She didn't belong in the world.

But she belonged with Terrible. He knew her and he still loved her, and damn he was wrong to do that but it was Truth, and she found that thought deep inside herself, a tiny nugget of gold buried in shit. She needed to do this for him.

So she turned that hate—those flashing horrible images of every one of them, all of them who'd hurt her, who'd used her, who'd laughed, who'd treated her like the garbage she was, into power. She took those images in her head and made them strong. She turned that love—and fuck, she did love him, she'd never in her life met anyone who made her feel the way he did—into power, and shoved it with all of her might into the key.

Her heart skipped in her chest; she heard it in her ears. Too much power. She couldn't handle it. Red lights exploded in her eyes, in her head, searing pain shot through her.

And above it all was the power making her shake, the endless, bottomless well of emotions inside her turned to energy so strong she couldn't stand it, so strong it ripped her apart. She was afraid to let it go, afraid to let it take over, afraid to let it have what it wanted because it wanted her, all of her, everything. It would consume her soul if she let it.

She didn't let it. Instead, she pushed it into the key as hard as she could. It reverberated out from there; she felt it hit her blood, hit the walls, hit the floor, wrapping her in her own power, changed from what it had passed through. Her heart kicked so hard in her chest she thought she would die. Maybe she was dying, because blackness rolled through the room, obscuring everything, coming to claim her, and she collapsed into it, exhausted, and let it have her.

Chapter Twenty-three

"C'mon, Chessie, open yon eyes, know you awake, c'mon, gotta—"

Movement. She was moving. She was lying down, but she was—running. Terrible had her in his arms and he was running down the hall, that awful narrow hall on that ship, and when she opened her eyes she caught a glimpse of the ceiling above her, of Terrible's worried expression, before she closed them again.

He turned and stopped; a pause while his body jerked and a door slammed. He must have kicked it shut, and the sound of it brought it all back: the bodies, the magic, the pain in her arm and in her mind and soul, the dizziness and the clearing clouds.

And the knowledge that it had worked. Somehow it had worked.

A new voice, one she hadn't heard before: "Hey! Who the fuck—"

Terrible set her down, rather less gently than usual, but she figured that could be excused when she heard the sound of a fist slamming into flesh. She opened her eyes to see a man fall, Terrible standing over him, ready to deliver another blow.

The man on the floor—she guessed he was Razor, seeing as how his shaved head had images of razor blades tattooed onto it—glared up at Terrible. His right hand reached back toward his pocket, where the handle of a knife protruded; Terrible kicked his arm away before he reached it.

"You Razor, aye? Came to have a chatter with you."

"Don't want to—"

Another kick. "Ain't give a fuck. Just come to give you some knowledge you needing, dig? Get outta Downside. Take you boat and whatany other shit an get the fuck out."

Razor wiped at the thin line of blood trickling from his nose. "Don't think you unnerstand, see, I gots me—"

The snap of a gun being cocked, and Terrible stood aiming at Razor's head. "Naw, thinkin you the one ain't understand. Don't give a fuck who backin you, payin you bills. Done now."

Razor glanced at Chess, back at Terrible. His hands rose into the air—the universal "Please don't hurt me I'm not armed" pose—but something in his eyes, in the set of his mouth, bothered her. He didn't look worried. He looked like he had an ace up his sleeve.

And the door wasn't locked.

Chess got up on unsteady legs and wobbled toward it. Anybody could walk in, and when Razor's voice followed her, she knew that's exactly what he was counting on. "Hey! Where you going, bitch? This—"

She'd been expecting another kick, another punch. She hadn't been expecting the gunshot or Razor's thin, high screech. The lock clicked shut; Razor writhed on the ground, squealing, clutching at his shin.

"Don't see what you so fuckin pissed about," he said, when his whining subsided. "Know that boss of yours got a big offer, plenty of cash, and shares in more later.

Plenty of cash. Were you I'da taken it, cause this way you don't get shit."

"What about the people?" Chess couldn't keep her mouth shut anymore. "What about all those people you're killing, turning into fucking zombies? Do they get money? Or no, they get to die, right?"

"The fuck you care?" Razor's brows drew together. "They just junkies. So they die, so what? Ain't like they worth a shit, they—"

Another gunshot report slammed off the walls, another scream from Razor.

"Just gimme the tell." Terrible's voice was cold, as cold as Chess had ever heard it, and anger poured out of his mouth along with it. "Who the one does the magic? Tell me now, maybe you live, dig. Iffen you don't . . . I put more holes in you, throw you in the bay."

Razor glared at him again, the kind of glare Chess had gotten used to seeing when it came to Terrible: the kind that started defiant, then turned to fear and acquiescence. Good. Fucker. As if he was any better. As if he could judge anyone, any of those people in the hall, any of those people just trying to get through the day.

"Don't know," he said finally. "I just get the stuff. The speed an them walnuts I'm s'posed to give em. Tell em they good-luck charms. Dumb fuckin junkies believe it, fuckin wastes of life they all is. Scratch a junkie find a piece of shit, aye? Can you—"

The gun went off again. For the last time.

Chess and Terrible stood in silence while the sound echoed off the walls, in her ears, quieter and quieter until it finally stopped.

She didn't know what to say. Should she say anything, should she—

Terrible cleared his throat. "Guessin . . . guessin we oughta search in here, aye? See if we can find any useful."

"Yeah." It felt colder in there than it should; her body

felt weak and shaky, but whether that was from the magic before or from—well, from what had just happened, she didn't know.

Pause. "Maybe oughta sit you down, Chessie, still lookin kinda—"

"I'm fine."

"I can do all the—"

"I'm fine."

And she was. A little trembly, her movements a little jerky, but fine.

At least she was until she got around the heavy desk in the corner, closer to the tall steel cabinet behind it. The nuts were in there. They had to be, because magic practically haloed the thing, a dark smudge in the air she could almost see. "I think they keep the nuts in here."

"Aye?" She was used to him moving quietly, to him just appearing nearby, but she still jumped when he was suddenly at her side. She could have turned around, wrapped her arms around him, and held on, buried her face in his chest until she felt normal again.

Could have. But didn't. And she didn't because— She didn't know why. Because she was scared. Because he'd killed someone a few seconds before and she knew he didn't like it when she saw that, and she knew why he'd done it and he knew she knew, and she didn't know if he wanted her to say anything or what. So she avoided the subject. "Yeah. Let's get it open and take a look."

It wasn't locked. She half-expected the nuts to come pouring out when the doors opened, but no, they were in plastic bins—inert plastic bins—lined up on the shelves inside.

The energy, though, the malevolent power of them? That poured out of the cabinet thick and strong, a slow-moving tidal wave spreading over her body and making her shiver. She could practically feel each walnut inside as it— Wait.

Terrible grabbed her hand before she could touch the pile of nuts in one of the tubs. "What you doin?"

"I'm—I need to touch them. A couple of them. I think I figured something out."

"Ain't you wanting them gloves you got? Could—"

"No, I'm fine."

She wasn't fine. But she was right. She picked up one nut in each hand and held them at arm's length to her sides, feeling the connection between them arc through her body. "It's— They're connected. It's a mass control spell."

Pause. "Aye, ain't you—"

"No. Sorry, no, I didn't realize it before. How it works, I mean. Yes, it's a control spell, but it's all connected. Shit, of course it is, how did I not figure this out before, it's—" She caught a glimpse of his face, patient but maybe a touch confused, and forced herself to stop babbling.

"Sorry. Here's the thing." She set the walnuts on the floor, sat down in front of them. "It's a master spell. All of these, all of the nuts, are connected. The magic is connected, and it's connected to one particular master spell—one sorcerer."

"So . . . he uses this bag, runs he some other bags from it? Like them Lamaru brought the Dreamthief?"

"Yes. Well, no, not exactly, because those bags were set up as a fence, remember, to hold the Thief in place. But it's a lot like that. There's a master spell somewhere. The sorcerer transmits his intent into that one, and it goes from there to all of these, to the people holding these or who have one in their houses or whatever. Some people probably tossed theirs, or haven't been close enough to them for the spell to really take effect. But most of the nuts are out there, and the people who have them feel the command because it links to the magic in their bodies. They feel it and follow it."

"Aye, I dig." He lit cigarettes for them both. "Gives

em the drugs, they get the magic in they bodies. Then this one controls em, and he runnin the whole thing from he master bag?"

"Right. With the bags, he doesn't have to touch each person or anything like that. He just touches his bag or gives it a magical command or whatever, and the magic seeks out the other bags and the people with those ingredients in their system, and they follow the command. It creates a circle."

"They know? Like they feel what he wants doing?"

"No." That was the worst part. The horrible part—well, all of it was horrible, but this was the part that made her shiver extra hard, that made her cheeks flush. "They're completely driven by the drugs. They're not— They're probably not even conscious of it. It's like they're dead inside, like their souls don't exist. No free will, no nothing, they're just compelled."

If he knew how much that idea bothered her—and she was pretty sure he did, how could he not—he didn't say it. Instead he laid his hand on the top of her head, gave it a quick rub. "Fuck of a thing to do to people."

"Yeah. Um, yeah."

"Thinkin the master spell be in here? Doin all he work from here?"

"I know *he* sure as hell didn't have the ability to control the spell." She tipped her head toward Razor's corpse, lying on the floor with a look of surprise across his pockmarked face, the off-center bullet hole in his forehead like a third eye seeing right into the City.

"Aye? How's— Shit, I ain't even gave you the chance touchin him or whatany, see if he got magic." He shook his head, his gaze fixed on the floor. "Just got me so mad, Chessie, weren't—"

"It's okay." Why had she waited so long to touch him? That had been a stupid thing to do, because the second she did, the second her fingertips touched his throat, he reached for her, pulling her into his arms to hold her tight. Warmth spread through her body, giving her enough strength to hold him back just as tight. "It's okay, really."

"Aye, but still . . . coulda got more—"

She kissed him, not a long kiss—no matter how much she loved him, three feet away from a dead body, with presumably a gang of magic zombies waiting outside the door, was not the place for an extensive show of physical affection—but a solid one all the same. "We already know who's behind it, right? I can't think of any other information we needed from him."

He nodded, but she saw the doubt in his eyes. "Aye, well, see what else we can get here, anyway."

"Right." She pulled away. "Can you see on that top shelf? Something's up there. And maybe if there's anything on top of the cabinet, too."

"Aye. Got some here, lookin like ingredients, aye? Like shit you use."

"Here, let me—" she started, but it was too late. Thankfully all he brought down was another plastic tub, smaller than the others. "That's it?"

"Almost." He reached into the closet again, with his bare hand, and before she could tell him not to he grabbed whatever it was. She should have expected that; she did expect it.

What she didn't expect was for him to stagger when he lifted it from the bland ivory-painted metal on which it rested. What she didn't expect was for him to go pale. What she didn't expect was for him to . . .

To start glowing, to start *flickering*, was the best way she could think of to express it. As if his soul was throbbing inside his body, bigger and smaller, bigger and smaller, lit with the faint awful light that ghosts cast in darkness. As if his soul was getting stronger, trying to break out of his body.

What the fuck?

Chapter Twenty-four

> The possibilities are endless! Soon you'll be making magic as part of your daily routine, and you'll wonder why you waited so long to get started.
> —*You Can Do This! A Guide for Beginners,*
> by Molly Brooks-Cahill

His eyes found hers; she didn't think she'd ever seen fear in them before but it was there then, it was, and something inside her screamed before she could get her throat to make a sound.

He dropped the spell bag— It was a spell bag, the thing in the closet, that's what it was, fuck! At least he had the presence of mind to do that. Dropped it and stumbled away from the closet, his face ashy-pale.

She grabbed him and half-pushed, half-carried him to the chair at the desk, her muscles straining under his weight. He was fine, she knew; he was recovering his strength even as they moved, his color coming back, his eyes focusing again. But . . .

That wasn't supposed to happen. The sigil she'd designed with Elder Griffin had held. It had been tested under the strongest circumstances—at least the strongest ones she could imagine—and it had held.

So what the fuck was the spell in that bag, that it had done whatever the hell it had done?

"I'm right," he said, pushing her away even as he sat heavily on the slick leather seat. "Right up, Chessie, aye?"

But he wouldn't meet her eyes, and color crept up his throat, up his cheeks, past the thick sideburns reaching halfway down his jaw.

"What—" She looked down at the bag on the floor. What the fuck was in that thing, what had it done? "Are you sure, are you okay?"

He nodded.

The worst thing she could do was press the point. His humiliation clawed at her in the tiny space; she could feel how much he wanted her to ignore it and forget it. But she couldn't. She couldn't because it was her fault, because what Elder Griffin had told her about him dying echoed in her head like a fucking record that wouldn't stop skipping, and none of that would be happening if it weren't for her. She'd done this to him. She'd done this. No matter what magic had just occurred, this was her fault.

She'd loved him, and she hadn't been able to let him go, and that had destroyed him.

But she also needed to know what was happening, what had happened. "What—"

"Felt like . . . the lights started goin brighter, if you dig. Like doin speed or aught like it."

Okay. Okay, what did that mean? "That didn't happen before, right? When Lex's guy threw the speed at you, when you touched the bags. It didn't affect you like that."

He shook his head. His color had returned, she could see; he looked as if nothing had happened at all. So whatever it was, it only happened while he was actually touching the spell. Just like the passing out had only happened when he touched whatever magic he happened to be touching, and then only if it was dark magic.

But he had Elder Griffin's sigil on him, and that had kept him from passing out. He hadn't passed out, which meant his soul hadn't left his body.

The relief of that thought lasted about half a second. "You felt like you were getting stronger or something, was it like that?"

He shrugged.

"So—" She turned to the spell, still on the floor where he'd dropped it, and reached into her bag for her pick case. Time to cut the thing open, see if maybe something in there would explain it.

Terrible sat beside her—not beside her, exactly, a bit off to the side—and watched as she rubbed her sweaty palms on her jeans to no avail before forcing them into a new pair of latex gloves.

Powder. Speed? Powdered ectoplasm? She wasn't sure. Maybe if she could get a better look . . . "Can you turn the lights out?"

When darkness enveloped the room, it became clear that more than one type of powder was in the bag. Well, there were various other items she'd inspect in a minute, of course, lumps of dust-covered darkness ominous in their anonymity. But for the moment her focus was on the powder and on the fact that some of it glowed with ectoplasm and some didn't.

Next step. Yes, focus on steps, on the fact that she knew how to analyze a spell. That way she wouldn't focus on the panic threatening to rise from her stomach into her chest and head and make her freak out. Focus on the steps so she wouldn't focus on the sick waves of magic pulsing from the spell, so she wouldn't focus on the equal sickness of the mind behind it.

Her flashlight sat in her bag, right where it should be; she tugged it out and switched it on. Indirect light might show her some details, and she could examine everything more closely that way, too.

"Look. It's not all the same color."

He shifted at her side, leaning over—not too close,

she noticed, which was good, because she didn't want to have to tell him to be careful.

She gestured with a gloved finger. "See? This is ectoplasm, I guess—it's mixed with it, at least. That's why it's got a bluish cast to it. But this . . . this is almost green. Right?"

"Aye."

Her first instinct was to scoop some of it up into one of the inert plastic tubs she kept in her bag, but what was the point? By the time the Church could do an analysis—if she could even get them to do one, which she doubted—it would probably be too late, since she didn't think her chances of surviving the night were very good.

Oops, there she was, thinking about it.

She pinched some of the greenish powder in her fingers. Soft, like talc or something. Not mixed with speed, then. This was a substance of its own, on its own.

Terrible grabbed her arm as she started to bring her hand to her face. "What you doin?"

"I'm just—I need to see if it has a smell or something. It's really soft and it doesn't clump. So not only does that mean it's not mixed with speed, it means it's probably organic, if you know what I mean? It's not a chemical powder. And I don't think I've ever seen one that color before."

He pulled his hand away. The flashlight cast his face in faint yellow, highlighting the unhappiness of his expression. "Ain't in there for fun, though, aye? Ain't aught you should be breathin in."

"It's fine."

He had a point, though. So instead of bringing it close to her face, she touched it with her bare hand.

That sucked. A jolt of fiery energy, dark and angry, raced up her arm; her fingers went numb. That was some heavy shit.

Terrible obviously noticed—how could he not, when she flinched and made some sort of sound, she wasn't sure what? "You right? What's on there?"

"I—I'm fine, yeah." Fine except for the numbness creeping up her arm. What the hell was that shit?

She wiped her fingers on the carpet to get the powder off her skin. "It's really strong, whatever it is. It has its own power, I mean, not from the spell, although the spell might be making it stronger."

"You got what it is?"

"No." She shook her head, rubbed her fingers together in an effort to get feeling back. And to stall. She hated admitting to him that she didn't know something. "No, it's not something I've ever worked with, at least I don't think so."

"Thought there weren't aught you ain't worked with."

It had been at least five minutes since she'd kissed him, hadn't it? So that was as good a time as any. For a second the horrible magic in the room and the creepy tingling in her fingers disappeared, replaced by something else, something good, something that made her smile. Like a counterspell, like stronger magic that chased the weaker stuff away. The best kind of magic, the kind she'd do anything to keep. "No, we learn about dark magics and everything, but some of that's pretty rare. The Church absorbed a lot of it and—oh shit. That's it."

"What?"

"That's—right. Here, hold the light, okay?"

She shoved it into his hand without waiting for an answer and started pawing through the mess on the floor, rubbing the lumps clean on the rug so she could see what they were.

A shriveled chicken claw wrapped in cloth, soaked in dried blood to harden it. A ball of white wax stuffed with fingernail clippings and shreds of snakeskin. A short thick braid of hair, made from smaller braids, all different kinds of hairs, and stiffened with what she thought was the liquid equivalent of the greenish powder. A bent nail. Knotted threads.

"Serious shit, aye?"

"Yeah." She poked the braid with her bare finger to make sure. More aching numbness. "Yeah, this is . . . It's a blocking spell. Like an immunity spell, if that makes any sense? If you're holding it, then even if you have the speed in your system, even if you have a walnut, you won't feel the command. You won't feel the magic."

"Why? Why he needin something protect him, why he ain't just leave the speed alone, dig?"

"Don't know, really." There had to be something else. One other piece. "Maybe he likes doing speed. Maybe it's not supposed to just protect against the walnut spells but against any spell. Maybe it adds power to him somehow; that's possible."

She started sifting through the mess again with her gloved hand. Where was it, it had to be there . . . Yes!

A single hair, tied in knots. It vibrated at her through the latex covering her skin; her entire body felt it. It was nauseating. "And this is his."

Terrible leaned over to inspect the hair, which practically glowed in the flashlight's beam. "You do aught to he from it?"

"No, it's already been used in a spell." And she didn't want to, anyway. Didn't want to think what might happen if the Church found out about it, what something like that might do to her. She'd already thought of how some magic stained people, how it could change their energy. She didn't want that to happen to her.

Changing energy, like how she'd changed Terrible's, and how Elder Griffin had found out about it . . .

Sitting there staring at the foul mess of evil on the carpet suddenly didn't appeal anymore. Her skin crawled. She wanted to get out of there. Immediately. Didn't want to look at it anymore, didn't want to think about it anymore.

She had no choice on the latter, but she did on the former. She scooped up the spell ingredients as best as she could with her gloved hand, shoving them back into the spell bag. Might as well get one of those inert plastic containers anyway, and put everything into there. She might need it later; in fact, she would totally need it later.

She'd need some of that speed, too, if the awful dark suspicion blooming in her chest was right, and she was pretty sure it was.

She'd have to find the master bag and destroy it if they wanted to set any of those people free. She'd have to find the *sorcerer*, because he probably had the master bag.

And now she knew how to do it.

"Hey," she said, closing the lid of the tub and trying—probably failing—to sound cheerful. "At least we know where they're operating from, and we know who's in charge. That's something, right?"

"Aye." He sounded as if he wanted to say something more. Thankfully he didn't. "How you figure we get outta here?"

Right. All those people on the other side of the door, and no way she could overpower them a second time; she felt half empty inside, like a burned husk. "Maybe there's another entrance or something, a secret way out?"

"Givin me a wonder, though. How them make it past em all, dig? Razor an whoany he got workin for him. Ain't can have em de-magicked or aught like that afore he come in every time, aye?"

"Maybe the spell isn't about him. Or maybe they aren't on alert when—"

"Naw, naw. Don't see them havin time to call an

get the spell goin, dig, afore we got us on the boat. So ain't can be they s'posed to go after us for specific, aye? Thinkin them on the ready all the time, an Razor got some way he moves around that ain't disturb em or go near em."

She hadn't even thought of that.

But if that was the case—and she imagined it was, that he was right—she might have some idea how Razor did it.

She pulled the tub back out of her bag, shuddering at touching it even through the inert plastic. So gross, so foul, to use people like that, to enslave them like that.

Enslave them with a master spell that was around somewhere, connecting them to it, and she had a good idea how to find the sorcerer but she didn't know how much good it would do her. Yeah, her Church ID could get them back to Blake's house or the sorcerer's, maybe scare them a little, but she didn't have any authority to make an arrest and she sure as hell couldn't call the Squad and ask them to do it. They wouldn't believe her.

Even if she gave them the bag they wouldn't believe her, because it wasn't connected to Blake directly. The bag was connected to the sorcerer. To the walnuts, to the speed. Shit! "That's how they found them. The people in Bump's houses. Damn, that's how they traced them. They found them through the spell, they . . ."

She trailed off. He was not going to want to hear what she was thinking, not at all.

Terrible must have seen something on her face even in the darkness, or felt something in the quality of her silence, because he touched her shoulder. "What plans you makin?"

"What? Oh, no, just thinking about how I can use this to find the master bag, is all, and—"

"Chess." His fingers tightened. "What you planning?"

Damn him. Why did he have to know her so well?

"Um, I might be able to use the walnuts, or this, to trace back the magic and find him, but . . . to do it by using only the bag will take a while. Would take a while."

She licked her lips, tried to make her voice sound as steady and confident as possible. "But if I can connect with the spell, be part of it, and push it—"

"No."

"It's the only way I can—"

"Shit."

He stood up; his face was turned away from her. "Know what thought you got, aye. An don't— How the fuck I'm supposed to let you—"

"You don't." She stood up, too, and grabbed his arm with her bare hand. "You don't *let* me. This is the only way for me to find the bag and beat him. You know that. You know it could be anywhere, it could be on the ship, it could be in any room in any building—hell, it could be in a fucking helicopter for all we know. We don't have time to hunt it down like that. But if I can be part of his spell, I can turn his magic back onto him, I can—"

"End up like Samms," he finished. He still didn't turn around. "End up like any of em."

"That's not going to happen," she said—"she lied" would be more accurate, because she was pretty sure it was a total fucking lie.

But what choice did she have? Her, or hundreds of people? Her, or hundreds of people who didn't ask for what they'd gotten?

She'd had a choice. And she'd made it, three or four years before; she'd seen occasional use turning into chipping and from there turning into something more, and she'd agreed to let it have its way with her. These people might not have, not that way. And when it came down to her or them . . . who was the most worthless in that situation? Who deserved it the most? The people who didn't even know what was happening, the ones who'd probably never done anything to deserve it—never done anything truly bad—or her?

Not to mention . . . Terrible. And Lex. Another choice she'd already made. Some lives were just more important than hers. Some lives, she'd lose her own to save.

But he didn't need to know that. At least not yet. "Listen, I can handle this. I can protect myself. I know how. I have to do this, because we don't have time to do anything else. He's going to know we were here. He's going to know what I did to his little army, he'll know we found this bag, because of the type of spell it is. He's going to be looking for me. I have to find him first."

Pause. Long pause. "Iffen you right an he knows we finding the bag, he ain't waiting, aye? Whatany shit he planning, he start it now."

"Yeah, I—"

"So you got that Lex's man coming for me, aye? An iffen shit goes down tonight, 'swhen he do it. Tonight. In the middle of all else."

She'd hoped that wasn't going to be the case, but . . . "Yeah. I know."

"Means I ain't can be with you. When you do this." He glanced at her; his eyes glittered in the half darkness. "You ain't let me causen of the spell. An I ain't wanting to be, causen I ain't wanting to lead Lex's man right at you. Aye?"

"No. I have to do it alone, you're right. You can't— It shouldn't really affect you, but in case . . ."

He grabbed her, his strong hands on her upper arms, painfully tight. His mouth fell hard on hers, rough, his hand finding the back of her neck to fist in her hair and pull her even closer, forcing her to her tiptoes.

It hurt. She didn't care. She kissed him back just as hard, digging her fingers into his shoulders, forgetting everything else around her—around them—for that one long, sweet, painful moment.

They weren't going to be together during the fight. They weren't going to be accidentally separated as they had the month before, when Slobag's witch had made his move and when Terrible had made it in time for the ending. This was different, would be different. Terrible would be fighting for his life against the only man who'd ever come close to matching him, and she'd be—well, she'd be somewhere, fighting her own battle.

Probably losing her own battle. She hoped she wouldn't, but she knew she probably would; what the fuck else was going to happen? She could trace the magic back, she could destroy it, but whether or not she could survive it afterward . . . She'd barely managed to fight the magic on the ship, and this would be so much worse.

But as his arm wound around her waist, as she was filled with the smell of him, the taste of him, the feel of his body hot and hard against her, she didn't care. Because right at that moment she had him, and right at that moment she could finally let herself rest, could stop worrying, could get past all of the things that scared her and let herself go.

Even there, in that strange room, on time borrowed from someone else. They'd have plans to make and things to do when they left; every minute that went by was a minute stolen from the night's preparations— a minute they handed to Kyle Blake and his horde of zombie slaves.

It was worth it.

What wasn't worth it, unfortunately, was the idea of having sex next to a corpse. So she forced herself to break the kiss and step away, pushing at him with reluctant hands. "We need to go."

For a second she thought he was going to argue; then

he glanced over at Razor lying on the floor and nodded. "Aye. Right, then, let's get us movin."

Shaky again, her movements not quite as smooth as they should have been, she got the lid off the tub and held it in front of her like a serving platter. "Okay. Open the door."

Blank faces jumped to angry life when the door swung aside; angry faces changed to dull acceptance when she got closer to them. It worked. Holy fuck, it worked. It deadened them out, stopped them from attacking.

Stopped them within a few feet, at least. She and Terrible exchanged glances; his arm went around her shoulders, pulling her close to his side, as they made their way through the crowd. Outside the few feet around them, the bespelled pushed and lifted weapons; a few of those close to her fell, beaten over the head or kicked or whatever else by those outside the spell tub's sphere of influence.

It felt almost like walking down the aisle at a wedding, or what walking down the aisle looked like, anyway, since she'd never done it. Outside the protective circle, chaos reigned. Inside it, where she held Terrible close and he held her back, all was still and calm, the crowd parting so they could walk through it. She'd never experienced anything like it.

She hoped she never would again. Too bad that was as false a hope as—well, as just about any other hope, any other sweet lie people told themselves. She would have to experience it again, probably that very night, because what she'd told Terrible was true.

The sorcerer knew they were coming for him. And he was going to do whatever he could to get to them first.

Chapter Twenty-five

Into that great empty space beneath the earth's surface the Church placed those angry souls, and calmed them, and peace reigned above and below through the Church's power.
—*The Book of Truth*, Origins Article 75

Crawling down the rope ladder was even worse than crawling up it, even with Terrible below her steadying the thing as much as he could. The journey in the horrible little dinghy or whatever it was didn't seem any better, either, especially not since the sun had lowered in the sky. She didn't want to see the faint red streaks starting around it as ominous, but she couldn't help it. A bloody sky over Downside . . . Well, hell, when wasn't it, really?

But she couldn't suppress the shiver that ran through her when she looked at it, when she thought of it.

Back into the tunnel, completely dark now from the setting sun and with the floor under about an inch of water—Terrible tossed his earlier captive into the dinghy—and back up into the taxidermist's office. Shit, she just wanted to go home; she was so tired of trudging here and trudging there, of the whole mess— What the fuck?

Something flew at them; Terrible leapt forward and caught it. Again the sound of flesh against flesh, again Terrible fighting, and something thudded in her chest when she realized who he was fighting. Lex was there.

Lex and his assassin—Devil, or whatever the Cantonese word for that was. How the fuck did they get there?

She'd probably find out—at least, she hoped she would. Terrible's fist snapped Devil's head back. Devil's foot swept sideways, slamming into Terrible's leg just below the knee. Their anger, their violence, filled the room; she could feel them, beating against her skin, assaulting her, and fear crawled up her stomach to lodge in her throat.

It didn't last that long, even though every second of it felt like hours to her. Terrible hooked his foot around Devil's ankle, punched him in the face; Devil stumbled, bent over.

When Devil came up, he had something in his hand, something that gleamed dull in the low light. A gun.

Chess started to shout; before she finished drawing breath for it, Terrible's hand moved again, pulling his own gun. They stood there, glaring at each other. A standoff.

She acted without thinking. Not that it mattered; she'd have done the same thing if she had thought about it, if she'd stopped and considered all of her options.

But there wasn't time, because Devil and Terrible were glaring at each other, their hatred filling the dusty room, and she yanked the gun Terrible had given her from the pocket in her bag, pulled back the slide to cock it in the same movement, and aimed it.

At Lex. "Tell him to drop it."

Lex might have looked surprised. Then again, he might not have. He almost looked as if he was smiling. "Why?"

"What?"

He shook his head. "You ain't shoot me, Tulip."

"You want to bet on that?"

No. He'd better not want to bet on it, because she wasn't so sure herself. Not after what happened in his bedroom. Not when his fucking paid killer stood there only a few feet away from her.

She'd made a choice. She'd made it months ago. She hadn't realized—well, she'd realized, but not completely, if she was honest—how seriously she took that choice until that moment. Did she want to make it? No. Did she want to shoot Lex? Fuck, no.

But she would, and she knew it, and she let him see it in her eyes before she gave him an out. "We need to talk to you about what we found today and what's coming. Probably coming tonight. You need to know, because it affects you."

That solved the problem of how to suggest to Terrible that they might want Lex's involvement with what would likely happen later. But she was right about that. She knew she was. The drugs, the murders, had been on Lex's side of town, too, and just because they were all headquartered on the *Agneta Katina* didn't mean Lex's side of town wasn't going to have a problem.

"They're planning to take over Downside. All of Downside. That means you, too, Lex. And you can't stop them without me."

Nobody moved for a long moment. Chess's arms started to ache, but she couldn't let them falter. Couldn't let them move even the tiniest bit, because if they did, it would look like she was wavering, and Lex would see that as weakness.

Finally he sighed. "Aye, fine, then. Oughta all drop the guns, we should. Let's have us a chatter."

They stood inside the abandoned taxidermist's; well, where the hell else would they go? Wasn't like any of them wanted to be seen talking to one another on the street. Frankly, Chess was surprised Lex had shown up at the docks at all, but then she figured he'd heard how empty they were through one of his spies—or just through the rumor mill—and figured he'd be safe. Which he clearly was, since she half-expected tumbleweeds to roll down the streets.

Somehow that emptiness didn't make her feel any safer, though. Maybe it was the knowledge of what was inside the *Agneta Katina,* or the knowledge that the person or persons responsible—Blake and his sorcerer, Blake and his gang—could be watching from any one of the blank-faced buildings lining the streets.

Or maybe it was that Devil watched Terrible like a beast about to pounce, and Terrible watched both Lex and Devil in exactly the same way, and she thought she might very well drown in the sea of furious testosterone and repressed violence filling the space in which they stood.

But they were standing, and Terrible caught her eye, gave her an almost imperceptible nod that sent relief flooding through her system. Good. At least he knew why she was doing what she was doing. Why she was telling Lex what they'd found, which she did in the quickest way she could, concluding with, "So Blake knows we're after him, he's going to know we were on the ship, and I think—we think—he's not going to wait anymore. He's going to do whatever it is—set them all out killing each other, killing whoever they can—tonight. And they're not going to stop at Forty-third."

"Shit. Tried buyin me out, too, he did. Made me the offer maybe five, six weeks past, just after—when I take over, dig." Lex paused, shifted his weight. "Ain't gave it much thought, what with street men being killed an all."

The last line was spoken with a suspicious half glare at Terrible, who returned it with the kind of blankness Chess knew all too well. Hmm. Not that it was her business—it decidedly was not, and she didn't want to know about it, not really—but still. Hmm.

She cut into the heavy silence. "So, we need a plan for tonight. They're going to know we were on the boat. They're going to know we're expecting something, that we know what's going on. Hell, they're going to know there's a witch involved. But they might not know where we are, where we're planning on coming from."

For the first time, Lex and Terrible *looked* at each other instead of glaring. The silence stretched between them, broken by a rat or something rustling in the piles of garbage and old bones lining the walls. Chess didn't turn to see.

"Guessing I could send some down here," Lex said finally. "We get them streets all filled up though, aye? Set watches, what you thinking, Terrible?"

Oh, how Terrible was hating this. She knew it from the look on his face, the set of his shoulders, the prickly feeling of his energy. But he nodded finally, glaring at Devil. "Aye."

Pause, while they all absorbed that. Yeah, Lex and Terrible had worked together before, but that had been off the books, as it were. To save her, and to save the City and the Church. This was different.

"Okay." She shifted her feet, ignoring the sound of some fragile bone breaking under her shoe. "Okay, then. So tonight—I think, I bet—they'll come out of here, the bespelled people, because they have to move fast. We—"

"Why we ain't set the fucker on fire, Tulip? Them bodies burn up right, aye?"

Was he serious? "We can't."

"Why come?"

Her mouth opened; it took her a second to answer him. "Those are— They're people, Lex. Actual people, bespelled people. They're innocent. We can't just kill them."

"Them coming to kill us."

"They're victims. We can't burn them to death. Besides . . ."

Terrible took his gaze away from Devil—he'd been watching him as if he were a cockroach he couldn't wait to stomp on—long enough to glance at her. "That many bodies, the Church hears on it, aye?"

"I don't see how they wouldn't. I mean, not everyone on the ship is even necessarily from Downside, you know? They could be anybody who came down here to score. It could bring a lot of attention."

"Aye, dig it now." Lex nodded. "So you break them spell, an they all free?"

"Yeah. If I break the spell they'll be themselves again. Hopefully they'll go home, chalk it up to a bad experience. Some of them might contact the Church, but I doubt it—they're not going to want to get busted for drugs, and they'd have to admit what they were doing if they told. They'd probably get tested, anyway, with a story like that."

"How you break the spell, then?"

That was the million-dollar question, wasn't it?

All three of the men were watching her—or, rather, all three of them were waiting for her to speak. Only Lex actually looked at her. The other two stared at each other, their aggression sparking in the air like tiny bombs. Devil, she noticed, hadn't spoken a single word. She couldn't decide if that made him more threatening or made him look like a moron.

Of course, if he thought he could beat Terrible—without his sneaky fucking tricks, at least—he *was* a moron, but oh well. His problem, not hers. She edged closer to Terrible so her arm brushed against his. She needed the contact, especially for the answer she was about to give. "I don't know. I'll figure something out."

Damn, she hoped she sounded more confident than she felt.

* * *

Terrible glanced in the Chevelle's rearview again. "Thinkin it work?"

"I don't know." Three Cepts ought to do it, right? Lift the clouds but still leave her able to think fast, move fast, if the need arose—when the need arose, because she was pretty sure it would. "I guess we'll find out."

Part of her wanted the sun to set, wanted to get to the rooftop where they'd agreed to meet and get it over with. The other part didn't want to do anything but run home and hide. She wasn't ready. If she had one more day, just one more . . .

He turned, heading back toward her place. "So the sorcerer, he doin shit you ain't seen before? Where you figure he learn on it? Always wondered, dig, where them pick this shit up."

"He could learn it anywhere, really. Even the books we study have this stuff in them, we just don't work with it. And the really dark magic books are restricted, but that doesn't mean they're not out there. All you need is to be strong enough to work the spells."

"Lots of power, then?"

"He's pretty strong." That was an understatement. She shoved the pills into her mouth, washed them down with water from her bottle, and hoped he wouldn't ask the question she knew he was about to ask, have the thought she knew he was about to have.

Sure enough, he did. "You stronger, though, aye?"

"Church magic is always more powerful. I mean, I'm not worried."

Another lie. If she wasn't terrified she wouldn't need more pills, wouldn't be wondering if she could sneak a couple of lines of speed in. If she wasn't terrified she wouldn't be feeling worse with every passing second.

Separating the victims from what controlled them would take some serious fucking power, power she didn't know if she could summon. Power she was afraid of summoning, because it was the kind of power that could overload her—especially with the amount of shit she put into her system, no point in being dishonest about it—and it dawned on her that this could be the last day she ever saw, and she didn't like that one bit.

He lit a couple of cigarettes and handed her one. Such a familiar motion, something he did all the time, something that always made her feel taken care of. Like he was always thinking of her, always watching out for her.

But then he spoke, and although his voice was casual—so carefully casual—the words sent a chill into her heart she wasn't sure even her pills would chase away. "What I seen in the City . . . ain't the whole thing, aye? Bigger'n that. An ain't always like it were then, all the shit goin down and ghosts racing around an all. Aye?"

Oh fuck. What could she say, what was she supposed to say? She didn't even want to hear that question; she sure as fuck didn't want to answer it.

But she did. And she gave him the third lie, the biggest lie, because it was all she had at that moment; because she knew he was picturing Lex's assassin and an army of soulless magic-controlled killers just as much as she was, and she knew he'd be absolutely horrified if she let on that she knew what he really wanted. And why, which was worse. "It's much bigger. And, you know, there's so much there, so many of them . . . You find people you knew and everything. It's really, really peaceful and happy and everything."

Saying it made her feel sick. She took a long drag off the smoke while she tried to pretend nothing was wrong, that he hadn't admitted anything at all, and that she hadn't told probably the biggest lie she'd ever told him—bigger, even, than any about Lex. "We were in the anteroom, if you know what I mean. It's bigger than the area you saw. There's a lot more to it."

He nodded as he spun the wheel to urge the Chevelle around another corner. "Always had the wonder, dig."

"Yeah." Her voice sounded too thin; she cleared her throat. "Everyone does."

He didn't say anything further. Instead, he parked the car across the street from her building and set the brake. "Aye, then. Guessing we finish getting weselves ready."

Less than an hour later, she stood with Terrible on the rooftop of a building three blocks away from the *Agneta Katina,* with the sunset diminished to streaks of bronze and orange behind them as night took over the sky. Waiting.

Waiting first for Bump, who arrived only a minute or two later in full regalia: slashed pants, fur boots, dirty diamonds, and all. The heat of the day had congregated on the rooftop, too, and Chess's whole body felt sticky, but it didn't seem to affect Bump. He looked as cool and calm as ever.

So did Terrible, of course, but Chess knew him well enough to know what lurked behind that. His anger about what she was going to do, his anxiety about it, hovered beneath the surface of his energy.

She grabbed three Cepts from her bag and washed them down. A futile effort to calm her nerves, yeah, but at least it was something. Something she could control, something she knew the effects of, because she had about twenty minutes before she jumped down the rabbit hole, and who the hell knew what would happen then.

Well, no, she knew what would probably happen. She was probably going to die.

Funny, she'd thought that so many times. So many times growing up, so many times since then. This was the first time she'd actually seen it coming, seen it from a great distance and not because she'd been grabbed or caught or whatever else. Her own death waited for her like a bed she'd crawl into at the end of the night, and she could only hope she managed to finish what she needed to finish before the sheet settled over her head.

The three of them stood without talking for about ten more minutes, until Lex showed up. Alone. Great. Chess scanned the rooftops around them, the city of flat empty spaces laid out like a multileveled checkerboard all the way to the bay and the silent ships resting there. Lex's killer was out there somewhere. Hiding. Watching, most likely—most definitely—to see where Terrible went.

"So here's the fuckin plan we got on," Bump said to Lex by way of greeting. "Them buildings be filled up, dig, all fuckin filled by Bump's men getting them waits on. An them watchin up, too, got theyselves fuckin signals them send."

Lex nodded.

"We figure on them dead walkers leavin them boat after sundown an fuckin headin out, yay. Maybe them look out for we, maybe not. But them ain't killable, dig, so we only fuckin hold em here 'til the Ladybird gets she fuckin magic done."

Lex turned to her. "What magic's that?"

She shifted on her feet, leaning closer to Terrible. "I'm going to try to push the spell back at him. I have one of the spell bags. I think I can find the others if I— I'm going to take some of that speed and—"

"Shit." Lex shook his head. "Ain't thinkin that's such a good plan, I ain't. Sounding to me—"

"Nobody asked you," she said. Coldly.

Bump broke the short silence that followed. "Ain't got no shit to fuckin worry on, dig, Ladybird good enough to handle any all comes she fuckin way."

Before Chess could react to that surprising—and totally misguided—little vote of confidence, he snorted. "Bump ain't fuck around with no cheap pickup witches, see, some fuckin dude pulled off the street all crazed up on whatany mental pills some dame gives he."

Of course. Not confidence in her. Smugness at a chance to get a dig in at Lex. Or, rather, at Slobag, Lex's late father, and the fact that he'd died because he'd tried to get himself a witch of his own and it had gone horribly wrong.

Lex's mouth tightened. Not a lot, but enough that she noticed. "Seems to me—"

She cut him off. Something told her that whatever would come out of his mouth next, it wasn't going to be good. "It doesn't matter how it seems to you. It's the only way I can break the spell tonight, so it's what's going to happen. And if I can break the spell fast, all of the slaves—or whatever you want to call them—will be free, and they'll probably just want to go home. Maybe nobody has to die tonight."

Except her. And possibly Terrible. She saw that in Lex's eyes, the way he avoided looking at Terrible, and her heart sank further. Terrible was right, then—well, she'd known he was, she'd known the same thing he did. Even as they stood there Lex's man could be watching, lurking somewhere with Terrible's head in his crosshairs.

And there was nothing she could do about it. Not a single fucking thing.

Lex shrugged. "Gots mine all set up on them streets beyond, ready for signaling iffen them see any, too. An iffen them find more of them magic bags you gimme the tell on."

"Right. And hopefully either I'll be able to text you to let you know when I find the sorcerer in the spell or I'll be able to tell someone."

Bump's phone rang, an interruption she welcomed. Not only did she not want to discuss the plan with Lex, but his concern looked a bit odd and suspicious in front of Bump, didn't it? Lex wasn't supposed to know her well or care about her at all.

She was a bit surprised, actually, that he'd been as obvious as he had been, but she figured he didn't give a shit about what Bump thought anymore.

Unless there was some other reason, which there probably was. But she didn't have the time or the energy to think about it.

"Cable Joe still ain't here." Terrible peered around the roof with narrow eyes. The sun had completely disappeared, leaving only the blank emptiness of the starless city sky. With it came the breeze, stronger now, lifting her hair from her shoulders and chilling the back of her neck. Or maybe that wasn't only the wind. "Said he'd be here on the sundown."

Lex raised his eyebrows. "Others comin up here?"

"Keep an eye on Chess," Terrible said. "An pass on any knowledge she gets."

Because he'd insisted. And she'd agreed, because, really, it didn't matter. Yeah, it was a bit of a comfort to know she wouldn't go accidentally tumbling off the roof, but given the sort of end she suspected waited for her, tumbling off the roof might be a lot kinder.

Lex, too, looked around them, swiveling his upper body in an exaggerated fashion like a drunk fighting a strong wind. "Ain't seeing him up here, I ain't. Figured on you getting somebody worth trust, look after Tulip this night. Maybe you ain't able to—"

"Lex!" She threw herself between Terrible and Lex just in time to stop Terrible's swing.

Lex already had his hands up, his hands and the corners of his mouth curving into that irritating grin she wished she could slap off his face. "Havin me a joke, there, aye?"

"Keep jokin," Terrible said, his voice a low growl. His fists clenched and unclenched at his side. "You keep fuckin jokin, Lex, you an me have ourselves some laughs after all this, aye? See how many fuckin jokes—"

"Stop it. Okay? Just—cut it out."

Part of her didn't want to interrupt them. Lex thought it was so much fun to bait Terrible? Fine. Let him see what happened when she didn't jump in between them, when she didn't hold Terrible back. What the fuck did she owe him, anyway?

Her life, unfortunately. Which was why she hadn't let Terrible beat the shit out of him before—well, no, it was why she hadn't let Terrible *kill* him before, because she knew that if and when it ever came down to violence between them—or rather, if and when it happened *again*—that's where it would end.

But at the moment . . . "What the fuck, Lex? Do you want your jaw broken again, or are you going for something bigger this time?"

"Only tryin bring some fun into the troubles, is all." Lex was still smiling. Still smiling, but he didn't fool her. She'd seen the flash of panic on his face when Terrible threatened him. Seen, too, the way his gaze quickly cut over the rooftops to the left of where they stood. So she'd been right. His assassin was watching them.

She turned around and caught Terrible's gaze, then turned hers deliberately in that direction. He nodded and shrugged in return. Right. Not new information.

"Now we all finished on that one," Lex said, "who's keeping them eye on Tulip? She all set on doin this, guessing, an seeming to me like you man ain't showin up here. So—"

Bump's voice broke through his. "C'mon have youselfs a look. Them fuckin coming now, dig? Here they come."

Terrible and Lex ran for the low roof wall where Bump stood. Chess didn't. Shit. She was supposed to have taken the speed already; she should have done it sooner, she shouldn't have been standing around trying to put it off another minute, just one more minute. Yes, she needed for the magic to be active in order to chase it—needed an actual line to follow—but she could have done it sooner. Those last few minutes could have meant the difference between life and death. Not for herself but for dozens of people. Hundreds of people.

She trudged across the roof. The slight breeze felt like a hurricane trying to force her back, strengthened by her own reluctance. Her hair tickling her face annoyed her; she grabbed a ponytail holder from her bag and twisted it on.

As she finished with it the street below came into view. What had been the street. She didn't see the cement anymore, or the docks. What she saw—what they all saw—was a mass of silent humanity moving in unison. Swarming across the dock, swarming between the buildings, a slow-moving river of death claiming the streets inch by inch.

They were coming, indeed.

Chapter Twenty-six

> They looked across the field and saw the dead coming, their
> bodies casting light over the dying grass, and they knew
> their time had come.
>
> —*The Book of Truth*, Origins Article 83

They didn't shout or groan; they didn't stumble. They just walked, like tired commuters at the end of a long day, but instead of briefcases and bags they carried knives and sticks, hatchets and steel pipes, that caught the moonlight and sparked it back.

Their stillness was echoed on the roof. Nobody moved; her breath caught. Even Bump looked shaken when she glanced sideways at him.

But only for a moment. He leaned back and lit another hand-rolled, letting smoke drift from his mouth as if he couldn't even be bothered with the effort of exhaling. "Well, lookee there. Be a fuck of a night, yay?"

She laughed. They all laughed. Not because it was funny—it wasn't, particularly—but because they wanted to, because it broke the tension in some indefinable way as they watched the steady flow of quiet horror wend its way along the narrow pavement. All they could do was laugh, really. Otherwise . . . well, she would scream, but that might have been just her. Probably was just her, at least where Terrible was concerned, because when she looked at him he stood perfectly relaxed, his anger and anxiety gone, watching the death-shrouded streets with the kind of calm that always made her feel safe. Made her feel safe then. She reached out and took his hand, and he squeezed it in return.

The first wave of sound had crashed through the silence below, the first wave of Bump's men shouting as they started trying to hold the horde back.

Chess broke out in goose bumps as she looked at Terrible. "You have to go now."

It wasn't a question, but he nodded. Slowly, his eyes holding hers in a tight grip she felt through her entire body. "Aye. Gotta get down there, baby. Gotta get moving."

He meant it regretfully, she knew, and she felt his regret and his worry for her. But at the same time she felt his excitement, his anticipation. He wanted the fight. Wanted it the way he wanted her in the darkness, in bed. He wasn't scared of Devil; he wanted that fight, too.

Fear shot up her spine. Despite what she'd said to him she was scared, was afraid he wouldn't win. It wasn't fair of her, no, but what was she supposed to do, how was she supposed to feel? He was . . . everything to her, everything, and she'd given up everything for him. Even Elder Griffin. Her heart, her honor, the Church, everything. And if he went, if something happened . . . He couldn't die, really; the sigil on his chest meant it wasn't possible. But how would he survive in a broken body, a destroyed one?

She didn't want to think about it. Luckily she had skill in pushing unpleasant thoughts aside, in "forgetting" things difficult to forget. But as he separated from the small group at the rooftop wall, as the group itself broke up, her hand caught his arm anyway. "Terrible. Be careful. Okay? Be careful."

His gaze passed over Bump, still watching the crowd below, and Lex, picking up his cellphone. "No worryin on it, Chessiebomb. Be all right up, aye?"

Like she believed that. His gaze faltered as she stared at him; she caught a glimpse of his own worry under that excitement. Not worry because of Devil or the enormity of the fight before him, at least she didn't think so. Worry because he wasn't stupid enough to believe there was no reason to worry, and worry because he knew what she was going to do and what the risks were. "The City ain't so bad, anyroad, aye? Like you gave me afore. Don't plan on endin up there, dig, but iffen it happen . . . guessin it happen."

He leaned forward and kissed her then, a hard, strong kiss that made her knees weak even as it stiffened her body with terror. She knew that kiss, even though she'd never felt one like it before, not really. Knew what it was. It was goodbye, just in case. It was a memory being made, words going unsaid.

It was a farewell based on a lie, and when he started to walk away she couldn't do it anymore. Couldn't hide it anymore, the thing she'd kept hidden from everyone, even from him, for so long. The last secret she held. He knew so many things about her, knew so much, but she'd never admitted this to him. Never admitted it to anyone.

She followed him to the edge of the roof, to the open hole from which descended a staircase to the lower floors, with her heart in her throat. It sank further down when she grabbed his arm. "Terrible."

"Aye?"

How the hell could she say it? Or how could she say it without crying, because her eyes stung and the words seemed to come from inside her stomach, forced through her throat by sheer willpower. "Terrible, I . . . I lied. I lied to you before. I lied."

Shit, she hadn't even touched the bag of speed and already she was crying. Maybe the tears weren't running down her cheeks yet but they were about to; she could feel them waiting behind her eyes, burning in their desire to escape.

"What?"

"What I told you earlier. It was a lie. The City—it's an awful place, it's scary, Terrible, and I'm scared to go there, I'm scared of it. I'm sorry I lied but it's so fucking cold, it's so awful—"

The tears weren't waiting anymore, weren't staying behind her eyes. They spilled down her cheeks and her voice cracked, and she hated hearing it. Was ashamed of hearing it, not because she knew Bump and Lex could see she was upset—who gave a fuck about them—but because Terrible could see it. And Terrible mattered.

His strong arms closed around her, pulling her to him so her head pressed against his chest. "Naw, naw. Ain't so bad, aye?"

"But it is." Now that she was saying something, now that she was admitting the truth—the truth she'd never even hinted to another living soul—she couldn't stand to have him not understand her, not get what she was telling him. "What you saw that night—it's so much worse, it's all like that. It's so—it's so cold and empty, it scares me, the thought of being there forever—it's not supposed to scare me, it's my job and I'm supposed to think it's peaceful but I can't. I don't, it's—"

"Hey." His big hands curved around her face, his fingers catching her pulled-back hair and tilting her cheeks up so her eyes met his. "Ain't so bad, Chessie, causen you ain't be alone, dig? You ain't go there on your alones. An I figuring, I end up there maybe you come down see me. You can do that, bein a witch an all, aye?"

"What? I mean, yeah, I'd come down to— Of course, but—"

"An that's the only one matters, dig. Can deal with it on my alones, baby, causen you visit me. But the other way . . . you thinkin I let you stay there by youself? Thinkin I stay here iffen you ain't around no more?"

"What?" Her voice sounded so thin, so dry. She had to be hearing him wrong or not understanding what he said, because it sounded . . . it sounded as if he was saying something huge. The noises around them, the shouts and the clangs of metal on cement and the shrieks of frustrated psychopomps whirling and diving in the night air, disappeared. "I don't . . . What?"

They shouldn't be standing there talking like that; they shouldn't be standing with their bodies pressed together on the rooftop, in the open. But she couldn't think about that or about anything else as his eyes met hers, serious and dark.

"I ain't . . . Don't know how to say it up right. Never—Fuck. Thought you was dead once before, you recall? Never felt so bad in my life, not ever. Then on the other day, thought you was gone an just . . . I ain't can do it, bein without you."

He rubbed his neck, pressed his palm into his furrowed brow and took a swipe at his eyes. Cleared his throat, twice. "Don't want to. An even if I did, ain't can leave you down there on your alones. How I can do that one, aye? Leave my Chessiebomb there without me. 'Specially knowin you scared on it."

The words kicked every other thought out of her head, so they echoed in the empty space. The empty space in her soul, the empty space she'd filled with drugs and shame and misery, suddenly full of something else. Full of those words.

Full of fear, too. This was what scared her. This was what she'd been running from deep inside, the knowledge of what kind of commitment he was making to her, what he wanted in return, and her uncertainty that she was capable of giving it to him. Her fear of what it meant to give it to him. This was what she'd been fighting with herself over since the day he'd come to her apartment and told her he loved her—hell, since the day he'd come to her apartment and she'd washed his shirt in her sink and realized that he understood her, since the day on the beach when she'd realized she trusted him, since that night at Trickster's when she'd realized she wanted him, that she felt something real for him.

All that time, this was what she'd been scared of. And as she stood there looking into his eyes, seeing the dampness of hers echoed there, she understood—fully understood for the first time—that what she was truly afraid of was that if she could be happy, if she could love someone and be loved back, that meant maybe she wasn't as bad as she'd always thought. Maybe she was worth something, and if she was worth something, it might mean making some changes.

And maybe those changes weren't about becoming some strange different person but about being herself in a different way, and there was nothing to be afraid of in that at all. She was ready for that. She could try to be ready for that.

All of that flashed through her mind, the sort of lightning-strike understanding that only happened when it could change a life, when the answer to a question had been there, ignored, for so long that it finally burst into existence.

Just as the words burst from her. "I don't want to be here without you, either. I can't— I don't want to be anywhere if you're not there."

"Naw, naw, Chessie, ain't wanting you— Only had the thought you come down see me, ain't meant—"

"No. No, I don't want that. Being here without you— I'd rather be in the City. With you. I don't want to be without you. I don't care where, I can't do it, I don't—"

His hands on the side of her face lifted her to her tip-toes, lifted her almost off her feet. Maybe he actually did; she didn't know, because she was floating, flying, his mouth on hers sending her off the roof and into that blank lonely sky above. The sky that suddenly didn't look so lonely, the sky that was maybe . . . peaceful.

"Love you, Chessie," he murmured. "Ain't never . . . Fuckin love you, more'n anything."

"I love you, I love you so much." Her eyes still burned; her cheeks were wet with tears. She stood on a rooftop in Downside not too far away from Bump and Lex, who were probably standing there watching her, while a paid murderer waited to earn his money by ending Terrible's life, while an army of unkillable magic-enthralled junkies waited on the streets below, while she was about to join their ranks and try to end the magic holding them all by herself.

It was one of the best moments of her entire life.

Not a long moment, or not long enough; she could have stayed like that forever, pressed against Terrible's strong warm body with his lips on hers and his back solid and hard under her palms. But he pulled away, his hands cradling her face, and rested his forehead against hers. "Needing somethin from you, though. One thing."

"What?"

"Rather be with you *here*. So whyn't you make sure you stay yourself alive, dig? Don't get dead, Chessie-bomb."

She made a sort of half laugh, half sob, as she dug her fingers into the hair at the nape of his neck. "Don't you, either. Please. Okay?"

"Aye." He lifted his head and took a small step back. Her body felt cold without his against it. "Ain't gotta worry on me. Ain't even can die with this thing on me, aye?"

It might have sounded like an odd question given what they'd just discussed. But she knew what he was really saying, what he was asking. And maybe it was wrong of her to answer it honestly, but she couldn't help it. "I don't think you can die with it on you, no. But if it was gone—yeah, that would do it. Without it— Removing it would kill you."

He nodded. "Aye, figured so."

They stood looking at each other for another few seconds; there didn't seem to be much more to say, not at that moment. Not when the enormity of what they'd said still pressed its weight on her, terrifying and exciting and comforting all at once. So many feelings, too many; normally she'd be reaching for her pillbox right about then to dull them out so she could breathe.

That was what she wanted to do. But she didn't, because she was about to take a dose of something that very well might kill her, and because . . . well, because for some reason those feelings—the love and trust and commitment ones—didn't seem unbearable, scary as they were. She could handle them. So she would.

At least for now.

And they needed to go. They'd already taken too much time. Not wasted. She could never think of it as a waste. But they'd taken it, and they couldn't take any more.

"Right," he said. He gave his eyes a quick rub, then slid his hands down her arms to take hers. "Let's get us on with it, aye?"

Bump and Lex hadn't been watching them, or at least they had the decency to pretend they hadn't. Neither of them looked up until Chess and Terrible were standing at their sides—or between them, because they'd retreated to opposite corners like boxers between rounds.

"Getting fuckin worse on down there," Bump said. He said it accusingly, as if Chess had somehow orchestrated the whole thing. "When you get the fuckin shit broke up, Ladybird? Wanting this fuckin done out, dig?"

Normally she'd grit her teeth at something like that,

but she couldn't be bothered. Now that the moment was over, the whole scared-shitless thing started up again. The noise from below returned, as if she'd just taken her hands off her ears. She took a deep breath. Might as well get it over with. "Now. I'm going to do it now."

Terrible shook his head. "Cable Joe still ain't showed. Don't want— Lemme get some else up here, aye, find—"

"Whyn't I stay on?" Lex said.

Bump snorted. "Ain't can guess why you still fuckin here all the same, yay, an why you getting you the thought we let you—"

Terrible cut him off. "Aye."

"What?"

Terrible looked from Lex to Chess and back again. "Aye. You stay. You watch her. Keep her safe."

Bump's eyebrows shot up, almost to the edge of his frizzy hairline. "You fuckin put on the joking, yay, Terrible? Ain't even fuckin know he—"

Terrible ignored Bump. He hadn't taken his eyes off Lex, and Lex had been staring back at him just as intensely. Chess didn't know exactly what was being communicated with those looks, but she had a pretty good idea. "You stay with her, dig? You watch her."

"Ain't goin nowheres she ain't."

"An you text me, aught happens. Chess, give he yon phone."

If the situation hadn't been so serious, she might have laughed at the dumbfounded look on Bump's face. But it was, so even that couldn't make her crack a smile. She brought up the addresses on her phone and handed it to Lex, pointing to which code was Terrible's. Lex nodded and put it in his pocket.

"Right, then." Terrible pulled two cigarettes from his pocket and lit them. "Better get on the move."

She took the one he offered her, trying not to think of it as the last one. It wasn't the last one, it wasn't. It couldn't be. "Yeah. Why are we all standing here when there's so much fun we could be having?"

The men gave her a polite laugh, even Bump. Silence fell while they all stood there looking at each other, waiting to see who would be the first to break the little circle, who would be the first to end the relative safety in which they stood.

It was Terrible. He took her arm and pulled her away, back to the staircase. "Don't want you thinkin on me, dig? Just get what you need done."

"You, too. I'll be fine. Don't worry about me."

He glanced at Lex. "Aye, well. Figure he ain't let shit happen to you. Knows he don't get to make he fuckin jokes on me iffen you ain't around."

She smiled. "No, that's true."

"Chessie . . ." Terrible looked at her, up and down, a long searching look as if he was trying to memorize her face. Which he probably was, because that's what she was doing; well, she already had his face memorized, but she was trying to memorize the moment, the sensation of his hand touching her cheek. Trying to freeze it all in her mind so she could experience it again whenever she wanted to, the exact feeling of it, the exact way the wind still blew across her skin and the moonlight hit his face.

He lowered his hand, and it was over. "See you on the later then, aye? No matter what."

She forced herself to smile, forced herself to blink back the tears threatening to fall again. He didn't need to see that. He needed her to be strong, needed to know how much she believed in him. "Yeah. No matter what."

One last quick kiss, one last quick word with Bump and one last look at Lex, and he disappeared down the stairs.

Chapter Twenty-seven

You may not falter. You may not lose your focus. You represent the Church, and you belong to the Church, and in the eyes of those you encounter you *are* the Church.
—*The Example Is You*, the guidebook for Church employees

She finished the smoke Terrible had given her and turned to Lex, standing a few feet away with his hands in his pockets. "Okay. You ready? Let's get this done."

He grinned. "Been ready all the day, Tulip. Just givin you the wait."

She glanced at Bump, but he was on his phone again. Good. Lex needed to watch that shit. It was one thing to do it to annoy Terrible; it was another to do it in front of Bump, who might well wonder why Lex had given her a nickname when they'd supposedly only met a couple of times.

Oh, what the fuck was she worrying about that for? Like it mattered. She probably wouldn't live through the night, anyway.

The packet of speed sat in her bag, wrapped in a shroud of inert plastic in an effort to dampen the energy it gave off. The plastic didn't help much, but she hadn't figured it would, because she'd grabbed what seemed to be the strongest packet of speed from her Blackwood box. The low wall wrapping around the roof had broken in places, but one corner was still intact, and a bit higher than the others. It faced the wind, too, so when she ducked down into it the breeze died and she could use her hairpin without worrying too much.

"How much you gotta do?"

"I don't know." Holding the packet sent tremors up her arm, that sick feeling of dark magic washing over her. "Not too much, I don't think. Just enough to get it into my blood."

"Thinkin you have a problem with it, seeing as how you already got magic in you blood and all?"

Shit, she hadn't thought of that. "I guess we'll find out, huh."

Lex crouched beside her, reaching out to touch her arm. "I be watchin on you, aye? No need for worryin."

"Don't think I'm not still pissed at you."

"Hey." His fingers closed around her arm, urging her to look at him. "Know you is. But that one's business, aye? Still gonna watch you. Ain't wanting shit happen to you, I ain't. True thing."

She met his gaze. The moonlight spilled over the top of his spiky head, over his shoulders, but not his face; it remained shadowed by the walls around them.

"I know," she said finally. "I know you don't."

That didn't stop him from trying to have Terrible killed, of course, but she didn't mention it. Not because it didn't matter, but because it would lead them down some other conversational path, a strange and uncomfortable one she didn't want to travel. She didn't think Lex was in love with her—she knew he wasn't, unless he was extremely good at hiding it—but obviously he hadn't wanted their relationship to end, and obviously he was rather put out by the fact that it had ended so she could be with Terrible.

This was too fucking weird, having some sort of Moment with Lex. He seemed to think so, too, because after a second he let go of her, leaned back. Moonlight washed over his face, wiping it clean of whatever serious emotion might have been there. "Get this shit over with then, aye? Got places I could be."

She went along with it. "Girls waiting for you?"

"Could be. Ain't wanting em get all bored an go home."

"Maybe they could have a pillow fight in their underwear while they wait."

He laughed. "Hopin they is, leastaways."

Pause. Okay. Time to get on with it. Rather than use her hairpin—she didn't think her hands were quite steady enough—she went ahead and dug the tip of her car key into the packet.

When she glanced up at Lex, he'd turned away, watching the psychopomp birds swirling in the sky. If only Terrible could have stayed, could have been with her . . .

But he would be. He'd be waiting for her after it was all over. No matter what. She pulled out the memory she'd fixed in her head earlier—the sound of his voice, his fingers on her cheek—and held it close while she lifted the key and snorted back the bump.

Her nose caught fire for a split second before going completely numb. Numbness up into her sinuses and, when she pulled air hard through them, into her head and the back of her throat. That bitter batterylike speed taste was there, but under it was something awful, something that made her want to gag. Something like—like death and rotting vegetables, mixed together and coating her throat.

The taste grew stronger in her mouth as the speed itself hit her bloodstream in earnest. The familiar kick of her heart, the way it felt like bubbles spreading through her bloodstream, but this time something else rode those bubbles, something creepy and dark. As if her heart wasn't speeding up from joy but was trying to run away.

Was this what the others had felt? It couldn't have been; it had to be the magic already in her blood reacting with the magic in the speed, because nobody would have done more if this was what it felt like.

Her skin burned, the magic tattoos up her arms and across her chest reacting to the threat now inside her, in her veins. Burned hard and hot, as if she was back in that white room at the Church, getting inked all over again, while the Elders and her fellow employees watched and chanted to raise power. She looked at her arm and half-expected to see it blistering from the heat.

She didn't realize she was panting, that she was sweating, until Lex touched her shoulder. "Tulip? You right, there? What's on with you?"

"I'm fine," she managed. "I just— You're right, it's reacting weird, it—"

The magic took hold then, tearing into her flesh, hooking cat-sharp claws dipped in poison into her brain. Feeling her out. Testing her.

Her vision went white. The pain disappeared. In its place was a feeling she knew very well, too well. A craving. More of that speed, she had to do more. Wanted more, as if she hadn't had any in months, in years. She had to have more.

Some dim part of her understood what it was. Not a real craving, a magical one.

"That's so smart," she whispered, fumbling around to fit her key back into the packet, still clutched in her sticky palm. "So fucking smart, shit."

"Aye? What?"

"It's—it's part of the magic, part of the spell, it makes you crave more. To build it up in your system, I guess."

Even as she said it she was lifting the key again, loading more sick magic into her nose, into her body. Chasing the magic, chasing the high, because the high had to be coming, right? *The* high, the ultimate one, the one as good as the first one ever. Some whispering voice inside her, inside the speed, promised that high, and she was going to get it; that magic promised her she could find its source and she was going to get that, too. She hadn't forgotten.

The death-taste, worse the second time, stronger. The shaking, the burning. Her brain was leaving her head, her body leaving her control. It was so peaceful . . . so peaceful for once. Like being wrapped in cotton, soft around her, swaddling her tight like the mother she'd never had.

She bet if she did one more bump she'd feel it even more. It would get her closer to the source, too, help her find what she was looking for. So she did, barely tasting it this time. Maybe one more? Somewhere beneath the padding of artificial peace she felt her body shaking and twisting inside, felt her skin still burning and tears running down her cheeks.

She lifted the key again; something caught her hand, stopped it from finding her nose. What the—

"Ain't that enough, now?"

Oh, right. Lex. She'd forgotten about him for a minute there. "Just one more, I think—"

"Lookin mighty shaky, Tulip. Maybe you oughta—"

She squinted at him. When she spoke, her mouth felt funny, as if she wasn't enunciating properly. As if her tongue were made of rubber. "One more, one more's going to do it. I'm—I'm sure of it."

He let go of her hand. "Aye, right up, then. Only then we get the move-on, aye? Start findin whatany we s'posed to be on the find of. Lookin wrung out, you is."

As if she cared what she looked like, when she was on the verge of the greatest high she'd ever had, she knew she was. The magic promised it to her. That promise insinuated itself through her body, deadened her mind, made her body feel mushy and irrelevant while at the same time excited and tense. As if she was about to have sex, as if Terrible was sliding her panties down her legs on her bed and his hands were hot on her bare skin, his lips exploring her upper thigh like he had the other night. . . .

Terrible. Terrible, and Lex crouching at her side, and all of them down on the street. Shit. She needed to focus. Okay.

The last bump hit her throat; magic filled her body. So high, and so good, but this time she didn't let go. This time she fought the immediate craving, the desperation for more, and concentrated on what was behind it. Concentrated on the magic.

"We need to get down," she managed. Her voice still didn't seem like her own, and with every passing second the need for more grew stronger. Maybe she should do one more bump before they left the roof, just to make sure she had a good enough grip on it? Another there, and one at the bottom of the stairs— Shit, no wonder those packets they'd taken from the group outside Trickster's had been so empty, no wonder there had been so many of them in Marietta's socks.

She didn't realize she'd been scooping out another bump until Lex grabbed her hand again. "Aye, let's get us down there. You got hold of it, you thinkin?"

Did she? She felt it, that was for sure, but she didn't feel as if she was part of the spell yet, didn't— Oh shit. Of course.

The inert plastic tub was still in her bag, the tub containing the spell they'd found earlier. She'd taken it apart but hadn't salted it or separated the pieces under running water or anything else, so it should work, and the magic in the speed needed the walnuts to set it off, right?

Right. She dug out the tub and handed it to Lex. "When we get down there, like around them all, we'll need this. You'll need to open the tub and hold it. It'll neutralize the spell on them. Only on the ones close by, but it should be enough to get us through the crowd."

"Gonna fix you up? Make you lose the magic?"

"Yeah, it will, and I don't know how much. So—go over there and stay until I call you, okay? Don't get too close to me until I say."

If she was going to be able to say, that was. She had no idea if she'd need to be away from the thing in Lex's hands in order to trace the magic back, no idea if she'd need to be near it in order to speak. "Um, actually, if I start moving without saying anything, go ahead and bring it over to me. Okay?"

He nodded.

Now the walnut. She could just carry it, yeah, but the nut was just a container, not an actual part of it, and she needed to get as deep inside as she could. So she grabbed one of those and opened it, had the presence of mind to brace herself before she stuck her finger into the mess of blood and parts inside.

Numbness. That same icy shocking numbness, tearing through her, making her body disappear. Kicking her out of her body, to be more specific; she couldn't feel it anymore, couldn't see, couldn't do anything. Couldn't hear. Was Lex still there? Was she still there, was *there* still there, was she anywhere? Fuck, where was she, what was happening?

The magic inside her, around her, didn't soothe anymore. It trapped her, entangled her like seaweed at the bottom of the cold deep ocean, and she was drowning. She struggled against it, fought against it, but it only held on tighter.

Shit, that was it. What little conscious mind she still possessed knew what was happening: She'd completed the spell, she was inside it now. She'd chased it and, instead of catching it, it had caught her. It held her in vicious steel arms that wouldn't let her go; it had stolen her and she belonged to it. Maybe she shouldn't have done so much of that speed, maybe that last bump had been too much, she'd gone too far into it and she couldn't escape—

No. Fuck, no. She was the one in control; she was the one who'd made the decision and she would get herself out of this. She'd get them all out of this, all of them who'd bought a little speed and suddenly found themselves under someone else's control. This was magic, and she could do magic; if there was one thing she could fucking do that was it. She wasn't just a junkie, she was a motherfucking Churchwitch.

Somewhere in the distance, she thought she heard Lex calling her name. She tried to answer. "Give me a minute."

Had he heard that? She didn't know, still couldn't see or hear. Had no idea if she was on the roof or what; her body remained inaccessible to her. The only way she knew for sure she wasn't dead was that she wasn't being picked up, wasn't in the City.

And yeah, the night might very well end with her there, but not this way. No fucking way was she going to give up so easy; if Terrible wasn't going to let her be alone down there, she sure as fuck wasn't going to make him join her because she'd lost without putting up a fight. It wasn't just her own life that depended on her, wasn't just the army of nameless blank faces on the streets below. Terrible's life depended on her staying alive, and she was going to do it.

So she pushed. Pushed as hard as she could, pushed with all the anger and determination a lifetime of shit had given her. She'd faced worse than this and she'd survived, and she'd be damned if she'd let this beat her.

Somehow she found a thread of . . . something. Something in the magic, something she could grab hold of. Yes! The heart of the spell, the line that connected it to its caster.

This wasn't something she'd done very often. The

Black Squad had training on this, but since her work usually involved nonmagical crimes—or at least it was supposed to—she'd had only the basic classes on it. But she found it. That was the important thing. And she could follow it—or she could if she could get hold of her own increasingly fuzzy mind, find some way to lessen the magic's grip.

Almost immediately upon thinking it, the weight on her lifted. Her eyes were hers again, her body in her control. Not entirely, no; the magic was still there, oh it sure as fuck was, that deep-down pull on her wanting her to—to walk, to go, to pick up something and start hitting with it. It wanted her to— No, it wasn't clear enough, not yet.

Not until she went back under. Because at that moment she felt her feet again, her arms and hands; felt one of them held in a tight grip she knew without thinking was Lex's. That fucking sucked, because what she didn't feel was that thin line of magic, the line she could trace. It was gone, and she wouldn't find it again until she was back under. All the way.

"You was takin youself a walk," he said. "Guessing you got it pretty strong, aye?"

"Where are we?"

"Still onna roof. Ready get off, head on down?"

She nodded. "Yeah. Go ahead of me, okay? I'll follow you."

He gave her a look—warning? Concern? She couldn't tell—and started walking. He made it about four steps before the magic slid over her again.

The magic and the craving. Fuck, she wanted another bump, a whole line. Her body screamed for it, so loud she could almost hear it. One more bump. She needed to bring the magic back up, needed to make herself feel better. Shit, she needed that so damn bad.

"On the street," she thought she heard Lex say. "Followin you now."

So she had been moving. She had been going somewhere; she'd been following the magic. She hoped, anyway, that she'd been chasing it and not obeying it.

Haze covered her eyes, as if she saw everything through cloudy film. Bodies moved, fighting all around her; she heard shouts as if they were miles away. She wanted to join them. It was a need almost as bad as the need for another bump, another line, that need pulling at her like a beast with its prey, trying to rip her flesh off her bones and devour it. So overpowering, it was so fucking strong, so desperate. How long was she going to be able to fight it? How long would she be able to remember what she was supposed to do, why she was under?

For that matter, how long were Bump's men going to hold on? All those people, all those bodies—their faces looked smudged and artificial to her, like golems—a swarm of them, endless like the clouds, all of them fixated on one thing. No one could last against that kind of determination. Nothing could last against it. They were running out of time. Not that they'd had much to begin with.

She needed to find the spell. She needed to step away from Lex. Fine, but how the hell to do that and not give in to the magic?

Maybe she didn't have a voice; she probably didn't. But she'd try it, anyway. "*Arketa restikah, arketa restikah. Baruel, baruel, matasae matasae. Arketa restikah . . .*"

Was it her imagination or did she feel the bonds around her start to loosen? Could she see a little?

The *Arketa* was one of the weakest chants in the Church arsenal, but she didn't want a strong one. She couldn't overpower the magic totally or chance having it disappear, because she had to follow it, but she needed to think, to see. To access her body and voice, and her power.

Should she ask Lex for iron? There were filings in her bag, of course, but he could— No. She didn't want him digging around in there, for one thing, and for another that might be too much, too strong.

So she kept going with the *Arketa*. At the fourth repetition she came back enough to see, to feel her feet and the ground beneath them; at the sixth she found her hands again. And . . . yes, she still had the line, she could still trace the magic. Shit, yes, just what she needed. She knew it, she knew the Church would have an answer.

What she didn't know was where she'd been going, what she'd planned to do, or why she'd headed— Of course. The ship. She was heading for the ship.

She hadn't found the master spell when they were on board earlier, but then she and Terrible hadn't gone everywhere, had they? There were still a few floors she hadn't even been on, and they'd only entered the captain's room; there were plenty of others. She'd be willing to put money down that what she needed was there.

"The *Agneta Katina*," she said, stopping her chant and letting it stay stopped. "We need to go there, that's where we need to be."

Magic flowed through her again, her grip on the end of it tight enough to make her insides ache. She needed another bump. It wouldn't ease the pain, no—speed didn't do shit for pain—but it would make it easier, make her feel better, cheer her up. Like speed always did. It would help her forget everything else, and this particular speed was especially good at that, wasn't it?

Even in her blitzed and blissful state, though, she knew taking another hit would be a bad idea in that crowd. How much were they craving, how badly did they need more?

Well, shit, how badly did she need more, and it had been only, what, ten minutes? So, yeah. Not going to take it out on the street. Follow the line, get somewhere private. Hell, follow the line and get onto the boat; she needed the tunnel for that, so she needed to get into the taxidermist's.

The magic line grew thicker, stronger, as she made her slow careful way along it. Very careful. If she could feel him, it was only a matter of time before he felt her, and once he felt her he could—well, he could do any number of things, none of them good.

Speed up, then, no pun intended. The line of magic vibrated gently, the line with so many offshoots, so many people connected to it. Like a thousand voices screaming across a great distance, screaming in fear and pain and frustration. And one of those voices was hers.

Shivers of bright sharp energy zipped through her body at odd intervals, little shocks that came out of nowhere. She must have been bumping into more speedzombies. They hadn't been that far from the docks, why was it taking so long, what was happening?

She hadn't found the sorcerer in the magic yet. Didn't want to find him until they got closer—hell, didn't want to find him at all, unless they couldn't find the master spell. That was what she needed to be working on. Finding that spell, finding the other walnuts. All of those little threads, tributaries in the river of horror—they were people, yes, but they were spells. Slipped into pockets, tucked under couch cushions or beds. Tied—she felt them, saw them in her head—to rafters in abandoned buildings, stuck under chairs in bars and diners, hidden in cars. They littered Downside; they were everywhere.

She started the chant again and found herself still clutching Lex's hand, surrounded by total darkness. "Where are—"

"That dead-animal place." He was smoking; red light

illuminated his face for a second as he took a drag. "Figured on takin us offen the street, I did, take that tunnel you come up out before. Them zombies gave me the callypunch, dig?"

"Yeah." Her fingers shook as she dug out the speed and bumped up again; her body's screams were too loud, too much to ignore any longer. Of course, when that death-and-old-asparagus taste hit her throat, she wished she had ignored it, but wasn't that just fucking typical of her: to want something so badly, and then to instantly regret getting it.

"Got he yet?"

"Almost. I— The spell, there's so many of them, but it feels really close, it feels like the master spell is really close, so— Fuck!"

Her body caught fire. Not literally, at least she sure as fuck hoped not. She couldn't see it. Couldn't see anything as the magic inside her swelled and shrieked. Something had just— What the hell had he done?

Through the pain she felt her knees hit the floor, the disgusting floor coated with slime and bacteria. In her speed-and-magic-crazed mind she pictured them, millions of them, germs like maggots with evil grins full of teeth, swarming up her legs, biting her, eating her.

She screamed—she thought she screamed, who the fuck knew if her voice actually came out or not—and swatted at them. Tried to swat at them, at least, because she didn't know if her arms were working, either.

He'd found her. The sorcerer had found her; he knew she was coming for him, and he was fighting back.

Chapter Twenty-eight

> They were never prepared for emergencies, as the Church always is.
> —*A History of the Old Government, Volume III: 1800–1900*

He knew what scared her, too. The magic gave him access to her mind; those sharp-toothed bacteria, those malevolent germs, grew bigger, stronger, grew long spindly arms to wrap around her and human faces straight out of her darkest memories. They howled and screamed at her. They sank their needle-teeth into her flesh and disappeared into her bloodstream.

She stopped reciting the *Arketa* in her head, and white washed over her vision again. It didn't block out the foulness crawling all over her body, the things that had lived in her right palm when she'd cut it on the Dreamthief's amulet, insects and worms, roaches and flies. All of those she could still see through the mist.

Dull pain blossomed in her cheek, distracting her long enough to make her remember. Somewhere she realized Lex had hit her—well, she realized it when the pain happened again. It didn't hurt that much; she had no idea if it would have if she'd been able to really feel. But it hurt enough to bring her back to herself for a second—to make her realize he'd somehow managed to short out the protection spell or whatever it was Lex carried—and that second was all she needed.

It was also all she got. She'd just started the *Arketa* again when the white before her eyes changed to black, and a sick miasma of neon colors swirled before them, like being trapped in a nightmare kaleidoscope. He was fighting her, all right. He was trying to obscure anything she might see, anything she might find, throwing images and shit at her to hide himself.

No fucking way was she going to let that work.

She grabbed hold of the cord, that invisible cord of magic, and yanked it as hard as she could.

The line vibrated. She felt it in her head, felt it reverberate along all of the connected lines. If it had any effect on the crowd of bespelled bodies outside, she couldn't tell, but the way it shook gave her something, and it was all she needed.

It gave her the master bag, the heart of the spell. It wasn't on the *Agneta Katina*. It *was* the *Agneta Katina*. The whole fucking ship. He'd painted it with ghost-and-magic-infused paint; he'd hidden the spell ingredients all over it, from stem to stern, and he'd activated it.

Holy fuck, the entire ship was a spell bag. How the hell was she supposed to destroy that?

The bay. The bay was running water, right? And running water could break a spell, purify its parts. So she had to get the ship submerged in it, that was all.

She had to sink a motherfucking freighter, and she had to do it on her own.

Another wave of horror washed over her, more sights and sounds she didn't want to see or hear again in her life. More shit crawling all over her, so real it made her already pounding heart start jerking around like an electrocuted nerve. He was fighting back, fighting harder, shit, she couldn't breathe—

"Arketa restikah, arketa restikah . . ."

It wasn't working. She felt—she practically heard—him chuckle as he sent more power throbbing down the line at her, enough to knock her down, to send her flying from her body.

More pain across her face. She wanted to tell Lex to quit fucking slapping her but really, what else was he supposed to do? She didn't have the breath, anyway, and when she did she had more important things to tell him.

"The ship," she croaked, or at least tried to; she could only hope he was able to hear her. "We have to destroy the ship."

She thought he replied, but whatever he said was lost, too quiet for her to hear over the airplane-engine roar of magic in her head. An explosion, that's what she needed. Fire could destroy the spell, too.

But the ship was steel. Steel didn't burn. She didn't think steel melted, either, and even if it did, it would be at temperatures way hotter than any she could generate.

The cord vibrated. An order. He was ordering his crowd to do something, to— Shit. He was ordering them into the building. Ordering them after her.

Sight and hearing came rushing back to her, just enough for her to see them outside, hear them pounding on the wood over the street-level windows. It barely registered in her mind before Lex started running, pulling her along after him, into the workshop and the tunnel below— No, not into it. She heard him say something, but she didn't know what it was, and it didn't matter because she saw it, too. Water. The tide was in, the tunnel impassable.

Lex kicked open the back door of the workshop and dragged Chess into the alley behind it. Thank fuck, at least that was empty. Too bad it wouldn't be for long; she could feel him watching her. He'd send them after her, they'd keep coming, and no way could she fight them all off. No way could Lex or all of Bump's men fight them off. They didn't think, didn't feel, and the power the sorcerer had put into them would keep them moving even after their bodies were ruined, crushed. . . . They were an army no one could defeat.

Her mind screamed for escape; her body screamed for more speed. He wanted her to do more, wanted to pull her deeper under his spell. She fought it as hard as she could, exhaustion creeping into her head even as her limbs buzzed and jerked from the drugs already in her system.

"Lex." Could he hear her? "Lex, it's the boat. The boat is the spell. We have to destroy the boat."

Whatever reply he might have made was lost in the wave of magic thundering over her again. So much, and so strong; she couldn't fight that, couldn't beat him, and couldn't destroy the *Agneta Katina*.

Lex had pushed her all the way down the alley behind the taxidermist's so they were on the docks again, and the horde had turned to them. They were coming, this was it, they were coming— The key.

She had the key.

She had the key, and she'd managed to short out the magic earlier. She'd shorted out the spell in the center of it, and she hadn't been part of it. Something was happening in the conscious part of her mind, some sort of idea forming. She had the key, and she'd been able to overpower the spell, even if for only a short moment.

And she hadn't been part of it then; now she was. Did that give her an advantage? She wanted to think it did but she couldn't think anything, she was so tired of thinking, tired of fighting.

Colors over her eyes, pain in her chest from her heart slamming itself against her ribs, aching in her limbs from trying to move, from fighting the spell's control and the almost overwhelming desire to do another bump, another hit, to chop herself a fresh thick line and vacuum it up, lose herself in it for good. More images flashed before her, like a movie she never wanted to see again in the last moments of her life.

No. She dug her heels in, dimly aware of another pain in her jaw; whether it was from Lex or from gritting her teeth so hard, she didn't know or care.

Magic flowed all along the cord, connecting her to the sorcerer, to all his other victims. Of course it did; the cord was made of magic, wasn't it? Was it? Confusion flowed along and mixed with the magic. Where was she, what was she doing? Was she part of the spell, or was she imagining it all? Was she dreaming? Before her eyes were faces, lights, spreading pools of red and blue and green; was it real? Was the dim shadowy shape of a ship she could just make out beyond the colors and lights real?

She spun at the end of the cord, leaving her body, riding a wave of smooth cold magic embedded with shards of glass. Being controlled, fighting against it, but knowing she couldn't win, and her instincts were to curl up, block it out, leave her body, because she'd been there so many times before.

But she could feel them, all of the others. Feel them following orders, coming for her, as if they were all part of a vast singular consciousness. She wanted to come for herself; she was hunter and hunted, and the confusion of it helped her break free. Helped her fight back.

She reached into her bag, shouting the *Arketa* in her head as loud as she could. It took her a minute to remember it; the words got lost on her tongue. But the spell's power receded enough for her to take a breath, for her to realize that Lex had pushed her up a flight of stairs, that she was in some kind of tower on the docks. His voice in sharp Cantonese made a familiar background as she grabbed that moment of clarity and held on to it with all her might.

She dug in her bag for the key, barely noticing the

way its energy zinged up her arm. She grabbed whatever else she could find, not even sure why she was grabbing some of it: cobwebs and a chunk of snake, a black mirror and a small pouch full of bones and claws. Ajenjible and sapodilla seeds, corrideira and powdered salamander eyes.

The pile of spell ingredients before her grew, while she slipped in and out of consciousness and kept tossing things onto it. Everything she had, a huge mishmash of odds and ends, and it dawned on her that some spells would explode if they were turned back on themselves.

Most dark spells would do that, in fact.

Shock transmitted itself down the cord to her. Fuck, he'd heard her thoughts, felt what she was doing. The tower in which she stood started to rock, pushed and pulled by bespelled hands with supernatural strength.

Time to make a choice. She might have enough power to use the key, to overtake the spell and set the horde free, even if only for a brief time. She might have enough power to feed into an anti-spell to make the original spell—and the *Agneta Katina*—explode.

But she didn't have enough power to do both.

She chose the ship.

He felt her choice; fresh power burst along the cord, burst into her body, kicking her out of it. She watched it crumple, watched Lex picking her up, from what felt like a very great distance.

Watched Lex grab his gun and start shooting at the boat, heard other gunshots echoing off the steel. More men—Lex's men, Bump's men—on top of buildings, shooting at the crowd, shooting at the boat. Yes! Thank fuck for Lex, Lex and that twisted brain of his. A distraction was what she'd needed and he'd given her one, and she thudded back into her body and gasped, "Get me on the ship. Hurry up," as she threw her magic items back into her bag.

The next few minutes—it could have been minutes, it could have been hours; she had no idea—passed in a haze of power and exhaustion. What sounded like hundreds of gunshots still broke the eerie silence around them, and the tower rocked harder. Lex pushed her up against the windows, his arms on either side of her, pressing her against the glass. She managed to open her mouth—so dry, it was so fucking dry—and croak out, "What are you—"

"Hang on, Tulip," he replied, and she looked down and saw it wasn't just the bespelled horde at the base of the tower but Lex's men, and it dawned on her what he was doing.

"Oh, you're fucking kidding—"

The tower went down.

Glass exploded around her, tiny shards embedding themselves in her skin, tiny stings of pain everywhere. She welcomed it. It focused her, dragged her back into her body as another massive pulse of magic slammed down the cord and into her head. She focused on the pain, forced herself to stay with it, and opened her eyes to find herself hovering a few feet above the angry surface of the bay.

Her hands had found the metal bars framing the now-empty windows; she gripped the bars tighter, her body aching with tension and effort, and tried not to fall into the water.

At least until she realized that she needed to fall into the water, needed to do it fast, because the horde was crawling along the fallen tower. She was going to end up in the bay no matter what; the question was whether she did it on her own steam or because they pushed her, and something told her that if they pushed her, she wouldn't be getting out alive.

The rope ladder hung off the side of the *Agneta* only a few feet away. She could reach it. She'd have to reach it.

Of course, chances were good someone would slice it when she was halfway up, but as with so many other things, she didn't have a choice. So she let go of the bars and fell into the icy blackness below.

Fuck, she hated the water. It covered her, knocked the wind out of her. She tried to open her eyes but couldn't see, tried to surface but couldn't tell which way was up. Hands grabbed her, yanked at her hair; she fought against them until she realized they were Lex's, and just as her lungs felt ready to explode, her head broke the surface.

That wasn't much better. Already the horde splashed into the water around her, coming for her. Lex dragged her—she'd never realized he knew how to swim, let alone that he was pretty good at it—toward the boat, much faster than she could have made it alone. It seemed like an endless struggle in the freezing cold sea of blackness, trying to keep hold of Lex while furious magic tore down the cord and into her soul.

But the sorcerer hadn't cut the ladder. It wasn't until she closed her hand around it that she realized why. Of course he hadn't cut it. He wanted her to come up there, wanted to kill her and be done with it, with her. Wanted, maybe, to pull her deeper into his spell and use her power to make it even stronger.

Her muscles shook with effort as she dragged herself up the rope, her palms burning from the rough fibers, her legs aching. Yes, he was waiting for her up there, waiting to kill her, because the magic binding her receded enough for her to think and that had to be the reason.

She could still feel it, though. Still feel him ordering his horde around, driving them into the water, driving them to further violence. More gunshots behind her; she knew without looking that the horde had turned on Lex's men, that they'd started fighting again in earnest.

Where was Terrible in all of that? What was he doing?

Not the time to think of it, not when she hit the little loading deck where she and Terrible had been earlier, with Lex right behind her. The rope twisted and jerked in her hands; more men followed, but whether they were Lex's or the bespelled she had no idea, and she couldn't pause to look. Instead, she ran down the hall to the stairs and up.

He was going to be waiting for her as soon as she got to the top deck. She knew it. She knew it, she knew it. She braced herself for the hand in her hair, the slash of steel across her throat.

With one last desperate plea to no one that she make it onto the deck alive, she hit the last flight of stairs and raced to the top, found the door to the deck, and burst through it.

Empty. No one stood there, no one waited for her, and the thought had barely registered when an explosion deafened her, a loud metallic gong right by her ear.

He wasn't waiting for her there, no. He was waiting in the wheelhouse, in that tower on deck, and he was shooting at her.

All of that flew through her mind in a barely coherent rush as she threw herself sideways, hugging the steel wall. Where to go, where to go? Running toward the wheelhouse would bring her closer to him, where she'd be an easier target, but where the hell else could she go? No place to hide, not that she could see.

Men tumbled onto the deck behind her, surrounding her, pushing her along. More gunshots. Bodies fell; screams rose into the air; and she kept running.

If she left the deck and reentered the boat to do her spell, she'd be better able to hide. If she was belowdecks when the spell exploded—if it did, please let it explode—she'd almost definitely die.

The whole boat housed the spell, the whole thing, but

somewhere in there had to be the heart of it, whatever totem or ingredient or whatever he was charging it with.

It was in the wheelhouse. That's why he was there. Not just to watch her but to guard his spell.

Okay, then.

She pivoted and ran back, charging the tower with her head down. More clangs as bullets hit the metal beneath her feet; she saw naked steel appear beneath chips in the paint, moonlight shining off the bare spots like stars trapped in the floor.

Lex pushed in front of her when she hit the wheelhouse door. He yanked it open and shoved his gun in, nearly deafening her with the sound of shots in the small space. Not all his, either. Fuck, this was it, she was going to die—

No. The connection—the cord of magic—had been silent for so long she'd almost managed to forget it existed, but something about the way Lex's men jostled around her, the way they moved in unison, reminded her. No, she might not have enough power to short out the spell, but neither did she need to. She was *inside* the spell. She wasn't its master but she had power of her own, and she knew how to get more, and she didn't need to short out anything or take over anything in order to do it.

He'd given it to her. The smug son of a bitch had given it to her, and she was going to take it.

If she hadn't been so scared she would have laughed. As it was she closed her eyes, took one long, deep breath, and reached out.

She reached out to all of them, all of them connected to her by the spell that trapped them. She reached out and found their energy, weak as it was, found the power connecting them, wrapped her hands around it, and yanked. Hard.

Energy flooded into her, so much energy her vision went black. She struggled with it, trying to force it into something smooth, something coherent, and when the sorcerer's rage came through to her clear and strong she absorbed that, too. Absorbed everything, as much as she could, until she felt as if she'd explode if someone even touched her, as if her skin was stretched tight around a glowing ball of magic.

She couldn't beat him and his spell with her own power, no. But she could do it with his.

At least, she really fucking hoped she could.

She barreled through the door, shoved the power up the cord as hard as she could, and aimed it all at him. Through the line she felt him stagger with it, felt him brace himself, and while he was doing that she raced up the stairs on feet she barely felt.

And found Mr. Carmichael—Kyle Blake's "assistant," the elegant gray-suited man she'd met at his house— struggling to stand as he braced himself on some sort of instrument panel behind him, magic throbbing all around him in a haze she could practically see. Magic *he* generated; it was him. Of course.

The instrument panel; the wheelhouse. The heart of the ship. The heart of the spell. She felt it the second her feet hit the floor. Felt its seductive dark call snaking through the air, adding to the power already inside her.

Carmichael wasn't the only one in the room. But he was the only one who mattered. Lex's men had headed straight for him, straight for his guards; the air in the small space filled with violence and the sound of flesh against flesh, with groans and last breaths. Chess ignored it. He'd come for her in a second, Carmichael would, he'd throw off Lex's men and come for her, and she had to get her spell—her anti-spell—ready before he did, because she couldn't beat him. Even the borrowed power thrumming in her body wasn't good enough, because it was his power; she'd managed to surprise him with it and knock him off balance, yes, but she couldn't hold him off for long.

Where was the power source?

Bodies knocked into hers, forced her to crouch and brace herself as she searched, her skin prickling as she felt his eyes on it. He was coming, he was coming, she didn't have time to set everything up; all she could do was hope for the best.

From her pocket she pulled her knife. From her bag she pulled the mirror and snake, the herbs wet from their dip in the bay but hopefully no less powerful. Where to set them—

Hands in her hair, yanking her, knocking her to the floor. Carmichael's furious face above her, his eyes blazing with rage as he lifted a shining blade over her head, ready to bring it down.

The second he touched her, the spell inside her—the speed and the magic—washed over her again. She was connected to him, connected so deep, and when that thought hit her mind she realized that he was the power source. The boat housed the spell, but he was its master. Things moved beneath his skin—what the fuck was that? How was he even alive, how the fuck did that work—

Lex slammed Carmichael in the side of the head with his gun; Carmichael fell sideways, catching himself before he tumbled off Chess. His knife fell sideways, too, slicing into her arm, and as her blood fell on his skin, as it fell onto the floor of the wheelhouse, she saw the horror in his eyes and guessed at what it meant.

If she was right, she'd win. If she was wrong, she'd die. She grabbed the magic items she'd dropped, clenched them in her fist, and pressed them to his arm—to the rivulet of her blood on his arm. "*Kesser arankia*. With blood I bind."

Carmichael screamed. The energy jolting down

the cord still connecting them jerked, it jerked and it changed, and she felt his terror, felt something swell behind it.

"*Septikosh, mellikosh, hatarosh—*"

Carmichael tried to jump off her. She grabbed him with her numb right hand, letting her blood flow faster onto his skin, and brought her left up in an arc beneath it. Her left arm, and her left hand, holding her knife.

Power exploded the second her blood hit his. His screams grew louder, higher, shrieks of agony. She thought she might have been screaming, too; she wasn't sure, but she knew she'd stopped when he crumpled off her to the floor.

Now he was bound to her and she could feel what he was, how inhuman he was, that he'd done things, evil things, to gain power and turn himself into the spell's master. He'd become something else, something held together and bound by magic, and that meant he was something she could destroy.

Her blood in his veins. Her power in his veins. He shrieked, his voice horrible and sharp as the others watched. He . . . curdled, somehow, on the floor. Like a slice of cheese left out too long, shriveling into himself as he screamed.

No time to be compassionate. She managed to catch Lex's eye and gasp, "Time to go," before she took the energy she still held inside her, the energy from all those people caught in the spell's trap, and shoved it back into Carmichael as hard as she could. Shoved it into her binding, into the anti-spell she'd cobbled together, and just before the *Agneta Katina* exploded she felt the spell release its prisoners.

Chapter Twenty-nine

Blackness. Silence. Freezing cold and so dark she couldn't breathe. She opened her mouth to scream but water rushed into it; she choked, her limbs flailing, trying to figure out— She was in the bay. She was in the bay, and she was drowning.

Trying to fight the urge to breathe, the urge to move, was like trying to fight the urge to take another pill after she'd crashed from the last dose. Almost impossible. But she did it, she forced herself to go limp, and holy fuck, it worked. She surfaced, lifting her face to the sky, and struggled, choking and gasping, to breathe.

The water in her lungs didn't want to let her. She coughed so hard she thought she might lose those lungs altogether, that they might fly out of her mouth to join the detritus of the *Agneta Katina* rising and falling around her.

Flames rose off the surface of the water; the *Agneta*'s skeleton, wreathed in fire, groaned as it sank inch by inch. Chess searched for the cord inside her, the spell, and didn't find it. It was gone. It was gone and she was alive. She'd done it, and she could find Terrible and they could go home, and she'd done it.

Now she just had to get back to shore, and that didn't look like an easy distance. Her bag—holy shit, the strap was still wrapped around her, thank fuck for that one—hung off her like a corpse, her wet clothes clinging heavily to her skin.

Where was Lex? Shit, where was Lex?

She'd told him to get off the boat, but she had no idea if he'd had time to do so, if anyone had. No idea if anyone else had survived the explosion. What if— Shit, if Lex died . . .

Not the time to think about it, especially not when her legs and hands had started to numb out from the cold. Make it back to dry land, that was what she needed to do. She'd find Lex there, or he'd find her there, because he would *be* there. She couldn't—wouldn't—contemplate the idea that he wouldn't be.

Swimming had never been an activity she'd enjoyed. Swimming in the dark waters of the bay, fragrant with dead fish and sewage, didn't make her like it any more. Especially not when her brain refused to stop showing her images of sharks and sea monsters, of diseases that loved to breed in unclean water and were probably burrowing into her—shit, into the open wound on her arm, and whatever others she hadn't felt yet—with her every movement.

Finally she reached the dock and climbed up onto it, scraping her hands in the process. Still no sign of Lex. She couldn't see any of his men, either; at least, she didn't think she could. Too many people crowded along the street, watching the *Agneta*'s corpse lower itself into the bay, for her to pick out any familiar faces.

Shit, she didn't have her phone. She'd given it to Lex, and he— Well, he was most likely on his way back to her place, or waiting for her, maybe on the rooftop where they'd all met up earlier.

That's where she'd head, then. Now that the spell had

ended, the fight would end, as well, so it shouldn't be hard to— What the fuck?

The fight hadn't ended. The fight was going on, loud and vicious, but it wasn't Carmichael's horde doing the fighting. It was Bump's men. And Lex's. They'd worked together until the threat had passed and then turned on one another. Shit.

She made her slow, cautious way along the outskirts of the battle, aware with each passing step of another ache, another injury. It felt like she'd been hit by a twenty-ton block of ice; every inch of her felt raw and tender, and all the speed had worn off, leaving her jittery and dehydrated.

And she couldn't do more; all of her own clean drugs would be ruined from her twin dips in the bay. Fuck. She had more at home, yeah, but that didn't help her much. She couldn't exactly head back there right at that moment. First she needed to find Terrible, and Lex.

If she made a strange picture—stumbling through the fight, soaking wet and bloody—no one paid any attention. Fine with her. She didn't pay much attention to the men she passed, either, except quick glances to make sure none of them were Terrible or Lex. With each step, her unease grew. Where were they? Where was Terrible, where was Lex?

They weren't waiting at the foot of the building where they'd all been earlier; several of Bump's men were, which made her heart skip with hope for a second, until she asked if Terrible was there and they shook their heads.

Bump was, though, still standing on the roof where she'd left him. He glanced back when he heard her shuffling footsteps.

"Ay, Ladybird, lookin like you had you a fuckin time, yay. Broken them fuckin magic all up, though, guessing."

She nodded. "Where's Terrible? Have you—"

He took a step back from the edge of the roof, sweeping his arm sideways in invitation. "Have you a fuckin look-see. Found heself a fuckin match, he done."

She'd started to move before he finished the sentence. Shit, she'd forgotten. She'd actually managed to forget Devil for a few minutes there.

If only that meant he'd disappeared, instead of doing what he was doing, which was fighting with Terrible on the street below.

"Fighting" was a mild word for it. Her stomach jumped into her throat and stayed there, choking her, as she watched the two figures on the pavement. The crowd had parted for them; they moved alone in a circle empty of everything but the blood she imagined she could see even from a distance.

Of course she couldn't. She stood four or five stories up and the only streetlight was far outside the circle. But still she thought she could, that she could see it spattered on the ground, could see it obscuring their faces and soaking into their clothes.

Devil must have found him—or vice versa—not long after Terrible had left the roof; they'd clearly been at it for a while. Both of them stumbled. Both of them moved as if their arms were too heavy, their bodies thick and slow.

But both of them still moved, and she knew they wouldn't stop until one of them was dead.

And there was nothing she could do about it. The sigils on his skin, bound with her blood or her energy, weren't enough, didn't make a connection strong enough for her to feed any power into. Especially not from a distance.

So she just watched as Lex's man swung again, connected again, snapping Terrible's head back and then doubling him over with a fist to the stomach. Terrible's knees hit the street; he fell forward, clutching at Devil's legs, knocking him down.

Devil kicked Terrible. Terrible grabbed Devil's leg and twisted, pushing down as he did—at least that's what it looked like he was doing—but whether or not he broke the bone, she didn't know.

"Here." Bump held something out to her. Her phone. Some of the tension in her shoulders left; not a lot, because it felt as if every muscle in her body was spasming in sympathy with Terrible—in fear for him—but some of it. Lex was alive, then. He'd made it.

"Lex fuckin bring it me, only he left a minute past. Guessin he wanting to find he a fuckin place to get him watch on, also." Bump snorted. "Like he man got he a chance on Terrible."

But something in his voice . . . She gave him a sharp look. He didn't sound as confident as he should have, and for some reason hearing that note of worry in his voice worried her more than anything else. She remembered then what Terrible had told her, about how Bump found him as a child, took him off the streets and gave him a home, and she wondered if their relationship was as businesslike as she'd always assumed. Wondered, for the first time ever, how Bump actually felt about Terrible.

She would never ask. Even if she did, he wouldn't tell her, at least she couldn't imagine he would. But the thought was there just the same, an unwilling sense of . . . of kinship, an uneasy sense of unity as they watched and worried.

"Do you think—"

He cut her off. "Nay, have a look. All wrapping the fuck up now."

Devil lay on his back, with Terrible over him, grabbing his ears and slamming his head into the pavement. Again, and again. Devil's fist shot up to hit Terrible's shoulder; she didn't see the blade in it but knew it was there from the way Terrible's body jerked. Terrible fell back, and Chess couldn't watch anymore.

She'd never believed, really believed deep down, that Terrible could lose. It was impossible; it would be like discovering the Church had no power over ghosts at all but the ghosts were instead just deciding to go away, and the whole psychopomp-and-magic thing was a complex trick done with lights. A Terrible who lost a fight would be— She couldn't imagine what he would be, if he wasn't dead.

No. She didn't have to imagine. She knew. A Terrible who lost a fight and lived would be a Terrible who lost everything, because practically all of Downside stood watching, and he would never recover from having them see him beaten. He would never— He would never go on if that happened, would he? Their earlier conversation took on a different tone, a different meaning. She honestly didn't know if he would be willing to stay in a world where he'd been defeated. Even for her.

It wasn't until her feet hit the stairs that she realized what she was doing. It might make a difference if he saw her. It might not. But no matter what happened, she wasn't going to leave him down there alone. If he won she'd be with him, and if he lost . . . she'd be with him for that, too.

Shouts and yells assaulted her when she hit the street, much louder than they'd seemed from the roof. The crowd was so deep; she fought her way through it, her heart leaping every time the crowd reacted to whatever was happening. She couldn't see them, couldn't see anything but backs and faces alight with the observation of violence. The energy of the crowd, gleeful and excited, bloodthirsty and cruel, beat against her skin, made it harder to breathe. Touching them all made it even worse, but she had no choice. She pushed them aside, shoved them, kicked them, ducked down and thrust herself into spaces way too small for her. With her every step the crowd grew louder. Something was happening; what was happening?

It looked worse up close. All the blood she'd imagined she could see from the roof was there, covering Terrible, covering Devil. They both appeared on the edge of death, sluggish and sick, staggering around each other.

Terrible wouldn't be able to see her; hell, she doubted if he could see anything, but even if he could, he wouldn't take his eyes off Devil. Even knowing that, though, standing at the edge of the crowd made her feel better. She sidled along, weaving in and out between the onlookers, until she found a place to stand behind Devil. A place where Terrible might be able to catch a glimpse of her.

Devil swung. They both went down again, their bodies hitting the pavement with a horrible *splat*. Chess gasped; so did some of the people standing around her.

The two men moved on the street like dying crabs, their movements slow and jerky, leaving trails of blood behind them. Chess got a look at Terrible's face, swollen and broken, barely recognizable, and could hardly breathe. How could he survive that, how could anyone survive that?

Pain blossomed in her lip; she realized she'd bitten it hard enough to bleed. Her hands ached from twisting them together; well, her whole body ached, but she didn't care. Didn't have time to think about it or worry about it. She didn't take her eyes off the fight before her.

Devil's hand on the back of Terrible's neck, driving his face into the cement. Terrible caught Devil's arm, pushed it up, pushed himself up far enough to land another punch to Devil's face.

Then he saw her. She thought— No, she knew he saw her. She felt it. Just a flash of his eyes, a fraction of a second, but it was there, she knew it was there, and it made it so much worse when Devil took advantage of that distraction to slam his fist into Terrible's nose and knock him back down.

Terrible didn't move. He didn't move for what felt like forever—she couldn't tell how long it was—while the shouts of the crowd became nothing but a humming irritation beneath the thundering of her heart, the screaming in her head. He wasn't moving, holy fuck he wasn't— She couldn't breathe. It felt as if someone had taken a sledgehammer and slammed it into her chest. Yes, he had the sigil on him, and it would hold his soul, but what if his body was too damaged to recover, what if his brain was damaged, what if he— Shit. A bird.

A bird screeched overhead, and she couldn't help but look up at it, couldn't help but see it. A bird. A psychopomp here to collect a soul. Oh fuck . . .

Devil drew his fist back, ready to hit Terrible one final time while he lay defenseless. Hot bright hatred raged through Chess's body. She still had her knife; if he hit Terrible again, if he killed Terrible, she was going to slice that motherfucker's throat all by herself and dance in his blood. Her fingers closed around the handle.

Devil's fist started to fall. Terrible's hand snapped up, caught it; his head rose, his chest rose, and before Chess realized what was happening, Devil was on his back and Terrible's elbow landed on his throat with an ugly crack.

Silence. Silence broken by a thin, rattly gasping sound, a reedy dry whistle like someone blowing through an empty straw, one long exhale before it disappeared.

The psychopomp told her what had happened. It swooped down, almost grazing the heads of the now-roaring crowd. Devil was dead, his windpipe crushed. Terrible had won.

Terrible, now kneeling on the cement with his head bowed, his back rising and lifting with his heavy, deep breaths. His hands rested on his thighs; she watched droplets of blood fall onto them, not realizing until she was halfway across the clearing that she was moving.

So many reasons for keeping their relationship secret, and all of them good ones. Hell, for all she knew he'd be pissed off at her for going to him, and she couldn't really argue with him about it.

But fuck it. They hung out in public all the time, anyway. The fact that they never touched, never kissed, never looked into each other's eyes, didn't mean most of Downside wasn't probably convinced they were together.

And she didn't give a damn either way. She dropped to her knees at his side. His face was slick with blood and hot under her hands; she turned it toward hers, and kissed him.

He tasted of blood and anger and fear, and something else that blossomed there when his clumsy hands found her hair, her back, when he squeezed her tighter to him. Something that was just him, and he was hers.

The crowd around them was probably watching with great interest. Let them fucking watch. This was her time, and she was alive and so was he, and she was taking it.

His palms held her cheeks as he pulled back, his voice barely audible. "Chessie . . . fuck, glad to see you . . ."

She kissed him again, trying to find some spot on his face where it looked like it might not hurt. A sob broke free from her throat as she shifted position. "Me, too."

He sighed and rested his head on her collarbone, his body warm against hers. Warm and wet: Blood seeped through her damp clothes as his hands fell heavily to rest on her thighs. She ignored it and tilted her head so she could whisper, "I love you."

They stayed like that for—well, she didn't know how long, until murmurs and the sound of shuffling feet grabbed her attention. She glanced away to see the crowd dispersing. Or, rather, some of the crowd was dispersing. Some of it stayed right where it was, apparently fascinated. Right. Having people know was one thing. Providing free entertainment was another.

"Can you walk? I mean, can you—"

"Ain't . . . ain't sure. Ain't thinkin so, just yet. Maybe . . . gimme a few, aye? Just a few."

Something in his voice cracked her heart—his voice, and the words themselves. Another weakness he was having to admit; she knew it wasn't weakness, but she knew he'd sure as fuck think it was.

But she didn't care. She didn't think one bit less of him for it. She never had, not for any of the tiny insecurities or whatever he'd revealed to her. She loved him, and she could sit there with him and take care of him, and it felt right. Like something she could do, like something she wanted to do. Something she was good at.

Something she didn't need to worry about, because when the time came, she was doing okay, wasn't she? And when she wasn't . . . well, when she wasn't she figured it out pretty quickly, and when she wasn't he let her know, the same as when he wasn't she let him know. And together they seemed to be figuring it all out pretty well.

But something she already knew was that she loved him and that she wanted to make him happy. So she wrapped her arms carefully around him and said, "Yeah. Take all the time you need, okay? We have all the time you need."

Four days later she was sitting in the Church library, using the computer—look at that, she was even using the Internet more than once on this case, not that it was officially a case or that it was anything at all anymore— to read up on the tragic death of Kyle Victor Blake, who'd for some reason snorted a massive overdose of speed alone in his office the night before.

At least, the papers reported that he was alone. Chess had her doubts. She didn't want to ask; she never would. But she doubted it all the same. Especially after she'd stopped in the hospital that morning to see the now-awake Edsel and was told that, miraculously, someone had left ten thousand dollars in an envelope at his bedside. And that happened to be the same amount of money Kyle Blake's wife thought was missing from their safe—the same amount they estimated the pile of speed on his desk might be worth.

Chess knew that was bullshit, and she had a pretty good idea where that speed had come from. Hadn't at least a hundred or so infected packets of that shit ended up in Bump's possession, through being confiscated from the victims?

But again, not something she'd ask about. She didn't want to know.

That didn't stop her from reading the stories, from taking a long, long look at the picture that went along with them, the same smirking one as on the cover of Bump's magazine. Blake was smirking in the City of Eternity now, and he'd keep doing it, and maybe as he did he'd think about the people he'd killed and the people he'd tried to kill. Maybe he'd think about what a mistake he'd made fucking with Downside.

Or maybe not. Probably not. Didn't matter, anyway; he was there, and there he'd stay. And she couldn't bring herself to feel one bit sorry for him. Maybe that was wrong of her, but he'd tried to kill so many people. He'd hurt so many people.

Of course, if hurting people meant deserving the City, she deserved it more than anyone. But she already knew that.

And she was trying to get better, to be better. She'd

talked to Lex briefly, the day after the fight, just a few minutes to thank him for helping her, and no promises made of anything else. She didn't know how to handle that yet, didn't know what she was supposed to do.

She'd promised Terrible no more. And she wanted to keep that promise—intended to keep it, even if it meant giving up Blue, too.

But it hurt more than she'd expected to talk to Lex, to hear his voice on the phone. Yeah, he was a cocky bastard, and he seemed to love causing trouble for her, and he seemed to think it was a fun sort of game to try to coax her back into his bed. She didn't appreciate any of that. She sure as fuck didn't appreciate him hiring Devil; the thought of it filled her with rage.

But . . . he was also her friend. With that one glaring, humiliating exception—that one exception she knew he saw as purely business and not personal at all—he'd never refused her a favor, never hesitated to help her if and when she'd needed it, even if his way of helping wasn't exactly what she'd had in mind. He'd saved her life more than once. Honestly, she could almost say he'd saved her relationship with Terrible, because Terrible had told her that it was when he saw her with Lex the night of the battle in the City, saw how unromantic—or whatever—Lex was with her, that he'd realized she was telling the truth about Lex never being more than a bed partner and a friend.

And last, of course, he gave her free drugs, plenty of them whenever she asked and sometimes when she didn't, and that made him a friend indeed. Funny. It hadn't occurred to her until the other night that maybe that was part of Terrible's objection to him.

It didn't matter. Terrible did object, period. So unless she could change his mind somehow . . . yeah, she wouldn't be seeing much of Lex anymore.

But she'd thought that before, hadn't she? He kept

popping up in her life, and when it wasn't him it was Blue, and none of it felt like something she wanted to think of just then. Not when Terrible was finally up and out of bed and he was picking her up in a few minutes, and not when she was hoping to get him back *into* bed the second they got home.

And not when Elder Griffin was walking across the library. She didn't want to watch him but couldn't help herself, couldn't help the wave of sadness that washed over her when she did. If only he could forgive her; if only she'd never told him. If only he was a different sort of person, not one so . . . so fucking ethical, or honorable, or whatever.

But then if he was, he never would have thought she was a good person to begin with, would he?

His gaze fell on her; he stiffened and gave her a curt nod. "Good morrow, Cesaria."

"Good morrow, sir. I— How are you?"

"Well, thank you." He hesitated. "Very busy, I'm afraid. I must get to work."

And he was gone, crossing the room at a speed just over his usual gait, not looking back at her as he went.

She guessed he didn't need to. He'd seen her; he saw her clearly enough now.

That—that kind of seeing, that kind of clarity—was something that would never go away, she knew. Like with Terrible. She'd seen him one way for so long, and then slowly she'd seen him as he really was. Only in her case Elder Griffin wasn't realizing that beneath the surface she was perfect. He was realizing she was worthless. And he'd never be able to see anything else, at least so she figured. How could he ever forgive her?

How could anyone, though, really.

The walls of the Church library, usually so comforting, seemed to close in around her. Time to go, anyway. She cleared the browsing history on the computer and shut it down, grabbed her bag, and headed for the front doors. Headed past Elder Griffin's office. The door was closed. Yeah.

But the Chevelle waited for her in the parking lot, Terrible in the driver's seat and a couple of boxes in the backseat. The last few boxes of her stuff. Well, not the last of her stuff, because some of it was staying in her apartment, but the last few boxes of stuff she wanted to have with her and handy all the time.

The last few boxes of stuff she was moving into Terrible's place.

She couldn't take everything; as she'd told him before, she needed to keep her address, keep enough stuff there that if the Church checked on her it would look as if she lived there. She'd have to check on it regularly, going to collect her mail—not that she ever got much—and to dust, and to refresh the wards on the door, and all that other shit she'd need to do.

It would be extra work, yeah. But it was worth it. It was totally worth it, and she was ready.

She hopped into the car and leaned over to kiss him, his face still bruised Technicolor and his body still padded with bandages but alive and smiling at her.

"Hey, Chess. You right? Ready to go?"

Was she? Fear still hummed through her veins, fear and the uncertainty of where they went next, of how long he'd want her in his apartment, of how well she was going to handle it all. She was still who she was, after all. A junkie, a liar, someone who didn't know how to have a relationship, someone who really didn't deserve whatever happiness she managed to find. Someone terrified she'd do the wrong thing, say the wrong thing, terrified that she was going to fuck this up like she did everything else.

Hell, she'd managed to ruin her relationship with Elder Griffin, of all people, the man who'd approved of her, helped her, liked her, since the day they'd met when she was in training. The man who'd always been on her side.

But she'd started to realize it was impossible not to be scared, that Terrible was, too. That maybe in that, at least, she was normal.

And they were going to figure it out together, and that was what mattered.

So she took his hand. "Yeah, right up," she said. "Let's go."